A MIRROR AGAINST ALL MISHAP

JACK MASSA

 Triskelion Books

Published by
Triskelion Books
www.triskelionbooks.com

This is a work of fiction. All of the characters, organizations, and events portrayed in this novel are either products of the author's imagination or are used fictitiously. Any similarity to actual sorcerers, pirates, or witches, is purely coincidental.

A Mirror Against All Mishap
Copyright © 2017 by Jack Massa

All rights reserved. No part of this book may be reproduced or transmitted by any means now known or hereinafter invented, electronic or mechanical, including but not limited to photocopying, recording, or by an information storage and retrieval system, without the written permission of the publisher, except where permitted by law.

ISBN 978-0-9976461-3-9

Print Edition published December 2017

Cover Design by Shaun Stevens, https://www.flintlockcovers.com/

For John W. Kelly.
Because only a true friend
critiques your fantasy novel
using a spreadsheet.

PREFACE

A Mirror Against All Mishap is Book 2 of *The Glimnodd Cycle*. It continues the story begun in *Cloak of the Two Winds*—although you can begin reading here with absolutely no harm to your psyche. For information on the world of Glimnodd, including a Glossary and access to a map, see the Afterword.

Cast of Characters

Amlina - Wandering witch from Larthang, a nation of great witches. Seeking the rightful path.

Glyssa - Young warrior of the Iruk people. Seeking to heal her wounded soul.

Glyssa's mates, members of her klarn:

    Lonn (m), the klarn leader, strong, passionate, stoical.

    Draven (m), Lonn's cousin, brave and optimistic.

    Karrol (f), brawny, decisive, outspoken.

    Brinda (f), Karrol's sister, quiet and reserved.

    Eben (m), lean, quick-witted, mercurial.

Beryl Quan de Lang - Archimage of the East and Amlina's great enemy. Seeking revenge.

Zenodia - Administrator in Beryl's Temple of the Sun, but secretly a priestess of the outlawed cult of the Lost Moon. Longing for Beryl's overthrow.

Meghild - Pirate queen of Gwales, aged and crippled. Wishing for one last adventure.

Wilhaven - Bard of Gwales and man of many skills. In the service of Meghild.

Kizier - A human scholar trapped in the shape of a sea-fern.

Buroof - A talking book, once a human. Three thousand years old and morally deficient.

Torms -Winged people of the mountains; wild and savage.

Myro - Dolphin people of the sea; fond of music.

Others: brigands, princes, sailors, boatwrights, herdsmen, priests.

PART ONE
AT THE HALL OF THE BRIGAND QUEEN

ONE

A meltwind blew late in the night. The steady breeze from the sea grew to a roar, the gray cliffs and pine-covered hills shimmered in witchlight, and the ice in the fjord changed to blue water.

Glyssa watched from a high battlement as the curtain of sparks and blast of warmth passed over the castle. She had risen from her bed, wakened by a fearful premonition. Leaving the alcove where she slept with the other Iruks, she had stepped quietly through the great hall, where servants and retainers lay huddled near the fires. Barefoot, dressed in thin tunic and leggings, Glyssa ignored the cold, just as the sentry posted at the round-arched portal ignored her—a small, black-haired woman, a foreigner from distant parts. The guards had grown used to Glyssa's silent wanderings in the night.

Like a ghost, she thought, *a lost spirit.*

For nearly three months, Glyssa and her mates had been guests in this castle, the keep of Meghild the pirate queen, here on the western coast of Gwales. They had voyaged to this remote northern land in the company of the witch Amlina, after fleeing the city of Kadavel where Glyssa had been enslaved.

Memories of that time still tormented her. Her body had been taken over, her mind submerged and trapped in a foul, dark place. Reduced to a mindless one, a *thrall*, she could only watch in hopeless despair as her body moved at the will of another mind—an ancient, nonhuman sorcerer. After nearly two months, when her identity had all but vanished, her mates had arrived as if by a miracle and saved her.

She loved them for it. And yet, so many days later, she still felt apart from them. The Iruks hailed from the distant, south polar region of the world. Together, Glyssa and her mates formed a *klarn*, a band of hunters joined by oath and a group soul.

But Glyssa had felt little of the klarn-soul's presence since her rescue.

Her strength had slowly returned, and she tried constantly to be her old self, the Glyssa her mates remembered and loved. But inside her was an emptiness, a frozen void she could not dispel. Whenever her mind touched that icy place she became miserably frightened—or else enraged.

Now, as the meltwind passed away to the north, she felt a clawing, hopeless dread. The night was dark again, no moons or stars piercing the clouds. The fjord was lit only by the luminous blue water—the witchlight that gleamed through all seas and sea-ice on this world of Glimnodd. In that dreamy luminescence, Glyssa could see *cranocks* on the beach—wooden sailing ships the Gwalesmen used for trading and pirate forays. One craft, smaller than the rest, lay up on rollers. This was the boat the Iruks had commissioned from Meghild's shipwright. They had waited through Second and Third Winter, and now at last the boat was finished. Soon the klarn would sail from Gwales.

They still had not decided where.

Either they would return home, to the South Polar Sea, and resume their former life of hunting and raiding, or they would continue their partnership with Amlina and sail with her against her enemy, the fearsome witch known as the Archimage of the East.

Glyssa did not know which course frightened her more.

Or perhaps, what terrified her to her core was the feeling that it made no difference—that if she could not melt away this ice in her soul, then no life was worth living.

Her shoulders jumped at a footstep behind her. Whirling, she saw that it was Lonn, climbing the stone steps from below. He had risen from his bed and come to find her.

"Glyssa," he whispered with concern. "You'll freeze up here."

"I hadn't noticed," she murmured. "The meltwind blew."

Lonn craned his neck to stare over the rampart. "So it did. But it's still frosty cold."

He spread his arms and embraced her, wrapping the bearskin bed cover around them both. Pressed to his body, feeling his warmth, Glyssa noticed the chill for the first time and shivered.

"Dear Glyssa," he said. "I've told you before, if you must go wandering in the night, at least take a bed fur with you."

Glyssa said nothing, only clung to him tighter. Lonn was the klarn's leader—strong, soft-spoken, deep of thought and heart. These past months, Glyssa had slept many nights in his arms. If anything could bring her back from despair, she thought, it would be his strength and patient love.

"So the changing-weather's begun," he said. "And Amlina is in her deep trance, and expects to have a plan when she awakes. The klarn must decide soon if we will sail with her."

"Yes," Glyssa answered. "We must decide."

* O *

Candles flickered in tiny spheres of red glass. Prisms, mirrored balls, and feathered *desmets* hung suspended from the ceiling, swaying and twirling on impalpable breezes. Amlina the witch sat cross-legged on her bed and stared vacantly at the shifting lights and shadows. It was three or four days since she entered the *dark immersion*—the trance of dissolution into the Deepmind.

After many hours her mind had begun to coalesce, self-awareness gradually returning. Now, she had almost come back to the surface mind.

But she still had no answer.

A fretful sigh escaped her. She shook herself and came fully awake.

Cautiously, trying to control her frustration, she stretched her limbs, then rubbed her numb thighs and ankles. Presently, she climbed to her feet and walked unsteadily across the dim chamber. The room was circular, set in a tower—one of the few private apartments in Meghild's castle. Amlina brushed past the hanging trinkets, the lamps on the floor meticulously arranged to facilitate her deep trance. She came to a trestle table, picked up a ewer, poured water into a cup. She drank it down and coughed.

She wiped her eyes, ran fingers through her long, pale hair. Her form was slender, narrow-shouldered, almost childlike. Her face showed the delicate features of noble Larthangan stock, with high cheekbones and flashing, sea-blue eyes. She wore a silk shift under a brocade robe, and on her head a silver fillet set with moonstones.

She poured a second drink and gulped it down. Three or four days without water brought a powerful thirst.

On one end of the long table sat an ancient book with parchment pages and leather binding—the talking book Amlina had taken from the lair of the sorcerer Kosimo. Near her hand sat a three-foot high fern-like plant in an ornate ivory pail. Amlina leaned over and gently touched the plant's green stalk.

"Kizier," she said softly.

A single eye on the stalk opened and regarded her alertly. The plant creature was a *bostull*, a windbringer—one of the sentient races of Glimnodd. But this windbringer was something more. He had once been human, a wandering scholar, and he was Amlina's trusted friend.

"What have you learned?" Kizier spoke in a whispery voice.

Amlina sank wearily into a chair. "Nothing I didn't know already."

"Even the *Bowing* counsels it?"

"So it would seem."

Prior to entering deep trance, Amlina had enacted a rite called *Bowing to the Sky*. This technique of deepseeing was advised only when all other methods of choosing a path had failed. It required the seeker to affirm that she would relinquish all personal choice, accept whatever answer the Deepmind gave.

"But how can I?" Amlina said. "How can I even contemplate using such magic?"

"You can, if you truly wish to vanquish your enemy." A brash voice sounded from the far end of the table. "It is only logical: to destroy a great witch, you must invoke power stronger than hers."

The voice belonged to a talking book, who called himself Buroof. His opinion was no surprise—it was he who had proposed this course that Amlina so feared to travel. Her enemy, Beryl, was a mighty witch. She had long outlived her normal lifespan, had mastered not only Larthangan witchery, but much obscure ancient sorcery as well. For many days and nights, Amlina had meditated and consulted the book, seeking a strategy to defeat Beryl. Persistently, Buroof had pointed her to the almost forgotten magical arts of ancient Nyssan. After much consideration, he had selected one formulation in particular—a grand ensorcellment called *The Mirror Against All Mishap*.

But on learning the particulars, Amlina balked. An example of the most barbaric kind of Nyssanian sorcery, the Mirror required human sacrifice.

Like Kizier, Buroof had once been a human, a mage and scholar of vast learning. Long ago, his mind had been captured and caged in the book by a serd sorcerer. For nearly three thousand years, his mind had continued to thrive and learn, absorbing the knowledge of each mage, sorcerer, and witch who possessed the book.

But over those centuries, Buroof had apparently lost whatever capacity for human morals he once possessed.

"How can you still dispute the choice," Buroof said, "when even the Bowing confirms it?"

—5—

"Because it is *blood magic*," Amlina answered. "And, as I am a witch of Larthang, my very soul calls it unspeakably evil."

The book made a sound like a dismissive grunt. "For how many nights have I labored on your problem, young and naïve *witch of Larthang*? Yet, when I offer a viable solution, you are too qualmish to accept it. I honestly fail to see why I should assist you any further."

Amlina glanced at Kizier, one side of her mouth pulled back in a frown. She stood, walked to the far end of the table, and shut the book—pre-empting further comment from Buroof.

Her shoulders slumped, and her glance returned to the solemn, one-eyed gaze of the bostull. "Perhaps he is right, Kizier. Perhaps I am too squeamish."

"I do not believe that, Amlina. I do not believe that the only way to oppose Beryl is to plunge yourself into evil as deep as her own."

Amlina returned to her chair, drained by doubt and indecision. "Sometimes...Sometimes the Bowing sheds further light a day or two after the seer emerges from trance. Perhaps a way will be revealed that is...not so terrible."

Kizier blinked but said nothing.

"A forlorn hope, I admit." Amlina fell silent for a time. Presently, she spoke quietly, as if to herself. "We were so close to defeating her in Kadavel, in that cavern under the Temple of the Air. If only it had gone the other way..."

Instead, though wounded, Beryl had managed to escape through a Gate of Spaceless Passage, taunting Amlina and the Iruks before she vanished, vowing she would hunt them down and kill them without mercy.

In the months since, Amlina had been constantly on her guard, pouring energy into a protective aura, wary that Beryl might strike at any moment. But no sign of the Archimage had appeared—no mental attacks through the Deepmind, no flaming mask and gloves materializing in the air, no squadron of warships or troop of monstrous *drogs*. Perhaps Amlina's concealments held and Beryl could not find her. Perhaps Beryl's wound had weakened her more than Amlina suspected, and she was not so capable as before.

"Perhaps she will never come after us at all," Amlina murmured.

"Perhaps not," Kizier said. "And perhaps, if you return to Larthang, to the Celestial Capital, she would not dare to follow you there."

Amlina steepled her delicate fingers, stared at them blankly. She had considered that option, of course.

But what would she do in Larthang?

She had left her homeland as a young student, after failing to advance in the Academy of the Deepmind and earn the gray mantle of a mage-adept. She had wandered through the Tathian Isles, hoping to develop her skills and knowledge. Finally, that quest had led her to Far Nyssan and Beryl's court, in the city known as Tallyba the Terrible. She had hoped to learn from Beryl, become her student. But that idea was folly.

Amlina had disregarded the tales of Beryl's evil, believing them to be propaganda spread by the Witches of Larthang, because Beryl was an enemy who had stolen from them, mocked them, and escaped all retribution. But Amlina soon learned the tales were true, that Beryl did practice abominable sorceries, did drink the blood of human sacrifices to sustain her youth. Beryl appraised her in a few moments, and Amlina was fortunate that she truly did seek only to learn from the Archimage. At first, Beryl had her imprisoned, later forced her to serve as a kitchen drudge. But in the end, she did take Amlina on as a kind of apprentice.

For nearly seven years, Amlina dwelled in the Archimage's palace and learned a small portion of her arts. Amlina stayed on her guard, knowing she was in constant danger of being murdered, or else reduced to a mindless thrall. Then, when that peril seemed imminent, when Beryl seemed to have tired of her presence, Amlina fled.

She planned her escape meticulously, waiting until Beryl was in deep trance and stealing the Cloak of the Two Winds. The Cloak was an age-old magical treasure that Beryl had taken from Larthang long ago. Amlina knew she could use it to drive a ship quickly across the seas. She planned to return it to Larthang, hoping that to do so would win her prestige and a place of honor.

Of course, that plan too went astray. The Cloak was stolen from her by the Iruk pirates who captured her ship—when Amlina herself was in deep trance. The Iruks, in turn, lost it to the sorcerer Kosimo, who seized the mind of Glyssa and made her bring it to him in the Tathian city of Kadavel. Amlina had joined forces with the Iruks to hunt it down. They had rescued Glyssa and almost won the Cloak—until Beryl arrived and snatched it away.

If only it had gone the other way. Returning the Cloak to Larthang might have won Amlina not only status and honors, but protection from Beryl. More than that, it would have given her a feeling of accomplishment, a reason to believe that her wandering life amounted to something worthy, had not all been a pointless waste.

A soft rapping on the door snapped her from her reverie. She glanced at Kizier, frowning. Crossing the chamber, she noticed it was now morning, gray daylight slanting through the high, narrow windows in the stone walls.

She reached the door as the knock sounded again. "Who is there?"

"Draven."

A smile curved her lips. She slid the bolts and pulled the door open.

The Iruk grinned at her. "I had a feeling you had come out of your trance."

He had sensed her awakening, Amlina thought. In Kadavel, the Iruks had joined with her in a *wei circle*, searching in the Deepmind for Glyssa. This had established a psychic bond they all shared.

But with Draven, it was more than that. Much more.

"Come in," she said.

Draven was broad-shouldered, slightly taller than Amlina. He had black hair down to his shoulders, the long mustache that Iruk men favored, and dark eyes that always seemed amused.

As soon as she closed the door, Amlina hugged him. She pressed her cheek against his shoulder, felt the soft deerskin of his shirt, smelled the familiar warmth of his body.

Throughout the winter seasons she had often allowed herself this comfort, even shared her bed with him on some cold nights. They had not, of course, engaged in sexual congress. That was too risky—it could change, even weaken her powers. Besides, she knew it might drive a wedge between Draven and his mates. The Iruks' *klarn*, she had learned, had a psychic bond of its own, and it could be brittle.

She had explained all this to Draven, and he had accepted it without complaint. He gave to her freely, with an open heart, not asking for what she could not give in return.

His hand caressed her hair. "Are you well, my lovely witch?"

"Well enough, dear friend. Just hold me a moment. I need your strength."

He always felt so solid, so at ease and unafraid. She sometimes worried that, through her neediness, she might inadvertently drain his vitality. But the Iruks were a hearty race, and Draven's vigor seemed boundless.

He held her at arm's-length. "And have you decided on a course?"

She lowered her eyes, the pain of indecision rushing back. "Not yet."

"But you said that after the dark immersion—"

"I know. But sometimes these things don't go as expected."

She started to turn away, then gripped his arm. Beryl had sworn she would kill not only Amlina, but the Iruks as well. If they separated, and she went to seek asylum in Larthang, she might never know the Iruks' fate. That only made her choice more difficult. Along with her love for Draven, she felt an obligation to protect him and his mates as best she could.

"We test the new boat today," Draven was saying. "Once it is judged ready, the klarn will meet to decide whether or not to sail with you." He gave a small laugh. "But that might be difficult, if we don't know where you are going."

"Indeed." Amlina wondered again if the lingering effects of the Bowing rite might yet deliver some acceptable answer, might make her way clear.

"I will decide on a course soon. I promise."

TWO

Hundreds of leagues away, in the city called Tallyba the Terrible, Beryl Quan de Lang, Archimage of the East and Empress of Far Nyssan, sat in her audience hall. She was a tall, imposing woman, dressed in robes of scarlet and black and a blood-red turban set with jewels and feathers. She sat erect on her throne—the fossilized skull of some giant horned beast, polished to a gleaming white.

The throne was set on a semi-circular dais, nine steps high and thirty paces across. Beyond the dais, the hall stretched into an empty distance, columns of rose and gold marble supporting an enormous dome.

Beryl's councilors and their attendants stood before the throne. No one was permitted to sit in her presence. The councilors were an obsequious lot—men and women ministers in long robes and pendants of office, stern soldiers in polished gold armor, priests and priestesses of the Sun, in orange gowns and gold sandals, their heads shaven, their skins dyed red, and scarred from frequent, ceremonial blood-letting.

Beryl herself was the High Priestess of the Sun, the incarnation of the deity. In her ascent to power, she had eliminated all of the other priesthoods, demolished their temples, making herself the supreme ruler of Tallyba. That process had culminated over a hundred years ago. How many council meetings like this one had she sat in since? Beryl strained to focus her attention.

Toulluthan, the temple treasurer, was giving a report. He read from an account book held by an acolyte, and gestured from time to time with the jeweled scepter of his office. Toulluthan was tall and obese, rolls of fat quivering beneath his chin as he spoke. At his shoulder stood Zenodia, his second. Beryl read the look in her eyes as she dutifully watched her superior cleric. Zenodia was ambitious. She was likely plotting to displace Toulluthan if she could, and after that ... Well, Zenodia would bear watching.

For Beryl, it was the usual dilemma. Councilors must have a certain amount of ability and ambition to make adequate servants. Too much, and they became potential rivals and had to be killed. Always a tenuous balance to maintain.

Beryl brought her distracted mind back to Toulluthan. The treasurer was explaining why the temple's monthly expenses had risen. He stepped cautiously, avoiding the implication of any blame, while still communicating the obvious facts. By Beryl's decree, the number of captives awaiting sacrifice had been tripled over the winter seasons. These "fortunate ones" who would be honored to give their blood to the Sun had to be fed and clothed at the temple's expense. Often, they arrived in Tallyba in poor condition, Toulluthan implied—again carefully not assigning blame to the military commanders responsible for obtaining and transporting the captives from the provinces.

Beryl's forehead started to throb. She resisted the impulse to reach under her turban and rub the scar. This reminded her, yet again, of the root of her troubles.

Months ago, in Kadavel, she had been wounded in a fight with her former apprentice. Beryl had been an instant away from cutting Amlina's throat when the barbarian Iruks burst in and forced her to flee—to snatch the Cloak of the Two Winds and escape through a Gate of Spaceless Passage. Such travel, outside the bounds of the physical sphere, was debilitating. In the past, it had taken Beryl several days to recover from such dire magic.

But this time was much worse. More than three months later, her full strength had still not returned. Perhaps it was the wound, a cut on the forehead that Amlina inflicted in her desperate, clumsy attack.

Perhaps the fact that Beryl was bleeding when she passed through the Gate had taken an unforeseen toll.

Beryl shifted in her seat. She knew there was a deeper cause, a shadow in her mind. Amlina's betrayal, her skillfully arranged flight from Tallyba, the potency of her challenge in Kadavel—all had surprised and shaken Beryl.

For the first time in many decades, she had been made to feel vulnerable.

And that feeling abided. Unlikely though it seemed, Beryl was haunted by the notion that Amlina would someday come to Tallyba and kill her. No, it was more than a notion—a premonition, a potential stream of events glimpsed in the Deepmind.

Of course, Beryl knew the way to forestall that possibility was to strike first, to destroy Amlina and her allies, as she had sworn to do.

But first, Beryl must regain her full powers.

This was the reason for the increase in sacrifices at the temple. As the Incarnation of the Sun, Beryl drank the blood of the captives and absorbed their life-essence. In the past, five or six sacrifices a year had been sufficient to prolong her life and maintain her vitality.

But since her flight from Kadavel, she had required more, and more.

… Beryl realized the chamber was quiet. Toulluthan had finished speaking and everyone was watching her expectantly. She had lost focus yet again.

She cleared her throat. "Thank you, Toulluthan. I am sure you will continue to serve us well as treasurer and manage the problem to the best of your abilities." She let her gaze rest pointedly on him a moment longer, then shifted her eyes to her chief military commander. "And I am sure our General Quallich will make the necessary changes to ensure that our sacrifices are delivered to the temple in excellent health."

Beryl sensed with satisfaction the deferential fear that now possessed both men. She glanced around the circle, noting how the rest of her councilors stared at the floor.

"But I think I have worked you all hard enough. We will adjourn for the day, and resume the Council tomorrow."

She rose. The councilors bowed deeply, while their aides and servants prostrated themselves. Beryl walked across the polished dais and passed through a portal with a high, pointed arch. Entering the corridor beyond, she waved a finger over her shoulder, moving a switch that caused iron doors to slip from within the walls and clang shut.

Now, out of view of everyone, Beryl allowed her shoulders to sag. She must be more careful. She must *never* show even the slightest sign of distraction or uncertainty.

She needed to replenish herself. Even the monthly sacrifices were proving insufficient.

Beryl marched down the long, empty corridor, with its shining black floor and opalescent wall panels—each a door that only she could open. At the far end, she passed beneath another arch, then crossed an open courtyard under a wintry sky. Ahead stood the massive gray stones of the Bone Tower, her sanctuary.

Twelve guards stood at the entrance, hulking brutes with the bodies of large men and the heads of male lions. They were thralls, reshaped by Beryl's arts. Halberds were clenched in their clawed hands, and wide, curved swords hung from their belts. They stood motionless, staring straight ahead as Beryl passed. They would come alert only at her command, or if some intruder tried to enter the tower. Then they would slay without hesitation.

The interior of the Bone Tower was an empty, cavernous space. A stairway on the circular wall spiraled up to the distant ceiling. Often, Beryl climbed the steps, but today she was weary and impatient.

She walked to the center of the floor and removed a black glass bead from a pocket. She spoke a few words and dashed the bead on the floor. The glass shattered and a funnel of silver light appeared. As it expanded and spiraled up, it lifted Beryl, turning her body gently as it raised her higher and higher.

After rising more than two hundred feet, she passed through a round aperture, drifted to the side, and settled her feet on the floor. The chamber was forty paces across, illumined by glass lamps and by slotted windows set beneath the high, pointed ceiling. Along the circular wall, doorways opened to an outside parapet, and to shadowy alcoves and hidden rooms. Stationed at intervals along the wall were servants, motionless as statues. They too were thralls, enlivened only when called on to perform rote duties such as tending the lamps.

A creature with the body of a long-tailed monkey and a hairless human head skittered across the floor. The treeman, Beryl's confidante and pet, jumped into her arms, chattering excitedly—sounds that only she would understand as speech.

"Yes, Grellabo." Beryl patted his head. "We will drink again." She grasped the fur on his back and dropped him to the floor. The treeman chittered and jumped about, watching her expectantly. As she crossed the chamber, it followed on her heels.

Passing a long ebony table, Beryl let her gaze fall on a stack of scrolls and parchments. For many days, she had been studying and working in trance, endeavoring to fashion a magical design to restore her full powers. Progress had been slow and tortuous, but lately there had been breakthroughs. Soon, she believed, the composition would be complete. Then she could begin the rituals to prepare herself for what she hoped would result in a perfect rejuvenation.

In the meantime, she would have to make do with her customary methods.

Reaching the wall, she slid aside a black curtain. In the recess stood seven cages of gilded bronze. Two were empty. The other five contained young men and women between the ages of fifteen and twenty, standing naked with eyes closed, their minds vacant. Beryl looked them over before making her selection.

She reached out a finger to touch the lock on one of the cages. Metal clicked and the door wheeled open, hinges creaking. Beryl reached inside and grasped the wrist of the cage's occupant, a slender boy with smooth, umber skin and shiny black hair, a captive from one of the eastern provinces. The boy's eyes sprang open, revealing a look of fear. Otherwise he stayed perfectly still.

"Come, my child," Beryl whispered.

The boy's mouth twitched, and his eyes grew desperate. But he moved compliantly, stepping out of the cage and accompanying Beryl along the wall. The treeman scampered happily behind.

They came to a heavy table—two stone columns supporting a slab of pure onyx. Tugging her captive's wrist, Beryl directed him to climb up on the slab. The boy whimpered but obeyed. Beryl forced him to lie on his back. The treeman hopped onto the table and sat at the edge, head bobbing up and down as he watched eagerly.

Beryl tightened a black strap, like a horse's girth, around the boy's middle. She secured the wrists to cuffs attached to the strap. She let her fingers linger a moment on the boy's upper thigh, and hummed to herself, heart quickening with anticipation.

She stepped to a nearby cabinet. Opening it, she picked out a shallow silver cup and a razor. A mirror hung on the cabinet door and Beryl paused, scrutinizing her reflection. Frowning, she turned and walked back to the slab.

Putting down the cup and razor, she stretched to her full height and took several long breaths. She murmured an incantation, words of power in a dead Nyssanian tongue. Below her, the boy lay stiff, the eyes showing confusion and worry. He was still deeply entranced. He felt fear, but not nearly enough. Beryl leaned over and whispered in his ear.

"Awake, my little one. Come out of your trance. I want you awake now."

The boy blinked. His eyes focused on Beryl and widened in horror. "Oh, no," he whispered, shrinking away, pulling frantically at the wrist restraints. "No. No—Please."

Beryl clenched her fist in the boy's soft hair and yanked back the head. "Yes, my little hero. I am going to cut your throat now and drink your blood. It will hurt very much, and you will struggle, and choke. It will take you quite some time to die."

The boy screamed, thrashing madly. Beryl tightened her grip on the hair, arm straining, as she picked up the razor with her other hand. Her lips pulled back, teeth clenched, as she reveled in the boy's hysteria, the terror flowing into her body as a nourishing force.

She waited till the thrashing subsided to weak shudders, the boy whimpering pitiably. Then Beryl emitted a triumphant cry and swiped the razor hard over the soft throat.

Blood spurted, and the boy's mouth jerked open. Beryl locked eyes with him for a moment, relishing the look of shock and terror. Then she dropped her head and lapped up the gushing blood. She swallowed as much as she could, then set the cup beside the throat to catch more. By then the boy's spasms had weakened, though the blood still spurted with the heart's pumping.

Beryl stood panting, invigorated and excited. When at last the boy lay still, she released her hold on the tangled hair. The treeman had slipped up near the victim's shoulder and was quietly licking up blood.

Beryl returned to the cabinet and regarded her reflection in the mirror. Despite the bloody mouth and teeth, she looked better now, younger. Not fully herself, by any means, but replenished for the present—renewed enough to return to her studies and the fashioning of her grand design.

And when that ensorcellment was accomplished and her powers fully restored, then she would turn her attention to her enemies— Amlina and her barbarian allies. She would find them, enthrall them if possible and lock them in cages. At the very least, she promised herself, she would feast on their terror and drink their blood.

THREE

Castle Demardunn, ancestral home of Meghild's tribe, perched like a raptor atop a steep hill. In the gray morning, Glyssa and her klarnmates marched through the gatehouse, passing under the iron teeth of the portcullis. They tramped across the drawbridge, over a deep ravine fed by a mountain spring. On the far side they paused, where a spill of boulders formed an outer defensive bulwark. Below them, the log houses, workshops, and stables of the village stepped down the hillside to the blue fjord. The smoke of morning cook fires rose from chimneys in steep-pitched roofs, mingling with wisps of fog that glittered here and there with witchlight.

For a moment, Glyssa was reminded of the murky fog in which her mind had been trapped for so long when she was enthralled, the sparks of light like the pricklings of fear. But that was over long ago, she told herself. Now she was back with her mates, and today they were going to raise the klarn spirit.

The Iruks turned away from the village and picked their way among towering pines and mossy boulders. Leaning at times on their spears, they climbed a narrow, slippery path. High in the branches above, crows cawed to warn of the human intruders.

Lonn led the way, followed by Glyssa. Behind her walked the other two women of the klarn: Karrol, who was tall and brawny, always outspoken and forceful; and Karrol's elder sister Brinda, tough and strong, but of a quiet, reserved temperament. Next came the other two men: Eben, lanky and sharp-witted, sometimes hot-tempered; and Draven, blithe and handsome, always hearty and cheerful.

The mates wore deerskin garb and leather harnesses. With the warming weather, they had left off their hooded capes, overshirts, and fur leggings. Along with a spear, each had a sword and long dagger hung at the waist. Of course, Glyssa's gear was different, her Iruk garb lost long ago. She wore the soft leather tunic and knee-high boots of a Gwales sailor. Her weapons at least were familiar—the castle armorer having made it a point of pride to forge a sword and dagger exactly like those of her mates.

Near the top of the hill, below the high ramparts of the castle, they came to a clearing where a spring gushed from the rocks—the place where they had put the klarn-spirit to rest. The Iruks performed that ritual at the close of every hunt, and raised the spirit when it was time to hunt again.

They had last called the klarn-soul into their bodies on board the Larthangan ship, the *Plover*, nearly a month after fleeing from Kadavel. Sailing on ice along the mountainous coast of this northern land, the *Plover* had been accosted by a Gwales warship. Thinking they might need to make a fight of it, the Iruks had raised the klarn and made ready for battle. But Amlina had skillfully bluffed and negotiated with the Gwales captain. Perhaps she had bewitched the man—Glyssa was never sure about Amlina's arts. Standing on the quarterdeck, shouting through a megaphone, the witch explained that they were outlaws, fleeing the Tathian Isles. She offered gold in exchange for refuge, and boasted that her party had spears and magic to defend themselves, if the Gwalesmen preferred to fight.

Garm, the Gwales captain, was intrigued and offered Amlina the hospitality of his mother, Queen Meghild. His ship conducted the *Plover* farther north, to the mouth of this fjord in Meghild's domain. There, Amlina parted with the Larthangan ship, paying the captain richly, as she had promised. Transferring to the *cranock*, the witch and her party sailed up the fjord to Meghild's castle.

On hearing their tale, the aged and crippled queen welcomed them as guests. At first, the Gwales folk treated them with distant courtesy and a certain, dour wariness. But that changed as Meghild warmed to them. The queen seemed to grow genuinely fond of Amlina, and to regard the Iruks, pirates themselves, as kindred spirits. After some days, satisfied as to their safety, the Iruks had come to this clearing and performed the ritual to put the klarn to rest.

Now, three months later, as they were preparing to leave, it was time to raise the klarn again. The mates arranged themselves in a half-circle around the spring. One by one, they lifted their spears and thrust the points into the ground.

Glyssa produced a wooden drinking bowl borrowed from the castle. The ritual cup they had used in the past was lost—left behind with most of their possessions on their home island of Ilga. Lonn had seen in a vision that their lodge house on Ilga had been ransacked by vengeful neighbors. So Glyssa's cup, made from the skull of one of her ancestors, was lost now, likely beyond hope of recovery.

Feeling a pang of regret at this memory, Glyssa dropped to one knee and filled the bowl from the spring. She stood and solemnly offered the vessel to Lonn, who raised it to his lips and drank.

"Now is the time for hunting," he said. "We awaken the klarn and call its strength into our hearts, our limbs, our blood." With these words he poured a libation at the place where his spear-point pierced the earth.

Lonn handed the bowl to Karrol, who repeated the ritual. Glyssa stared as the bowl was passed to Brinda, then Eben. With each pouring Glyssa attuned her mind to her mates, straining to feel their spirits rise into her with the klarn-soul.

And she *did* feel it, faintly at first, then more clearly—their courage and excitement at starting a hunt, their mutual trust and devotion. When Draven passed the bowl to her, she took it gladly. She spoke the ritual words and carefully poured the libation, watching the clean water spill over her spear.

She looked up to find all the mates watching her intently. She cleared her throat and sought to reassure them with her smile.

"Let us go and test the boat," she said.

* O *

In a cheerful and excited mood, the Iruks marched down the hill through the village. A dog barked at them from inside a fence, but the people they passed merely nodded, if they acknowledged the Iruks at all. The Gwales villagers had long ago grown accustomed to their queen's strange guests.

"Rather lucky for a meltwind to blow when we're finally ready to sail the boat," Eben remarked. "Most of the voyage figures to be on soft water."

Glyssa knew that to be true. Whether the klarn decided to sail with Amlina or home to the Iruk Isles, the voyage would take place in First and Second Summer. Except for an occasional short-lived freeze, the seas would likely remain melted.

"I expect it will float like a bathtub," Karrol grunted. "Like all Gwales craft. But I'm more worried to see how it handles on ice." Karrol had been skeptical about the size and design of the new boat from the start.

"It will freeze again soon enough," Lonn answered. "We'll have ample chance to test on both."

"Sure," Karrol said. "If we're lucky, a freezewind will blow while we're out today. Then we'll learn how hard it is to chop the boat free of the ice."

Lonn, who would pilot the boat, snorted at this. "The Gwalesmen sail their ships up onto ice with no trouble. Are they better sailors than Iruks?"

"In a Gwales boat, who knows?" Draven laughed. "But we'll see."

The mates reached the base of the hill and trekked along the shingle beach. Near the edge of the village, they approached their new boat, perched on the rollers that had been used to haul it down from the shipyard.

The craft was a *cranock*, similar to the ships Gwalesmen used, though smaller than most. Still, at sixty feet, it was half again as long as the hunting boats the Iruks were accustomed to. Iruks built their boats of bone and hide, as their home islands lacked timber. The Gwalesmen constructed their ships with oaken keel and planks, some of the vessels over a hundred feet long. Like an Iruk hunting boat, the small cranock had a single mast, and twin outriggers stretched out from the hull. The outriggers gave the boat stability on water, while their iron-shod bottoms served as runners when sailing on ice. Unlike an Iruk boat, the cranock had raised fore and aft decks, with sheltered compartments below for storage or sleeping.

The boat sported the painted figurehead of a phoenix, a sacred bird of Larthang. Amlina had provided a sketch to the wood-carver, and had worked designs over the carving for magical protection. In anticipation that the Iruks might sail with her, Amlina had shared the cost of commissioning the boat. If the Iruks elected to part ways with the witch, they would repay her portion.

Talees, the bald shipwright, waited beside the boat with two of his apprentices—brawny young men in plaid wools and leathers. "Here she stands, my Iruk friends. What think you?"

"A pretty craft, to be sure," Draven said, scanning the sleek lines with admiration.

"True enough," Lonn said. "But our liking will depend on how it handles."

"She'll sail as *treen* as any boat her size," Talees replied. "Treener than most."

Generally, the Gwales folk spoke a dialect similar to the Low Tathian the Iruks knew well. But on occasion they might use a word or phrase of *Gwelthek*, their ancestral tongue.

"*Treen*?" Eben asked.

"Aye, sweet and nimble." Talees explained. "She's ready to launch, if you'll just help us push."

The Iruks and the apprentices arranged themselves at the outrigger planks and the rear of the hull. Glyssa stood next to Lonn and set her back against the stern. Talees used a mallet to knock away the restraining blocks. At his word, everyone heaved, and a moment later the boat went rattling over the rollers and splashing into the fjord.

Glyssa's mates gave whoops of excitement as they high-stepped through the chill water and climbed onboard. Lonn and Talees mounted to the aft-deck and took their places at the tiller, standing beside two windbringers in wooden pails. Aided by the shipwright's men, the Iruks unpacked the canvas sail—the soft-water sail—and threaded it to the yard. Draven and Karrol took positions at either rail, holding the sheets, the steering lines. Glyssa and the others dragged on the halyard, running up the sail.

There was no need to rouse the windbringers from trance, since the wind was steady, blowing up the fjord from the southwest. With the halyard secured, Lonn pulled the tiller hard to starboard and shouted for Draven and Karrol to trim sail. The yard swung round to port, the mast leaned, and the broad sail bowed as it caught the breeze.

The cranock glided away from shore, gathering speed. Along the rails the mates were grinning and cheering. Glyssa climbed to the rear deck to stand beside Lonn, resting a hand on his shoulder. She breathed in the cold air, felt the salt wind on her face. It felt good to be sailing again.

During the winter months, the Iruks had gone on two excursions as guests of Meghild's warriors, journeying up the fjord to hunt deer and tusk-bears. They had learned the lines and rigging of the cranock as they helped crew the boats. But now they were sailing on soft water, and the boat was their own. In the days ahead, they would need to sharpen their skills to a level of mastery, in preparation for venturing out on the open sea.

For the next two hours they put the boat through maneuvers—changing tacks, running close-hauled, adjusting shrouds to the tilt of the mast. Glyssa darted about on the deck, hauling on lines and unraveling knots, enjoying the work of crewing the boat and glimpsing, through the klarn-soul, the thoughts and feelings of her mates.

All of them seemed pleased with the boat. Lonn allowed that it handled well—not as fleet and nimble as an Iruk craft, of course, but swifter and more responsive than the large cranocks they had sailed before. Draven was joyful as usual. Eben, perched on the masthead as lookout, warily scanned the waters, even as his keen mind judged the boat's pitch and roll. Even Karrol and Brinda seemed thrilled with the sailing, though Glyssa sensed in them, beneath the surface, a growing mindfulness and worry over what would happen next—what decision the klarn would make about their future.

Sensing all this recalled to Glyssa's mind past voyages, the exhilaration of hunting, and the firm sense of belonging, of sharing the klarn-soul. Glyssa had been the most adept at that sharing, the first to feel when a mate was moody or aggrieved. The mates had relied on her to gently hold the klarn together. She hoped now, with all her heart, that she could fill that role for them again.

"Freezewind!" Eben yelled from his perch atop the mast.

Snapped from her reflections, Glyssa followed his gesture to the south, where a veil of white sparks moved on the horizon. She was standing beside Lonn at the helm, as the boat tacked in that direction.

"Right," Lonn tightened his grip on the tiller. "Now we'll have a tougher test."

He shouted to Draven and Karrol to adjust the sheets, and he pointed the bow closer to the wind.

"Aye, that's right," Talees advised. "One or two points off-wind, then hard on it when the sparks come."

"And it will climb the ice then," Lonn shouted—half-question, half-statement.

"She'll rise if you sail her rightly," Talees answered with a wild grin.

Glyssa moved back against the rail to give Lonn room. She watched the shimmering wind advance toward them up the fjord. The water grew rough, the hull bounding and jolting on the waves.

Glyssa sucked in a breath as the crucial moment approached. The magic forged into the freezewind produced a buoyancy, which allowed even large ships to ride onto forming ice if handled well. But the handling was all. If Lonn's timing was off even a little, the craft might become ice-bound, even damaged by the shuddering force of the freeze.

The instant before the witchlight reached the prow, Lonn pointed straight upwind. Everyone ducked, as the shrieking howl passed overhead. The hull quaked, lurched upward, and slid onto the new-made ice.

Shouts of celebration went up from the Iruks and Gwalesmen alike.

"Are you satisfied now, my Iruk captain?" the shipwright cried.

"Lower the yard," Lonn called, for the canvas sail was now flapping violently and the boat starting to slide backwards. "Break out the ice-sail."

As the mates jumped to it, Lonn turned to the shipwright. "Yes, my friend. It's a fit craft you've built us."

Glyssa laughed with joy and patted Lonn's back. She started to go and help with the sail, but Lonn grabbed her arm to detain her for a moment, leaned over and kissed her on the lips.

* O *

With the ice-sail raised and trimmed, Lonn moved to the pilot's bench amidships. To steer on ice, an Iruk hunting boat relied on the sail and the drag of the rudder, but the cranock, like all larger vessels, used cables and levers that actually changed the pivot of the runners. These were controlled by a second tiller, which Lonn now swung to point the boat off the wind.

For several more hours the Iruks tested the boat, repeating maneuvers at the higher speeds of sailing on ice. The new-formed ice was rough, with frozen waves and pressure-ridges, so the ride was far from smooth. It took Lonn time to master the ice-tiller, and to coordinate turning the runners with his mates' trimming of the sail. At one point, when they were coming about, the boat heeled dangerously off the ice. Eben might have been thrown from his perch had he not, as a precaution, lashed himself to the masthead.

Still, the cranock handled better on the ice than any of them had expected. By mid-afternoon, the mates decided they had put the boat through enough trials and could call the day a success. Lonn pointed the prow toward the wind, and they followed a course of long, easy tacks back toward the castle.

The weather had turned colder, and Glyssa crouched against the rail, a scarf protecting her face from the stinging wind. Her mood became gloomy, apprehension creeping into her mind. The boat had passed inspection, and so the waiting was over. The klarn would have to decide on a course. Glyssa clung tight to the wood rail, as if to keep from falling yet again into that icy void in her soul.

Soon after they spotted Meghild's castle perched on its craggy hill, Eben sang out from the masthead. Three ships were sailing up the fjord from the opposite direction. Peering into the bright haze, Glyssa spied them in the distance—tall cranocks with distinctive, bold red sails.

"Lord Penredd, home from raiding," Talees the shipwright said to Lonn. "Best give him wide berth to make his landing."

"Why?" Karrol called from her station at the rail. "We're closer to the town and faster too."

"And less experienced with our boat," Lonn answered. "Besides, we're guests, remember. And Penredd's never been pleased about it. Swing the yard to port. We'll head upwind and wait till after they've landed."

The mates moved to carry out the order, Karrol a bit grudgingly. Penredd was Meghild's grandson—a renowned captain, and a vain and boastful warrior. Where the other princes, Garm and Leidwith, had shown courtesy to the Iruks, Penredd had been surly from the start. He'd made it clear he disliked the visitors, and seemed especially resentful of the queen's growing fondness for Amlina. Glyssa was relieved that Lonn had not risked antagonizing the prince.

"You are wise, my friend," Talees said to Lonn. "Prince Penredd is known to be easily affronted."

FOUR

"Careful, my dears. Careful of an old woman's bones!" Meghild the queen sang out in her reedy voice as she shuffled and limped down the passageway. She leaned heavily with one forearm on Amlina's shoulder, the other on the strong shoulder of the bard, Wilhaven.

"Sure, my lady," Wilhaven answered soothingly, "your precious bones are safe with us."

Meghild was a tall woman, once famed as a warrior equal to any man in ferocity. Now, in her dotage, she was bent and rawboned, crippled by a lifetime of hardship and war.

Amlina, with her slight frame, struggled to support the queen's lurching steps. But she carefully avoided showing any strain. Conducting the queen to the feast hall was an honor the witch would not shirk, and she knew well the wisdom of revealing no weaknesses before these wild brigands of Gwales.

Fortunately, Wilhaven carried more than his share of the queen's weight. He was of medium height but wide-shouldered and strong, a warrior as well as a bard. Blonde and bearded, dressed in a rich maroon doublet and hose, he easily supported Meghild's arm, even with his harp in its velvet bag slung over his other shoulder.

Soon, to Amlina's relief, they reached the great hall, loud with the sounds of merriment. Twin tables running the length of the chamber were crowded with warriors and courtiers, bearded men in tunics and doublets, women in fine gowns with jeweled brooches and armlets of gold. Servants carried pitchers and trays between the tables and the cook fires that blazed in two hearths along the walls. A multitude of oil lamps burned in huge, black-iron chandeliers that hung from the vaulted ceiling—the excessive use of lamp oil a testament to the castle's wealth. At the far end of the hall, beneath a high gallery, hung the red and gold wolf banner of Demardunn, Meghild's Tribe.

From beside the doorway, a herald called out to announce the queen's arrival. Immediately the clamor subsided and all who were seated rose to their feet. Amlina and Wilhaven helped the queen to her place at the center of the high table, set across the top end of the hall. Meghild let out a grunt as she braced her knuckles on the table's edge.

"Welcome, my lovelies," she called. "Welcome to this feast in honor of our beloved Penredd and his noble company, who this day have returned to us with riches of gold and fabric, oil and ale. But the greatest treasures they bring are surely their own noble selves, their sweet presence a comfort to the heart of their queen." She raised a goblet to salute Penredd and his two captains, who stood near her at the high table, and then the crewmen of his ships, who occupied one of the long tables, over a hundred men in all.

"*Yr wyf yn cyfarch eich dewrder.*" The queen recited a toast in Gwelthek. "Now be seated, my lovelies, and enjoy yourselves!"

Amlina and Wilhaven gripped the queen's elbows and helped her sit down in the carved, high-backed chair. Meghild sighed and smiled at them both.

"Sit down, my dears. And thanks."

"Sure, it is an honor, my queen." Wilhaven bowed to her graciously.

Taking her seat, Amlina scanned the great hall as the babble and motion of the feast resumed. She spotted Draven and his mates, seated partway down the table to her right, opposite from Penredd's crews. Even at this distance Amlina could read tension in the Iruks' faces and postures. Of course, they had tested their new boat today and, from what Draven told her, were pleased with it. Now they were wondering where and when they would sail. This thought brought

Amlina back to her gnawing dilemma. The talking book, the *Bowing to the Sky*, both directed her to this path she dreaded to travel—the path of blood magic.

"You are preoccupied tonight, Amlina," Meghild's voice plucked her from her thoughts.

"Yes, my queen," Amlina glanced down at the platter of roast meat and vegetables that had been set before her. She had no appetite. "I am...pondering my next move."

"Hmm." Meghild carved at her meat with a knife. "You know you are welcome in my hall as long as you wish to stay. Your ministrations have eased my pains. Beside that, I enjoy your company."

"You are kind, great lady, and I am grateful." Amlina was far from expert in the healing arts. But through the application of pure deepshaping techniques, along with a herbal remedy suggested by Buroof the talking book, she had managed to relieve some part of Meghild's chronic suffering.

Boisterous laughter erupted from the far end of the table—Penredd reacting to some jest. The prince was a loud, violent man in his late twenties, with a dark and predatory look. He nursed a simmering hostility toward Amlina.

She tilted her chin toward that end of the table. "Some in your keep, at least, will be happy to see me go."

"Penredd?" The queen asked as she chewed her food. "Or others as well?"

"No, I was speaking only of your grandson," Amlina replied. "The other princes, have been most courteous, as have all of your retainers." Meghild's two sons were both currently away—Garm on a raiding expedition, Leidwith on a visit over the mountains to a neighboring tribe.

"Well," Meghild waved the knife. "Penredd is young and proud, anxious to prove his mettle, as befits a warrior. He will learn courtesy in time...unless someone kills him first." She chuckled at her own jest.

Amlina smiled wanly, caressing the rim of her wine cup. "I suppose that is the way with warriors."

"Ha! And with witches too?"

"Oh, no. In Larthang we are drilled in courtesy from an early age. If anything, we are excessively courteous."

Meghild's eyes sparked with amusement. "Aye, your manners are most refined, Amlina. And yet, you sail with a pack of barbarian pirates, and are locked in a death feud with the most bloodthirsty witch known in the world. I think beneath that Larthangan refinement, you are as tough and ruthless as any brigand—even myself."

"Am I?" Amlina did not picture herself that way. True, she had always been strong-willed, compelled by exaggerated ideas of her abilities, of what she might accomplish. Those notions had driven her across the world, from Larthang to the Tathian Isles to Far Nyssan. Did that make her tough and ruthless? Could she be ruthless enough now, to follow the path open before her? *Could it be the right thing to do?*

Meghild was studying her, one eye cocked. "What is your plan then?"

"That, I am trying to decide," Amlina confessed. "If I should retreat to Larthang and hope to find protection there, or if I dare to sail against my enemy, and risk the baneful magic I would have to invoke."

The queen stared into her eyes a moment, then lifted her goblet and took a long drink. Setting the cup down, she wiped her mouth with the back of her hand.

"Well, I know which I would choose—Any risk for a chance to face and kill my enemy. By the Three Sisters, what I would not trade for one more voyage! Were I not trapped in this ruin of a body, I would gladly sail with you against the Queen of Tallyba, though it meant my certain death."

Hearing these words, Amlina felt a cold tremor in her stomach. *The death of a queen in trade for the death of a queen. A fitting exchange to invoke the Mirror Against All Mishap. Sometimes the Bowing to the Sky gave a clearer answer after a day or two.*

Would Meghild really make that trade? Could it be the right thing to do?

The tremor inside Amlina grew stronger, like the tone of a temple gong.

* O *

Across the hall, the Iruks had taken their fill of meat and bread and now sat quietly drinking ale. While normally they were merry, even boisterous in the feast hall, this night they were solemn. Glyssa sensed the awakened klarn-spirit hovering over them, turning their thoughts inward.

Earlier in the day, as they climbed the hill to return to the castle, Karrol had broached the subject that concerned them all.

"So the boat is ready and we can sail—tomorrow if we wish. It's time to decide where we are going."

"We are waiting on Amlina," Draven reminded her.

"I know that," Karrol answered. "But how long will it take her to make up her mind?"

"We'll need to provision the boat," Lonn said. "And a few more days of practice sailing would be wise. There is no need for hurry."

"Fair enough," Karrol said. "But after a few days, if we are still waiting, what then? I just don't like not knowing."

The uncertainty troubled all of them. But for Glyssa, it was more that—an incipient terror she struggled to keep at bay.

Now, resting her chin in her hand, she pondered the faces of her mates and wondered what choice each of them might make. Draven was easiest to predict: he would want to follow Amlina. He was in love with the witch; all of them knew it. Lonn would choose whatever course he thought best for the klarn—he saw that as his duty as leader. Brinda said little, but Glyssa knew that she longed to go home, to hunt and sail on Iruk seas. Eben was harder to figure: He would weigh all factors carefully before deciding. As to Karrol, she felt a certain gratitude and loyalty to Amlina, but of course her loyalty to her sister Brinda must be stronger. The only thing certain about Karrol was that she would argue forcefully, whichever way she felt.

The feasting continued, many of the revelers growing rowdy, while others cradled their heads on the tables and fell asleep. The Iruks slept in an alcove off the great hall, so there was no point in retiring to seek quieter quarters. Besides, the servants continued to refill their tankards.

As an entertainment, a few of Penredd's crew staged mock duels in the floor space between the long tables. They fought with shields and wooden swords, stumbling at times, the worse for drink, while the onlookers roared with mirth.

But then Penredd himself leaped from his seat, took one of the swords, and challenged all comers. Now the combat took a more serious turn. Penredd showed no languor from drinking, and attacked his opponents with ferocity and rage, vanquishing one and then another.

The Iruks watched the duels with a certain derisive amusement. Eben suggested that the warriors showed only token resistance to their prince. Karrol muttered that, drunk as she was, she could take Penredd and two of his brigands at the same time. The Iruks were proud of their fighting skills and considered them superior. While the Gwalesmen did combat with long swords and shields, hacking and stabbing and relying on brute force, Iruks fought with subtlety and quickness. Their curved hunting swords were deadly at both point and cutting edge, and they never used shields. Instead their other hand might hold a spear or dagger, allowing them to parry or strike with either hand.

Suddenly, the hall was hushed. Looking up, Glyssa noticed that all eyes were fixed on her and her mates. From the center of the floor, Penredd stared at them.

"It seems that our Iruk friends mock us," he announced. "I see them simpering behind their hands. Perhaps one of them would like to try me?"

"No, Penredd!" Queen Meghild called from the high table. "These warriors are my guests."

"Just a friendly challenge, grandmother." Penredd defied her. "We all know how they boast, claiming their dodging and weaving style is superior to ours. I merely offer them a chance to demonstrate. But there is no need ... " He turned his back on the Iruks, spread his arms wide as he faced his crewmen. " ... if they are afraid!"

As the brigands of Gwales roared with mockery, the Iruks bolted to their feet. Karrol was halfway across the table, before Glyssa grabbed her arm.

"No, let me," Glyssa said. She had drunk less than the others. Besides, she feared Karrol might become enraged and injure the prince.

"Glyssa, are you sure?" Lonn clapped a hand on her shoulder. "One of us can—"

"No, I am sure." She flashed him a grin. "Let the smallest of us go. I welcome the exercise."

"Don't worry, Lonn," Eben laughed. "Glyssa will take him."

"I'm sure of that," Lonn answered. "But we don't want to humiliate him."

"Ha!" Karrol roared. "Don't humiliate the prince, Glyssa ... Not too much!"

Glyssa strode across the table and hopped to the floor. "Ho, Lord Penredd!" she called. "Are you ready for your lesson?"

Uproarious cheering sounded through the hall. Penredd turned to her, startled. But he recovered at once and gave a mocking bow. Glyssa glanced at the high table, where Meghild sat back now, relaxed and laughing—though Amlina watched with clenched jaw.

Penredd gestured to one of his men, who came forward and offered Glyssa a shield and wood sword. She took them, made a show of weighing them in her hands, then tossed the shield away.

"This will suffice," she announced. Lifting the sword, she slashed the air, weaving a blurred pattern.

Penredd frowned, then threw aside his own shield and raised the sword. Glyssa crouched and stepped sideways, balanced on the balls of her feet. The hall had grown very quiet.

Iruks were schooled to the sword and spear from an early age. Aspiring to become a warrior, Glyssa had always applied herself fervently to those lessons, compensating for her lack of brawn with quickness and determination. By the time she came of age, her agility and daring made her the equal of any of her klarnmates in sword craft. Through the winter months, she had practiced daily with her mates in the castle courtyard, approaching those sessions with a kind of desperate ferocity, the exercise bringing welcome relief from her internal struggles. So now, as she faced this mock combat in the feast hall, her skills were honed.

She feinted, dipping a shoulder, drawing an overhead slash from Penredd that she easily dodged. She leaped back, avoiding his vicious backhand cut. From both tables came muttering, laughter, shouts of encouragement.

The combatants circled, the prince's eyes blazing with anger. Glyssa thrust low, toward the sword hand. When the response came she pivoted in a blur of motion, ducked behind the prince and slashed him soundly on the back of the thigh.

The Iruks cheered their approval as Glyssa danced away.

"Were this a real fight," she called aloud. "Your leg would now be crippled. Do you wish to continue, my lord?"

Penredd spoke from his fighting stance. "A slight cut—hardly enough to slow a Gwalesman. We are far from finished."

Glyssa crouched, the wood sword pointed. This time Penredd attacked with fury, two quick jabs that made Glyssa retreat, then a sweeping cut that nearly caught her head. But Glyssa ducked beneath it and thrust long, her limber body close to the floor as her point struck the prince hard in the groin. He bent with a grunt and stumbled backward. A gasp went up from his crewmen, while elsewhere cheers and applause sounded.

"I fear I might have injured your man-parts, my lord," Glyssa shouted, "were this a real fight."

Penredd snarled. "Aye, you are a tricky little fox. But had I my shield, that thrust would never have touched me. Once more!"

Glyssa shrugged and balanced herself again. Penredd stalked forward, feinted twice, then slashed at her chest. Glyssa lunged low, aiming for the groin exactly as before. But this time Penredd dropped his sword, grabbed Glyssa's blade with one hand, then her wrist with the other. He yanked her arm high and back, wrenching her shoulder. As she tried to twist away he wrapped both arms around her middle. Glyssa was trapped, her back to his body as he growled triumphantly and lifted her off the floor.

"Now my lithe fox, you see this *is* a real fight. And you have lost!"

The Gwalesmen were hooting with laughter. At the far table, the Iruks jumped to their feet.

Penredd tightened his grip on Glyssa, holding her in a mockery of a lover's embrace, one forearm crushing her breasts.

"Oh. Have I damaged your woman-parts?" he cried, and squeezed harder.

Glyssa gasped with pain. She squirmed and strained, but the man was far too strong. Helpless rage welled up in her, black and dreadfully cold. Suddenly she was back in the icy place, back in Kadavel, trapped in despair. From far away she heard her own strangled cry.

With wavering vision, she saw that her mates had charged across the floor, ready to spring at the prince.

"Let her go now," Lonn ordered, his tone deathly calm.

But Karrol did not wait. She stepped in without pausing and punched Penredd square in the face. His head snapped back and his arms flew wide. He staggered a half step and fell, sprawling on his back.

FIVE

Glyssa had collapsed to her knees, gulping for air, her mates hovering over her. Penredd's crewmen were shouting, scrambling over the table.

"Enough!" Meghild bellowed from the high table. "There'll be no brawling in my hall!"

Amlina stood beside her, relieved at how swiftly and forcefully the crippled queen took charge of the situation. Meghild was on her feet, glowering as she shouted to the assembly.

"Back to your seats, my lovelies. Now, I say! And two of you men conduct Prince Penredd to his chamber. I believe he's had enough amusement for one night."

The prince was lifted to his feet, blood running copiously from his nose. He glanced about, angry and confused. Amlina gathered he was only partly conscious. His men stared furiously at the Iruks, but backed away as Meghild had ordered. Amlina was grateful for the queen's rule requiring that weapons be left outside the feast hall.

"Wilhaven, a song!" the queen commanded. "Something light and soothing."

As the Gwalesmen returned to their seats, the Iruks relaxed. They had helped Glyssa to her feet. Lonn tried to take her arm, but she pushed him away. She staggered, then ran to the far doorway, fleeing from the hall.

* O *

Glyssa raced through the dark, up the winding steps of a corner tower. She emerged on a high battlement, alone under the stars. The despair that smothered her was horrible, worse than at any time since her rescue. She would never be the same again, she knew that now—as she knew in her heart she could bear it no longer.

She climbed onto the wall, in the space between the merlon stones. Far below, her eyes could just discern the boulders at the edge of the moat.

Just lean forward, and this agony will be over forever.

She hesitated, thinking of what her death would mean to her mates, to Lonn most of all. But what good was she to them now? They would grieve of course, but wasn't that better for them than this—bearing with her this unending, hopeless misery?

She tilted forward. The wind sighed in her ears.

She was grabbed by the wrist, and then a forearm curled around her waist. She was pulled back and fell on top of someone. Twisting, she looked into Brinda's face.

"No, Glyssa. Don't you know how much we love you?"

Glyssa gave a piteous, keening cry. She sank against Brinda's body, sobbing.

"I am weak, Brinda. I am no good to the klarn."

"Yes, you are. Dear Glyssa, you are our heart!"

"But I can't be that any more. You don't understand. My own heart is lost to me."

Brinda soothed her like a babe. "We will help you reclaim it. We will find a way, I promise."

* O *

When Wilhaven had played and sung for some time, and the atmosphere in the hall grown peaceful and languid, Meghild announced she would retire. Amlina and Wilhaven assisted her from the feast hall and up the dim corridor.

The queen's apartment consisted of a single broad chamber at the rear of the keep. Tapestries adorned the stone walls, and a dark velvet curtain opened on a dais where the queen slept. As Amlina closed the door, two maidservants stepped from behind the curtain.

"Set me down on the couch, my dears." Meghild said.

As they guided her haltingly to the divan, the queen called to one of the maids to bring wine. Wilhaven lifted the queen's legs so she could recline, while Amlina arranged the cushions. Meghild settled back with a sigh.

"A song, if you please, Wilhaven—something to quiet my nerves. You stay too, Amlina, if you will." The queen waved her to a chair. "Unless you have pressing matters elsewhere?"

"No, my queen." The witch sat, straight-backed, at the edge of the armchair. "In fact, I have something I wish to discuss with you."

"Oh, aye?" Meghild scrutinized her. "Are you concerned about your Iruk friend roughing up Penredd? You needn't be. He got what he deserved. Perhaps it will teach him a lesson ... Or is it that you fear the Iruks are not satisfied, and may seek further redress for the insult?"

"What? Oh, no. I am sure their honor is satisfied. They are quick to anger, but not apt to hold grudges. I regret that the incident happened at all. Glyssa should have known better than to fight with Penredd."

Meghild shrugged. "They are warriors. They could hardly ignore the challenge."

"Yes, but Glyssa has ... " Amlina hesitated. "She is vulnerable. There is a rift in her soul that has not healed."

The queen looked somber. "She did seem humiliated. I am sorry. Please express my regrets to them all for Penredd's behavior."

"Yes. I will."

Amlina took a cup of wine from a proffered tray and stared into the ruby depths.

"What did you want to discuss with me?" Meghild prompted.

The two maids stood nearby. Wilhaven sat at the foot of the divan, tuning his harp.

"It would be better if we speak in private, my queen."

"Hmm." Meghild gestured at her attendants. "Leave us, my dears. I will call when I need you. No, you stay, Wilhaven. I have no secrets from my bard."

Wilhaven had set down his harp and started to stand. Now he settled back and, with Meghild, gazed inquiringly at the witch.

And so we come to it, Amlina thought. She was about to step off of a bridge, to fall into unknown depths.

"I was struck by what you said in the feast hall. That you would give anything for one more voyage, that you would sail with me against my enemy if you could, though it meant your certain death."

"Aye?"

Amlina peered hard into the queen's eyes. "Did you mean those words, Meghild? Do you mean them now?"

The chamber fell silent, Meghild and Wilhaven both staring at the witch. When the queen's lips moved, her voice was hushed and eager. "Is there a way?"

"There is. But understand: your death *would* be certain."

Absorbing these words, the queen hesitated, pondering for moment. Then her visage darkened, eyes glaring. "Explain yourself, Amlina. Tell me all!"

Amlina winced at the queen's ferocity. But there was no turning back.

"What I propose is to journey to the lost city of Valgool, in the upland wastes of Far Nyssan. There, and only there, by invoking an ancient spirit of that place, it is possible to fashion a great ensorcellment called the Mirror Against All Mishap. If I am successful in weaving that design, I will then sail to Tallyba and attempt to kill Beryl. But you must understand, my queen, the chances of success are uncertain. I might never reach Valgool; I might fail at creating the Mirror; or the power of the Mirror might expire before I can reach Tallyba. Or, Beryl might use some magic I cannot guess at, to overcome my designs. But the worst part is—for you—that you will never know the outcome. You see, this is blood magic; it requires human sacrifice. The death of a queen to achieve the death of a queen: that is the reflection the Mirror demands. I would never ask this of anyone—it violates my principles as a witch of Larthang. But tonight, in the feast hall, you spoke words that made me think you would accept such an opportunity, welcome it, in fact. And so, I lay the offer before you."

Amlina had stared at the floor as she spoke. Now she forced herself to confront the queen's gaze. Meghild was pale, lips pressed shut. She glanced at the bard, whose hand covered the harp strings as though to keep them still.

"Perhaps you think I lack the courage for this," Meghild said at last. "But you would be wrong."

"My queen," Wilhaven cried. "I beg you to consider with care: your life, your duty to the tribe."

"Aye, I know. It is no light thing to cast your life away. But this existence I have is but a painful wreck of my former life. As for Demardunn, it deserves a warrior on the throne. Leidwidth my son will make a fit ruler."

"Not so fit as you, my queen," Wilhaven said. "Forgive my bluntness."

"Fit enough," Meghild growled. "Besides, what difference if he takes my place now, or a few years hence? No, the more I look at it, the more sure I feel. If your witchery can restore me, Amlina, so that I can sail once more, stride the rolling decks of a cranock, then I will gladly go with you and die in lost Valgool."

Amlina locked eyes with her, wondering again if this was the right thing to do.

"But I have one condition." The queen raised a finger. "That my bard here accompany us on the voyage. So that, assuming he survives, he may compose fit poetry to record Meghild's last adventure, to sing in all the halls of Gwales. Would you accept that charge, Wilhaven?"

The bard's eyes were downcast, his voice subdued. "Aye, my lady, if you are fixed on this course, then it would be my honor to sail with you."

"There you have it," Meghild eyed the witch challengingly. "Now tell me the truth: How will you rejuvenate my body to make this voyage possible?"

Amlina's gaze shifted again to the floor. "That won't exactly be necessary. All I will need is your head."

SIX

"You need to explain that, Amlina," Meghild said calmly. "And in a way we can understand."

The witch climbed to her feet. "The Mirror is difficult to create," she said, pacing the floor. "But not so difficult to understand. Essentially, it protects the bearers from all harm, reflects that harm back at the ones who launched it. If I were protected by the Mirror and Wilhaven here struck at my head with his sword, then space would bend and the sword embed itself in his skull. If a deepshaper cast a design at me to turn my bones to jelly, then it would be cast back and her limbs and spine would collapse.

"So much for the Mirror's effects. As to its fashioning, just as in an actual mirror, each element of the design must be a reflection of something else. To create it requires the formulation of an *eidolon*, a spirit-body, which would be a reflection of your physical body. This eidolon will be animated, directed, by your brain. This means that your head must be removed, still living, and mounted on the shoulders of the eidolon."

The bard stared aghast, but Meghild's eyes showed eager excitement. "Will it allow me to stand, to walk, to breathe the air?"

"It will, according to the ancient texts. It will also, from the moment of its animation, draw power from the *Ogo*—that which we call the Deepmind. This pure, unformulated power will engender the Mirror Against All Mishap, at the moment when the eidolon—and you, my queen—are obliterated atop the ruined pyramid in lost Valgool."

"I see," Meghild said. "And you are certain you can make this eidolon work, and it will house my mind?"

Amlina shook her head. "No. As I admitted before, the whole project is uncertain. The currents of the Deepmind are true, the laws of magic are certain. But steering those currents, invoking those laws—that depends on the power and skill of the deepshaper. I *believe* I can fashion an eidolon body that will house your mind. That is all I can say for certain."

Meghild stared, pondering, appraising the witch. Wilhaven's eyes were downcast, his face solemn and dark.

"Very well," the queen said, at last. "I will risk it. When do we start?"

Amlina could not help but smile. "You are brave and indomitable, my queen. I honor you for that."

"Bah!" Meghild brushed aside the compliment. "It is little enough I am risking. Assuming your magic works, how long will I have to live in the spirit body?"

"That," Amlina said, "is a crucial factor. For just as many days as the eidolon lives, from the moment of creation to destruction, for just that long will the Mirror itself last after it is formed."

"Then you will want to prolong the time."

"Yes, for as long as possible. But there is another factor. The Mirror is both blood magic and moon magic. It can only be created under a specific alignment of the moons—including not only Grizna and Rog, but Tysanni, the mythical third moon that vanished in the Time of the World's Madness."

Wilhaven twanged a sharp note. "And how can a vanished moon align with anything?"

Amlina shrugged. "Some believe Tysanni did not fly off into space, as is commonly believed, but only became invisible, and still follows its course through the sky. In any case, there are records of its appearance on historical dates, and these allow astronomers to calculate where in the sky it would be, even to this day."

"And that is sufficient for your moon magic?" the queen asked.

"Yes. Moon magic is common in Nyssan, including such as relies on aspects to Tysanni. For creation of the Mirror, the three moons must be aligned in a configuration known as a *Baleful Trine*—a configuration that occurs once every four or five years. It will next occur on the 19th night of the first month of Second Summer."

"Then we have roughly two months," Meghild said.

"Precisely 73 days." As a bard, Wilhaven was trained in calendar calculations.

Meghild shifted her legs and sat upright. "There are charts in that cabinet by the wall. Find me one that shows Kleeg and the northern seas."

Amlina walked over and opened the carved doors of the cabinet. She sorted through a number of parchment rolls, then carried one over to the queen. She sat on the divan beside Meghild, who spread the roll on her lap.

"Aye, here we are." Meghild's gnarled finger traced the outline of lands and waters across the northern ocean. "About two small-months to reach Kleeg, in the soft-water season. Then across the Bay of Mistrel ... Fogs are likely there, so say another 10 to 15 days ... That makes about 37 days to get here, Borgova, on the eastern edge of the bay. Valgool, as I recall, was supposed to be somewhere beyond these mountains."

"Yes ... here." Amlina pointed to a spot on the map. "According to charts shown to me by Buroof, the talking book."

"Then we'll travel up this river as far as it is navigable, then overland through the mountains. That is the realm of the *torms*, you know? The winged-folk are savage and speak no human tongue."

"So I understand," Amlina replied quietly. "But Buroof claims to know their language."

The queen's eyebrows lifted. "Interesting. Well then, assuming safe passage through their mountains—and it will be summer at least, so the passes should be open—it should take maybe another 20 days to reach the ruins of Valgool. And that means ... how many total days for the journey, Wilhaven?"

"Close on 57 days by your figuring, my queen. And if the alignment of moons comes in 73 days, that gives us 16 to spare."

"Very good," Meghild said. "I will need a small-month to settle my affairs." She showed a wicked smile. "After that, Amlina, my head is at your disposal."

* O *

Nervous, exhilarated, bone-weary, Amlina returned to her chamber—to find the Iruks waiting. Grouped around the trestle table, they turned to her expectantly as she entered and shut the door. From his place at the end of the table, Kizier the windbringer regarded her somberly with his single eye. He instantly sensed her mood.

"Amlina, is everything well?"

"Yes. I've just come from the queen." She ran a hand through her pale hair as she stepped toward them. "But why are you here, my friends?"

"We need to talk with you, about Glyssa," Karrol said. "You must help her. She is ... she needs your help."

The Iruks hovered over Glyssa like bears protecting an injured cub. The small woman sat with shoulders hunched, staring vacantly through eyes red from crying.

The witch slumped into her chair. "What help would you have from me, Glyssa?"

It was necessary that Glyssa speak for herself, to confront the chaos inside her. Amlina knew this much, at least, and so she waited through the painful silence.

"I cannot speak of it," Glyssa said at last. "I am too afraid, too ashamed."

With a twinge of fright, Amlina glimpsed the abyss in which Glyssa was trapped. The witch pulled back, deliberately shielding her emotions. Empathy now would be no help at all.

"There is no reason for shame, Glyssa. But the fear: I understand that all too well." She glanced at Draven, then Lonn. "I have known for some time of Glyssa's predicament. Since even before we came to Gwales."

The Iruks stared at her with surprise.

"It is true," Kizier said. "Amlina and I have spoken of it. We have both been concerned over Glyssa's suffering."

"Then why have you done nothing to help her?" Lonn demanded.

Amlina frowned. She rose to her feet, leaned over the table, and opened the talking book.

"Buroof: I, Amlina, summon you to speak."

A white haze flickered over the pages, and with it came the ancient smell of the book—mixed of dried parchment, incense smoke, countless magical energies.

"I am listening, Amlina of Larthang."

"My allies, the Iruks, are present, along with Kizier," Amlina said.

"Hmm. Yes, I perceive them. An active set of minds, not dull, but unschooled— distastefully ignorant."

The Iruks were watching, grim and perplexed. The book had spoken in Larthangan.

"Converse with us now in Low Tathian, so they can understand."

"Oh, very well," Buroof replied with ill humor. He switched to the common trading tongue: "Why have you summoned me?"

"Have I not spoken with you before, concerning souls that have been enthralled, and the ways of recovery from that condition?"

At the far end of the table, Glyssa lifted her head, eyes alert.

"Yes," the book said.

"In many cases," Amlina continued, "full recovery occurs within days of the mind-cage being broken. Is that not correct?"

"True," Buroof allowed. "But in many other cases, full recovery never occurs, and the thrall is left a babbling idiot or speechless imbecile."

"But there are also cases, are there not, where recovery is only partial? Where conditions of fear, confusion, or desolation linger?"

"Yes, as we have discussed. This seems to happen more often if the captivity has been long, or the enslaver particularly powerful."

"And what magical techniques are known for healing such afflictions?"

Buroof answered impatiently, "As we *also* have discussed, there is scant knowledge on the subject—which only stands to reason after all. Why should a practitioner of these arts be interested in helping thralls recover? What benefit to them in such foolish altruism?"

"Spare us the rhetorical questions," Amlina said. "Explain instead the historical cases where full recovery for such sufferers *has* been achieved."

"*Purportedly* achieved," Buroof corrected. "And there are only two creditable traditions. One, at the temple of Nei-Chan in northwest Larthang, in the 16 Century of the current era, thralls who had been enslaved by the Red Viper Cult were supposedly healed, over time, by strict adherence to a monastic life."

"Yes, and the other tradition?"

"That would be Moorlina Kel San, the legendary and saintly Archimage of the East in the 4th century. Upon deposing Jan Tei, her notorious predecessor, Moorlina is said to have taken it upon herself to free all those whose minds Jan Tei had enslaved. In some cases, according to the histories, this could only be accomplished by training the former thralls in the arts of deepshaping, so that, over time, they were able to heal themselves."

Amlina shifted her gaze to Glyssa, whose stare now was compounded of fear and confusion—and perhaps a glint of hope.

"Thank you, Buroof. That is all." Amlina closed the book. She filled her lungs and let out the breath, scanning the Iruk's faces.

"Now you understand. Kosimo the serd was a potent sorcerer. He left a mark on Glyssa's soul. The only treatments known to history for her condition are a life of complete withdrawal from the world or training in the magical arts. In both cases the hope would be that, in time, Glyssa could heal herself."

The Iruks eyed her somberly. Karrol shuffled her feet. Lonn laid a hand on Glyssa's shoulder. Glyssa simply stared straight ahead.

"I do not see Glyssa withdrawing to a monastery," Kizier finally said. "But surely the other path is a possibility."

"That's right," Lonn said. "You initiated me, and later the rest of the klarn. Why not Glyssa?"

Amlina sank into her chair. How could she make them understand? "When I initiated you, and we formed a wei circle, it was with a certain, narrow purpose. That work only touched the surface of what we are talking about now. To train Glyssa in the arts of deepshaping, to the point where she could integrate and control the energies of her own soul: the task would be long and difficult at best, the chances of success ... unpredictable. And I am certainly not the best teacher. Honestly, you would do better to sail to Larthang and to use your gold to place her in an academy, or hire an expert tutor. But then—"

She stopped herself. She had known it was possible that she must part from the Iruks, but had not till this moment confronted her feelings. She feared going on without them, knew she would miss their strength and blithe courage, dreaded most of all the prospect of losing Draven.

She forced herself to go on. "—But that would mean we must part ways. For I will be sailing to the other side of the world. It has just this night been decided."

She told them of her plan, to take the head of Queen Meghild to the lost city of Valgool, to use it to invoke the Mirror Against All Mishap. The Iruks listened intently, grim and thoughtful, yet with a light kindling in their eyes at the promise of such a wild adventure.

The decision was also news to Kizier, but from him Amlina sensed only doubt and worry.

"You are resolved on this course?" Draven asked. "Even if we do not go with you?"

Amlina suppressed her misgivings. "Yes, I am resolved. If you will not join me, I hope some of Meghild's men might volunteer to sail with their queen. If not, I will hire a crew."

The bleak expression on Draven's face made her wonder if he might even break with his mates and follow her. Then Amlina's eyes were drawn to Glyssa, and the emotion she saw there, the fear and anguish, but also the stubborn courage, touched her heart. There was emotion in her own voice as she spoke.

"My friends, I cannot say what the end of this voyage will bring, but I dearly hope you will come with me. If you will, I promise to use my arts and all the strength of my soul to help Glyssa ... if that is what she chooses."

She rose unsteadily from the chair. "Now I must rest. For the next small-month, there is deep magic to prepare. I mean to sail in twelve or thirteen days. You must decide for yourselves what is best for you, and for Glyssa."

SEVEN

The bathing hall of Castle Demardunn was a long, steep-roofed building set in a corner of the main courtyard. The Iruks, who were fond of bathing, came here nearly every day—first to soak in tubs of warm water, then to relax in the steam.

They chose the bathing hall for their klarn meeting. It was as private as any place in the castle. Besides, by speaking in Iruk, they were assured their words would not be understood by attendants or other bathers who might appear. Wrapped in linen towels, they sat on two benches, facing each other through clouds of white steam that rose from the heated and drenched stones.

Glyssa had passed a sleepless night, her mind returning again and again to the duel with Penredd, the horrible flight up the steps, the despair so deep it almost made her leap from the parapet. But she had not stirred from bed, afraid of disturbing her mates, certain that Lonn and Brinda and Karrol would all have woken if she had tried to leave. She despised herself for causing them such worry.

Lonn stood and cleared his throat. "As to the meeting. You all know the question. Who will speak first?"

Their faces turned to Glyssa, and their scrutiny was like something that smothered her. "I prefer for others to speak," she muttered.

After a moment, Draven sprang up. "Well then, my opinion is this: we owe Amlina much—for rescuing us when we would have drowned in the sea, for helping us find and reunite with Glyssa, for leading us to more treasure than we'd ever seen. We owe her loyalty; she is our friend and ally, and she needs us now. But more than all that, she has promised, from her heart, to help Glyssa. I know she said she might not be the best teacher, but what option do we have? To sail to Larthang and try to find a witch or school to train Glyssa? We would have no idea what we were doing." He spread out his hands. "Really, mates, I see very little question about it. We should sail with Amlina. That is my vote."

He sat down, jaw set firm, and looked expectantly at the others.

Eben stood next. "As for what is best for Glyssa, she needs to speak for herself. She has not said she wants Amlina's help, or will accept it. As for Amlina, it is true we have benefited from our alliance. But so has she. We fulfilled the deal we struck with her. So my choice would be to sail for home—except for one thing, which Draven did not mention. The Archimage swore she would track us down and kill us. So far it has not happened, but that does not mean it won't. If Kosimo the serd could reach us with sorcery, even on Ilga, then I must believe Beryl could do the same. I believe that if we must face Beryl, our chances are much better with Amlina than without her. So I vote to stick with her."

As soon as he sat, Karrol rose, her face red and sweating. "This decision is harder than Draven and Eben make it sound. Regarding Beryl, it might be far more dangerous for us to go with Amlina than not. Beryl might never choose to hunt for us; Amlina is her true enemy. But I do feel sympathy for Amlina. She saved my eye, and has been a good friend to us. Were it just for myself, and I think for Brinda too, I would vote to go home. We are Iruks; I want to see our mothers and be with our own people. But none of that—none of it—matters to me in comparison to what is best for Glyssa. So I need to hear from her before I vote."

She sat down and there came another silence.

"I agree with everything Karrol said," Brinda murmured, without standing up. "I have nothing to add."

The mates stared at the stones and the gentle, rising steam. Glyssa felt all of their minds on her, waiting. Reluctantly, she stood.

"I am grateful to you, mates, for caring so much about me. And I am sorry, and so ashamed, for the grief I have caused you." At this, they uttered protests and words of consolation. Glyssa lifted her hand and continued: "As for what we should do ... I do not know if Amlina can help me. But I know she will try, with all her heart. I felt that last night when she spoke to us. I've always been suspicious of her. She is so different from us. But she does care about us, and we owe her much. I think Draven loves her, and might even break with the klarn if we *don't* sail with her."

"I have not said that," Draven protested.

"No," Glyssa answered softly. "You have not ... Karrol, Brinda, I understand your wanting to go home. And if *you* were to dissolve the klarn and leave us, I would not blame you. But I hope you will stay with me. I need your love and strength if I am to mend myself. My vote is that we sail with Amlina."

She resumed her seat, holding back tears.

Lonn stood and peered around at their faces. "I do not think we need further debate. I am reminded of what Belach the shaman said to us, the last time we landed on Ilga. In his vision, we were as terns, blown before the storm, far from Iruk seas. It would seem the storm is not yet ended."

"He told us to hold to the klarn," Draven said.

"Yes." Lonn extended his hand, palm down. The mates all stood and placed their hands in a pile on his.

"We will sail with the witch Amlina and help her kill her enemy," Lonn pronounced. "And we will do all in our power to help Glyssa be whole again. This is the decision of the klarn."

* O *

That afternoon, after practicing with her mates with sword and spear, Glyssa went alone to Amlina's chamber. She knocked on the door and presently heard the witch's voice, sounding as if from a distant cave.

"Who is there?"

"Glyssa. Is it all right if I speak with you?"

In a few moments the door opened. Amlina's face was pale, her manner distant. "Come in, Glyssa."

Inside the round chamber, candles burned in red lamps on the floor, and the witch's mirrored balls and feathered things hung suspended on threads attached to the distant ceiling. The air smelled of incense and felt charged with invisible power.

"If I am disturbing you, I can come back later."

"No." Amlina smiled kindly. "I am working on the designs I must cast. But setting things in motion is ... toilsome. A respite is welcome. It might help my concentration."

She led Glyssa to the long table where the talking book lay shut and Kizier, in his ivory pail, stood with his eye closed, humming in trance as windbringers were wont to do.

"Would you like to speak with Kizier as well? I can wake him."

"No, I do not think so." Glyssa sat on the edge of a bench.

Amlina settled herself into the carved arm chair and stared at her placidly.

"I wanted to tell you," Glyssa said, "that the klarn met this morning. We have decided to accompany you on your voyage."

Amlina smiled, bowing her head. "I am most grateful. I would not have wanted to undertake this journey without you and your mates."

"I am grateful to you," Glyssa replied, "for offering to help me. I have felt so alone these past months. I know how silly that must sound, with my klarn all around me."

"No," Amlina said. "It doesn't."

Surprisingly, Glyssa felt the urge to confess to the witch, to reveal the weakness she dared not show to her mates. "I keep thinking I am getting better. But then something happens—like last night—and I fall into it again: fear and despair that I cannot conquer."

"I know, Glyssa. I will help you as best I can. But you must understand, the most I can do is teach you the arts of the Deepmind and guide you in helping yourself. The real work, the hard work, will be yours."

"I know that, because you have said it. Yet I have no idea what the work will be."

The witch's sea blue eyes stared at her in the dim light. "I thought of you this morning and I consulted with Buroof again, to learn more about the legend of Moorlina. She likened the condition that you suffer to a fishhook left in the heart. A deepshaper who enthralls a person captures them, she said, like a fisher with a hook and line. She could cut the line, as I and your mates did when we freed you from Kosimo. But she could not remove the hook without tearing the heart and killing."

"I see wisdom in that," Glyssa said. "When the sorcerer's mind first entered me, it felt like claws seizing my heart and belly. But if the hook is this cold emptiness I feel, and it cannot be removed, what is the remedy?"

"According to Moorlina's teaching, over time you can dissolve it, absorb it into yourself."

Glyssa sucked in her breath. "That frightens me. It is foul and evil."

"It is power," Amlina said. "Magical power that you can make your own, and then transform into whatever manifestations you wish. That is the art of the deepshaper."

Glyssa pressed her lips. "I see … But I fear that it will change me, that I will no longer be myself."

"Oh, it will change you, indeed. But if you walk this path with patience and faith, you will become more yourself, not less. Your soul will grow and flourish. You will become a larger being."

Glyssa did not fully understand the witch's words. Yet despite the fear they roused in her, she could see no other way. "It is what I must do," she murmured.

"It is strange," Amlina said. "How at times the forces of the Deepmind create echoes in our world. This work I have undertaken, that I have been guided to: it requires that I invoke a vast and terrible power, take it into my soul and transform it, even as you must do."

In that moment, Glyssa perceived what Amlina faced, and sensed the witch's doubt and fear—almost as if Amlina were part of the klarn. Compelled by the same devotion she would show to a klarnmate, Glyssa stood and laid a hand on the witch's slim wrist.

"Perhaps we can strengthen each other."

* O *

A short time after Glyssa left Amlina's apartment, Kizier opened his eye. Alerted by the absence of the windbringer's hum, Amlina looked up from the parchment she studied.

"I have good news," she said. "The Iruks are sailing with me."

"I am glad, for your sake." The bostull's voice was even more subdued than usual.

Amlina had assumed the windbringer would also join the voyage, but now suddenly she was unsure. "And you, Kizier?" she asked.

"I do not know, Amlina. I must admit, the prospect frightens me. Not because I fear failure, or what Beryl might do to us. But because I fear what the blood magic might do to you. I fear how you might be changed."

Amlina's throat constricted. "I am aware of the danger. I honestly did not believe I could make this choice. But Meghild's willingness, *eagerness* to go along has led me to see things in a different light."

"So?"

"Yes. Consider: for more than a century, Beryl has kept Far Nyssan enslaved, the people terrorized, their children taken as hostages and sacrifices. Surely, to rid the world of such evil is a rightful goal. Perhaps then, this is a duty laid upon me by the Ogo."

"Well, I suppose that could be true."

Or perhaps, Amlina thought, it was once again pridefulness, her exaggerated belief in her own importance. No, she must cast those doubts aside. A deepshaper who did not believe wholeheartedly in her intent failed before she ever began.

"I was thinking, Kizier, that if we succeed in killing Beryl, it would mean the designs she forged by sorcery would likely all break apart. That would mean that you would change back to human form."

The bostull's one eye blinked. "Yes, I suppose so ... Oddly, the idea is not entirely pleasing."

"No?"

"Indeed. I have found a certain serenity in the life of a windbringer, a passive attunement to the Ogo that is most comforting. Of course, I've also maintained human contacts. I have intellectual stimulation, my friendship with you, even with the Iruks. I've had the advantage, as it were, of living in both worlds."

Amlina showed a wan smile. "If you decide not to sail with us, you will lose your place in one of those worlds."

"True," Kizier remarked pensively. "I will become just another windbringer in the stern of some Gwales ship."

Amlina let him ponder that. She sorted through the parchments spread across the table, and found the map Meghild had given her.

"I wanted to ask you to look over the queen's map, and help me determine if we've estimated the time for the journeys correctly."

With the map set in front of Kizier, she pointed out the proposed route to Valgool and reviewed the number of days Meghild had predicted it would take. Then she traced the next phase of the journey, back through the Bay of Mistrel, south along the coast of Near Nyssan, around the Cape of Moloc, and finally on to Tallyba.

Kizier pointed out how the sea route would take them many hundreds of miles around the continent. By land, the distance from Valgool to Tallyba was actually much shorter. Of course, the overland route was through the *Khylum Destrae*, known as the Missing

Mountains, which had grown up in the Time of the Worlds Madness. No one knew what lay in that region, no deepseer had ever succeeded in piercing the mysterious veils that hung over the mountains, and the few explorers who ventured there had never returned.

"I almost considered the overland route," Amlina said, "thinking the Mirror might protect us from whatever beings or forces dwell in the Khylum Destrae. But even if it did, the chances of finding a route in time are doubtful." By the timetable Amlina had worked out with the queen, the eidolon would live for 60 days. That meant the Mirror Against All Mishap would exist for exactly 60 days after its creation.

"No, the question certainly is: will 60 days be time enough to reach Tallyba by the sea route?"

"Indeed ... Very difficult to estimate," Kizier commented. "And impossible to say with certainty. There will fogs in the northern waters, of course. And that time of year, the winds on the ocean may die for days at a time, especially around Moloc. Sixty days should be more than adequate time—but depending on circumstances, it might easily fall short."

Amlina shrugged. "I will just have to keep envisioning success."

"There's another factor," Kizier said. "All this assumes Beryl will *be* in Tallyba when you get there. But if she learns about the Mirror, and it's limited lifespan ..."

"She might withdraw from the city until the Mirror expires? No, I don't think so. For two reasons: First, knowing Beryl as I do, I don't believe she would allow herself to be driven from her capital by fear of her former apprentice. And secondly, when I was in deep trance, pondering whether to take this course, a strong vision came to me— that, for good or ill, I will confront Beryl one final time, and that confrontation will be in her Bone Tower."

Kizier sighed. "You are gambling much on the verity of that vision. And also on the fickle winds off Near Nyssan."

"Quite so," Amlina answered. "But as it is written in the *Canon of the Deepmind*, once the path is chosen, the steps must be taken with sureness. That is the way for all deepshapers."

"For anyone who would lead a worthy life," Kizier sighed, "even lowly scholars who have been changed into windbringers."

Amlina looked at him, hope rising. "Does that mean you will travel with us?"

"Yes, Amlina, I will not abandon you."

She placed a hand on the bottom of the bostull's green stalk. "I am grateful to you, my friend."

"It is best I see the end of the adventure," Kizier remarked philosophically. "Otherwise, if Beryl is slain and her designs overthrown, I might find myself on the deck of some Gwales ship, suddenly transformed into a naked scholar standing in a bucket of ice water. Can you imagine a more embarrassing scene?"

Amlina laughed quietly, and thought, *Whatever this journey might bring, at least I shall travel with noble companions.*

EIGHT

For the rest of the day, Amlina found that her work went easier. She consulted with Buroof about the formulas for the Mirror ensorcellment, and discussed with Kizier the pitfalls inherent in all blood magic. She wrote with quill and parchment, composing the incantations she would use for the preliminary workings—the forming of the eidolon and the taking of Meghild's head.

Absorbed in her work, she did not go to dine in the feast hall. But an hour or two after dusk, she received a summons from the queen. Amlina slipped on a quilted robe and fixed her hair with ivory combs. Arms folded in her sleeves, she descended the curving steps outside her chamber, wondering what the summons portended.

She found Meghild at the high table, surrounded by courtiers. Wilhaven the bard was there, and Frenrik, captain of the castle guard. Next to him sat Ishelda the law-speaker, a somber woman with plaited gray-hair. Amlina was surprised to see Leidwith, the queen's elder son also present. With him sat four other warriors, graybeards in plaid capes and felt hats, chieftains of the tribe. At the far end of the table sat Penredd, his face swollen and bruised. He glared at the witch for an instant, then lowered his eyes.

"Amlina, my darling, thank you for joining us." Meghild set down a silver tankard. "Will you take meat and drink?"

"Just water, my queen." Amlina sat in the chair Meghild indicated. She nodded at Leidwith. "Welcome home to you, prince."

"My lady." Leidwith returned the nod. He was a stout man, with specks of silver in his brown hair and neat beard. He had always treated Amlina politely, but tonight she sensed caution and unease.

"Yes, we were pleased to welcome him home today, from his visiting over the mountains," Meghild said. "His arrival gives me the opportunity to announce my plans, which is why I wanted you here, Amlina."

Now the witch understood the cause of the unease. Her glance traveled around the table, noting wary anticipation in everyone present—except for Wilhaven, who already knew the queen's plan, and Penredd, whose mood was sullen and rancorous.

Meghild rose from her chair, arms trembling. "My lovelies, it has long been in my mind that I ought to retire, that the throne of Demardunn deserves a fit and strong warrior, not a withered old woman ..."

She raised a hand to silence protests spoken by Leidwith, Frenrik, and others. "... And it has long been in my *heart*, that I would wish to sail again, to have one more voyage of adventure. Now, through her witchery, my friend Amlina will make this possible. Within the month, I will sail with Amlina and her party. Wilhaven will accompany us, and if there be enough men to outfit a second cranock, then they may come as well. But be advised, the journey will be long and perilous, deep into the highlands of Nyssan, and I do not expect to return."

Her words brought looks of shock and confused muttering.

"How is this possible, mother?" Leidwith demanded. "How will Amlina make you fit enough to sail?"

Amlina dreaded having to answer that question—or rather to conceal the true answer. Fortunately, Meghild took it on herself.

"The details of Amlina's magic are unimportant, and anyway beyond our ken. The concern of this council is the succession. I wish the throne to pass to you Leidwith, my elder son and heir. I hope, my lords, you will back my choice and work to ensure a peaceful succession."

In Gwales, Amlina knew, a monarch was elected by vote of able-bodied warriors. Disputes could easily lead to bloodshed, so a strong consensus was essential for a peaceable transfer of power. Everyone present at the table wielded influence, and Meghild was looking to solidify their support.

Leidwith stood, hands resting on the table. "My queen, I am sensible of the honor you grant me, but I must ask you to reconsider. Surely you know that I, and all of your people, wish you to remain our queen."

"Thank you for those sentiments, my son. But my decision will not be altered."

"But surely," Leidwith persisted, "your leaving should wait until Garm returns, so that the strength of the family is complete."

Meghild shook her head. "Garm will be at least another month at sea. For reasons pertaining to the plans I have made with Amlina, I cannot wait."

The faces around the table were anxious and perplexed.

Leidwith remained standing. "My liege, forgive my speaking plainly, but you put us in an awkward position. For an elderly queen to abdicate is one thing, but for her to sail off alone, with foreigners, it ... raises questions."

"What questions?" Meghild snapped. "What are you trying to say?"

When Leidwith hesitated, Penredd jumped to his feet. "What my uncle is trying to say is that you will shame us. To allow our queen to sail off in her dotage, with a Larthangan witch and a pack of barbarians? Our tribesmen, indeed all of Gwales, would question our strength and our honor."

"Bilge water!" the queen roared. "I am not so advanced in my dotage, Prince Penredd, that I cannot make my own decisions. I leave Demardunn strong and prosperous. Why should our people question my will, or care what prattlers in distant halls may say?"

The courtiers remained silent, plainly worried. Meghild's lips went thin. "Law-speaker, what say you?"

Ishelda stood and smoothed the front of her robe. "Certainly, it is the queen's right to abdicate her throne; the precedents are exemplary. And certainly, once that is done, she is free, as any free woman, to sail where she will. So much says the Law. But as to political implications, I believe there are valid concerns. It might be hard for Leidwith to consolidate the kingship if there are rumors and suspicions concerning the queen's departure."

Meghild scowled, anger drained away, her mind now calculating. "Wilhaven, you have been bard here, and in the castles of other tribes. What is your view?"

Wilhaven flashed a quick smile of appraisal. "Sure, and fools will flutter their tongues for many causes. But Leidwith is an able prince, and loyalty to Meghild is firm in Demardunn. I believe the folk will respect her wishes—provided they know them to be her *true* wishes. It might be well for the queen to send ships up and down the fjord, to summon as many as may come to an assembly, and to announce her decision to all from the village landing."

Two of the chieftains nodded. Leidwith still looked unsatisfied.

"Amlina," Meghild said. "What does your witch-sight say? Will calling an assembly assure a peaceful transfer of my throne to Leidwith?"

The witch had known Meghild would call on her. Now she felt the minds of everyone shift in her direction, their feelings of uncertainty, suspicion, fear. She screened out these impressions, sought to peer into the Deepmind, to discern what message she could. Her gaze fell on Prince Leidwith, who watched her intently.

"An assembly will certainly be helpful. But Leidwith must want the throne, and must support your decision." Still, Amlina could see there would be trouble, and her gaze was pulled inexorably to where Penredd slouched in his seat.

Meeting her eyes, the prince slapped the table in sudden fury. "I will listen no more! Whatever this witch says must be self-serving!"

"Penredd!" Meghild warned. "Take care!"

"I will not be silent, but will speak the truth, though others may fear to do so. Who knows how my grandmother has been bewitched? Who knows what evil fate this witch of Larthang intends for her? Will Demardunn allow a foreign sorceress to steal away our queen?"

"Nephew!" Leidwith cried. "You go too far. Take care lest you earn yourself more than a bloody nose!"

But Penredd was white with fury. "No! I advise you—all of you—to take care. You may do as you wish, even bending the knee to Amlina and her schemes. But I shall not be party to such cowardice."

He swept out an arm deliberately to spill his cup. Then he turned on his heels and stalked from the hall.

A stunned hush settled over the high table.

"You will need to bring him to heel, Leidwith" the queen muttered. "And soon. He is popular with many, and could be a threat to you."

Prince Leidwith sank into his chair, his countenance dark and troubled.

NINE

Glyssa traveled alone through an immense emptiness of ice and sky. At times the ice was smooth, and she was able to skate. Other times the surface was broken or crusted with snow, and she was forced to remove her skate-blades and walk. But always she hurried on, propelled by desperation.

Something was chasing her. She didn't know what—only that she had to keep as far from it as possible. She was also not sure where she was, although the place reminded her of the desolate wastes south of the Iruk Isles—which her people called the Ever Ice.

How had she gotten here? Where was her klarn?

Rolls of mist drifted over the ice, glittering with witchlight. Sometimes the mists enveloped her. Then she would remember, scenes that came in barbed fragments ...

She had gone with her mates to the witch's apartment. Amlina was going to initiate her, to begin her training in the arts of the Deepmind. Glyssa was frightened, the more so on seeing how drawn and hollow-eyed Amlina looked. The witch had been working for three days on preparations for the blood magic she was going to make. She moved slowly, and her voice was hoarse.

The Iruks sat on a circle of cushions on the floor. A lone lamp shone in the center, and above it the witch had placed a spinner—a thing with brass spokes that caught the heat of the lamp and rotated, casting lights and shadows over the walls. Staring at the spinner, hearing the witch chant verses in the Larthangan tongue, Glyssa had fallen into a trance.

Trance, she thought. Perhaps that scene had been real, and all of this was some dream. She turned and looked over her shoulder. The mist had dispersed, and far away, just over the dim horizon, she could sense the thing that pursued her.

Whatever it was, she must keep moving.

* O *

"There has still been no change?" Lonn asked.

The Iruks stood in the center of the witch's chamber, staring down at Glyssa. Her body lay sprawled on a pile of rugs and cushions, as it had for nearly five days. She scarcely seemed to be breathing.

"I've gotten her to drink a little water," Amlina answered. "But she remains deep in trance."

Amlina herself had just risen from meditation. Behind her, lamps twinkled and feathered desmets swayed on threads, hung in a pattern designed to magnify her mental strength. On the trestle table, the talking book lay shut, and Kizier stood in his pail, humming softly with his eye closed. Incense smoke wafted in the air.

"How long can this go on?" Karrol said. "She takes no food. She is likely to die!"

"She draws sustenance from the Deepmind," Amlina replied patiently. "As I have told you already, it can last for many, many days."

She settled into a chair, gripping the carved wood armrests. In the past days she had swung between bursts of frantic energy and periods of exhaustion. The wave of forces she had loosed in the Deepmind was rolling toward her. She would need all her strength to stay above that surging flood.

Perhaps it had been a mistake to rush Glyssa's initiation. On successive days she had performed two separate ceremonies: first the *Initiation into Deepseeing*, then the *Threshold of Deepshaping*. In Larthang, the rites were often done in consecutive days—but that was for novices with months of preparation. Still, Amlina had judged it best to proceed quickly. Glyssa's need seemed urgent. Besides, once they sailed, there would be no room on the crowded boat for performing elaborate rites.

And the sailing could not be delayed.

Lonn knelt beside Glyssa and brushed the damp hair from her forehead. "You are sure it is safe to move her?"

Amlina gazed at him for a moment, before comprehending his question. "Oh, yes ... Keep her warm. Offer her sips of water. Someone should stay with her at all times, in case she cries out."

"What if she does?" Brinda asked.

"Speak to her soothingly. Remind her who she is, as we did in that passageway under the temple in Kadavel. But don't try to call her back. Just remind her that she has a place here, and can return when she is ready."

"You speak as though she were on a journey," Eben remarked. "Can't you explain to us what is happening to her?"

More than the others, Eben always hungered for reasonable explanations.

Amlina settled her gaze on Glyssa and opened her mind to impressions. "She might be wandering, lost. But I do not think so. I sense she is on a quest ... More than that, I cannot say."

Frowning, Lonn looked around at his mates. "We would like it better if you were near her, Amlina. Are you sure she can't stay here?"

"No. That's impossible. I would not be able to attend her, in any case. I will be ... much occupied." For the next day and night, Amlina would be completing preparations for the blood rites. Tomorrow, after the red moon rose, she would take the queen's head.

"Everything must be ready for us to sail tomorrow evening. We will leave shortly after nightfall." Amlina paused, eyes shifting down. "I think Glyssa will be safer on the boat."

"You are expecting trouble then?" Lonn's inflection showed he too thought it possible.

"What have you heard?" Amlina asked.

Starting six days ago, Meghild had sent boats up and down the fjord, and messengers into the mountains, summoning her tribesmen to an assembly. Yesterday, speaking from a platform raised on the village docks, the queen had announced her abdication and her intention to sail from Gwales. She had asked that the tribe elect Leidwith as their new king. Predictably, her announcements had been met with surprise and confusion, many voices raised in protest or demanding to know more. Leidwith had tried to take charge of the assembly, but had failed to quell the uproar. Discussions continued around cook fires late into the night, and this morning many of the tribe were still camped along the shore, or sleeping on anchored boats.

"We have heard much muttering," Draven answered. "Rumors that Penredd is recruiting followers, that he will contest the kingship."

"He is stirring hate against us," Eben said. "Wilhaven warned us of it this morning. Many of the Gwalesmen stare at us now with open hostility."

Amlina nodded, lips drawn taut. "The queen is worried. She called the assembly to gather support for Leidwith, pledges to support him as king. But the tribe is divided, and many of the warriors have not gone home. She fears that Penredd will rally enough men to his banner to seize the throne."

"Then it would seem he would want us to leave with the queen," Draven suggested, "to make the throne vacant."

"Not so," Amlina said. "His whole case is based on the premise that I've bewitched the queen, and that Leidwith is too weak to stop us from taking her. To win the kingship, he will have to depose Meghild but keep her here, a prisoner."

"And carve us up for fish food," Eben said.

"No doubt," Amlina agreed. "As a show of strength, he would have us killed. Tomorrow night is going to be dangerous." She hesitated, then decided it was best to reveal all. "After the ceremony, when we are ready to leave, the queen will walk from this chamber in her spirit body. The sight is likely to be shocking, even appalling. It's impossible to say how the Gwalesmen will react. I hope they will not try to prevent us from leaving. But we must be prepared."

The Iruks' faces were drawn and grim.

"I've packed all of my belongings except what I will need in the next two days," Amlina continued. "I ask that you take them, along with Kizier, down to the boat today. The queen assures me there are men loyal to her who will guard my chamber, but I would wish that three of you also stand at my door, while the other two stay with the boat. Does that sound reasonable?"

"Two might not be enough, if they decided to fire the boat," Lonn said. "And what easier way to prevent us from leaving?"

"If they attack with a large force, all five of us will not be enough," Eben answered.

Lonn pondered, touching his jaw. "Suppose we anchor the boat out in the shallows? Make them march through the water."

"Yes, that should work," Karrol said. "With that position and enough spears, two of us could hold the boat against an army."

* O *

Glyssa stumbled over a ridge and fell flat. Picking herself up, she brushed the snow from her fur shirt and leggings. Her Iruk clothing—she thought she had lost it long ago. She felt no pain from the fall. She also had no sensation of hunger or thirst, or even the cold.

How long had she been traveling alone over the ice? She could not remember.

But as she trudged on, a memory did come ...

She was sitting in the witch's chamber, cross-legged on a cushion, barefoot, wearing only a thin shirt and leggings. Light and shadow, cast by one of the witch's spinning trinkets, moved ceaselessly over her body. Amlina sat before her, holding a small book with a red leather cover, translating the words as she read aloud.

"As you learned in the prior rite, O seeker of knowledge and power, you are merely a thought. This world called Glimnodd is a thought, one thought of an infinity. Infinite worlds and suns and seas, infinite bodies and minds—all are only thoughts of the Ogo, the One Mind, which comes to know itself by thinking. Know further this, as has been taught in our Ancient Order since earliest days: the One Mind is within you, with all its worlds and suns and creatures. To wield the power of magic, you must unite your mind with this One Mind, so that your thoughts are its thoughts. Thus may you shape the manifestations that the Deepmind eternally pours forth."

Amlina set down the book and instructed Glyssa to close her eyes.

"Now I shall touch the nerve centers of your body, and by my power release the power that is yours, that has always been yours."

Glyssa felt the witch's fingertips on the soles of her feet, as Amlina sang words in Larthangan. Glyssa's feet grew warm, then cold. Her body seemed to come alive in a new way, a flow of sensation moving through her that was cold and bright and reminded her of the pulsing of arched auroras in the polar sky. Amlina repeated the touch and the chant at Glyssa's knees, her groin, her lower back. But when the witch's fingers settled over her heart, the sensation changed—dreadful weight and pain, as though a sharp rock had appeared in her chest.

Amlina whispered: "I think we have found the fishhook, Glyssa."

The fishhook! Glyssa remembered now, the remnants of the sorcery Kosimo the serd had used to enthrall her, enslave her.

She was back on the ice. She glanced anxiously over her shoulder. She must keep moving.

She marched and trotted, scrambled over hillocks of snow. The thing beyond the horizon—perhaps it was the fishhook, perhaps it was the serd. Whatever, it was chasing her, and she must get away.

After fleeing for some time she skidded down an icy slope, to the shore of a frozen lake. The smooth surface stretched into the distance. Gratefully, she sat down and strapped on her skates.

Casting a nervous look behind her, she glided onto the ice. She settled into a smooth rhythm, bent low, arms swinging, legs making long, steady strides. Skating this way, she could cover a great distance.

The sun was behind her, low in the sky. From time to time she took note of its position, wheeling over her left shoulder. This confirmed her suspicion that she was crossing the Ever Ice, traveling south.

Far ahead on the icy lake, a black speck appeared. As she drew nearer, Glyssa perceived that it was a figure, animal or human. She feared approaching it in this wilderness, but she feared the thing behind her even more. Resolutely, she skated toward it.

Drawing close, she saw that it was neither animal nor human, but a spirit—A man-shaped thing with a black, feathered body and a raven's head. Glyssa thought it best to swerve aside, giving it wide way. But each time she changed her course, the thing appeared directly in front of her.

Glyssa skidded to a halt. She looked around in all directions, sensed again the thing over the horizon that pursued her. She took hold of her nerve and skated straight at the spirit.

As she approached, it seemed to watch her curiously, and she thought it might be human after all—a man in a shaman's cloak and mask. When she stopped a few feet from the figure, it spoke.

"Glyssa, daughter of Sorcha. What do you here?"

The voice was familiar. A gloved hand came up and lifted the beaked mask.

"Belach!" Glyssa exclaimed, recognizing the shaman from Ilga, her home island. "Honored Belach, I greet you."

A smile creased the wizened face. Eyes like black onyx beads appraised her.

"Are you dead?" he asked.

"No. I do not think so."

The shaman let out a piercing cry, flapped his arms once, and floated into the air. His body, stiff and still inside the feathered cloak, circled her, then settled back on the ice.

"I see now. You are on your quest. You seek to become a woman of power."

"Yes ... I was supposed to be trained by a witch of Larthang. But now I am lost." She scanned the northern horizon. "I am so afraid."

"Ah." Belach also looked at the north, then nodded sharply. He clicked his tongue three times. "Didn't the witch tell you that fear is the first enemy you must overcome?"

"I do not know. I do not remember."

"So?"

Glyssa recalled the icy place in her soul, the emptiness that had robbed her of her heart's peace. "How? How can I overcome the fear?"

Belach grunted. "Not easy. Only by facing it each time it appears. Do this enough, and one day the fear will be gone."

Glyssa gazed again at the horizon, felt the unseen thing that pursued her.

"You have only two choices," the shaman said. "You can keep running away. Or you can turn and face your enemy."

With that, Belach smiled at her kindly and vanished.

Alone in the emptiness, Glyssa stared hard, first at one direction, then the other. South, the way she was travelling, would lead her nowhere. North, the way she had come, would lead to her enemy.

Glyssa muttered a curse under her breath, turned, and skated back the way she had come.

TEN

She heard singing, muffled and far away.

Opening her eyes, Glyssa stared at gray, mottled canvas. She blinked, trying to understand. She was in a sleeping tent, lying under a fur. She shifted her head and saw—Draven.

"You are awake?" he said with surprise. "How do you feel?"

She tried to speak, but found her throat swollen, painfully dry.

"Here." Draven pressed the spout of a water skin to her lips.

Glyssa swallowed eagerly. She coughed, sat up, drank more.

"Where are we?" she whispered.

Draven laughed. "You are back! I am so glad. We were all so worried."

"How long was I ... ?"

"Six days—No six and a half. The sun just set. We are on the boat. We will sail tonight."

Glyssa started to rise, found herself stiff in every muscle. "Six days?"

Draven supported her arm as she climbed, grimacing, to her knees. She was dressed in tunic and trousers. Her wool cloak lay nearby.

"Amlina initiated you," Draven said. "Do you remember?"

Before she could answer, Karrol poked her head between the tent flaps. "Glyssa! Are you well?"

"I think so."

Draven and Karrol each took an arm and helped her out of the low tent. She stood on the deck of the klarn's new boat, which rocked gently in the shining water. She looked around at the hills and the darkening sky. The clouds in the west were stained with the last reds of sunset. She breathed in the cold, bracing air.

"How do you feel?" Karrol asked. "You were gone a long time."

Glyssa puzzled over the question. She recalled her meeting with Belach on the frozen lake. She remembered Amlina touching her skin, singing magic words, and power like cold fire flowing through her body. She felt that same power now, and at her heart, felt the same dreadful weight. But it seemed lighter now, diminished—an enemy she could face.

"I feel strong," she said. "Where are the others?"

Draven and Karrol burst into laughter. They both grabbed and hugged her at the same time.

"You are really yourself!" Karrol cried.

"Of course," Glyssa said. "Now where are the others?"

"They are guarding Amlina's door," Draven answered.

He explained that tonight, Amlina would perform the blood ritual. He and Karrol were assigned to watch the boat, and have it ready to sail after nightfall. A faction of Gwalesmen, led by Prince Penredd, opposed the queen's leaving and whatever witchery they supposed Amlina to be doing. Another group, led by Prince Leidwith, supported the queen's decision. Both factions were in the castle, and the dispute had simmered for two days. With Amlina and the queen planning to leave tonight, there were fears it would come to a battle.

"I don't like the klarn being separated," Glyssa said, "if there's to be a fight."

"None of us like it." Draven shrugged. "But we agreed we must have two guard the boat."

"Well, there are three of us now," Glyssa said. "I will go and stand with the others. Where are my weapons?"

Draven and Karrol exchanged doubtful glances. "Are you sure you're strong enough?" Karrol said.

Glyssa thrust back her shoulders. "Yes, I'm sure."

Draven unrolled a fur that contained Glyssa's clothing, sword belt and blades. But as Glyssa bent to pull on her boots, she felt dizzy and lost her balance.

"Here," Karrol caught her arm. "No battles for you tonight, mate."

"I'll be fine," Glyssa insisted.

"You haven't eaten in six days," Draven pointed out. "Have some meat and drink, then decide."

Glyssa had to acknowledge the wisdom of that. While Draven unpacked the food, she walked aft and stood on the rear deck by the tiller. Three windbringers had been brought on board and were humming softly together. Glyssa smiled to recognize Kizier in his ivory pail. She placed a hand on his stalk.

The bostull's eye opened and immediately shone with recognition. "Glyssa. You are back to yourself."

"I am happy to see you are with us, Kizier, and that you have two companions."

Noticing the interruption in their chorus, the other two windbringers had opened their eyes.

"Yes, I will do my best to introduce you," Kizier said. "Though I must confess, I have difficulty with their Gwelthek names: Next to me is Bryyverdydd and beside her is Ossvindufurvin. My friends, this lady is Glyssa, the kindest human you will ever meet."

The bostulls gazed at Glyssa incuriously and whispered words of greeting. Glyssa nodded in return. Typically, windbringers had little to say to humans.

Draven brought a platter of dried venison and hard bread, along with the water skin. Karrol remained amidships, keeping watch. Glyssa ate deliberately, cautious of her stomach after the long fast.

"How is Amlina?" she asked.

Both Draven and Kizier sighed.

"She seemed well enough when we left her," Draven answered. "Sunk deep into her witch-work, of course."

"She has taken on a great burden," Kizier said. "She sees it as a duty laid upon her by the Ogo. Perhaps she is correct. In any case, her thinking this as good as makes it so."

While Glyssa reflected on that, a voice shouted in Low Tathian from the beach. "Hallo! May I come aboard?"

"Come ahead, Wilhaven." Karrol called.

Glyssa set down her food and went forward with Draven. Wilhaven splashed through the shallows, kicking up gleaming waves. The water was waist high by the time he reached the boat. He tossed a long duffel bag over the side, then climbed up over the gunwale. He was dressed in leathers, a seaman's cloak, and a hat with a feather. His thigh-length boots dripped on the deck.

"Thank you, friends. I thought it best to stow my gear before heading back to the castle. Ah, Lady Glyssa, you are with us again. That is fine. Now our crew will be complete."

"I am glad to see you," Glyssa said. "Will you play for us, on the voyage?"

Wilhaven grinned and touched the harp-bag that hung from his shoulder. "In fair weather and foul, I promise."

"We heard you singing from down the beach." Draven said—and Glyssa realized that was the singing she had heard, the music that woke her.

"Aye, that you did," Wilhaven said. "I paid a little visit to the men watching the decks of those cranocks." He pointed over his shoulder, to where the hulls of three long warships floated by the village docks.

"We understand those ships belong to captains who stayed on after the assembly," Karrol said, "because they oppose Leidwith and the queen's leaving."

"Aye, you are not wrong. Penredd has been politicking many, and won some to his cause. Tonight, at the queen's request, I did a little politicking of my own."

"Successfully?" Glyssa inquired.

"Ha. We shall see what we shall see. Now, if you'll show me where I can lash down my things, I'll be heading up to the castle."

"Wait for me," Glyssa said. "I'll go with you."

While Draven showed the bard to a corner by the foredeck where he could store his gear, Glyssa ran aft to collect her weapons. She placed sword and dagger in their sheaths, and hefted a spear.

"Are you sure you are fit for fighting?" Karrol asked.

For answer, Glyssa drew her sword. She struck a defensive pose, sword and spear-tip leveled, then wheeled and lunged with the spear. The cold fire came to life and surged through her limbs. She felt stronger and braver than she had for months, since before she was abducted.

"Yes. I am certainly ready."

* O *

In the fading twilight, Glyssa and Wilhaven marched up the hill through the village. The streets were deserted. Muffled voices came from behind closed doors, and the chill air smelled of wood smoke and cooking meat. The crimson face of Rog hung over the cliff in the east.

At the rising of the red moon, Kizier had said, Amlina would begin the blood magic.

"Will we get there in time?" Glyssa asked the bard.

"Oh, aye. The rite will take two hours or more, according to the witch."

His tone was uncommonly terse, and Glyssa sensed a shade of discomfort—or aversion. "You do not approve of the queen's decision?" she asked. "You wish it were otherwise?"

"Aye, you read me well, Lady Glyssa."

"And yet you agreed to sail with us."

"Oh, I could hardly do otherwise ... You see, Meghild is not only my sovereign. I love her as my own mother. I was an orphan, fostered in her castle. When I showed a talent for music, she sent me to the College of Bards at her own expense. All that I am, I owe to her. Of course, I am grieved that she has chosen to sacrifice herself ... And yet, given her wild nature, I understand why she would seize such a chance."

In the dim light, Glyssa perceived a rueful smile.

"So, I will support her with all my strength," the bard said. "And so, we shall be shipmates."

Turning a corner, they came in sight of the tavern. A group of warriors stood in the light that spilled from the open doorway. They looked up from their tankards to stare suspiciously as Glyssa and Wilhaven hurried by. The bard showed them a curt smile, his hand resting on the hilt of his long sword. Glyssa knew he also had a dagger hidden in his cloak.

"Do you expect fighting tonight, Wilhaven?" she muttered.

"Aye, 'tis very possible," he answered through the side of his mouth. "Prince Penredd is an angry man, and an ambitious one—a very dangerous combination."

"Are there many who support him?"

The bard grunted. "Nearly half, from what I can tell. If Prince Leidwith were a more ruthless man, he would have crushed Penredd days ago. Now I fear Leidwith might be forced to fight, or else give in to Penredd's demands and try to stop the queen from leaving."

"If that happens," Glyssa said, "we'll have to fight our way past both factions."

"Aye, my lady," he laughed grimly. "So let's hope that it doesn't happen."

Past the last log houses and fenced enclosures, they climbed the slope leading to the moat. The castle loomed against the stars like some giant, brooding beast, waiting to devour them. Glyssa brushed aside the fear brought on by that thought. If she died tonight, it would be a warrior's death, fighting shoulder to shoulder with her mates. She could take comfort in that.

Fear was the enemy, and must be faced each time it appeared.

Their footsteps clattered on the boards of the drawbridge, rousing the attention of the two men-at-arms who stood below the portcullis. They lifted spears as Glyssa and Wilhaven drew near.

"Stop and be recognized."

The bard smiled, lifting his empty hands. "Sure, gentlemen, you recognize Wilhaven the bard, and this Iruk lady, a guest of the queen."

"Enter in peace," one of the guards said, though Glyssa noticed their faces did not soften.

She and Wilhaven were not challenged again as they traversed the dark passageway and crossed the courtyard. The main door to the keep stood open, and the guards stationed there merely nodded as they passed. It was the dinner hour, but the castle seemed eerily quiet. When they reached the great hall, Glyssa understood why.

In the firelight cast by the twin hearths, warriors and courtiers sat feasting at the long tables, and attendants served them from trays and pitchers. But there was none of the usual laughter and merriment. The little talk that could be heard was muted and sullen. Worse, Glyssa saw that most of the men wore chainmail and carried arms—violating the queen's prohibition against bringing weapons into the hall.

"Let us move now like mice in a room full of cats," Wilhaven said. "Quick and quiet and keeping to the walls."

Glyssa followed him along the back and then up the length of the chamber, passing close to alcoves and the wide hearth. But their arrival had not gone unnoticed, and the hall seemed to grow even stiller. As they neared the dais, Glyssa spied Leidwith and Penredd, seated at opposite ends of the high table, each flanked by warriors.

Penredd's eyes locked on her for an instant, and he leaped out of his chair. He pointed at her and his angry roar echoed through the hall. His words were in Gwelthek, but Glyssa understood well enough. He shouted that she was an enemy, a companion of the witch. Across the feast hall, a number of men growled in agreement, a few bolting to their feet.

"Peace to you all," Wilhaven held up his hands, smiling. "We go on the queen's business."

He turned and hurried Glyssa across the dais and through the arched portal. They paced quickly up the passageway, dimly lit by lamps set in niches. At the far end, before the door to the queen's apartments, they turned left. Up another corridor, they came to the doorway that led to the round tower with Amlina's apartment. Six soldiers in chain mail stood at the portal, holding spears and shields. One of them was Frenrik, captain of the queen's guard.

"Greetings, my lord," Wilhaven said to him. "Any news from up the stairs?"

"The queen went up at sunset," the captain grumbled. "We've heard nothing since except chanting through the door. What is the mood in the feast hall?"

"Ugly," Wilhaven responded. "Best that you be wary, captain."

Glyssa sidled past them and ran up the curving steps. She passed four more of the queen's men, leaning against the stone wall. Beyond them, on the landing in front of Amlina's door, stood Lonn, Eben, and Brinda.

"Glyssa!" Lonn exclaimed as she threw herself into his arms. "Are you all right?"

"I am fine," she laughed with joy, hugging the others in turn. "I am so glad to see you, mates."

"And we you," Brinda answered.

"But are you sure you should be here?" Lonn said. "There may be danger."

"I know." Glyssa felt the strength of the klarn-soul in heart. "But I have been apart from the klarn for too long. Now I am back."

* O *

They waited.

From time to time they heard Amlina chanting behind the oak door. Her evocations were not in the vibrant, singsong Larthangan tongue Glyssa had come to know a little. This language sounded hollow and ominous, imbued with a menacing power. Listening, Glyssa shuddered inwardly, for she recognized that Amlina was summoning dark forces akin to those Kosimo the serd had used to enslave her.

Glancing at her mates, she saw her apprehension reflected on their faces, though they remained stoically quiet.

After a while Wilhaven joined them, lounging on the step below the landing, his legs outstretched. He appeared completely calm and at ease.

Suddenly the chant grew deep and loud, the witch's voice rising to terrible, strangled moans. The guardsmen on the steps below cast frightened looks at the door.

"Steady, my lads," Wilhaven advised, then added something in Gwelthek that Glyssa found puzzling.

"What did you just tell them?" She spoke to the bard in Tathian. "Something about the queen and considering what song they would sing?"

"Aye, that was it exactly." Wilhaven smiled with a flick of irony. "You see, my lady, in our beliefs, each man and woman has a fate. But our word for fate is *danna*, the same word we use for song. Each person's song is written by three divine Sisters, who sit at the base of the Tree of Worlds."

"Then how can you advise them to consider what song they will sing?" Glyssa asked, "if that is their fate?"

"Oh, because the Sisters only write the song. It is up to each of us how we perform it—and in the performing, change it and make it our own. These lads are sworn to serve the queen, as I am. So I was encouraging them to sing bravely and well."

"That is interesting," Eben said. "To what degree is it possible to alter your song?"

"Well," Wilhaven laughed, "that depends on how canny and determined you are. But tell me, what do you Iruks believe about fate?"

"We don't worry about it," Lonn answered gruffly. "We are aware of how the Tathians philosophize and debate such things. But the Iruk seas are cold and bleak, and we are mostly concerned with hunting and surviving."

"And drinking and mating," Eben added with a grin. "It's not all misery."

"We have our rituals and stories, of course" Glyssa said. "And we believe there is a Great Mother, from whom we come and to whom we return. But Lonn is right, we don't worry about what might or might not be fated. We just do our best to live bravely."

"And so you do, from all I have seen," Wilhaven noted with respect. "And to my mind, *that is* your song."

Glyssa gave a slight smile. She had not been brave lately, to be sure. But now at last she believed her courage was returning. "A strange song it must be," she said, "to have brought me and my mates from the far South of the world to the far North."

"Aye." Wilhaven's eyes sparkled. "And now sailing to lands barely known, in the company of a witch of Larthang and a queen of Gwales. It may be a truly glorious song by the time it is done."

A crash like thunder boomed inside the chamber. The Iruks went rigid, eyes wide. Wilhaven scrambled to his feet and, below him on the stairs, the guardsmen jerked down their spears as though for protection. The chanting resumed, but now the voice was not Amlina's. Rather, it sounded like many voices—roaring, bellowing, howling. The appalling clamor went on and on, seeming at once to be calling something huge and monstrous into the world, and to *be* that monstrous thing.

Then, suddenly, all went quiet.

ELEVEN

Gripping their spears, the Iruks eyed each other and waited. Moments passed. Glyssa felt sure that the ritual had ended.

Eben whispered, "Maybe we should ..."

"No," Lonn said. "Amlina's orders were clear."

Time crept by. The queen's men on the stairs, who had looked to be ready to charge the door, now leaned, solemn and tense, with their backs to the wall. Glyssa breathed deeply, trying to stay calm.

A scraping noise made everyone start. Bolts were thrown. The door creaked open.

Amlina appeared, hollow-eyed, her face and hair splattered with gore. She was dressed in boots and a long coat. In her arms she held the talking book, with extra parchments stuffed among the pages. Her voice was a hoarse whisper.

"We must go now, quickly."

"But what of the queen?" Wilhaven demanded.

"I am coming, my dears!" The tone was unmistakably Meghild, and yet it was not her voice. This voice held an eerie, inhuman quality that made Glyssa shiver.

The thing that was now the queen floated through the doorway. Meghild's gray hair and wrinkled face sat atop a tall body of quivering, translucent light. The arms and legs were fluid shapes that fluttered in and out of existence. Below the gashed neck, drops of blood hung frozen, cascading down to a gold sphere that pulsed like a heart.

In her dread and amazement, Glyssa recalled what the witch had told her: that after the ritual, the queen would reside in a spirit body. *Eidolon* was the word she had used.

"We must go," Amlina said again.

"No! Monstrous!"

The guards on the stair had caught sight of the eidolon. Others were poking their heads through the doorway at the bottom of the tower.

"That is it not the queen!"

"It cannot be."

Abruptly the guards turned and fled, falling over each other as they rushed down the steps.

"Cowards!" The eyes of the eidolon blazed. "Unworthy men!"

Wilhaven dropped to one knee. "My queen. It might be wise if we left by your secret gate, the tunnel under the moat."

Meghild's head looked down at him. "My clever Wilhaven. You at least are loyal."

"Aye, my queen. But your new appearance is startling—to say the least. And Penredd has gathered forces that oppose your leaving. If we go through the feast hall, I fear there will be bloodshed."

The eidolon sucked in breath, chest swelling, the fantastical limbs shuddering with power. "No! Meghild will not sneak from her own keep like some traitor. What kind of start would that make, Wilhaven, for the saga you will write about me? Come, my lovelies. I shall depart through my own front gate."

At the ends of her legs, feet like lion's paws appeared, and the eidolon lurched down the steps. "How marvelous to walk again, to feel such strength!"

Wilhaven shrugged and followed her. The Iruks held back, unsure.

"What do you think, Amlina?" Glyssa asked, her fear pitching higher.

The witch's face looked dazed. "We'd best follow the queen."

"Aye, follow me, my loyal ones." Meghild called from the bottom of the steps. "And hold your weapons ready!"

* O *

Swords and spears in hand, Glyssa and her mates rushed down the curling stair and through the corridor. As she ran, Glyssa's dread was a throbbing pain around her heart—the fishhook, bleeding off her courage.

The luminous spirit-body glided ahead of them, Wilhaven stalking at its side. The queen's guards were nowhere in sight. Turning onto the passage that led to the feast hall, Glyssa heard a swelling uproar ahead. Through the archway, she glimpsed a throng of armored men and the gleam of drawn swords. Then Meghild stepped over the threshold, drawing gasps and moans of wonder as the warriors shrank back.

The Iruks charged through the doorway and spread out beside the queen and Wilhaven, Amlina coming a step behind them. At the forefront of the mob of Gwalesmen, Glyssa spied Leidwith on one side, Penredd on the other. The queen's guards who had fled now hovered behind the front ranks. All were staring wild-eyed at the shimmering eidolon.

"Make way for the queen!" Wilhaven shouted.

"What have you done?" Prince Leidwith howled in dismay.

"They have killed our queen!" Penredd pointed his sword. "Slay that monstrosity. Slay the witch!"

"Keep back!" The eidolon screamed, flinging up arms that ended in glittering claws. "I be Meghild, daughter of Isthhaven, son of Luth. I be queen of Tribe Demardunn, and I command this castle!"

Most of the Gwalesmen stepped back, a few dropping to one knee.

But Penredd shouted defiance. "Whatever that thing is, it is not our queen. I warned you all that something monstrous would happen. Now, if there is manhood in you, I say destroy that abomination, and kill the witch and her barbarians!"

He raised his shield and started forward, sword leveled. After a moment, the men closest to him did likewise. Leidwith and all the rest still hesitated, gaping.

The Iruks crouched in fighting stances, spears and blades pointed.

Amlina moved behind the eidolon and laid a hand on its back. "Cover your eyes!" she cried, then shouted five syllables of evocation.

Glyssa, eyes shut and shielded by her forearm, perceived a flash of red through her eyelids and felt a searing heat on her face. Howls of shock and pain rolled through the hall, then came the clatter of weapons dropping on stone.

"Hurry now," the witch said. "Their blindness will not last."

Glyssa opened her eyes to find men groaning and blinking throughout the hall. Some clutched their heads or reached with groping hands. The eidolon stood quiet and still, its light diminished. Amlina had used its energy, Glyssa realized, to cast the blinding magic.

Then Glyssa spied a flash of movement, armed men moving toward them.

"For the honor of Demardunn, kill them!"

Penredd and three of his followers must have understood the witch's warning and shielded their eyes. Now they advanced with murderous intent. Their shields and chainmail would give them an advantage over the lighter-armed Iruks. And, at the rear of the throng, Glyssa saw other men moving forward.

"For the glory of your queen, stay back!" Wilhaven stepped lightly toward Penredd, sword and dagger pointed. Lonn, Eben, and Brinda darted forward to stand with the bard.

Glyssa stood rigid, paralyzed by the clawing terror in her chest. *No! She must not fail her mates now.* And yet she could not move.

Helpless, she watched as Penredd, growling like a bear, jabbed his sword at Wilhaven. The bard parried, but had to dance back, then immediately dodge a stab by the warrior on Penredd's right. That thrust left the man open for an instant, and Brinda lunged with her spear. The point found the man's belly, piercing the mail and sending him staggering back.

Lonn and Eben had rushed the two warriors on the other side, their fierce attack forcing the men to retreat. Wilhaven, teeth bared in a mocking smile, now stood his ground against Penredd. But Glyssa knew that the bard would be no match for the heavier, better-armed prince. Penredd's shield swept aside the bard's long sword. Next instant, a vicious thrust scraped Wilhaven's upper arm as he tried to twist away. In seconds, the bard would be slain, and then Amlina ...

"No!" With Glyssa's cry, something broke inside her. It might have been the klarn-spirit, or the cold power birthed in her by the witch's initiation. Whatever it was, suddenly she could move.

Raising her sword, she screamed Penredd's name and rushed him. The prince pivoted to face her. Glyssa used her spear to smash his sword aside and flung herself onto his shield. Her weight threw him back, off-balance, and Glyssa stabbed his face, her sword laying open his cheek and slicing his ear.

Penredd screamed and fell, Glyssa sprawled on top of him. She clambered to her feet and crouched over the prince as he writhed, clutching his face through gushing blood.

Seeing Penredd fall sapped the will of the other warriors. They shrank back and lowered their swords. The fight had lasted only seconds.

"Come, we are leaving!" Amlina cried.

Now it was a mad dash through the hall. The Iruks pushed and jostled aside the still-blinded warriors, while others who were not blinded, merely watched. Amlina and Wilhaven followed the Iruks, each holding an arm of the eidolon queen as she lurched and tottered along.

Lonn and Glyssa led the way down the castle steps and across the courtyard. By the time they reached the gatehouse, the eidolon's body had regained some of its ghostly light. The sentries at the portcullis fell back in amazement and made no challenge as the party hurried by.

Down though the darkened village they went, with dogs barking but no one abroad to view their unearthly passage. The eidolon, it's light returned, no longer needed support, but flowed down the streets with long-legged, wheeling strides.

"How wonderful to be free again!" Meghild cried.

Glyssa ran with blood thrumming in her ears, exultant with the thrill of battle and their escape.

But when they reached the docks, a glance up the hill showed torches and lanterns moving out from the castle.

"They are following us," Eben said.

"Aye." Wilhaven clutched his wounded arm. "Penredd's not a man to give up, even with his face split open."

They ran down the beach, past the piers and the three warships, to the place where their boat lay anchored in the shallows. As they strode into the gleaming water, Lonn shouted for Karrol and Draven to raise the anchor.

Slogging waist-high in the fjord, Glyssa glanced back to see the eidolon pause on the shoreline, then step into the water—or rather, *over* the water. For to Glyssa's astonishment, the spirit-body cascaded over the waves, never breaking the surface. Ahead, Draven and Karrol had stopped on the deck to stare dumbly at the eidolon.

"Make ready to sail," Lonn shouted at them. "We've no time to lose!"

Amlina and Wilhaven were the last to reach the boat, and Glyssa and Brinda leaned over the rails to haul them aboard.

Eben had already gone to help Draven and Karrol haul up the yard, while Lonn ran aft to man the tiller. Glyssa could hear him rousing the windbringers and imploring them to lend their efforts.

"How is your arm?" Glyssa parted the bard's upper sleeve to examine the wound.

"Sure, it's just a scrape," Wilhaven answered with a grin. "'Twill make a pretty enough scar, though."

After helping her mates secure the lines, Glyssa grabbed her spear and ran to join Lonn at the helm. Amlina, Wilhaven, and the queen stood with them on the rear deck as the boat slipped away from shore. The lamps and torches of their pursuers had reached the docks.

Glyssa saw that the wind was against them, blowing up the fjord from the sea. Even with the help of the windbringers, the best Lonn could do was head to the opposite shore, sailing as far from the village as could be. But they would then need to tack into the fresh wind. Penredd's crews were already clambering aboard the three warships, which were moored upwind. They would have no trouble intercepting the Iruks' boat.

"I believe they will catch us," Lonn stated matter-of-factly.

"Sure, I would not be worrying," Wilhaven replied.

Meghild's head tilted to look down at him "So, my bard, that means you accomplished the little errand I sent you on this afternoon?"

"Aye, dear queen. The watchmen succumbed to my lullabies and to the sweet, drugged liquor. And then the knots joining tillers to rudders succumbed to my hacksaw."

Glyssa recalled how she had woken from her trance to hear Wilhaven singing from down the beach, and how he said he had visited the three warships loyal to Penredd's men to "do some politicking."

Now, in the witchlight that hovered on the fjord, she saw the result. Sails raised, the three cranocks drifted back from the docks. But when they tried to turn they floundered in the waves, as sailors cursed and shouted. One ship swung until its prow crashed back into the dock. The other two waddled sideways and collided, the snap of outrigger planks sounding distinctly over the water.

"Ooh, worse than I expected." Wilhaven winced. "'Twill take a small-month at least to make those repairs."

"Ha-hah!" Meghild laughed jubilantly. "So much for Penredd and his fools. And so, my lovelies, we are away, our voyage begun!"

"Yes," Amlina sighed. "We are safely away, I think."

With that, the witch's eyes rolled up behind their lids, and her knees buckled. Glyssa and Wilhaven grabbed her arms to save her from collapsing.

"Poor Amlina has worn herself out," Meghild said. "Best you take her to where she can rest."

Glyssa and the bard half-dragged, half-carried the semiconscious Amlina forward on the rolling deck. The eidolon floated behind them, drawing mute, tight-lipped stares from Karrol and Draven who were stationed at the sheets.

"You'll soon get used to it," Glyssa told them with a laugh.

They conveyed Amlina to the crawlspace under the foredeck, which had been outfitted as her cabin, and left her lying on a narrow bunk. As they crawled out of the hatch, Draven arrived, his expression full of concern.

"She'll be all right," Glyssa told him. "I know she will."

"I will watch over her," Draven said. "Brinda and Karrol have the sheets."

Glyssa clasped his forearm and smiled.

Wilhaven climbed onto the foredeck and stood with the queen. Her tall, glimmering form hovered at the prow, watching over the water.

Glyssa went aft to stand at the helm with Lonn. He looked at her fondly and laid a hand on her shoulder.

"You are well, my Glyssa?"

The cold wind caressed her face, and she breathed in happily. "Yes. Much better now."

"You'll have to tell me where you were these past six days."

"That I will," she said. "But not tonight."

Lonn called the order to come about, and pulled the tiller hard as the yard arm creaked round the mast. As the boat leaned on its new tack, Lonn gazed at the prow, where the eidolon stood by the phoenix figurehead, like a beacon lamp lighting their way.

"It might be an interesting voyage," he said.

Glyssa laughed. "Yes, I think it might."

Sometime later, Grizna the peach-colored moon rose behind them. At dawn they reached the open sea.

PART TWO
TO THE RUINS OF LOST VALGOOL

TWELVE

In the morning the weather turned foul. Wind from the southwest drove gray clouds over the sky, and curtains of rain lashed the deck. The cranock rode nimbly enough on the rolling swells, and only a few waves splashed over the bulwarks. That was not the problem.

The crew would sleep in shifts. At mid-morning, Lonn left Karrol at the helm and Draven and Eben stationed at the ropes, while he, Glyssa, and Brinda crawled into the sleeping tent—only to discover their bed furs soaked in a pool of ankle-deep water.

Angry and exhausted, they tore down the tent and spread the furs to dry as best they might on the upper part of the deck. Their grunting and cursing roused Wilhaven, who had been dozing in his dry spot next to the foredeck.

"Aye, I ought to have warned you." Wilhaven yawned, scratching his beard. "In rough seas the bilge collects around the mast. Not the best place to set your sleeping gear."

"We're leaking from the bottom!" Lonn complained.

"Oh, indeed," the bard said. "That's to be expected in this weather. Don't your Iruk boats need bailing?"

"Only a little, in heavy rain or very rough seas," Glyssa answered. "Our hide boats are watertight."

"Well regrettably ours are not perfectly so." Wilhaven was untying several long-handled scoops designed for bailing. "Which is why a cranock comes equipped with these admirable tools."

He handed one of the bailers to Eben and tossed another to Lonn.

"There was no leaking when we sailed in the fjord," Eben pointed out.

"Sure, and there the water was calm and the boat brand new." Wilhaven set to work. "It's the cracks between the planks, you see. They stretch and swell in rough water. You'll want to patch them with new moss and tar, I'm thinking. Best to stop and do that before we leave the coast."

"Wonderful," Lonn growled, setting to work with the bailing tool.

Glyssa picked up the fourth bailer and joined them. She imitated Wilhaven, sweeping the pail into the bilge water and slinging it over the rail in a single smooth motion.

"By the way," Wilhaven asked cheerfully, "what name have you given your ship?"

"Name?" Lonn said. "We Iruks do not name our boats."

Wilhaven looked astonished. "Oh! But a cranock has a soul. A soul that is compounded from the spirit of the trees that gave their planks and tar, the hemp plants that gave their fibers for canvas and ropes, the beasts that gave their leather and hides for ..."

"We get your point," Lonn grumbled. "But we do not name our boats."

"I have a suggestion," Karrol called from the tiller. "We can call it the *Leaky Ladle*."

Despite his ill humor, Lonn joined his mates in grim laughter.

But Wilhaven looked aggrieved. "Sure, and it would be a pity not to name such a fine ship."

"You are our poet," Glyssa said. "Why don't you name it for us?"

"Well ... with the captain's permission?"

Lonn shrugged. "You can name it if you want to. But to us it will just be 'the boat.'"

"Fair enough, my lord, and thanks." Wilhaven paused in his bailing and looked toward the bow. There the light-body of the queen hovered before the waves, as it had all night and day.

The bard's tone grew soft and serious. "Amlina chose the phoenix as our figurehead. And like that legendary bird, Meghild has risen from her own death to live and stride a deck again. I name this ship in her honor: the *Phoenix Queen*."

Despite themselves, the Iruks were moved by his reverence.

"That is lovely," Glyssa said. "The *Phoenix Queen* it is then."

* O *

Lying flat, tilting and lurching, Amlina opened her eyes. A gasp caught in her throat as she scanned the darkness, not sure where she was or how she got here.

Fear seized hold as she remembered—chanting and shrieking, summoning that terrible force until it filled her soul, possessed her. Then screaming and hacking with the sword, blood everywhere ...

Amlina shuddered and thrust herself up, fully awake. She was in the small crawlspace on the boat. Of course, they were at sea now—a rough sea, to judge by the steep rocking.

She shut her eyes. For some time she breathed deeply, suppressing the panic, the awful urge to be sick. The act was done, the design cast. Now she must hold to her course and trust it was the rightful thing, cling to her faith in herself.

She shifted her legs off the bunk and sat for a few moments. A water skin hung on a peg near at hand. She opened it and drank. The ceiling was too low for her to stand upright. Rather than stumble with lowered head and shoulders, she crawled on hands and knees to the hatch.

Pushing it open, she emerged on the deck—and immediately braced herself against the foredeck to keep from toppling. The sky was overcast, the cranock riding up and down on heaving swells. Away to the left, gray cliffs marked the coast of Gwales.

At the middle of the boat, Wilhaven and Draven were bailing with long-handled pails. Karrol and Eben stood on the rear deck, beside the tiller which was lashed in place. Amlina glanced over her shoulder and spotted the eidolon of the queen, hovering like a statue of light at the prow.

Draven came toward her, stamping on wide-spread feet to keep his balance.

"Amlina." He touched her shoulder. "How are you feeling?"

"I will be all right." She wiped her forehead, then stared down at her fingers, remembering.

"I sponged the blood off," Draven said, "while you slept."

She offered him a feeble smile. "Thank you for that. How long did I sleep?"

"It is afternoon," Draven answered. "This weather kicked up soon after we left the fjord. Our tent got soaked and put everyone in a foul mood. Lonn and Glyssa and Brinda are trying to sleep in the storage hold. I'd best get back to bailing."

He returned to work, leaving Amlina holding the rail. Her stomach was empty; she'd eaten nothing since early yesterday morning. But the heaving of the boat made the thought of food sickening. She was thinking she might best go back to the crawlspace and lie down, when Wilhaven approached.

He leaned close to her and spoke quietly. "I am glad you are awake, my lady. I am concerned about the queen. She seemed so full of life during the night. But now when I speak to her she is spiritless, distant, hardly there at all."

Amlina followed his gaze to where the queen's translucent figure rose and fell with the waves. The witch sought to recall what she had studied about the energies of the eidolon body. "In fact, she is *not* entirely there. Part of her existence resides in the Deepmind, from whence she draws the force of life. But maintaining the light body in this world is a strain. She needs to rest."

"Aye, but how can she rest?"

"I will speak to her. Bring a lamp and a bowl filled with sea water—clean, not from the bailing."

The bard nodded and set off. Amlina climbed the three steps to the foredeck. Moving on hands and knees, she reached the prow, braced herself on the rail, and rose to her feet.

The eidolon seemed dimmer now, in the pale daylight and silvery luminescence of the sea. The wizened face stared straight ahead, lips parted, eyes dull.

"My queen, are you well?"

The witch waited a long moment, then spoke again. "My queen. It is Amlina."

The head rolled down, eyes staring. The voice sounded faint and faraway. "Amlina, my dear ... I so wanted to be here. I am so happy that I am."

"How are you feeling?"

A slight shake of the head. "I almost feel that I am not here, that I am dreaming ... But then it seems the whole world is a dream."

"So it is perceived by many who are privileged to see as you can now see."

"But I want ... I wanted ..."

"My queen, you need to rest. To enter a state like sleep, where you can dream in truth. Then, when you rise, you will feel stronger and more awake. Will you come with me?"

She glanced anxiously at the sea. Then her chin dropped. "Of course, if you think it best."

Amlina clambered over the slippery foredeck, the eidolon floating behind her. Wilhaven waited at the hatchway, holding the lamp and bowl. The witch opened the hatch and ushered him inside. The queen hesitated, staring into the darkness with apprehension.

Amlina spoke cheerfully to reassure her. "I am sorry for the cramped quarters, my queen. Please do me the honor to enter."

"Oh, I've slept in smaller spaces," Meghild answered, then sank down and floated inside.

Wilhaven struck the lamp and set it down where the witch indicated. Amlina opened one of her trunks and brought out candles and two desmets. She lit the candles from the lamp and pinned the feathered trinkets to a beam overhead. She set the bowl of seawater on a shelf and asked the queen to draw near.

"The sea is a symbol of the Deepmind," she said, "the Ogo from which all things emerge. With your permission, my queen, I will draw your light body down into this water, your head to rest on the surface, and so you may dream and revitalize yourself."

Amlina placed a cushion on the floor and sat, her back against the frame of the bunk. She locked her eyes on the eidolon, took three long breaths, and began to sing.

Her words called power up from the depths. When the power had grown to a glowing force inside her body, she lifted a hand and sent out her intention. Her song took on the tone and rhythm of a lullaby.

Slowly, the form of the eidolon folded itself into a glimmering mist that spiraled and swirled as it drifted toward the bowl. The head floated with the mist, and came to rest just above the surface of the water, eyes shut in deep repose.

Amlina let out her breath. Wilhaven stared at her mutely.

"She will rest now," Amlina whispered. She touched her forehead, then climbed unsteadily onto the bunk. "I had better rest as well."

Wilhaven blew out the lamp and candles, then crept quietly from the cabin. Amlina lay flat on her back, exhausted and slightly dizzy.

But after a short time, her eyes flew open and she sat up again. She needed to reinforce her designs of concealment and protection. She had not replenished them in several days. Worse, the vast forces she had unleashed with the blood magic would have sent ripples across the Deepmind, disturbances that would be all too apparent to a skilled seer—such as the Archimage of the East.

For the next hour, Amlina sat erect in the dim cabin, eyes closed, lips whispering, fingers weaving patterns of magic in the air.

* O *

A MIRROR AGAINST ALL MISHAP

The Seat of Supreme Splendor hovered in the temple sanctum, a brilliant replica of Glimnodd's orange sun. Its blazing light shone on the polished black floor and spiraling white columns. The light dazzled the eyes of the orange-robed priests and attendants grouped around the huge onyx table, forcing many to shade their brows or look away. Beryl enjoyed their discomfort—up to a point. She had to be careful to modulate the intensity of the sphere in which she floated, so that her minions could pay heed to her orders.

In a calm, imperious voice, she listed the requirements for the unprecedented ceremony she would perform to restore her vitality—the lamps and banners to be hung in the temple; the arrangement of drummers and gong players around the furnace pit; the parade of acolytes who would slice open their forearms to contribute a few drops of blood to the fire.

After months of effort, Beryl had finally completed the grand design—composed the verses to be chanted, devised the energy forms that she would create and then encase in trinkets to be released at the proper moments. But on one point she had stalled. The design necessitated a considerable supply of animalistic vitality, more than a single human body could provide. And yet, it required that the life-force be focused within one sacrificial entity.

Then, while in trance, the answer had come to her.

Now, as the temple officials listened in grave silence and scribes scratched furiously on parchment, she explained that last, crucial element.

"In addition to the foregoing, the youngest and most vital of the sun lions will be brought to the temple. It must be carefully bound, not drugged, so that its vital energies flow undiluted. At the climax of the ceremony I will cut its throat. It must then immediately be skinned and butchered. I will clothe myself in the skin, while the meat is consumed in the fire pit."

Beryl scanned the assembly, noted the parted lips and shocked expressions. The orange, white-maned lions were sacred, embodiments of the solar light. Never before had one been sacrificed—the very idea could be called blasphemy. The queen waited in silence, to see if anyone dared oppose her. Though Beryl herself was the living incarnation of the Sun, she had never before gone so far in violating tradition. She had actually been worried that her plan might spark an outcry.

"Do all of you understand me?" she said.

Around the onyx table the clerics gave murmurs of assent, heads bowed, none daring to meet her eyes.

* O *

Outside, Beryl's gold palanquin waited at the bottom of the temple steps, flanked by her entourage and a company of soldiers. The Archimage descended the broad gleaming steps with her erect, unhurried gait. Stepping into the palanquin, she reclined on the silken cushions. When the sliding panels were closed, she was able to relax and massage the throbbing scar on her forehead. She was pleased to have this meeting done—and without apparent opposition. Now she could concentrate on the rituals to prepare the energy forms—and herself—for the culminating ceremony. When Grizna, the large moon, was full again, her vitality would at last be fully restored.

The palanquin was lifted onto the shoulders of bearers, who began the slow march back to the palace. The summer air was warm and humid, stifling in the closed sedan chair. Sniffing that air, Beryl sensed again the grim urgency to complete her rejuvenation.

Over the past days she had felt a new force in the currents of the Deepmind. Long experience told her that somewhere in the world, a powerful sorcery had been unleashed. To Beryl, this foretold a new rival, some deepshaper who might one day challenge her as the preeminent mage in the world. It had even occurred to her, in the drowsy moments emerging from trance, that this deepshaper might be Amlina, her former apprentice. Beryl dismissed that notion as unlikely. While Amlina surely had such potential, Beryl did not believe she could possess the knowledge—or more importantly, the will—to create such a dark and powerful disturbance.

But then again, Amlina had surprised her before.

THIRTEEN

Glyssa knocked and immediately heard Amlina's voice within, calling for her to enter. Pulling the hatch open, she bent at the waist and stepped across the threshold. The cramped cabin was similar in size and shape to the crawlspace below the rear deck, where Glyssa and her mates now slept when not on watch. But the feeling of this enclosure was far different. Candles flickered in glass lamps; desmets hung from the beams and swung gently with the swaying of the boat; the air held a perfumed fragrance. But more than all of that, Glyssa perceived magical energy—which, to her awakened mind, came as a brushing on the skin, a faint tingling behind the eyes.

"Welcome, Glyssa," Amlina said. "Come and sit down."

The witch sat cross-legged on a cushion next to her bunk. Behind her, on a shelf, Glyssa saw the head of the queen, floating in a cloud of light over a black bowl. Glyssa removed her boots and settled herself on the cushion facing Amlina. A tiny lamp burned on the floor between them.

"First I must apologize," the witch said, "for not speaking with you sooner—and for not being there to help you when you came out of your trance. I have not done what I should, as your teacher. But now that I am more myself, I promise to do better."

For the first two days of the voyage, Amlina had hardly emerged from her cabin. Then, to regain her strength, she had entered the *dark immersion*, and remained another four days and nights in that state of death-like insensibility. During that time, the Iruks had landed at a settlement near the southern tip of Gwales. Under Wilhaven's supervision and with the help of local tribesmen, they had repaired the boat, patching the interstices with new moss and pitch. A day later, they rounded the cape and set off across the wide channel that separated Gwales from the Tathian island of Lustre. The weather since had been fair, with a steady wind from the northwest and seas far less choppy.

"I am glad you are better," Glyssa said. "Draven was very worried. But somehow, I knew you would be all right."

Mention of Draven's name brought Amlina a fleeting smile. "Yes. I am more in balance now. But tell me how you are feeling. You seem calmer than before."

"Yes. I am more steady. The first night after I awoke I felt very strong, exhilarated by the battle and our setting sail. But since then ... well, the fear has crept back. Not as strong as before, but still bleak and hopeless. Each time it does and I become aware, I try to face it. That is what Belach advised me."

The witch frowned. "Who is Belach?"

"Oh," Glyssa laughed. "Of course, you do not know." She related what she had experienced in her visions, the desperate fleeing over the ice, the meeting with the shaman from her village.

As Amlina listened, her gaze grew severe. When Glyssa had finished the tale, the witch got up and retrieved the talking book from a shelf behind her. Resuming her seat, she set the book in her lap and flipped open the cover. She spoke words of summoning. After a moment, the pages glimmered in the dim cabin, and the book answered. Amlina spoke to it in Larthangan, her voice low and urgent.

"What are you saying?" Glyssa demanded. "I do not understand."

"Oh, I am sorry," Amlina said. "I was starting to tell Buroof about your meeting with the shaman. It's not something I expected, and I'm not sure what it portends in terms of your training."

"What is it you want from me, Amlina?" Buroof asked impatiently. "And should I continue to speak Larthangan, to hide my responses from the barbarian?"

Amlina sighed. The book had disingenuously asked the question in Tathian, so that Glyssa would understand it clearly. "No, I do not wish to conceal anything from Glyssa. I am trying to understand about her vision, and to ascertain what if anything needs to be done."

She explained how Glyssa had fallen into trance immediately after the *Threshold of Deepshaping* rite, and had not awoken for six days. Glyssa then repeated all she recalled from those days, culminating in her encounter with Belach.

"So in summation," Buroof said, "you took a primitive young woman, who was already damaged by enthrallment, and subjected her to the traditional Larthangan initiation rites, with absolutely no preparation, and all in the space of two days. A most reckless decision, I must say."

"I am aware of my many failings, Buroof," Amlina replied. "My question to you is: what light can history shed on our situation? The fact that she fell into a trance, and there encountered an entity that might or might not have been a magician of her people—"

"—Speaks to the fact that you gave no thought to her cultural context."

"I know! But there must be cases on record where initiates with foreign backgrounds encountered beings from their own traditions."

"Certainly. But not without first receiving a full and adequate grounding in Larthangan principles. No, Amlina, here you have broken new ground of incompetence."

Amlina gave up and shut the book.

"I'm sorry, Glyssa. Buroof is right in that I ought to have prepared you better. Of course, I would have, had there been more time ... "

"I don't understand your concern," Glyssa said. "Belach helped me. He gave me the courage to return to this world."

Amlina gazed at her intently, as if peering deep into her soul.

"I see that," she said. "The problem is, we have no way to tell if it was truly the shaman that you know, or some other entity pretending to be him. Many spirits inhabit the realms of vision, and skilled deepshapers may journey there and take on any form. This being might have helped you to gain your trust. It may wish to use you, to wield power in our world, even to possess you, as you were possessed in the past."

That thought made Glyssa shiver. She wanted to insist that the guide she had met truly was Belach, that she felt this in her heart. But Amlina knew much more about the spirit world than she did, and so she was uncertain.

"What must I do?"

"Begin your training," Amlina said. "I will teach you exercises to draw power from the Deepmind, to move this power through your body. We need to dissolve that fishhook in your heart; that is still our goal. You must practice the exercises every day. Sometimes, they may put you into trance. While you are in trance, or while asleep and dreaming, you might meet again with this entity. If so, be wary. If it speaks, ask why it has come to you and what it intends. Try to judge if it is really your shaman, or something else. Above all, do not follow it anywhere or give it any of your power."

When she first entered the cabin, Glyssa had felt strong and stable within herself. Now the witch's somber warnings had stirred up her fears. Hopelessness and dread yawned within her like a dark abyss.

"All right," she said. "I will try."

Amlina again seemed to read her thoughts. "I did not mean to worry you, Glyssa. The truth is, you have done very well—and without any of the help you ought to have had. Training for a deepshaper is difficult, and often there are pitfalls and quandaries. But when I look at you, I see strength and remarkable bravery, and ..."

"What?" Glyssa asked.

The witch offered a tenuous smile. "I see again how fortunate I am to have you and your mates with me on this voyage."

* O *

In the days and nights that followed, Glyssa practiced the witch's exercises with the same determination as she had always applied to training with sword and spear. She stood still and chanted, clearing her mind of all except the sound of her voice. She moved her hands in slow spirals, focusing on the muscle force stretching from shoulders to fingertips. She meditated on the sea waves, imagining that her thoughts created their ceaseless movement. Twice a day, she sat on the rear deck, back straight, eyes shut, and envisioned a hovering light around her, a cold and infinite fire. Then she drew the fire into herself, moving it from place to place along her spine, circulating it through her limbs.

For the most part, the fire flowed readily. But whenever she brought it to her heart, she felt the blockage, the fish hook, like an icy stone. Touching that place with her mind awakened the fear and despair. Each time those feelings arose, Glyssa confronted them fiercely, affirming that she was an Iruk warrior, and fearless.

The *Phoenix Queen* sailed on, traversing the North Channel and emerging into the open sea. The sailing season had arrived in these northern waters, and they frequently sighted other vessels—fishing boats from the coastal towns, a few freighters from the Tathian Isles, cranocks out of Gwales. On Wilhaven's advice they steered clear of all craft—and, being outfitted as a raiding ship, were themselves never approached.

The wind stayed fair from the east or south east, and with the repaired bottom and mostly mild seas, there was minimal need for bailing. This fact cheered the Iruks considerably. The mates worked in shifts, six hours on and six off, with three of them crewing the boat at all times. Lonn arranged that he and Glyssa were always on duty together, so when they went to sleep in the hold below the rear deck, they could huddle together and share warmth. Lying between him and another of her mates, rocked by the sea, Glyssa found a deep sense of safety and contentment. She had worried a bit that her initiation and training by the witch might pull her away from my klarn. Instead, she found her connection to them, and her awareness of the klarn-soul, seemed to grow stronger.

When they had been nine days at sea, the weather changed. The wind shifted to the north east and white clouds blew across the sky. Wet snow flew for half a day, and then a freezewind came. Once the boat rose onto the ice with no trouble, the change was welcomed by the voyagers. For the three days it lasted, the ice brought faster sailing, and eliminated the need for bailing altogether.

Frequently, Glyssa met with Amlina in her cabin. The witch would practice the magical exercises with her, and listen as Glyssa described her experiences. Amlina expressed relief that Glyssa had not sunk into trance again, and had no more encounters with the spirit entity. In general, she spoke encouragingly, claiming that Glyssa was progressing well.

Aside from those visits, Glyssa seldom saw Amlina. The witch remained in her cabin, coming out on deck only briefly to take the air and exchange a few words with Lonn or Wilhaven about the condition of the boat and the progress of the voyage. Draven, or sometimes Glyssa, brought Amlina hot food and tea in her cabin, but the witch, always abstemious, seemed to have even less appetite than normal.

During the day, the head of Queen Meghild rested in its bowl on the witch's shelf. But at night the queen would emerge from the depths of her repose. Then the cabin hatch would creak open and the shining eidolon rise to walk the decks, the pulsing light of its body a weird counterpoint to the witchlight on the sea. Sometimes the queen would greet the Iruks, call them her crew and her dears, speak to them of the sea or the stars. But more often, the eidolon walked as though in a trance, staring out to the horizon with a lost and distant air.

Glyssa found the eidolon fascinating. But increasingly, the sight of the queen unsettled the other Iruks, especially Karrol. Whenever she was on duty and the eidolon appeared, Karrol would look away, and could usually be heard to mutter how she would be happy when this voyage was over.

For his part, Wilhaven roamed the decks both night and day. He slept in short snatches, in his little enclosure by the foredeck, and appeared whenever an extra hand was needed for bailing or reefing the sail. Sometimes he took the helm, to relieve Lonn or Karrol. More often, he perched himself on the foredeck, beside the phoenix figurehead, singing softly and playing his harp.

Late one night, when both moons were high and the sea exceptionally quiet, Glyssa stood on watch and listened to his playing. Queen Meghild had been at the prow with Wilhaven for some hours, but had recently retired. Now the bard strummed a mournful tune and sang in his honeyed baritone. The words were in Gwelthek, but Glyssa clearly perceived the mood of yearning and lament.

Suddenly, she heard other voices, wild and eerie, sounding from the sea as if in answer to the bard's song. Peering over the rail, Glyssa saw snouts and dark heads bobbing in the waves, and glimpsed eyes that shone with intelligence. Brinda, who shared the watch, stood beside her at the rail and shook her head, mystified. Whatever these creatures were, the Iruks had never seen their like before.

Glyssa ran to the foredeck, where Wilhaven continued to sing amid the strange accompaniment.

"Do you hear them?" she cried. "Can you see them?"

"Sure," the bard said. "The myro you mean."

"They are myro!" Glyssa exclaimed. The Iruks had heard tales of the dolphin people from Tathian sailors in the taverns of Fleevanport. But they had never known whether to believe them.

"Do you not have dolphin people in your southern seas?" the bard asked.

"Indeed no. They are wise, are they not? Sentient?"

"Oh, aye. And they seem to like the harp. They have sung with me before, on other voyages."

Enchanted, Glyssa gazed over the bulwark. "What are they singing?"

Wilhaven chuckled, "Sure, I cannot tell. A few mages and sea priestesses are said to know their language, but not I."

The chortling and whistling about the prow grew louder now and ... insistent.

"I think they want you to keep singing," Glyssa laughed.

"Well then," the bard raked his fingers over the strings. Then a thought struck him. "Why don't you ask them what they would like to hear?"

"I? But I don't know their speech."

"You are training to be a mage, aren't you? Perhaps they will converse with you. Speak to them with your thoughts, and listen, not with the ears, but the heart."

Glyssa hesitated. She thought the idea absurd. And yet, the myro were so lovely, their voices so plaintive, she felt enticed to try. She shut her eyes, took two deep breaths, and cleared her mind as the witch had taught her.

Lovely dolphin people, what are you saying?

She felt a quiver around her heart, and then the keening voices resolved themselves into words. Eyes still shut, Glyssa heard her own voice repeat the words to Wilhaven. "We are the people of the sea. We want to hear your music. A happy song, a laughing song. No sorrow under these round moons, in this bright sea."

She opened her eyes to find Wilhaven gazing at her with delight.

"Aye then, to be sure, we mustn't disappoint our audience."

He struck up a lively tune, and sang merrily in Gwelthek. Glyssa clapped her hands, imagining young men and girls in Gwales, dancing to such a tune in their fire-lit halls. Out on the sea, the myro whistled and giggled. Their glistening heads rose on the waves. Then one jumped clear of the water, it's dolphin body twisting in the air before splashing back down. Another performed the same trick, and then another, leaping in wild joy at the music.

When the song ended Glyssa shook with laughter. Through eyes wet with tears she watched the myro swim away. Their voices came to her mind again, and she translated them for the bard.

"We thank the air-singer for his song. Farewell for now. Farewell."

"Air-singer?" Wilhaven crowed with delight. "Sure, and I like that title for myself. I believe I will use it from now on." He set down his harp and regarded her brightly. "I thank you, Lady Glyssa, for interpreting the speech of the myro."

"Oh," Glyssa shrugged. "I only said what I thought I heard in my mind."

"Aye, it is proper not to boast," Wilhaven allowed. "Still, I recognize and honor your blooming talent as a mage." He paused a moment, twisting his mouth. "That piece I was singing before? It is the beginnings of my song about Queen Meghild's last voyage. It was in my mind that the tale would concern three powerful women: Meghild herself, Amlina the witch of Larthang, and Beryl the Archimage of the East. But now I begin to think a fourth woman will figure prominently: Lady Glyssa of the Iruk folk."

FOURTEEN

The Temple of the Sun had always been the largest and grandest in Tallyba. But since the Archimage had come to power and abolished all of the other gods, the vast gold and white edifice had been expanded and rebuilt four times. It was now the most imposing structure by far in all of Nyssan.

The dome itself would have covered a fair-sized town. Beneath the dome, six concentric chambers—high-ceilinged, painted with murals—led to the enormous central arena. Around the arena rose eleven galleries supported by pillars of orange marble. In the middle of the spotless white floor, a circular fire-pit ninety feet wide was set directly below a ninety-foot opening in the dome.

At noon, when a shaft of sunlight fell through that opening, illuminating clouds of cedar smoke, Beryl began her long-anticipated rejuvenation. The Archimage crossed the arena in measured steps, through the crowd of attendants and musicians who waited in silence. Dressed in bronze-colored robes and a turban that shone like a ruby, she stopped at the edge of the blazing pit, lifted her arms in wing-like sleeves, and began to chant.

Temple clergy stood on a half-circle of steps behind the fire-pit. Among them was Zenodia, second-ranked priestess of the sun and assistant to the temple treasurer. She was a stout young woman, dressed in an orange robe, the skin of her face and hands dyed red. Wisps of orange hair hung below the shaved crown of her head. Her calm eyes and neutral mien gave no hint of the smoldering hatred in her heart.

She watched tight-lipped as Beryl's brash voice invoked the power of the Sun, singing verses that rose and fell, punctuated now and then by beating drums and clashing cymbals. Zenodia's eyes widened as the queen smashed glass trinkets on the stone lip of the furnace, spawning jagged creatures of light that howled and screamed as they leaped into the fire. With each rolling verse, each *drog* destroying itself, the power in the arena grew, until Beryl herself seemed made of jagged light—a terrible, pulsing incarnation of the Sun.

At the appointed time, one row of priests and then the next marched down to the edge of the pit to add their offerings. When Zenodia's turn came, she dutifully slipped the ceremonial razor from her robe, held up her arm and cut herself, letting the blood drip into the fire—adding one more to her many scars.

When all of the clerics had given their blood, the ritual approached its culmination. Bound with chains, its eyes masked, the white-maned and tawny-furred lion was wheeled in on a cart decorated with flowers. Feeling the heat of the flames, the great cat tensed and shuddered, roaring plaintively. The attendants stepped back as Beryl approached the cart, a gilded sword in hand. The drums beat faster.

With a shrieking ululation, Beryl called upon herself, the divine and invincible Sun. She gripped the lion's mane and twisted the head, exposing the throat. Screaming, she hacked with the sword again and again, the lion bellowing, its blood splashing onto Beryl's arms and chest.

Zenodia looked away, trembling with rage. *How long?* she thought bitterly. *How long must my people suffer the abominations of this foreign tyrant?*

Sucking in her breath, Zenodia suppressed her emotions, forced herself to watch the unfolding blasphemy. Beryl, exultant, drank from a chalice filled with lion's blood, then poured the rest over her head. The Archimage stood with her back to the furnace, her body glittering with ruby witchlight, as the lion's carcass was butchered and skinned. High priests placed the steaming pelt over her shoulders and fastened it there with gold brooches. Beryl lifted the lion's dripping head in one hand, the gold sword in the other. Flinging her arms wide, she proclaimed herself the invincible Sun.

"I live forever!" she shouted. "I rule over all!"

Orange light burst from her, unbearably bright. A gasp of awe fled through the arena, and all present shielded their eyes.

* O *

Late that afternoon, Zenodia left the temple complex through a postern gate. A black cloak covered her priestly robe, its pointed cowl concealing her face. Her head still ached from the aftereffects of the ceremony. Her heart still seethed with rage. She walked alone down the grand avenue of the citadel, past imperial offices, storehouses, scriptoriums, and barracks. Behind her on the hilltop stood the palace complex, Beryl's Bone Tower at the center, dominating all.

Zenodia passed through the Gates of the Sun. As she descended across the city, well-appointed shops and stone houses with walled gardens gave way to poorer quarters. The avenue ended in a maze of narrow streets and cramped alleys. She was nearing the harbor now, and the smells of smoke and grime mixed with the rank air of stagnant water. As dusk settled, men and women hurried home to lock their doors. Zenodia marched on with calm determination. Her hooded black cloak, with its implication of magical prowess, protected her from thieves and cutthroats.

At last she approached a boarded shop-front on a dank, cobbled street. She rapped sharply on the door. A peephole slid open and hostile eyes stared out at her. She pulled back her cowl.

"Zenodia," she said. "I must see her."

The door opened and a bald, pot-bellied man bowed stiffly as she entered. "How went the great ceremony?"

"Successfully, it seems, for the tyrant."

The man grimaced and held a finger to his lips. "Shhh! Not so loud."

"Sorry," Zenodia whispered. "I am heartsick with anger. I must see Mawu."

The man, who wore a baker's apron, gestured to a doorway at the back of the shop. "She is here. Go through, my sister."

Zenodia proceeded to the back room of the bakery. Past racks of trays and bowls and the yawning mouth of the oven, she stopped at the far wall and opened what appeared to be a tall cupboard. Bending low, she crept inside and descended a curling staircase of ancient brick.

She entered a low-vaulted chamber that smelled of incense and mold. A single lamp cast faint illumination over wood benches and a makeshift altar. Above the altar hung an ancient, forbidden banner—the silver crescent of Tysanni, the lost moon.

The survival of the banished gods across Far Nyssan was an open secret. Even here in Tallyba, their outlawed cults still abided in hidden chambers and dim cellars such as this. The Archimage was known to be aware of their existence. It was assumed Beryl found it more convenient to let the cults survive in these squalid circumstances, rather than attempt to stamp them out altogether—thereby increasing the people's hatred and possibly inciting rebellion.

As for Zenodia, she had lived with the hatred from earliest childhood—like a canker exuding poison. Her grandfather had been a high priest of Tysanni. Her family had lost everything in the religious purges. She had grown up in impoverished exile, listening to tales of the rich and dignified world her people had lost to the tyrant. Gifted with intellect, she had studied diligently, learned all she could of the forbidden mysteries, as well as the state-approved religion of the Sun. She had entered the priesthood at nineteen, won appointment to the great temple in Tallyba, and in eight short years rose to her current rank. From the start, her intention had been to position herself close to the seat of power, to find some way to undermine and eventually topple the Archimage.

Zenodia had believed that her hatred for Beryl could not grow any stronger. But today, on seeing the sacred lion butchered, the queen drenched in its blood, prancing about in its skin, the canker had burst, flooding her with new poison.

"Welcome, daughter." A hunched figure sat at the edge of the first bench, facing the altar. She spoke without turning around. "I foresaw your coming."

Zenodia ran to the front of the vault, dropped to her knees. "High Priestess, I must speak with you."

"I know. I listen." Mawu was old and small, with braided white hair, skin dry and wrinkled. A faded tattoo adorned her forehead—the crescent of Tysanni.

"The rites went as expected," Zenodia said, choking back the poison. "Now it seems the queen has achieved her regeneration—and will be even harder to defeat."

"Yes, daughter. But as you say, it was expected."

"But the oracle—"

"The oracle makes no guarantees."

For more than three years, Zenodia had placed all of her hopes on an oracle delivered by the high priestess. It seemed to indicate that Beryl could be destroyed by another witch of Larthang. Zenodia, and others in the cult, had believed that the prophecy referred to Beryl's student, Amlina. When Amlina had disappeared from the palace, stealing the Cloak of the Two Winds, that hope seemed to die. But when Beryl had pursued the young witch, and returned many days later in a clearly weakened state, the hope had flared again.

"I know," Zenodia said. "And what the oracle sees may manifest in many ways, at unexpected times. But after the atrocity I witnessed today, I am so sick with grief and anger. I do not believe I can bear to live in this world."

Mawu's hand reached down and clasped the younger woman's wrist. "Courage, child! And patience. The gods gave their blood to create this world. So must we live in the world they made. That is our duty."

"I know. Forgive me, High Priestess ... If only I could still believe there was hope."

"Hmm." The ancient head nodded. "Would you like to consult the oracle then?"

"Yes. If I may."

Zenodia assisted the old woman to rise. Together they assembled a brazier on the altar, and placed a bronze bowl above it on a tripod. While Zenodia added charcoal and lit the brazier, Mawu collected vials and dried herbs from a cabinet. She filled the bowl with a mixture of cactus juice and wine, and uttered prayers as she crumbled and sprinkled in the herbs.

Soon the mixture was simmering. Zenodia knelt before the altar and waited. The high priestess bent over the bowl, hands braced on the edge of the altar, and inhaled the vapors.

Presently, she coughed and sputtered, and Zenodia knew the oracle had come.

"Who are you?" Zenodia spoke the ritual question.

"I dwell in the night and I watch. I see the circling of the moons, the crossing of the winds, the rise and fall of souls. What would you ask of me?"

Zenodia's hands balled into fists. "How can Beryl the Archimage, the tyrant who has enslaved us, be destroyed?"

Mawu sucked air between her teeth. "The queen ... the foreign queen ... Her witchcraft is mighty. She will thrive for a thousand years ... Unless ... unless these three prevail: the student who returns, the queen who is already dead, the spear that was melted and forged again."

Zenodia focused to commit the pronouncement to memory, even as she scowled in disappointment. The prophesies were typically recondite, requiring analysis, open to interpretation. But this—this sounded more like a riddle.

When she had guided Mawu back to the bench and sat with her while she came out of trance, Zenodia repeated the prophesy. The old woman listened and shook her head.

"The student who returns might well be that same Amlina," she said. "But as to the others. I do not know. I suggest we both of us meditate on the oracle and seek more insight."

"Yes, High Priestess."

"Take heart, my daughter. At least the oracle sees some hope."

Zenodia stared solemnly at the banner over the altar. "Yes, I will be patient, and seek further meaning in the oracle's words. And I will return to my duties and bide my time, watching Beryl and the forces around her. But I tell you this, Mawu, and I swear it before the moons and sun. A year from now, Beryl will no longer rule in Tallyba. Either that, or I will have died attempting to destroy her."

FIFTEEN

Fog, dense and gray, glittering with flashes of silver, like the sparks of witchlight in a freezewind or meltwind ... Except there was no wind, only stillness and the endless fog obscuring all ...

Amlina stared numbly into the gray cloud as her consciousness surfaced. She had entered the dark immersion for the second time in less than a month. Normally, a witch of Larthang timed her deep trances to coincide with Grizna's cycle—immersing once per month at the most. But Amlina had been desperate to compose herself, subdue her fear. And the fog ...

Her eyes popped open, dimly perceiving the dark wood and lamps of her tiny cabin. She remembered now: the fog was not just a construction of her trance. It existed in the physical world, surrounding their boat, impeding the voyage. The *Phoenix Queen* had crossed the open sea, passed the Cape of Kleeg, entered the Bay of Mistrel. Soon after that the sea-clouds had appeared, dense and increasingly frequent, far worse than Meghild and Wilhaven predicted. Fogs were common in the region, especially in the warm seasons. Meghild's timetable for crossing the bay allowed for some delays. But for four days and nights the boat had mostly been fogbound, forced to lower sail and float aimlessly on the slack current—while the moons moved inexorably toward the night of their critical alignment. Almost a full month had already passed since their departure from Gwales; little more than a month's time remained.

Amlina had hoped that in deep trance she might find answers: whether the fogs were simply misfortune or had perhaps been caused by witchery, whether they would lift soon, or if some magical intervention might be possible. But, lost in the bliss of forgetfulness, she had discovered nothing.

Except ... Amlina shuddered, fully awake now, remembering. The fog was an emanation of the Deepmind, representing something else—a thing that obscured her vision, engulfed and smothered her, rousing hopelessness and fear. She did not have to look far to know what that thing was. Her glance lifted to the head of the queen, floating in hazy light. *The thing that she had done, the blood magic.* Day by day, the power of the design was growing, and with it Amlina's responsibility, a weight that threatened to crush her.

The witch squeezed her scalp with both hands, as if she could force down the dread. She needed to eat and drink, to ground herself, preserve her strength. She rolled out of the bunk, blew out the lamps, pulled her coat from its hook and wrapped it around her shoulders.

She climbed out of her cabin to find the cranock enveloped in fog. Wet veils of it floated over the bulwarks. The sail was reefed, the boat drifting. She gripped the rail and made her way to the mast, where Draven and Glyssa were stationed.

"Hello," Draven embraced her. She sank against his shoulder, welcoming his warmth, feeling her legs go weak.

"Are you all right?" he asked.

"Yes. I am well enough." She spoke with a parched throat. "Some water? Perhaps some food?"

"Of course. I will get you something."

He fetched a cup of water from the cask on deck, then busied himself at the oil stove and food locker. Amlina sipped cautiously, steadying herself by gripping a shroud line. Glyssa came over and touched her arm.

"Were we fogbound the whole time I was in trance?" the witch asked.

Glyssa shook her head. "It lifted two nights ago. We were able to adjust our course by the stars. We sailed that night and the next day, before it closed in again. Did you learn anything from your trance?"

Amlina hesitated. But Glyssa was her student, and anyway, she saw no point in concealment. "Nothing definite ... except, I think I am to blame."

Startled, Glyssa searched the witch's eyes. "Because of your fears, you mean, your doubts over what you have taken on?"

Amlina's brows lifted with surprise. "Yes. Your training, I see, is not wasted. Your perception grows very keen."

"But how can you be causing the fog? I mean, why would you?"

Amlina frowned, fixing her gaze on the water swirling in the cup. "I do not say I am causing it exactly. Not deliberately. But as deepshapers, we attune ourselves to the forces that shape the world. When we have thoughts and feelings outside of our awareness and control, those too can influence what comes to us—even against our will. That is why we must strive for perfect self-knowledge, and train our minds to purity, focusing only on what we intend. In this instance, it appears I have failed, bringing us this obstacle, which I must find a way to overcome."

Draven brought her a bowl of stew and some hard bread, and sat down with her on the deck while she ate. With the boat swaying, the wisps of fog floating and sparkling, it almost seemed to Amlina she was still in trance, or dreaming.

But the hot food restored her somewhat, and when she stood she felt less lightheaded. She climbed to the rear deck and greeted Lonn. Having heard her conversation with Glyssa, he did not press her with questions. She knelt and touched Kizier, who was humming softly with the other windbringers.

His eye blinked open. "Amlina. How are you? ... Oh, I see we are still beset with fog."

"Yes."

"My companions and I have tried, I assure you. But calling any breeze at all is very difficult."

"I understand," Amlina said. The ability of bostulls to summon the wind varied by location and weather conditions. Fog in particular

A MIRROR AGAINST ALL MISHAP

was known to make them drowsy and ineffective. "Please continue to try."

"Of course. Do you sense that a mental influence might be involved?"

"I do," Amlina sighed. "That is a thread I must pursue."

Suddenly, she felt very tired again. "I think I best go and lie down."

* O *

Soon after the witch returned to her cabin, Glyssa and Draven climbed to the stern and touched Kizier's stalk. The round eye slipped open, dull and bleary. Glyssa sensed fatigue, perhaps worry.

"We are sorry to waken you again," she said. "But we wanted to ask about your talk with Amlina. Draven and I are concerned about her."

"Indeed," Kizier whispered. "So am I."

"She is tough," Lonn asserted, leaning on the tiller. "She will be all right."

But Draven shook his head. "She is not so strong as she pretends, Lonn. You do not see how vulnerable she is."

"She carries a great burden of magic," Kizier stated. "And it grows heavier as we approach the night when she will cast the Mirror. It is not like any working she has done before. From the start, I feared it might be too much, that the power might change her."

"How do you mean?" Draven demanded.

Kizier made a noise like a sigh. "I have known Amlina for a long time. When we first met at the court of the Archimage, she seemed naïve in a way, her heart pure and full of light. But you cannot serve as apprentice to one as evil as Beryl without becoming tainted, without certain seeds taking root in your soul. I fear Beryl's influence made Amlina more susceptible to the seductions of evil magic."

"I remember," Glyssa said. "Amlina told me she had been guided to take an evil power into her soul and to transform it."

"That is how she sees it," Kizier replied. "But by performing blood magic, she violated a fundamental tenet of Larthangan practice. Whether the guidance to do so came from some higher purpose in the Deepmind, or from motives in herself that Amlina is unaware of—that is the worrisome question."

"What do you mean?" Glyssa said.

"Ah. I am no deepseer, but as a windbringer I have certain perceptions. Amlina has a strong and determined soul. As a child, she suffered the abuse of a tyrannical mother. She was never allowed to express herself, as a child with her gifts must in order to flourish. At the first opportunity, she fled her family and enrolled in the Academy of the Deepmind. But she failed to flourish there again, too willful, they told her, disinclined to proper humility and obedience. And so she left Larthang altogether. But you know the rest, how she dwelled for a time in the Tathian Isles, then finally came to Beryl's court. Always she is driven, by needs and ambitions she does not fully understand. And now ... now I fear she may have been driven to something beyond her powers to control—or recover from."

"What can we do to help her?" Draven asked in anguish.

"I only wish I knew." Kizier exhaled mournfully. "But then, I am always wishing for things to be better than they are. That is how I became a windbringer, did you know? When Beryl wearied of me, as an ornament of her court, she said my constant, feckless wishing annoyed her. So she transformed me into a windbringer, saying I could henceforth wish for the winds."

The Iruks regarded him in gloomy silence.

"Ha," he said. "If only my wishing now could bring a wind to dispel this dismal fog."

* O *

A MIRROR AGAINST ALL MISHAP

The fog still hovered over the *Phoenix Queen* late that night, when Glyssa and Draven stood watch again. Queen Meghild was forward at the prow, her grayish light fading and brightening in strands of mist. Wilhaven sat at the queen's feet, softly plucking his harp.

Glyssa was silently chanting to herself when a noise startled her— a hatch swinging open. She spied Amlina climbing from her cabin. Even in the mist, Glyssa noticed something different in the witch's posture. Determination, she thought, and power.

Glyssa followed Draven, who immediately went to join Amlina.

"I am all right, my friend," the witch touched his arm and gave him a smile. "Glyssa, would you come with me, please? I am going to speak with the queen."

Glyssa followed Amlina onto the foredeck. Wilhaven climbed to his feet and nodded to them. Meghild stared into the fog, oblivious to their arrival.

"My queen," Amlina said, and when there was no response: "Queen Meghild, I must have words with you."

Atop the light-body, the face swiveled down. "Ah, Amlina." The queen looked perplexed. "This fog ..."

"That is why we must talk. We have been fogbound for most of six days. It is almost certainly not just circumstance."

"Sure, but what can be done about it?" Wilhaven asked.

Amlina continued, solemn and resolute. "I have sought an answer to that question in deep trance, and I have consulted the talking book. I have concluded the fog is a magical emanation, most likely resulting from suppressed thoughts of my own. That makes it much more difficult for me to address through deepshaping. I have fashioned a design, a simple invocation of the North Wind, to disperse the fog. But unless I have help from outside myself, my own weakness and uncertainty will likely thwart the effect." She stared into Meghild's dim eyes. "My queen, do you remember the night in your feast hall, when I drew down your power to blind the warriors who barred our way? I must tap that power again."

"Oh," Meghild moaned. "But I was so much stronger then. This body of mine was brand new. I am not sure I can do this, Amlina."

"The magic of the eidolon is perplexing," the witch answered. "In fact, the power in you is growing, not fading. But it is growing in the Deepmind, below the surface, as it were. The stronger it grows there, the less awareness you have of yourself in *this* world. It is possible that drawing your power from the Deepmind will actually *increase* your presence in this world. You might for a time feel much more self-aware and vigorous."

The queen glared suspiciously. "You say that is possible. What is the other possibility then?"

Amlina's mouth twitched. "It is also possible that tapping your power will weaken you, in both the Deepmind and this world, and your waking mind will further diminish. That might also mean your energy will not be sufficient to generate the Mirror Against All Mishap, and then our whole voyage will be a failure."

Glyssa's glanced shifted to the queen, who seemed intensely present now, carefully weighing Amlina's words.

"It must be your decision, my queen," Amlina said. "I hate to ask it of you—the more so because it is probably my failure as a witch that has brought us to this crisis. But unless we can dispel the fog, I do not believe we will reach Valgool in time."

"Bah!" Meghild growled. "What an inglorious end that would make for my last voyage. Is that not so, Wilhaven?"

"I have faith in you, my queen," the bard said quietly, "that you will make the best decision."

"Aye," Meghild muttered. "And be sure you record this in your song: that on this fogbound night, Amlina had the wisdom to see her weakness, and the courage to confess it. And that Meghild, given the chance, did not cling to a fading life, but chose instead the way of high risk and valor."

"To be sure," the bard said, "I will sing all of that proudly."

"Tap my power as you will," Meghild said to Amlina. "I am at your service."

"I thank you, my queen," the witch's voice held a tremor of respect, that Glyssa too felt in her heart. "Stand you ready then. Glyssa, I need your help also."

Glyssa's lips parted with a twinge of apprehension. "What can I do?"

The witch taught her a chant, eight words of Old Larthangan, which she translated as a summons to the North Wind—*Old Lord of the mountain, we call you.*

"As we speak the words, visualize the power building in you, spiraling up from the base of your spine, a pure light of intention. Then, when I lift your hand and touch the queen's body, send the power out as a summons into the north. Do you see?"

"Yes." Hesitantly, Glyssa took the witch's hand. "I will try."

* O *

Amlina closed her eyes, took a deep breath, and began the summoning. Beside her, Glyssa tried to mimic the chant, her voice uncertain. Amlina brought to mind the design she had formulated, visualized the force within exactly as she had described it, brightening as it spiraled up her spine.

At first the flow of light was steady and strong. But then the glow flickered, her will faltering. Despite her best efforts, lurking thoughts of failure appeared, sparked by the knowledge that she was to blame. The fog manifested her own weakness. She had risked everything, invoked terrible rites of blood magic, brought her friends on this desperate voyage—all driven by vanity, her foolish belief that she deserved an exalted destiny. And it had brought them all to this, lost and defeated by mere fog.

Amlina gritted her teeth, straining to vanquish the lethal doubts, to focus on her intent, her power. She felt Glyssa squeeze her hand, sensing her distress. The Iruk's voice was strong and certain now, intoning the words like drumbeats.

Perhaps we can strengthen each other, Glyssa had said to her once.

That memory steadied Amlina. She resumed chanting, her voice rolling with Glyssa's, forceful and potent. She drew the spiral up her spine, raised the power from the Deepmind until it blazed in her brain. Then with a primal call to the wind she lifted Glyssa's hand, touched the eidolon, and cast her magic away to the north.

Meghild screamed, shuddering as the power exploded away.

Amlina blanked out for a second, found herself on her knees. Glyssa gripped her elbow and helped her to stand.

Meghild had crumbled, the eidolon body bent over, its light dim and flickering.

"Help her," Wilhaven muttered.

"Yes." Amlina collected herself. She took hold of Meghild's arm. "Come, my queen. I will take you to rest."

The eidolon hobbled now like an old and crippled woman. Guided by Amlina, Wilhaven and Glyssa helped the queen step from the foredeck and into the witch's cabin. There, Amlina worked the magic to settle the light-body into the bowl of water, and placed the queen's head to float above it.

When she returned to the deck, a fresh breeze was blowing from the north, the fog shredding and flowing away.

SIXTEEN

Standing on the rear deck with Lonn and Wilhaven, Amlina watched as the *Phoenix Queen* tacked in toward the docks. The port of Borgova spread along the north shore of a broad river, an unwalled town of gray stone and ancient dark timber. Beyond the roofs rose green hills, and white clouds towered in a pale blue sky.

It was morning, the 36th day of their voyage; 24 days until the three moons would align.

The north wind had held fair for six days. Slight fogs had appeared, but caused no further delays. With the time they had gained sailing on ice for part of the sea-crossing, they were actually one day ahead of schedule. Amlina felt a weary sense of relief. The magic to summon the north wind had balanced her spirit. And, though the growing power of the Mirror ensorcellment still weighed on her, her mind was clear, her intention firm.

When they came within earshot of the docks, Wilhaven raised his hands and shouted out to the men ashore, asking the location of the best boatyard. He was directed to an inlet a short distance downstream. The cranock would need to be hauled out of the water and refitted for the journey upriver. The outriggers would be torn out to make space for oars. Thwarts for rowers to sit on were already built in, but the oarholes would have to be unplugged and oars provided. A cranock was designed for ready conversion to a river craft, and Meghild and Wilhaven had both said that the work could be accomplished in a single day.

As they sailed toward the inlet, Amlina headed for her cabin. All of the Iruks were on deck, bantering and laughing as they secured lines and packed up their gear. After so many days on the cramped vessel, they were looking forward to time ashore.

Ducking her head, Amlina entered the crawlspace. She had already packed one of her trunks with trinkets, a change of clothes, and the talking book. Now she added her purse, and an embroidered pouch containing her jewelry and dagger. A heavier bag held several hundred gold coins, which Meghild had given her prior to leaving Gwales to ensure adequate funds for the voyage.

The queen's gift had been necessary, since the small amount of gold Amlina had carried off from Kadavel had been spent—gone in generous payment to the crew of the Larthangan ship and in Amlina's share for financing the *Phoenix Queen*. The Iruks, of course, had taken much more treasure from the Temple of the Air and, so far as the witch knew, still had sacks of it stored with their gear.

Amlina placed the money-bag in a hinged basket and set a blanket over it. Then she knelt before the shelf where the head of the queen floated in its bowl. She whispered a few words in the extinct Nyssanian tongue, then said aloud: "My queen, it is time to awaken."

The eyelids lifted at once, the face alert. "Amlina. Have we landed?"

"We are nearing the boatyard. I must draw your light form out of the water."

"Bah! And wrap my head in an oilskin, hide it in a dark trunk. I don't want to sleep the whole time we are ashore. I want to walk the land and breathe the air." Since Amlina drew the eidolon's power to summon the wind, the queen had been more energetic, more present in this world—and also more willful and stubborn.

"I know, my queen. I regret the necessity. But in your present form, you are bound to attract undue attention."

"So wrap me in a cloak to hide the light. I won't say a word. I can be discreet."

Amlina sighed. "I've explained to you: If even a few eyes discover your true appearance, the wonder of it will cause ripples in the Deepmind—ripples that the Archimage is liable to discern. Our whole venture depends on concealing ourselves from her, at least until after the Mirror is cast."

"By that time, I will be dead," Meghild answered. "A queen does not beg, Amlina. But neither does she accept terms she finds unreasonable. I remind you of our bargain: that I should be able to sail and walk and take full part in one last adventure. Nothing was said of locking me in a trunk."

Amlina bowed her head. She could not deny the rightfulness of the queen's appeal. And she could not find it in her heart to deny it.

"Very well. We will draw up your light body and let you walk. We will purchase clothing in the town to conceal you. That will have to suffice."

"Ha ha!" the bodiless head cried. "Now I am satisfied!"

* O *

When Amlina returned to the deck Meghild followed, her eidolon body rising tall, wrapped in a blanket from head to foot. The queen looked around, eyes sparkling.

The sail was lowered, the cranock settled in shallow water. Before them on the shore rose the ramps and enclosures of the boatyard, crowded with workmen and vessels being built or repaired. Wilhaven stood on a boardwalk, gesturing in intent conversation with a burly man in a leather apron. Several workers stood behind them with hands on their hips. The Iruks had gathered at the rails to watch the confrontation.

"Amlina," Lonn called. "You had better go and help Wilhaven. I don't think the negotiations are going well."

The Iruks assisted the witch over the side. She marched through the shallow water and onto the boards. Folding her hands in her sleeves, she took a deep breath to settle herself.

"Greetings, gentlemen," she said. "Have we been able to come to terms?"

"Not hardly." The boatwright stared at her belligerently.

"This is Master Bruel." Wilhaven introduced the man. "He says they can do the work all right, and for twenty ellas, a reasonable price. But not for another small-month."

"Two small-months more likely," Bruel said. "This is our busy time."

"But the job is not large," Amlina suggested. "Perhaps if we offered a higher price?"

The boatwright crossed his arms. "You could offer me both moons and it wouldn't make any difference. I have contracts with local owners to fulfill. I can't delay them just because some foreigners sail into town and expect special treatment."

Inside her sleeve, Amlina moved her fingertips. She stared briefly into the man's eyes and summoned her witch's art of *passive persuasion*.

She offered a tenuous smile. "Forgive me for not introducing myself. My name is Olicia Wor-T'sing. I am a scholar from the Academy of Foreign Nations in Larthang. Once each hundred years, we are sent across the world to survey the peoples and climes and update the Academy's knowledge."

"So?"

"Well." She lowered her eyes, evincing embarrassment. "I am afraid we are far behind in our timetable—owing, I must say, to faults entirely my own. You see, I so love learning about people and their ways that we spent far too much time in the hinterlands of Kleeg. Now I must get upriver to survey your inlands as soon as may be. It would be a great kindness if you could have our boat outfitted by, say, tomorrow morning?"

The foreman's expression had softened, his mind lulled by her gentle voice. "I'd like to help you, but my regular customers ..."

"They will not be inconvenienced—a single day's work for a few of your men. Indeed, they may think you magnanimous for assisting a troubled group of travelers. And they need never know that you were paid *twice* the sum you asked."

Bruel's eyebrows lifted. "Well, I ..."

Amlina took a silver ring from her finger. "In appreciation of your generosity, I offer this token. It was forged by a witch at the Academy of the Deepmind and contains a charm said to bring good fortune in business affairs."

The foreman scowled dubiously. "Oh, really?"

"Here, see how it fits."

Reluctantly, he took the ring. When he slipped it onto his little finger, the scowl melted into a look of wonder and delight.

"Worn on the smallest finger—most propitious," Amlina said. "So you will have our boat ready by tomorrow noon?"

"Yes ..." the boatwright looked puzzled. "You did say *forty* ellas, correct?"

Amlina smiled. "Agreed."

* O *

Firelight from the stone hearth danced across the floor. Under the low-beamed ceiling, the dining room was crowded with tables and benches, customers and servers, eating and drinking, talking and laughing. The close air smelled of spilled ale, grilling meats, wood smoke.

Amlina and her companions sat at a table in a dim corner. They had dined on broiled fish, fresh vegetables, hot bread. Their mood now was languid and satiated.

"Oh, I've missed this, to be sure." Meghild waved her tankard at the noisy crowd. Though the eidolon had no need of food or drink, the queen was managing to enjoy her ale, the gold liquid passing down her throat to be immediately consumed and changed to light.

"All of us have missed this," Eben laughed.

"Aye," the queen answered. "But I don't just mean the inn and the drinking. I mean traveling, seeing new lands and people, breathing the air of different climes. I was stuck in that moldy castle nigh on ten years and thought to never sail again." She laid a glove on the witch's slim wrist. "You've made an old woman happy, Amlina."

"I am glad, my queen."

After leaving the boatyard early in the day, they had stopped at a clothier and purchased a long cloak, gloves, and boots to conceal the eidolon's light. Next, on the Iruks' insistence, they had found a bathhouse. While the travelers soaked gratefully in steaming tubs, their clothes were laundered, furs brushed and cleaned. Finally, they had come to this inn near the waterfront and rented two rooms for the night. Locked in her room, Amlina had meditated, woven her usual concealments, and then fashioned an additional *cantrip*—a mind trick extended to all of her companions, making them hard to notice and easy to forget.

With all of that accomplished and after the warm and nourishing meal, Amlina should have felt relaxed. Instead, apprehension tugged at her nerves. Restlessly, she scanned the other tables and along the walls, watching for anyone who might be paying them undue attention.

The babble in the dining room subsided as, off in a corner, an *elbow-piper* sat down to play. His instrument was a construction of pipes, keys, and an air-bag squeezed at the elbow. Amlina had heard it played before, in Meghild's hall. The tune was mellow and sweet, and the diners listened with quiet appreciation. Borgova had been founded long ago as a colony by Gwales traders. In later times, Tathians had come to dominate the sea routes, and now the town was a mixture of Gwales, Tathian, and native Nyssanian folk. But plainly the love of Gwales music lived on.

"Sure, and that lad needs accompaniment," Wilhaven said, amid the applause that followed the tune.

"Aye, my lovely," Meghild cried, as the bard took his harp from its velvet bag. "Let them hear the music of the eastern fjords!"

Amlina started to object, worried once more about being conspicuous. But glancing around the table, she stopped herself. After so many days and nights of hardship, her companions were enjoying themselves. She must not spoil that, she thought. She must let it be and trust that her concealments were enough.

Wilhaven stepped across the room and introduced himself to the piper. Together they played two pieces--another delicate air and then a lively, stomping reel that brought fervent applause and set a few of the customers to dancing. When the crowd demanded more, the bard offered to sing a ballad, one of his own recent compositions.

The song concerned a group of pirates, "rude barbarians from a distant shore," who wintered as guests in a Gwales castle. All went well, until a certain prince of the tribe took a dislike to the guests. This was a proud and arrogant man named "Pendraith." One night, when he'd had too much to drink, this prince broke the courtesy of the hall and challenged the foreigners to fight. After consultation, the pirates sent the smallest of their band to accept the challenge, a woman warrior named "Alyssa." She bested the boastful prince with ease, and left a scar on his cheek to remind him to treat guests with respect in the future.

Cheers erupted at the end of the song, several patrons jumping up to clap Wilhaven on the back. Scanning her friends' faces, Amlina saw smiles of smug satisfaction from the Iruks, a blush on Glyssa's cheek, fierce pride on the queen's countenance.

Startled, Amlina felt tears welling in her eyes. As a witch of Larthang, she was schooled in the concept of *rectitude*, the correct use of power. Since the start of this voyage, she had been troubled, unsure her choices were correct. But now, contemplating this remarkable group of friends from far-flung places, who had chosen to journey with her, united in her cause to rid the world of a great evil, she took comfort that her course might indeed be rightful.

* O *

Later that night, the Iruks marched through the streets of the town. Glyssa and her mates were dressed in clean clothes and carried all their weapons, cleaned and oiled. Although the night was warm, they had donned their hooded capes. Eben toted a water skin filled with ale. Lonn and Brinda lit the way with lanterns borrowed from the inn.

"I think it was a fine ballad," Draven was saying. "Of course it's not exactly what happened. Wilhaven changed some parts to make a better story."

"I realize that," Karrol answered. "I'm not saying he should sing exactly what happened. I'm just not happy with how he described us. 'Rude barbarians from a distant shore.' When were we ever rude to anybody?"

"I think he used 'rude' in a different sense," Eben said. "Not discourteous, but uncivilized. Because we're barbarians."

"Aren't *all* barbarians uncivilized?" Karrol argued. "Isn't that what the word *means*? Why not just say barbarians then? I get tired of the way people from other nations look down on us, just because they live in big halls and sail big ships. I'd like to see some of them survive in the Polar Seas ..."

"Wilhaven is all right," Lonn said.

"I know, Wilhaven is all right," Karrol said. "Amlina is all right. Even the ghost queen is all right. I'm just glad to get away from them all for a while. To be alone with my mates."

That was the reason for this late-night foray. Karrol and Brinda had suggested the mates leave the inn and find some deserted place where they could build a fire and raise the klarn spirit—to reestablish their unity after so many days at sea.

Passing the outskirts of town, they climbed a grassy hill. They had learned that the hills behind the town were commons, used for pasture in some seasons, little used this time of year. The night was clear, with both moons floating among the bright and unfamiliar constellations of the northern sky. Lonn stopped at the crest of the hill, where the ground was nearly level.

"This looks to be a good place."

The mates nodded agreement. Below them spread the town and beyond it the wide river, black and sluggish—only gradually acquiring witchlight as it flowed west and mingled with the salt water of the bay.

From a grove on the far side of the hill, the mates gathered sticks and fallen branches. Lonn lit the fire, then extinguished the lanterns. When the blaze was high and crackling, the Iruks stood in a circle and one by one thrust their spear tips into the ground.

With their hands still gripping the spear hafts, Lonn said: "The klarn has not been put to rest, and we do not rest it now, for the hunt continues. But gathered around this fire we awaken the klarn-soul, that we may feel it in our bodies, to bring us strength for the journey ahead."

"And so we may feel our bond," Glyssa was inspired to add. "And bring comfort and strength to each other."

Glyssa felt the klarn-soul thrumming inside her—an energy like and yet unlike the power that circulated in her with the witch's exercises. Glancing around the circle, she was astonished to find she could *see* the klarn's presence, a silvery aura hovering around each of her mates. It was witch-sight, she realized. Amlina's training was changing her into a seer.

The mates sat down cross-legged around the fire. Eben took a swig from the water skin and passed it to Brinda.

After passing it on, Brinda said. "I am glad we did this. We are going to need all our strength for pulling that boat up the river."

Back in the fjord in Gwales, the Iruks had seen a cranock outfitted with oars, so they understood about the conversion. But they had never sat at oars and had no experience rowing.

"We'll learn it quick enough," Lonn grumbled. But Glyssa knew he was masking uncertainty.

"Sure," Draven declared. "How hard can it be?"

"Back-breaking," Karrol said glumly. "That's what I heard Meghild's boat master say."

"Well, he would say that," Eben remarked, "just to impress us with the toughness of Gwalesmen."

A calm sureness came into Glyssa. "We will manage it," she said.

All of them stared at her.

"When you say things in that tone," Karrol said, "I feel sure you are right. Is that the witch power growing in you, Glyssa?"

She laughed softly. "I think it could be. Sometimes now I feel things and ... am just certain of them. Perhaps this is how a shaman, like Belach, perceives truths from the spirit world." She watched as her mate's auras flickered, ghost-like. "The training *is* changing me. That's for sure."

"It is helping you, I think," Draven asserted. "You seem much better than before we left Gwales."

Glyssa reflected on that. "Yes, I am steadier. I cannot say I am cured. The fear and emptiness still seize me sometimes; perhaps they always will. But I can control myself better now." The ale was passed to her, and she took a sip. Her mates gazed at her and she smiled. "One other thing I know for sure: I am happy to be here with my klarn."

They talked quietly around the fire, until they had drunk all the ale. Then Karrol stood and stretched. She walked a little apart, drew her blades and practiced her fighting stances. The others joined her. Joking and laughing, they matched feints and thrusts in mock duels, relishing the chance to exercise freely after so many days confined on the boat.

Glyssa fenced with Lonn, then Brinda. But she tired sooner than the others. She watched them for a while, then went and placed more wood on the fire. She wrapped herself in her cape and lay down, feeling drowsy and content.

When she woke, it was well past midnight. Rog had already set and Grizna floated in the west. Her mates were sleeping, all except Draven who sat hunched over the fire.

Glyssa crept over to join him. Draven eyed her with a wistful smile.

"You are troubled?" Glyssa whispered.

He lifted a shoulder. "Thinking about Amlina. Does your witch-sight tell you anything about her, Glyssa?"

She reached over and squeezed his hand. "I don't need witch-sight to see you love her dearly, Draven."

He snorted. "No, that's obvious I suppose. My feelings for her are hard to fathom, though. I want her as a woman, of course, but that's only the start of it. I feel a bond with her, a spirit bond, like we have with the klarn, but different."

"How different?"

Draven pondered for the space of several heartbeats. "The klarn is something we make up together, something we all agree to. But my feelings for Amlina come from a place deep inside me. Sometimes I wonder if she's bewitched me."

Glyssa reflected on that. "No, I don't think so. Not in the way of using magic to control you. But ... there is something in her that calls to you, a weakness she dare not admit, a need for someone to care for her, someone she can love and trust."

"Yes, that's it," Draven said. "I feel a tremendous need to take care of her, protect her ... to help her bear the burdens she carries." He was gripping Glyssa's hand tightly. "Do you think she will be strong enough to survive what lies ahead?"

Glyssa relaxed her thoughts, focused on listening to the impressions that came, the way the witch had taught her. "Oh, I think Amlina is like a downy feather—light and delicate, can be bent and twisted, but almost impossible to break or tear apart. I think the voyage has been hard for her. Waiting, inaction, these bring out her fear. But when the time comes to act, then she is strong and sure. Then she is the toughest of us all."

* O *

The Iruks arose before dawn and put out the fire. They spoke words of thanks to the klarn and affirmed that its strength beat in their hearts as one. Then they picked up their spears and walked down the hill, singing softly the chant they had sung when the klarn was first formed:
    Through wind and sharp wave
    Through ice and blood
    We hold to the klarn
    We are fearless
    Many hands, one heart
    Many eyes, one soul
    Many spears, one hunter
    We hold to the klarn
    We are fearless

SEVENTEEN

Beryl floated in an immensity of darkness, her body resting cross-legged as if seated on a cushion, perfectly still. From time to time a luminous sphere drifted into sight. She would draw it near with her will, and peer inside as into a bubble. Thus her deepsight penetrated veils of time and distance.

A small-month had passed since her rejuvenation. Nourished by the life-force of the sacred lion, her full powers had returned. Now at last she could turn her attention to other matters, such as that spike of dark power she had noticed entering the world many days ago. She had traced its source to some region to the north and west, but that was as much as she could discern. Whomever wielded this power was deliberately concealing themselves. This of itself was no surprise. Any mage capable of such workings would know the importance of secrecy.

But Beryl could not escape the nagging thought that this magic was hidden specifically from herself. And when she peered into the bands of obfuscation, she sensed the signature of Amlina's mind.

Beryl's former apprentice, it seemed, had conjured something vast and deadly.

Tonight, new ripples of the power had manifested, drawing Beryl's gaze. Either the ensorcellment had suddenly strengthened, or the concealments around it had weakened or flickered. From what Beryl could see now, the source of the emanations was on the move: still in the north but no longer so far west.

If it really was Amlina, where was she traveling, and why?

Another bubble of light drifted into view. Beryl attracted it with her mind. Here was a new insight: a second practitioner of the

Larthangan arts. This one was young. She had potential, but no developed skills—a rank beginner. Perhaps Amlina had acquired an apprentice of her own? Peering deeper, Beryl drew in a sharp breath of excitement. This neophyte had a flaw, a psychic wound.

Here at last was a weakness to exploit.

Beryl scrutinized the wound for some time, probing, prodding. Yes, she could use it as a vent to infiltrate the mind of this would-be mage. In this way, she could discover the secret of the dark power and know for certain who wielded it.

And, if in truth it was Amlina ... Well then, penetrating the mind of this apprentice might be useful indeed. Beryl could easily imagine turning this neophyte into a weapon—by making her a thrall.

* O *

Amlina was in Valgool, the night of the moons' alignment. She stood on the rubble of an ancient step-pyramid, her body suffused with power.

She had arrived in time. She had succeeded in summoning Kumokaon, the being who could create the Mirror Against All Mishap. He was a godling, native to the place, reptilian in nature. In the time of Valgool's ascendency, he had grown to vast size and power by partaking of countless blood sacrifices. In Larthang, he would have been called a dragon. Here he was simply known as 'the Devourer.'

But now, as Kumokaon hovered before her in circles of flame, eyes like blood rubies, teeth like swords, Amlina knew she had not succeeded at all. She lacked the strength to control him, to compel the dragon to do her will.

She woke from the nightmare to the sound of dreadful howling.

It took her a few moments to realize the howls belonged to the physical world—gallwolves in the hills. She sat in utter darkness. Although the cabin was warm, she groped for her coat and wrapped it over her shoulders. She had spoken with Meghild in the afternoon, explaining about the Devourer. Undoubtedly, that talk had engendered the nightmare. But now ... She sensed the queen's head was missing from the shelf.

Early in the voyage, Amlina's magic had been necessary to raise the eidolon body. But after a time, Meghild had learned to rise and wrap herself in the light form purely by the force of her will. Since then, she had risen whenever it pleased her, usually at night, to walk the decks of the cranock.

Blind in the darkness, the witch got out of her bunk, found her shoes. Bending low at the waist, she moved to the hatch. Stepping onto the deck, she found the night overcast, nearly as black as her cabin. A faint, lonely light shone above her on the foredeck—the eidolon.

On starless nights, away from the sea, it was remarkable how dark the world could become. It reminded Amlina of her childhood in the hinterlands of Larthang, the only period of her life when she had witnessed such impenetrable gloom. She found it unnerving.

The Iruks, she knew, found it appalling. They had never been so far from the open sea and its abiding witchlight. Yet, they had not once complained to her, just as they had not protested about their aching backs or blistered hands in the five days they had rowed up the river—although they grumbled enough to each other in their native tongue. As was their way, the Iruks showed stoic demeanors to everyone outside the klarn.

As the boat traveled up the river, the flat ground had risen into hills, increasingly rugged, farms and tended groves giving way to woods and pastures. Since navigating at night was impossible, the crew pulled into the shallows and anchored at dusk. They all slept the same hours now, except for one who kept watch. Tonight it was Brinda, who leaned with her back to the mast and gave Amlina a curt nod. Brinda was usually the most taciturn of all.

Away in the hills, a gallwolf howled, another answered, and then the whole chorus started again. Repressing a shiver, Amlina climbed to the foredeck and went to stand beside the queen.

"Ah, Amlina." Meghild gave her a faraway glance. "It's so dark up here, so far from the sea. Luckily, I make my own light now."

Amlina smiled faintly. But then her shoulders twitched at a sharp yowling close to shore.

Meghild laughed harshly. "No need to worry. They won't cross the water—no matter how much they might like to eat us." Her expression grew vague once more. "I have a certain sympathy for the gallwolves ... roaming in packs, hunting, as I did for so long as a pirate. But all of that seems long ago ... another life, another Meghild ... I am hardly Meghild at all anymore, you know? I am changing into something else."

Amlina stared at the gray face, the sharp shadows of jaw and cheekbone cast from the eidolon light below. The queen's volatile mental state gave her constant worry.

"But that's all right," Meghild said. "It is something else you need me to be. And Wilhaven will make it into a saga ... All of us must choose how we live our songs, you know."

"Indeed, my queen. And you have lived yours bravely."

"Hah. That I have."

The chorus of wolves howled in reply, mournful and bitter.

"Aye, they would like to eat us. But it's that other Devourer I am thinking of. What do you suppose it will feel like, Amlina, to throw myself into its mouth?"

"I do not know," the witch murmured. And she thought, *Perhaps we will all know, soon enough.*

* O *

Later that night, Glyssa stepped out on deck to take the watch. She had not been sleeping anyway, between the intermittent howling of the wolves and her own raging emotions.

With neither sealight nor stars, the night was fearfully dark. The only dim glow came from the prow, where the eidolon stood motionless. Learning against the mast, Brinda watched Glyssa approach.

"You can get some sleep now, mate," Glyssa said. "If you *can* sleep with all the wolf calls."

"They're quieting down, I think," Brinda said. "Besides, you know me, I can sleep through anything."

"How are your hands?" Glyssa asked.

Brinda glanced down at her blisters, which Wilhaven had treated with an ointment. "Not so bad. Yours?"

"Terrible." Glyssa laughed grimly. All of the mates had blistered palms and aching backs from the rowing. The thought of their suffering rose as a pain in Glyssa's chest. With it came guilt and a lonely feeling of shame. They had traveled so far, endured so much, all because of her.

Her voice had a ragged edge. "I am so sorry, to have brought you all such troubles."

"That is nonsense," Brinda answered firmly. "We hold to the klarn. It is what we must do."

"But I have made it harder—so hard for all of you."

"Through no fault of yours. It might have been any of us, and the klarn would have done the same." Brinda set a hand on her shoulder. "The only difference, dear Glyssa, is that for you we all do it more gladly."

That brought tears to her eyes, and Glyssa looked away.

Brinda gave her a hug. "Be cheered, mate. At the end of this voyage, we will kill a great witch and sail home with a boat full of plunder. And best of all, the klarn will still be whole."

"I hope so," Glyssa whispered, and returned the tight embrace.

She watched as Brinda headed off to bed. When the hatch closed, Glyssa took a deep breath, seeking to calm herself. But her attention settled on her heart, and there she felt once again the dreadful pain she had come to call the fishhook.

In recent days the pain had sharpened, like an old wound pulled open, trickling blood. Glyssa had first noticed it at the oars, as she and her mates struggled to accustom themselves to rowing. The discomfort, the sense of impending doom, had deepened each day they journeyed farther from the sea. Once, Glyssa almost thought she sensed a presence, another mind probing her, trying to slither into her soul the way the sorcerer had done. But she shrugged this off, deciding it was only fear from the past rising up to haunt her.

Fear was natural, she told herself, as they were heading into unknown and dangerous territory. But she was an Iruk warrior, who must face her fears and cast them aside.

* O *

The hills grew steeper, the current swifter. Three more days rowing brought the *Phoenix Queen* to the foot of cascading rapids. A settlement called Blaal's Landing had grown up here, the farthest point inland where boats could travel. Piers stretched out from the muddy riverbank. Log and wattle buildings rose in a hollow between grassy slopes. The village had no wall or stockade. But, remarkably, a ring of tall poles surrounded the settlement, supporting a canopy of stout netting.

"I've never seen anything like that," Amlina said. "As if they're protecting themselves from the sky."

"Aye, to be sure," Wilhaven answered. He stood on the middle deck, coaching the Iruks at the oars as they maneuvered toward the dock. "We are near the realm of the torms, you see?"

"So the winged people raid here?" Eben grunted as he shifted his oar.

"I don't know how often, this far down the river," the bard said. "But they are known to raid along the borders, carrying off sheep and woolgoats, even aklors."

They brought the cranock near the dock, and Lonn and Wilhaven used stout poles to guide them alongside. As they tied lines from bow and stern to bollards, a few villagers gathered to watch them. Dogs ran up, barking with excitement. No other boats were moored at the landing, as this was not the season for trading wool and hides.

Amlina wore an embroidered gown of bright yellow and blue, silver bangles, earrings, and her moonstone fillet. Her baggage rested on deck, including a trunk containing some magic baubles, the talking book, and the head of the queen, cushioned and wrapped in oilskin. Meghild's presence in this world was fading again, as the eidolon's power strengthened in the Deepmind. She had not objected to staying concealed while the party made arrangements at the village.

More people were assembling at the end of the dock, staring at the cranock and muttering with uneasy curiosity.

"What language will they speak in these parts?" Amlina asked Wilhaven.

"Oh, the barbarous Nyssanian tongue, I should think. I have a pinch and smattering of it, perhaps enough to get us by."

"No need," the witch answered. "I will speak for us." She knew Nyssanian well enough from her seven years in Tallyba.

She climbed over the gunwale and onto the pier, the others following. The Iruks wore their leather armor and carried spears. Wilhaven had his dagger and sword. As the travelers approached the end of the pier, the crowd grumbled fretfully. Several men pushed their way to the front, armed with staves and butcher knives.

"Let's be friendly now," Amlina muttered. She smiled, lifted a hand, and called out in Nyssanian: "Greetings."

A squat, broad-shouldered herdsman took a step forward. He wore leathers and a fleece vest. His wild black hair and beard were flecked with gray, and his wide smile crafty. "Greetings, richly-attired little woman, and to your stout companions. I am Izgoy. I am boss here. What brings you so far up the river?"

Amlina stopped a few paces from him. "My name is Olicia Wor-T'sing, from distant Larthang. We are travelers, seeking knowledge. We wish to hire pack animals, and a guide to take us into the mountains."

Surprised and suspicious muttering rippled through the throng. Izgoy's feral grin scarcely flickered. "Into the mountains, you say? And what would you think to find in the mountains?"

Amlina perceived no advantage in dissembling. "We wish to cross to the high plateau. Our destination is the ruined city of Valgool."

Moans and gasps escaped the villagers. Izgoy chuckled. "Valgool? No one goes there. It is full of ghosts. Besides, you cannot cross the mountains. The winged folk live there. They will tear you up and eat you!"

Amlina regarded him calmly. "Nevertheless, that is our destination. The guide need only take us to your border and point out the route. We will find our way from there." She had pulled out her purse and now her fingers played with gold coins. "I will pay you well: A guide to take us to the mountains, two aklors to carry our gear."

Now the headman's eyes sparkled like his teeth. "Ha ha! Of course I will help you! Three pieces of gold for the aklors. Three more for the guide. I will send my own son—but mind you, only to the border."

"Four gold pieces in total," Amlina said. "That is more than generous. And one other thing: your people must keep watch on our boat and care for the windbringers—fresh water every few days. If any harm comes to them or the boat, or anything is stolen, my warriors here will be very angry when we return."

Izgoy scanned the stern faces of the Iruks. Then he burst out laughing. "Don't worry about your boat. You will never miss it, because you won't be coming back! The torms will see to that."

Amlina fixed him with an icy stare. "On the contrary, we will return. And our boat must be as we leave it."

"All right, all right." Izgoy threw up his hands. "I will guarantee your boat and the care of the windbringers, for four or five months, till the trading season. Fair enough?"

Amlina nodded. "Acceptable."

Izgoy wagged a finger. "But I tell you this, little pale girl who is so sure of herself: I would not wear that jewelry in the mountains. The torms are fond of shiny things, and will rip off your arms and ears to get them."

* O *

The travelers stayed that night in Izgoy's house, a round dwelling with a single chamber twenty paces across. A wood fire burned at the center of the dirt floor, smoke rising through a hole in the roof. Glyssa and her companions shared the fire with the headman, his extended family, and assorted village leaders. They feasted on roast lamb and sipped a strong, sour liquor made from fermented sheep's milk. The scene reminded Glyssa of a gathering in an Iruk lodge house.

And yet she felt uneasy. The Iruks kept their weapons close at hand and their baggage at their backs. Amlina had expressed confidence that the villagers would keep the bargain the headman had made. Still, she advised, there was no harm in keeping on guard.

Through the smoke, Glyssa surveyed the assembly. Amlina sat at a place of honor beside the headman. On his other side were two elderly women; Glyssa gathered they were shamans. They stared at the strangers with grim, hawkish eyes, though they smiled benignly whenever Glyssa caught their glance.

"I wonder if these torms are as fearsome as people claim," Eben said, refilling his cup from a wooden bowl. As usual, he was drinking more than the others, and it was beginning to show. "And if they are so formidable, what good is that netting over the village?"

"Amlina asked Izgoy about that," Draven answered. "He said a few torms fly over from time to time and drop carcasses or dung on the village, just to make a nuisance of themselves."

"These winged folk sound more like an annoyance than a danger," Lonn said. "Anyway, I imagine we'll meet up with them sooner or later."

"I look forward to it." Karrol slapped down her cup. "I haven't had a fight at all since we left Kadavel. Remember, I missed that brawl in Meghild's castle."

"Hardly a brawl," Eben answered, bleary-eyed over his cup. "A few swipes and a dash really. Wouldn't you say, Wilhaven?"

The bard sat with his back to the trunk that contained the head of the queen. "Aye, that I would. And I'd also say this sheep's milk is stronger than ale, and we'd all do well to drink less than too much of it."

Eben grunted.

"Wilhaven is right," Glyssa said. "Remember, we travel in the morning."

"I suppose." Eben reluctantly set down his cup. He stretched out with a groan. "I'll sleep well enough. Too bad we couldn't have a bath though."

"Yes, too bad," Karrol grumbled. "It seems bathing is a custom not yet invented in these parts."

When the fire burned low, the villagers rose and took their leave. As Izgoy's family made up their beds, Amlina joined the Iruks and Wilhaven on their side of the fire. They all lay down to sleep, except for Lonn who took the first watch, his sword resting on his knees.

EIGHTEEN

In the morning white mist clung to the hills, and a cold drizzle drifted down. It was the fourth day of Second Summer, 15 days till the alignment of the moons.

Amlina and her companions returned to their boat, accompanied by Izgoy and one of his sons, Durfsky, who would be their guide into the mountains. Durfsky was a sturdy young man, with the same curly hair and heavy eyebrows as his father. He stood head and shoulders taller than Izgoy, but bowed his head and listened deferentially when the elder man spoke.

Wilhaven and the Iruks lashed down the oars and gathered the last of their baggage for the march inland. Amlina took the opportunity to weave extra protection over the craft, envisioning a cloud of awe and apprehension to descend on anyone approaching the boat. She gave explicit instructions to Izgoy regarding the watering of the bostulls. Windbringers were a rarity this far from the sea, so she made sure their needs were clearly understood.

When the witch finished speaking with the headman, Glyssa was crouched in front of Kizier, saying farewell. Amlina knelt beside her.

"Once again, my friend, we must say good-bye."

Kizier eyed her gravely. "Yes. I shall miss you both. But I take comfort in the knowledge that you will look after each other."

Amlina caught Glyssa's eye, and both of them smiled. The witch thought again of how strong in spirit Glyssa was, and how dedicated she had proven herself to the hard disciplines of training. Yet, in that moment, Amlina also glimpsed a cruel vulnerability. Glyssa had been badly damaged by her enthrallment to the serd. No telling how long that wound might take to heal. Amlina gripped Glyssa's hand and they stood up together. They left Kizier with the other bostulls, humming quietly in trance.

Izgoy led the party to a corral at the edge of the settlement. Inside the enclosure stood a small herd of aklors—wooly, six-legged beasts with long necks and barrel-shaped bodies. They were shorter and stouter than the breeds Amlina had known in Larthang and the Tathian Isles. Izgoy pointed out two that he recommended as excellent pack animals. The witch called on her intuition and selected two others instead.

Durfsky fitted reins on the chosen animals and led them out of the corral. Assisted by the Iruks, he loaded and tied the group's baggage onto the creatures' backs—bed furs, the canvas sleeping tent from the boat, the witch's trunks and bags, enough food and oil for several days march. The travelers expected to purchase more food from herdsman in the hills, while streams and springs would provide fresh water.

With the gear secured, they bade Izgoy farewell and set off. Durfsky led the way, Amlina a step behind, then the Iruks single file. Lonn and Wilhaven brought up the rear, each tugging the reins of an aklor.

The trail curled into the hills. The mist dispersed, but the rain only fell harder. Before long they were trudging and slipping in mud, soaked and miserable. In the afternoon they came on a large herd of sheep and woolgoats huddling in the wet grass. Four herders sat sheltered in a lean-to and had a fire going. Amlina gave them a coin in exchange for cooked meat and an opportunity to rest under their roof.

Having eaten and dried out a little, the travelers set off again. The rain fell unrelenting and the path, already slick, grew steeper. The sure-footed aklors had no trouble, but Amlina and her friends often slipped, and sometimes had to scramble on all fours, muddying their hands and garments. To keep their spirits up, Eben started a chant, and his klarn mates soon joined him. Presently, from the rear of the train, Amlina heard Wilhaven's baritone, matching the Iruk words, though he did not know their language. The Iruks seemed to find this funny, and laughed grimly amid their chanting.

Their song is binding us together, Amlina thought. Hesitantly, she too joined in.

Finally, the rain slackened. A fresh breeze blew from the west, and the clouds lifted, revealing a blue-gray sky. Snow topped peaks came into view, looming in distant hazes.

Exhausted from the long march, the party made camp early at a place where a freshet flowed through a stand of pines. With no hope of finding dry firewood, Amlina lit an oil lamp. In the twilight, Durfsky tethered the aklors and gave them feed and water. The Iruks unpacked bed furs and set the tent canvas out on the ground to make a dry place for sleeping. The travelers shared a small meal of mutton and hard bread. They were just preparing to sleep when a muffled voice sounded from inside the pile of luggage. Meghild was awake and demanding release.

Wilhaven and the Iruks glanced uncertainly at Amlina. Durfsky stared wild-eyed at the source of the noise.

Sighing, Amlina stood and addressed her friends in Tathian. "I am going to let the queen free. The sight of her will no doubt frighten our guide. Be ready to hold him, in case he runs."

Kneeling, she laid a hand on Durfsky's shoulder and spoke to him in Nyssanian. "Do not be frightened. You are about to see a wonder. I am a witch of Larthang, and a certain spirit travels with us. I am going to release her and let her walk free. You have nothing to fear. So long as you keep your bargain with us, no harm will come to you." She stared hard into his eyes. "Do you understand me?"

Durfsky nodded, awestruck.

Amlina opened the trunk and took out the oilskin. She spread it on the ground, revealing the queen's head. When Meghild's eyes popped open, Durfsky gave a sharp cry and tried to rise. Lonn and Karrol pressed strong hands down on his shoulders, and Glyssa spoke to him soothingly. Wilhaven picked up his harp and strummed a mild tune.

Meghild's eyes swerved around as Amlina cast the magic to formulate the eidolon body. The head rose on a column of pale light, which undulated and thickened as long arms and legs appeared.

Durfsky frantically made hand signs to ward off evil.

Meghild threw back her head and sighed. "It feels good to breathe again, my lovelies. Where are we now?"

That night the eidolon hovered and paced around the perimeter of the camp, the ghost-light making up for the lack of a fire. As usual, Wilhaven or one of the Iruks stood guard. At Amlina's suggestion, the one on watch kept a particular eye on Dursky, lest he try to sneak off in the dark.

* O *

The weather held fair the next morning, with a chill mist drifting over the hills but no more of the pounding rain. At mid-morning, the party stopped at a stream where the Iruks insisted on bathing in the icy waters and scrubbing their muddy clothes. Amlina and Wilhaven settled for washing their hands and faces and changing into clean garments.

As they continued upcountry, they encountered scattered herds of woolgoats and aklors and flocks of sheep grazing on the hillsides, watched over by herdsmen and their dogs. At one point, Eben spotted paw prints in the soft ground, which Wilhaven surmised were left by gallwolves.

Late in the afternoon, they topped a ridge and came upon the ruins of a castle or temple—a half-circle of tumbled limestone blocks, partially buried and coated in moss. The witch identified the ruins as a remnant of the Nagaree Empire, of which Valgool had been the capital.

"The Nagaree were a race of powerful sorcerers, skilled in blood magic," she explained. "Their domain once stretched all the way to the Bay of Mistral, as well as over the mountains and the high plateau. Their empire perished in the Age of the World's Madness."

"Aye, vanquished by the torms," Wilhaven said, "or so the tale is told."

They stood surveying the massive ruins and the rugged landscape to the west.

"Indeed," Amlina said. "The torms came into being during the Madness, when the world fell into chaos from the unrestrained use of magic. But the annals differ on the details. Some have it the torms were a tribe of mountain folk subjugated by the Nagarees, who performed pernicious experiments to blend their stock with birds. Others maintain the torms were originally a faction of Nagaree wizards, who sought to empower themselves with flight but whose efforts went awry. All we know for certain is that the torms now rule the mountains, and nothing remains of the Nagaree greatness but ruins."

* O *

Two more days march brought them to the fringe of the mountains, the boundary of human lands. From a hilltop, Dursky pointed out a trail, the remains of a Nagaree road, that meandered through a steep valley and then up a rocky slope. Farther off, he indicated a gap between snow-capped peaks—the route to Valgool.

Suddenly he glanced at the sky and thrust his hand toward a distant winged figure that wheeled against the clouds. "Torm," he said, then turned without another word and headed back the way they had come.

The companions stared mutely at the far-off winged creature—little more than a speck—as it glided down in a long, slow spiral and then disappeared behind a ridge. Glyssa glanced at her mates, who offered shrugs or fierce grins. Amlina nodded solemnly and led the way down the hill.

The trail led through the valley and onto a bare shoulder of rock. There Eben spied another torm, drifting high overhead. Presently, two more appeared, and the three circled, cawing at each other, before one flew off toward the peaks.

From that time on, two or more of the winged people were always present, gliding in effortless circles far overhead, watching silently as the travelers trekked higher into the mountains.

"Why don't they come down and face us?" Karrol grumbled after a few hours. She was at the rear of the train, leading one of the aklors. "If they want a fight, we'll give them one!"

"Perhaps they are curious about our intentions," Wilhaven said. "They know they can attack whenever they please."

"They seek to unnerve us," Glyssa observed.

"Yes," Amlina said. "I think that is so. When we finally meet them, we must show no fear and no aggression. Remember, Buroof will speak for us. He knows their language—or so I hope."

"Well enough," Karrol said. "But if they don't understand the talking book, they can mince words with our spears."

As they trudged on, Glyssa could feel her mates' nerves fraying. Bred as hunters, the Iruks found the role of quarry a kind of affront, the inability to face their foes a nearly-intolerable frustration. The klarn's unspoken stress added to Glyssa's unease, which seemed to grow sharper each day. Often now, she had to compress a lump of fear around her heart as it threatened to burst into panic.

She woke late that night from a troubled dream in which some cunning, nameless beast was stalking her. She sat up, breathing hard. She reminded herself that, of course, all of them were being stalked, by the torms.

On the far side of the campfire Karrol stood guard, a spear resting on her shoulder. Queen Meghild had been set free at nightfall, and her shining body wandered the edge of the camp, flowing in its smooth, unearthly way.

Glyssa shut her eyes and tried to calm herself with meditation. But as her breathing slowed and her mind settled, she sensed someone watching. Blinking, she stared hard and spied a dark shape just outside the circle of firelight.

The torm had crept up unobserved. It had a slender human shape, covered in feathers, with boney arms and legs ending in claws. Its head was like an eagle's, with fierce golden eyes fixed curiously on the eidolon.

Suddenly, it sensed Glyssa watching. The head jerked and for an instant the eyes caught hers. The creature hissed, spread its wings, and flew into the night.

The noise startled both Karrol and Meghild. Glyssa ran over to them.

"Did you see something?" Karrol asked, her spear leveled.

"Yes. It was a torm."

"Bah!" Meghild cried. "My first chance to see a torm, and I missed it!"

"Don't worry," Glyssa said. "I don't think it will be your only chance."

* O *

When they struck camp in the morning, five torms circled overhead. As the travelers marched higher into the mountains, the number grew to over a dozen. The party walked mostly over bare rock now, with nothing to indicate the trail except an occasional stone marker left by the Nagaree. They kept on track by always moving in the direction of the pass, sighting it whenever they rounded a shoulder or topped a ridge. Occasionally, they spotted mountain goats, or a lone, wild aklor. Otherwise they were alone in the vast stony landscape—except for the winged men who stalked them. The air hung clear and eerily quiet.

Toward midday, they came to a deep gorge. Sheer cliffs rose on both sides, with a stream gushing far below. The pass they sought stood somewhere on the other side, but they could see no way across. After talking it over, they agreed their best option was to follow a ledge along the cliff, hoping it led to a crossing.

As they filed carefully along the canyon wall, more torms gathered. Many spiraled in the distant sky. Others glided down, cawing and screeching, to perch on the rocks above. The Iruks eyed them warily.

"It occurs to me," Eben said, "that they are herding us into a trap."

"Indeed, it seems that way to me," Amlina answered, scanning the cliffs on either side. She made a decision and sidled back along the ledge. "If that is the case, we might as well show them something of our power."

With Brinda's help, she untied her trunk and lowered it to the ground. She removed Meghild's head and called up the magic to raise the eidolon body. As Meghild's light-form loomed into view, caws and squawks rose in a tumultuous wave, echoing through the canyon.

Meghild looked about in confusion. "Daylight? Where are we, my dears? And what is that maddening noise?"

"I was told you wanted to see the torms," the witch answered. "They are all around us."

"Aye, so they are!" Meghild surveyed the heights above, grinning. "Have they attacked, or are they inclined to parley?"

"Neither as of yet," Amlina said. "But I think it will be soon now."

Before shutting her trunk, Amlina removed the talking book. She carried it in her arms as the company moved off, Meghild now striding in their midst. The frenzied screeching of the torms diminished to a continuous, urgent chirping. More and more of the winged people were flying in to crowd the ledges and outcroppings overhead.

Presently, the path widened. Ahead stood an archway framed by ancient, weathered carvings. Amlina led the way through a short tunnel. They emerged on a wide shelf—a paved plaza bordered by tall, broken statues. Massive monuments and galleries, clung to the canyon walls on both sides, with the openings to numerous caves— the ruins of a Nagaree town. The space swarmed with hundreds of torms.

"There is our way across." Amlina tilted her chin toward a stone bridge that spanned the gorge. A dense throng of the winged people stood on the bridge and in front of it, while others glided in the air above.

"Remember now: show no fear and no aggression. We must make peace with them if we are to survive."

Spears shouldered, the Iruks stared with awe at the sheer number of their adversaries. Even Karrol made no boasts about fighting their way through. Amlina stepped to the front of the company and opened the book. She spoke to it in Tathian, so Wilhaven and the Iruks would understand their words.

"Buroof, I Amlina summon you. We are in the land of the torms."

"Obviously" Buroof answered. "I can hear their unholy cacophony. I congratulate you, Amlina. I didn't expect you would make it even this far."

"Never mind that. What are they saying?"

The book paused to listen. "Oh ... burbling about who you are and who among them gets the honor of killing you. Also wondering about the shining figure and if they can capture it alive."

"Hah!" Meghild cried. "Won't they be surprised if they try!"

"... And now they are talking about myself and arguing over what sort of creature I might be. Those birds on the gallery beyond the bridge seem to be elders. They speak with the most authority, but there is no real government here. They will make their decisions as a mob, and probably not peacefully."

"All right," Amlina said. "Speak to them as loudly as you can. Tell them this: that I am a mage with great power and these warriors are my companions. That all we seek is to pass unmolested through their territory. And that I will give them gifts of shiny coins in return."

She lifted the book high and faced the open pages toward the noisy crowd. Buroof's voice sounded high-pitched and loud, chattering and shrieking. The assembled torms hushed for several moments, then resumed their clamor.

"They say that no one speaks their language except themselves. They question if I am one of their tribe that you have imprisoned in this book."

"Reply that you are not, but that we have vast knowledge and power. Repeat that we only wish to pass in peace and offer gifts in return."

When Buroof had delivered this message, a lengthy and raucous debate ensued. Many of the torms screeched at each other, batted their wings, flashed claws. Finally, seven of the elders flew across the ravine and touched down in front of Amlina and her party. They flapped their wings and cheeped angrily until the noisy confusion subsided. The elders peered sternly at the witch and her companions, and then one of them made a pronouncement.

Buroof interpreted: "He claims to speak for all the torms and he declares this: No one may cross the land of the torms unless they be a torm. However, as we have the language of the torms, this presents a dilemma. Oh, and he admires those sparkling things that dangle at your ears."

"Hmm." Amlina set down the book, removed her earrings. "Glyssa, would you go please and lay these at his feet?"

As Amlina picked up the book, Glyssa edged forward, spear pointed, and placed the earrings on the ground. She backed cautiously away. The elders stared with avaricious eyes at the jewelry, then squawked and bobbed their heads. Another wave of tweeting and screeching rolled through the plaza.

"Now some declare they like us better, because of the gift," Buroof said. "Others maintain they should kill us at once and take all of our shiny possessions."

Eventually the elders seemed to reach a consensus. The one who had spoken before screeched and flapped his wings until the canyon grew quiet. When he spoke, Buroof translated.

"After due deliberation, the council has decided to adopt us into their tribe. But first we must pass a test of worthiness."

"That is marvelous!" Queen Meghild cried.

"Aye, so it is!" Wilhaven answered.

"What is the test?" Amlina said.

The reply came: "The prescribed test is to fly to the nearest mountaintop and return with a stone equal to one's own weight. However, as we plainly lack wings, they have ... generously and graciously ... decided on an alternative. Which is, we must cross this bridge and safely reach the other side."

"Well, that sounds easy enough," Lonn said over Amlina's shoulder.

"Yes," the witch answered. "Too easy. Buroof, ask if there are any conditions to the test."

The torms seemed riotously amused by the question.

"Of course there are conditions." Buroof spoke the reply. "You must walk across without the use of eyesight. You will all be blindfolded."

Amlina craned her neck. "I cannot see the bridge clearly as it is crowded with torms. Ask them to clear it."

This request was greeted with hostile cheeping. But after some argument, the elders directed that the span be cleared. Reluctantly, it seemed, the torms on the bridge flew off to find other perches. Amlina examined the vacated bridge. The walkway was wide enough, but centuries of disrepair had left it perilous for crossing on foot.

Many of the stones were broken or missing, and a single misstep could easily result in a plunge to the rocks far below. Still, with her witch's sight, Amlina judged she could make the crossing blindfolded without much danger.

"Tell them we accept the test," she told Buroof. "But that I alone will walk the bridge, representing our whole company."

This suggestion did not sit well with the torms and incited another round of raging debate. Several of the elders spread wings and rose in the air a few yards, peering down at the travelers. Amlina waited patiently, staring calmly at the elders. Finally, they arrived at a decision.

"The torms accept the concept of choosing one to represent all," Buroof said, "but insist on their prerogative to do the choosing. You, Amlina are not acceptable, as you are the leader and presumably the most powerful. If all are to be judged worthy of their tribe, then the smallest and weakest must pass the test."

As Buroof finished, all of the elders lifted long arms and pointed talons at Glyssa.

NINETEEN

With a stab of fear, Glyssa observed the torms pointing at her, felt their golden, predator eyes boring into her. A memory flashed in her mind: Belach appearing in her vision as a human-shaped bird. *Each time you meet fear, it must be faced and overcome.*

"Glyssa—" the witch began.

"I know. I must cross the bridge blindfolded, or all of us will be attacked. Very well, I will do it."

Her mates started protesting that one of them could take her place, but Amlina interrupted.

"Listen to me, Glyssa. Your eyes will be covered, but mine will not. When you begin the crossing, quiet your mind and focus your thoughts on me. I will guide you. I will be your eyes."

"Yes," Glyssa whispered. "I understand. I will try."

Amlina nodded, her lips clenched. She instructed Buroof to communicate that the challenge was accepted. The book screeched this message forcefully, and the torms responded with furious excitement. Many took to the air to flap and tussle with their neighbors. Others flew low over the witch's party, broad wings swooping close. In the chaos, Glyssa could scarcely hear the elders, flailing and squawking. Finally, they succeeded in quieting the assembly and clearing the space in front of the bridge.

Two torms fluttered down, one of them holding a hood of black cloth. As they moved to fasten the hood over Glyssa's head, Amlina halted them with a gesture. The elder was speaking again.

Buroof interpreted: "The elder says there is one further condition. While the small one attempts to cross the bridge, two hunters will harry her."

"You mean she must fight them off while blindfolded?" Amlina cried in astonishment. "That hardly sounds fair."

When Buroof had translated these words, Glyssa heard cawing that resembled laughter.

"Ah, the torms are amused," Buroof said. "They do not understand what you mean by *fair*. Apparently the concept has no equivalent in their language."

"She won't have a chance," Lonn said. "Amlina, you must find another way."

"Better to fight our way across," Karrol muttered through set teeth.

"Aye, my lovelies." It was the voice of the queen. "Better to die fighting them."

The Iruks drew their swords.

"No!" Glyssa shouted. "Let me try it. If I fail, you can all die fighting after."

She turned to Amlina, who twisted her mouth, then nodded.

"Let us try," the witch said. "We have a chance, I think."

She closed the book and set it under her arm. With her free hand, she took hold of Glyssa's wrist and started toward the bridge. The rest of the party followed, the Iruks moving reluctantly, hefting their weapons and glaring at the torms who swooped in to crowd around them.

"Focus on clearing your mind," Amlina whispered. "Once the hood is in place, remember my touch and seek to follow that memory to my mind, my perceptions. The blindfold will actually help you in this, as it will keep you from distraction."

They stopped at the edge of the ruined bridge. Glyssa surveyed the pavement, striving to memorize gaps and broken masonry, to pick out a safe path. The noisy chirping had subsided to a hushed murmur of excitement and expectancy. The elder torms stood nearby. One spoke a command and waved a claw. The torm who carried the hood stepped forward. Glyssa tilted her neck. The torm fitted the blindfold over her head and tied it at the throat, talons scraping her skin.

Glyssa choked back panic. She was blind now and breathing was hard. Inside the hood smelled of molting feathers.

Amlina squeezed her wrist a last time, then let go. "Draw your sword, Glyssa. Listen for my thoughts. We will cross the bridge together."

Glyssa sucked in her breath. She gripped the hilt and slid the sword from its scabbard. With blade and spear pointed high, she stepped blindly onto the bridge.

All around she heard the torms, shrieking and cawing. Her knees felt weak, but she took another step. Inside the hood she shut her eyes, seeking desperately to recall Amlina's touch, to feel the witch's mind.

Lifting her foot for the third step, she heard the witch's voice like a whisper.

We are linked in the Deepmind. We are one.

Glyssa's stomach lurched. A sensation like a gust of wind lifted her mind, yanking it backward out of her body. Gray light flashed, and then she could see. A few paces in front of her, a small hooded woman crossed the bridge, sword and spear in hand. She was seeing herself though Amlina's eyes.

Watch out! Amlina's thought cried inside her skull.

Glyssa ducked just in time as the torm hunter swooped, talons on feet and hands reaching. She swung her blade and the hunter wheeled away, shrieking.

The other one!

Glyssa saw it through Amlina's eyes, diving from the other side. It took Glyssa a moment to translate the vision into action in her own body. That left her only time to drop flat onto her belly. The claws missed her, and Glyssa rolled over and thrust the spear with a fierce yell.

Distantly, she heard her mates cheering, their shouts all but drowned by the frenzied squawking and cawing of the torms. Through the witch's eyes, she saw the two hunters rise into the air, confused by how she had met their attack.

Taking advantage of their surprise, Glyssa scrambled to her feet and staggered forward. She took several lurching steps, still struggling to match her muscles' actions to the eyesight from outside of her body.

Almost halfway across, she saw the hunters dive again. They were attacking together this time, but Glyssa was ready. She let them come close, then sprang ahead, turned and crouched all in one motion. Swiping with the blade to keep one of the torms away, she thrust the spear hard at the other. She felt the point pierce its body and the torm screamed. It flapped its wings violently to free itself from the spear, then collapsed onto the stones. It backed away on skittering feet, covering the belly wound with its arms.

Through Amlina's eyes Glyssa spied the other hunter, hovering now, unsure. She seized the opportunity, pivoted, and ran. She was within a few paces of the end of the bridge when her toe struck a raised stone and she stumbled. Her body sprawled on the pavement and she heard a sharp scraping sound. The upper half of her body sank, masonry shifted beneath her, and then her hands were clutching empty air.

Part of the bridge had collapsed. Even as this thought registered with its terror, her legs slipped and she knew she was falling into the gorge. In desperation her mind reached back for Amlina. Suddenly, Amlina was there, and Glyssa felt a force, like a strong hand. It clutched her collar and dragged her body forward. Her hands and then her knees scrabbled onto solid stones.

Clambering to her feet, she heard the screeching of hundreds of torms, and her mates shouting to her. But when she reached for Amlina's mind, she felt only a splitting pain.

Somehow, the witch had pulled Glyssa to safety. But the unexpected effort had been too much. Now Amlina was down, perhaps unconscious.

And Glyssa was blind. She couldn't even tell which direction she faced. And one hunter still stalked her. Fearing its approach, Glyssa raised both her weapons high, waving them as she circled, trying to think what to do.

Frantically, she reached for Amlina's mind, hoping to re-establish the link. At first, she found only darkness and a splitting pain in her skull. But suddenly the veil lifted, and she could see again. Once more she saw the canyon and the torms everywhere, and her own body at the far end of the bridge. More, she felt a rush of strength and support—the klarn!

She was seeing herself through the eyes of her mates.

Just as she realized this, she heard them shouting for her to duck. The torm was attacking again. Glyssa dodged below the talons. She swiped viciously with the sword. The torm screeched and rose on its wings. Glyssa turned and darted the last few steps.

Amid the uproar of squawking and the flapping of countless wings, she heard her mates cheering on the far side of the chasm. She reached to remove the hood, but felt torms crowding around her and clawed fingers untying the cord. The hood was lifted off, and she glimpsed a chaos of wings, feathered bodies, cawing beaks. Claws gripped her upper arms, and she was lifted into the air. At first she thought they meant to drop her into the gorge after all. But as they flew higher, high above the canyon walls, and numerous torms soared around her, she realized they were celebrating, cheering her victory, welcoming her to their tribe.

O

Amlina climbed to her feet, squinting, straining to clear her vision. Draven and Wilhaven supported her arms. She had blacked out after … after seeing Glyssa fall and the bridge give way under her. Amlina had reached out with her mind, pulled Glyssa to safety in an instinctive act of pure shaping. But channeling such power without preparation and in a moment of fear had exacted a cost. Her eyesight wavered, and her head hurt as if pierced by a needle.

All around her the winged people were chirping and flapping in mad excitement. The Iruks were shouting—Glyssa had been carried away. Amlina looked up, spotted torms soaring far overhead. Two of them held Glyssa's body, her legs dangling. The witch picked up the book from where she had dropped it, flung open the cover.

"Buroof! Speak to the torms. Ask them what is happening. Tell them to bring Glyssa back to us!"

Amlina held the book open, facing the elders who stood nearby. Hearing Buroof's speech, the elders chortled with amusement. Several of them answered at once.

"They say not to worry," Buroof told her. "The small one will not be harmed. You are all part of their tribe now."

Another elder pointed at Amlina and chirped, eyes flashing.

"He says that you used witchcraft to win the challenge. That was unexpected. He admires your trickery."

Amlina rubbed her forehead. "Ask that they please set Glyssa down safely."

"Look!" Lonn pointed his spear. "They are carrying her away!"

Glancing aloft, the witch saw the group holding Glyssa fly off beyond the cliffs.

The elders chattered and Buroof translated: "Have no fear. They are taking her to the … the nearest word, I think, is *aerie*. I take it to be their gathering place—or perhaps 'high place of ceremony.' All of you will be brought there, to be welcomed into the tribe. They are sending for conveyances now."

* O *

The conveyances proved to be woven baskets, which the torms normally used for transporting animals and freight. As soon as the baskets were set on the ground, the witch and her companions were abruptly picked up in twos and threes and dropped inside—all except for the eidolon, whose light body simply flowed through the basket wall, to the astonished delight of the torms.

"What about our baggage and the aklors?" Amlina shouted to Buroof.

The book made the inquiry and received a reply that the goods would be brought, the animals tended. "Though, by *tended*, I think they might mean *eaten*." Buroof observed.

Before Amlina could react to that, she was thrown off her feet as the basket jerked into the air. Four of the winged people bore it aloft with ropes coiled around their bony arms. Amlina's head swam as she gripped the rim of the basket and struggled to stand. Dozens of torms flew around them, screeching. In a tumult of flapping wings, the baskets were carried up out of the canyon and away over the cliffs.

The view was stupendous—soaring ridges of gray and green ascending to snow-capped peaks, steep valleys and gorges, lakes fed by tumbling streams, all flushed with the rose and gold colors of sunset.

"How wonderful!" The eidolon of the queen murmured, standing beside the witch.

From the other baskets, Amlina heard the Iruks, laughing and shouting with nervous amazement.

"This is fantastic," Draven cried. "We are flying."

"*That* is obvious," Eben answered, sounding less than comfortable.

"I'll be happy when they set us down again," Karrol called.

"Not I!" Meghild keened with delight. "O Amlina, this alone is worth everything to me."

Amlina herself felt dazed by it all, her head still aching.

Soon the winged people approached the ruins of a Nagaree castle built at the top of a jagged peak. Scores of torms had already gathered, and more were flying in from all directions. They circled in the air, strutted on the ground, perched on battlements and walls. As the baskets glided low over the courtyard, Glyssa waved excitedly from amid the feathered throng. When they touched down, she ran up to greet them. Whooping with joy, the Iruks jumped out of their baskets and hugged her.

"No, I wasn't frightened at all," Glyssa explained in answer to their breathless questions. "That is, not after I made it across the bridge. I could tell they did not mean to harm me. Still, I am glad you all got here at last. Even with my new friends, I was starting to feel lonely."

"You did well, Glyssa." Amlina embraced her warmly. "I am so glad you are safe."

"And you. I felt your mind lift me when I started to fall—and also that it hurt you to do it. Are you all right?"

"Well enough," Amlina brushed a hand through her hair. "I seem to have blacked out. And I don't know how you crossed the rest of the way. You must have been blind."

Glyssa beamed, clutching the shoulders of Brinda and Lonn. "It was my klarn. When I could no longer see through your eyes, I reached out and found I could see through theirs."

Remarkable, Amlina thought. She wondered again at the mysterious bond the Iruks shared, and at the unsuspected talents Glyssa continued to show.

The group of elders filed toward her with their waddling gait. They spoke with rapid chattering. Amlina opened the talking book to request translation. The elders were welcoming her and her companions to the place of ceremony and directing them to follow.

They walked through the milling assembly of torms who crowded close, cooing and chirping, some reaching out to brush them gently with a pinion. The whole attitude of the winged people had changed to one of soothing mildness. They now seemed to regard the travelers as friends—or rather, as clumsy fledglings deserving of solicitude and protection.

Amlina and her party were conducted to a place of honor, a stone porch in front of a ruined wall. As twilight gathered, bundles of sticks and heavy logs were laid out for a bonfire. The elders conversed with the witch, spreading their wings and peering brightly as they chattered. They asked where the party was bound, and seemed mightily impressed that their destination was Valgool. The torms never ventured there, they said, as the place was haunted by ravenous killers—Buroof translated the name of the creatures as *ghost dogs*. Nevertheless, the elders promised to convey the travelers to the outskirts of the city. When Amlina asked about the aklors, she was assured there was no reason for concern. The animals had already been butchered and would be served as part of the evening's feast.

After the bonfire was lit, the assembly listened intently as one elder then another made grandiose speeches. This was a great day. Never before in memory had wingless people been welcomed into the tribe. Amlina and her companions were directed to stand. One by one, they were approached by a coterie of elders, who presented them with symbolic feathers and pronounced their new tribal names. Snorting with amusement, Buroof translated. Amlina was called "White-pinioned Witch"; while Glyssa was named "Small Lethal Claw." Meghild laughed with delight to be dubbed "Wind of Light and Blood."

When they were seated again, more torms came forward and presented gifts—shiny stones, fragments of metal, broken jewelry. Amlina had coins and beads fetched from her trunk to give in return. The feast was prepared by dropping dozens of torn and shredded carcasses into the fire—aklors, wild goats, hares, and voles. This nominal effort at cooking was in honor of the witch and her party, since the torms generally ate their meat raw. When the undercooked fare was brought to them on huge trenchers, the Iruks fell to with hearty appetites. Amlina had no stomach for it, but gratefully sipped spring water from a stone cup. Around her, the torms sat on the ground, tearing the bloody meat with beaks and talons.

As the feasting continued, the winged people celebrated with entertainments. Pairs of hunters flew and clashed in mock combats. A line of percussionists tapped complex rhythms on wooden disks with their beaks. Finally, a chorus sang what appeared to be a ballad, their weird, melodious voices blending in circuitous harmonies. When Buroof suggested that courtesy dictated the humans also participate, Wilhaven was pressed into service. He offered a soulful love song, which seemed not to impress the torms, though they chirped and nodded politely at its conclusion. But when he followed with a set of wild tunes, the torms responded with enthusiasm, leaping up and flapping their wings in time, some lifting off to swoop and dance in the air.

Finally, the festivities subsided. The fire burned low and most of the torms flew off to their nesting places. The elders bade Amlina and her friends good night and departed, leaving a few hunters to guard them and tend the fire.

The travelers unpacked their bedding and spread it on the ground. Meghild confessed herself weary from the day's excitement, and Amlina performed the magic to shrink and enfold the eidolon. She wrapped the queen's sleeping head in the oilskin and locked it safe away. Then, exhausted, Amlina stretched out and closed her eyes.

But sleep eluded her. Her head still ached, and she found herself staring up at the sky, which glittered in the mountain air with hundreds of stars. Rog drifted near the zenith, and Grizna was a curved blade over the peaks to the West.

Ten days remained till the fateful alignment of the three moons. Now, with the torms' promise to fly them to the vicinity of Valgool, Amlina thought it most likely they would arrive in time.

But the long journey had taken a toll on her. So had the agonizing burden of bearing the blood magic. Weary and deathly weak as she felt, would she have enough strength to complete the design and forge the Mirror?

TWENTY

Music of flutes and strings flowed from the chamber at the end of the mirrored corridor. Zenodia walked stoically, hands folded in sleeves, face expressionless. At the corners of her vision, her reflections marched from mirror to mirror—coming and going like the false images she presented to the world. Zenodia paid them no heed.

Her attention was fixed on settling her spirit, casting out fear. For a priestess of her rank to be invited to Beryl's salon was uncommon. It portended something—whether good or ill remained to be deciphered.

Passing the last of the mirrored panels, squeezing down a flutter of panic, Zenodia stepped into the ballroom. The chamber was wide, flanked by galleries, illumined by huge chandeliers. At the far wall, a patio disclosed a vista of snow-covered peaks flushed with the colors of sunset—although the actual hour was nearing midnight. Fifty or sixty figures milled about the polished floor, their convivial babble mingling with the stately music. Impossible to tell at a glance how many were human or thrall, how many mere constructs. Certainly the ethereal, blue-skinned musicians were thralls, their lives reduced to occasions such as this, when they were woken from trance to perform. Of course, Beryl's monstrous lion-headed guards were thralls as well. But among the few ministers and courtiers she recognized, Zenodia spied others: gold automatons who strolled about with serving trays, richly-dressed persons whose visages of fox or parrot were plainly not masks, a human-faced cactus in a pot on wheels—thralls reshaped by Beryl's whims, or drogs created wholly by her arts?

This is her message, Zenodia thought. *All of us are her puppets.*

Her gaze found the queen, reclining on a couch of orange silk, smiling as she watched the festivities. Since the rejuvenation rite, Beryl had been vibrant, seemingly enjoying herself—even to the point of resuming these weekly fetes. She wore a simple gown of gold silk. No turban: her clipped brown hair was adorned with a coronet. Her hideous human-faced monkey, the treeman, nestled at her hip, her fingers idly stroking its fur.

Beryl's eyes met Zenodia's, and her smile widened. Zenodia bowed her head, marched with measured steps. Reaching the space before the couch, she prostrated herself, forehead touching the cool tiles. The action elicited murmuring and a stray giggle from the courtiers gathered around the queen.

"Ah, Zenodia," Beryl said kindly. "Those formalities are not practiced here. Rise, my dear young woman."

The queen crooked a finger. An automaton brought a stool and placed it near her feet. "Sit here," Beryl said. "I want to talk with you."

The ivory seat placed Zenodia a foot below the queen's eye-level. She struggled to hold on to her nerve. The treeman eyed her malevolently.

"I am glad you could join us tonight." Beryl's gesture encompassed the ballroom. "What do you think of my little party?"

"Remarkable, of course," the young priestess ventured. "I do not believe I have seen many of these ... people before."

A quirk of amusement flicked over the queen's mouth. "No. You wouldn't have. But then priests and priestesses move in prescribed circles. In fact, I believe you are the only cleric I invited tonight."

Zenodia stared back calmly. "That did not escape my attention."

"No," Beryl mused. "I don't think much does."

"I try to stay vigilant, majesty. So that my humble service may be of value."

"Oh, yes. I hear very good things about your work. Masterful with the accounts, punctual and diligent in ritual observances. All in all, an exemplary assistant treasurer."

"Thank you, majesty."

"But what do you do for enjoyment? Any lovers?"

Zenodia drew in a sharp breath. "As a priestess, I must be chaste."

"Oh, of course," Beryl said, as if she'd forgotten that essential. "But there are other stimulations: erotic poetry, wine, euphoriants ..."

Careful, Zenodia warned herself. *Be very careful.* "I do not indulge in those things. I take satisfaction in studies and my work."

"Most commendable," Beryl said flatly, as if losing interest. Beside her, the treeman stirred, walked in a circle following its tail, then settled again against Beryl's thigh.

The music had stopped. A crossbar was being wheeled to the center of the floor, the crowd parting to make room. When the wheels were locked, a creature flew in and perched on the bar. It had the body of a naked man, the yellow wings and head of a nightingale.

"Perhaps you enjoy opera," the queen said.

The blue musicians struck up a melody, and the nightingale creature began to sing—an aria lamenting a lover's death. The voice, high and pure, mingled the notes of a bird's tweeting with the pain of a human heart. Despite herself, Zenodia felt tears rising in her eyes.

When it ended, Zenodia copied the courtiers' genteel applause.

"Beautiful, was it not?" Beryl was watching her closely.

"Yes, majesty. Beautiful and very sad."

"So you *do* have a heart under that dyed skin," the queen said. "I am pleased to know it." She touched a finger to her lips. "I wonder what your master Toulluthan will think of the fact that I invited you here tonight and not him."

Another test. Zenodia answered cautiously: "Perhaps he will worry that you are considering deposing him and elevating me in his place."

"Hmm. Quite possibly. What do you suppose he might do about that?"

Soberly, Zenodia returned the queen's gaze. "Perhaps he will turn on me, plot to discredit me in some way. He might even have me poisoned."

"Doesn't that worry you, Zenodia?"

"Indeed it does. But as you invited me, majesty, I could hardly refuse. Much better to risk my master's displeasure than yours."

"Very wise." Beryl smiled with a hint malice. "But I wouldn't worry too much. I will have a word with Toulluthan, make sure he understands my high opinion of you. As for his feelings, well, it's good for my retainers to be reminded that they only serve at my pleasure. No one is irreplaceable, Zenodia. Remember that."

At this, the treeman stood up, chattering angrily.

"Oh, no, dear Grellabo." Beryl laughed, petting the bald head. "Of course, *you* are the exception."

* O *

A short time later, Beryl abruptly ended the festivities. Rising, she bade the courtiers good night and left the ballroom through a doorway behind the dais. With the treeman scampering behind, she descended a back stairway, crossed the walled courtyard under the stars, passed through the ranks of her lion-headed guards, and entered the Bone Tower.

The Archimage sometimes found it tedious, however necessary, to attend to the many trappings of rulership—council meetings, banquets, temple ceremonies, entertainments. Even the games of manipulation, of pitting courtiers and factions against each other, sometimes palled. True, the scene with Zenodia had been somewhat amusing, poking and prodding the little assistant treasurer to see what weaknesses she might reveal. Otherwise, the evening had been a bore.

Still, Beryl knew the importance of keeping up appearances, of constantly presenting a tireless, indomitable facade. And yet wearisome—especially at times like this, when an unsolved problem nagged for her attention.

How long since she first felt the stirrings of the vast, dark power in the north? Nearly two months. And now fifteen days since she had discovered, among those in the sphere of that magic, a neophyte mage with a wounded soul. For just that many nights, Beryl had probed the wound, seeking to infiltrate the neophyte's perceptions.

True, there had been some progress. Beryl had glimpsed Amlina's physical form, verifying that it was indeed Amlina who had cast this potent ensorcellment. She and her party were traveling now somewhere in the mountains of northern Nyssan.

But why?

Unanswered questions needled at Beryl as she climbed the curving steps of the tower. She recalled how little effort it had taken to pierce Amlina's defenses in the past. In Kadavel, she had found and attacked her renegade apprentice with flaming mask and strangling gloves. Of course, they were in the same city then, the physical proximity making it easier to forge a strong link. But it was more than that: Amlina's mental barriers had grown dense, much harder to pierce. No doubt, this was due to the dark power she had evoked.

That left the neophyte. Beryl had learned that it was one of Amlina's barbarian allies, the one who had been enthralled by the serd in Kadavel. That accounted for the psychic wound. Beryl's probing had succeeded in opening the wound, causing the young woman considerable misery and distress. But despite all her concentrated efforts, Beryl had learned nothing more of Amlina's exact location or intentions.

Tonight, Beryl would apply stronger measures.

Reaching the top of the Bone Tower, the Archimage strode across the circular chamber, the treeman still following on her heels. But when Beryl approached a narrow door framed by black iron, Grellabo stopped, his posture tense. When Beryl slid the bolt and pulled open the door, the treeman hissed and skittered away.

The chamber was a circular vault, six paces across. At the center, a stout column of black marble formed a small table. On top stood a pitcher, a goblet, and a single lamp, all fabricated of ruby glass. Beryl lit the lamp with a word and a gesture. Red light flickered on the stone walls, revealing a host of brackets supporting knives, swords, razors, and scalpels of every size and description. Beryl used another gesture to close and bolt the door.

After pouring water into the cup, she stood for a time, mentally raising power. Around her on the walls, the weapons and implements quivered and came to life, rising from their brackets, scalpels and razors first, then knives and swords. They floated into the air and slowly circled, riding the currents of Beryl's thought.

The Archimage watched them, feeling the energy rise and swell. Suddenly, she plucked a razor from the air and used it to carefully slice her finger. She squeezed the small cut, allowing twelve drops of blood to fall into the goblet.

Beryl swirled the cup in her hand, the circling of liquid matching the revolving of sharp steel in the red-lit air. Staring wide-eyed at the bloodied water, she focused once more on the apprentice mage, whose name she had learned, was *Glyssa*.

Far away in the north, Glyssa was sleeping, her mind at its most vulnerable. When Beryl had fixed the girl in her thoughts and could clearly see the psychic wound, she spoke.

"Glyssa, I call you. My blood is now your blood, my mind now your mind, my will now your will."

Beryl drank down the contents of the cup. Sensations washed over her—visions, feelings, thoughts. Glyssa was heartsick and afraid. But also formidably tough. This toughness came not from Amlina, but from Glyssa's own heritage—and from her companions. Her warrior band shared a kind of group spirit. Beryl had been aware of it before, had probed and measured its strength.

But now she perceived something else ... another figure. Beryl caught a glimpse of black feathers, a beak. Some bird-spirit or elemental ...? Beryl tensed and peered harder. Glyssa was instinctively resisting her. Straining, Beryl whispered the chant.

"My blood, your blood. My will, your will."

In the vault, the blades whirled faster, scraping and clashing in the air. Beryl felt burning pressure, pain behind her eyes. She pushed harder, harder.

"Belach." A name and an image—a magician, an ally Glyssa trusted. One whose power protected her.

"Ah!" Beryl lurched back, the vision obliterated. Blades clanged and clattered as they struck the stone floor.

Beryl panted, blood dripping from her nostrils. She wiped her upper lip, stared at the red smear on her fingers. So, another mage protected Glyssa. A shaman of her tribe, to judge by the feathered garb. Beryl had his image, and his name.

"Belach."

A lesser deepshaper would have seen this as yet another obstacle. But Beryl recognized the opportunity: a being that Glyssa trusted in the Deepmind, one whose power could be bound and stolen, one whom Beryl could impersonate—a key to finally learning what she needed to know.

It would take some time to fashion an adequate ensorcellment. Beryl decided to begin at once.

Time, she sensed, was running short.

TWENTY-ONE

Amlina gripped the rim of the basket and stared down at the ruins of Valgool. They had flown across the mountains in a day and camped last night on the edge of the high plateau. Now, in mid-afternoon, the course of their flight had brought the lost city into view. It sprawled beside a dry riverbed, in a web of ancient roads. Square warrens of crumbled walls and fallen roofs surrounded the remains of a citadel, a step pyramid rising at the center. Even from a distance, the witch felt a lingering power, a presence of bleak and restless evil.

The torms lowered the baskets to settle on the ground a mile from the city. There were over thirty of the winged bearers, four for each of the eight baskets that had made the journey. The leader of the party lifted Amlina out of the basket and set her on the ground. He chirped some words, which Buroof translated, Bidding the witch farewell and affirming that the flock would return in eight days time. By now the other torms had alighted. They lined up, waddled forward and ceremoniously touched a wing to Amlina's shoulder, peering intently into her eyes. They then marched around, touching each of the party in the same manner, before spreading their wings and lifting off.

The travelers watched in silence as the torms flew away into the pale, cloudless sky. The plain on which they stood was empty and eerily quiet. Even in high summer, the air on the plateau was chill and arid. Amlina repressed a shiver. The Iruks and Wilhaven looked at her expectantly. She glanced down at the book still open in her hands.

"Buroof. We stand within sight of Valgool."

"That is where the torms agreed to convey you, so why are you telling me so?"

"Because of the evil immanence I feel in this place. The torm elders mentioned it was haunted—by creatures that you called *ghost dogs*. What manner of beings are they, material or elemental?"

"Material, but with savage elemental energy. They are reanimated corpses, in the Nagaree language called *kul shirra*. In the age of the Old Empire, many of the warriors sacrificed on the pyramid were brought back to life to serve as soldiers for the priestly caste. Their hearts were torn out and replaced with constructs of light, which endowed them with extreme longevity. Now, whenever warm-blooded beings enter the city, the kul shirra attack and devour them. But surely you have prepared adequate designs to protect your party from these creatures."

"No," Amlina answered with a grimace. "You never mentioned such protections would be necessary. Why did you not warn me?"

Buroof signed with exasperation. "Because you never asked. I can't be expected to warn you of everything. Really, Amlina, of all the mages I have belonged to in the span of 29 centuries, you are undoubtedly the most ineffectual."

Amlina looked away in disgust, pain throbbing behind her eyes.

"What is the delay?" Karrol demanded. "Why are you standing there talking to the book instead of leading us into the city?"

The witch had conversed with Buroof in Larthangan, not considering that her companions would understand little if any of the discussion.

"We will have to camp here tonight," she said. "There are protections I must prepare before we enter."

* O *

Late that night, Glyssa walked the perimeter of the camp, armed with a single spear. Her sword and dagger, like most of the klarn's weapons, had been taken by Amlina. Glyssa could see the witch's shadow, cast by an oil lamp inside the small tent. Amlina's shoulders were hunched, her long fingers moving as she wove magic over the blades and spears—designs to make the arms more effective against the enemies they would likely encounter in Valgool.

Except for that one lamp, the camp was dark—illumined only by stars and the faintly wavering body of the eidolon. Firewood was not to be found on this barren plateau, and the party needed to preserve their supply of lamp oil.

Glyssa gathered the woolen cloak tight at her throat. The night was cold, though not nearly so cold as winters in the South Polar Sea. Her mates lay sleeping, huddled on the ground under bed furs—all except Lonn who shared the watch with her. As they passed each other he reached out his hand. Glyssa smiled and let her fingers brush his, happy for his touch.

She walked on, past the weird figure of the queen. Meghild's head floated atop a column of light that flickered into shadows. Since being roused by Amlina at dusk, the queen had not spoken at all, only stared with a lost, dreamy gaze at the distant ruins of the city. Meghild had wildly enjoyed the ceremony and feasting with the torms, but since then had seemed dull and faded. Her mind and soul were once again leaving this world, Glyssa surmised, draining into the Deepmind.

Glyssa scanned the darkness, wishing they had a fire or that the eidolon shed more light. Though she heard nothing, she could not escape the feeling of being stalked, as though some fearsome beast was creeping out there in the darkness, waiting for an opportunity to pounce.

No, she told herself, it was the shadow within that unnerved her—the lingering dread she had come to call the fishhook. The fear had fled from her, banished in the flush of triumph from crossing the bridge and the exhilaration of flying with the winged people. But in the last day and night it had crept inexorably back. Glyssa wondered if she would ever be free of it.

Lonn stepped up beside her, glumly staring into the night. "I wish Amlina would finish her magic-making so we could have our weapons back." He too was armed only with a spear.

"I know," Glyssa whispered.

Lonn clenched his lips. "I'm beginning to feel like Karrol, that I will be happy when this voyage is over."

Stoical by nature, Lonn seldom voiced feelings of unease. His confession was a mark of how the hard journey, and now the eeriness of this place and talk of ghost creatures, had worn on him.

Glyssa experienced again a twinge of guilt. Her awful weakness was the reason her mates had to come on this journey. She reached over and squeezed his hand. "I am glad you are here with me."

His smile warmed her heart. "My Glyssa, I would rather be in the worst of places with you than the best of places without you."

His eyes held hers for just an instant, then a scream tore the air.

They both whirled to look at Meghild, whose mouth hung open with shock. Creatures were rushing into the camp—naked, gray things that moved with a slithering, four-legged run. Amlina had called these things *ghost dogs*, and Glyssa thought the name most apt. She no sooner spotted them raging through the camp than one fell on her shoulders, dragging her to the ground. She glimpsed red, feral eyes, raised her arm just in time to keep jaws from snapping on her throat. She thrust the spear at the thing's body, but had no leverage.

Lonn kicked the creature off her and pinned it to the ground with his spear. "Mates, wake up!" he roared. "We are attacked!"

Glyssa rolled over, scrambled to her feet. Another of the ghost dogs rushed her. She crouched low and ran it through. It looked shocked for a moment, then growled and kept coming, reaching for her with swiping nails.

"Amlina!" Lonn shouted as he ran across the camp. "Our weapons!"

Grunting in disgust, Glyssa braced her foot on the ghost dog's belly and yanked the spear free. The creature stumbled backward and fell. Looking around, Glyssa spotted more of the things leaping on her mates. Waking to this nightmare, the Iruks were shouting and struggling to fight.

Glyssa started toward them, tripped and fell. The creature she speared had lunged again and grabbed her foot. Glyssa rolled over and brought her point up just in time for her foe to impale itself. Still not killed, it gurgled and raked at her face with its claws. Growling, Glyssa heaved it off of her. She got to one knee and drove her spear point through the creature's neck again and again. Only when the head rolled free from the body did the thing at last lay still.

Standing, Glyssa saw that the battle had turned. Amlina had rushed from her tent, carrying weapons that she tossed to the Iruks. The mates hacked and stabbed, swords and spears gleaming blue with witchlight. The magic-imbued steel seemed to burn the flesh of the ghost dogs, who dodged and yelped with pain. Wilhaven had rushed over to protect the queen—though it appeared none of the intruders had assaulted her. When Karrol decapitated one creature with her blade, the others—six or seven—turned and fled howling into the night.

Glyssa hurried over to join her mates, whose shoulders slumped as the fury of battle left them. Brinda and Eben grimaced, clutching bitten forearms. Lonn stared down at the witch who knelt over—Glyssa's gut twisted. Draven lay unmoving, legs splayed. Amlina's hands pressed down on his neck, which was torn and leaking blood.

"Help me," the witch cried. "Bring something to stop the bleeding, or he will die."

* O *

Stunned and silent, the Iruks stood over their fallen mate. Through the klarn soul, all of them could feel the wound, feel Draven's life slipping away. Karrol moved, half-heartedly, to find the medicine bag in the klarn's gear. The bag contained needle and sinew to bind wounds, strips of rabbit skin for bandages. But from what Glyssa had seen, it was hopeless—too much of Draven's flesh was torn away.

"Here, my lady, let me look." Wilhaven spoke softly, kneeling beside the witch. He shifted Amlina's hands and examined the wound. "If we stitch it up at once, we may save him. I have supplies in my kit. Bring another lamp or two."

He went to rummage through his pack, returning in a few moments with a small canvas bag. He spilled the contents on the ground: needle and thread, a skein of bandages, small bottles and vials. He directed Amlina to press lower on the neck, then poured spirits over the wound. Draven's mouth lolled open and he whimpered in pain.

"This is my fault," Amlina cried. "I did not think they would attack so far from the city."

"Sure, and how could you know that either way?" Wilhaven asked. "We are in unknown lands, my lady."

Dexterously, he threaded a needle and set to work stitching the wound. The Iruks stood over him, staring in numb, desolate grief. Glyssa sensed again that it was hopeless: the wound too severe, too much blood lost. Meghild had drifted over to stand at the edge of their circle. The queen too stared in silence, with a solemn, dejected expression.

After some time, the bard finished with the needle. Lifting Draven's head, he wrapped bandaging around the neck. When the bandage was tied, he stood.

Amlina looked up at the Iruks, her eyes glistening. "Will you carry him into the tent, please?"

Lonn laid a hand on her shoulder. He and Draven were cousins, raised together since infancy. Their love was that of brothers. "Is there a chance your magic can save him?"

Amlina touched him with her bloodied hand. "I will do all I can, I swear it on my soul."

* O *

Two nights later, Glyssa again patrolled the edge of the camp, sword and spear clutched in her hand. A fire of sticks and grass burned behind her, casting her long shadow over the ground.

They still had not entered the city. Instead, the morning after their arrival, three of the Iruks had marched off to explore some low hills in the north. They'd returned in the afternoon carrying fuel and fresh water. On a second foray, they'd managed to bring down a small deer to supplement their rations.

The ghost dogs had not attacked again. From the talking book, Amlina had learned that the creatures were thought to be animate only at night, and that they shied away from fire. Glyssa could hear them though, yipping to each other, rustling in the darkness around the camp. The Iruks slept in shifts day and night, so that three warriors always stood guard. Tonight, along with Glyssa, it was Karrol and Wilhaven.

Glyssa walked past Karrol, who glanced at her drearily. The helpless inaction weighed on all of the mates, but perhaps on Karrol most of all. Although Draven still lived, he had shown no sign of recovering. Through the medium of the klarn-soul, Glyssa could sense his life flickering. She thought it only a matter of time.

Amlina had tended him day and night, emerging from the tent only a few times to take water and a little food. For long periods she could be heard singing over him, her voice rising and falling in lilting Larthangan chants. Once, Glyssa had peeked into the tent and saw the witch lying beside Draven under the cover, her arms wrapped around him, her body pressed close. In that moment, Glyssa had known how much the witch loved Draven, how desperate she was to save him.

The tent flap parted, and Amlina stepped out, straightening her back as though in pain. She shuffled wearily toward the fire. Glyssa and Karrol marched over to her.

"Any change?" Karrol asked.

Amlina shook her head. She took a drink from the water skin, grunted to clear her throat. "I am going to try something else. It requires me to go into trance. You must make sure I am not disturbed, no matter what you may hear."

"All right," Glyssa said.

"But for how long?" Karrol asked.

Amlina seemed unprepared for the question. "I don't know ... Three days, I suppose. If I am not returned by then, you may enter the tent. You will likely have to part with us both."

Glyssa took hold of the witch's wrist. "What are you going to do?"

Amlina showed a fragile smile. "As I promised, I will do anything to save him."

* O *

Returning to the tent, Amlina sat cross-legged on the ground next to Draven. She opened a small book bound in red leather—the *Canon of the Deepmind*. It was the basic volume of Larthangan lore, containing instructions in the "Five Revered Arts of Magic" and their "Thirty-Five Respected Applications." As a trained witch, she had read the volume through many times. But now she turned to a section near the end, a practice she had never attempted. Whispering to herself, she read the title: "The Way of Summoning the Dead Through the Deepmind."

Draven was not dead, not yet. But his soul was already on the journey. Amlina had exhausted all other means of healing him. This was her last, desperate hope, one she was determined to try, even at the risk of not returning herself.

She read the chant in Old Larthangan, murmured it over and over as she formulated her design, visualized Draven walking alone in the night. She saw herself meeting him, and then their walking back together—back to this world.

Soon, she slipped into trance.

In her vision she was sinking, slowly, as though in bubbling water. The space around her brightened, the bubbles becoming stars and clouds of starry dust. After a while she no longer floated but walked through the star-strewn sky. With an ache, a longing in her heart, she kept going, seeking her lost friend.

Time ceased to have meaning. There were only the stars all around her and the endless, lonely march.

Then, at last, she spied a figure far ahead, striding resolutely. Amlina quickened her pace, desperate to reach him. As she closed the gap she called his name.

"Draven. Draven!"

The third time, he stopped and turned around. She ran to him, hope surging wildly in her heart.

He looked at her, perplexed. "Amlina. How can you be here?"

"I came for you. I came to bring you back."

He gazed around, as if trying to recognize where they were. "Is that possible?"

"It is—if you'll come with me now."

"But ... I am on the Star Road. Are you dead also?"

"No. We are both still alive. It is not too late!"

Draven frowned. "You know, we Iruks believe that if a warrior dies while on a hunt, the soul travels on with the klarn. But I see now, it is only a bit of my strength that stayed with them. My soul is here ..."

"I want you to come back with me." Her voice broke into a sob.

"Oh, it is not so bad," Draven said. "I am returning to the Mother. There will be peace and rest, then after a while, I'll be born again into my people ... Isn't that right?"

"I don't know. Different peoples tell different stories. I only know I want you to return with me now. Your mates need you. I need you."

For the first time he seemed to consider the possibility of returning. "But I can't do that. I was too badly wounded. I would be a burden to the klarn, to all of you."

"You can recover. I am sure of it. Your mates want you to live, and so do I."

He peered around at the stars, as if listening. "I can see much from here. I can see that ... even this, even your coming here, is dangerous for you. You've risked the strength you need, risked everything you set out to accomplish ..."

"I don't care." She flung her arms around him, hugged him close. "None of it matters if I can't save you. Yes, I wish to defeat Beryl, to return the Cloak to Larthang. But if you can't go with me, it means nothing." She was crying now. "No one ... No one has ever loved me as you do. And I have never loved anyone else."

Draven's embrace grew firm, with the strength she remembered. "Oh, do not cry, my beautiful girl. If that is how it is, then of course I will go with you."

* O *

Amlina opened her eyes. In the sputtering lamplight, through a blur of tears, she saw Draven watching her serenely.

"Oh!" She leaned over, touched his forehead, his cheek. "You're awake." Sobbing, she lay down with her head on his shoulder.

He stroked her long hair, his voice a dry whisper. "You called me back, so I am here."

She wept harder, clinging to him like an injured child.

TWENTY-TWO

Next day they marched into Valgool.

Amlina led the way on the ancient, dusty road. She was dressed in her long, fur-trimmed coat, the moonstone fillet in her hair, the talking book clutched in her arms. Behind her came Wilhaven, with the basket containing the head of the queen strapped on his back. The Iruks followed, weighed down with packs and luggage, grasping their spears, warily scanning the empty plain and the trail ahead. Eben and Brinda both carried lighter loads, their bandaged forearms still sore from the bites they'd suffered in the attack. Fortunately, the other klarnmates had suffered only scratches and bruises.

Draven rode on Lonn's back. He had taken broth and a little meat in the morning, the color returning to his tawny complexion. He had insisted he'd be able to walk on his own, but after a few moments standing his legs had given out. His mates treated him with all gentleness and consideration, so relieved to have him back, to have the klarn whole again. They disputed happily over who would have the honor to "serve as his aklor," and joked about what services Draven would have to perform in recompense once his strength returned.

Every few paces Amlina looked over her shoulder to check on Draven. Her emotions rushed like a torrent in many streams—elation for Draven's recovery, dread at entering the haunted city, pricking doubt about her ability to accomplish her mission. The weight of the blood magic ached low in her belly, seeming to grow heavier with each step. And yet, the journey on the Star Road had not drained her after all. On the contrary, the passion roused in her for Draven, the alluring, overpowering love, nourished her intention and strength.

She no longer felt alone.

Past the tumbled outer wall of Valgool, they entered a broad avenue strewn with weathered bricks and piles of rubble. Collapsed buildings on either side displayed jagged facades and fallen beams. Lizards warmed themselves in the faint sunlight, and a fat black toad eyed them balefully. No rats were visible, no birds—no warm-blooded creatures at all. Below the empty sky, the city lay silent.

Turning a corner, the witch spied a hairless, human-shaped thing lying on a doorstep. Spotting the intruders, the ghost dog roused itself and crawled sluggishly away. Karrol and Eben dropped their baggage, drew swords and started after the creature.

"No," Amlina warned.

"Could be leading us into a trap," Lonn agreed.

"Possibly," the witch said. "But I don't think they're capable of harming us in the daytime. We'd best get to the pyramid and set up camp."

* O *

The step pyramid stood at the heart of the city. Built of granite quarried in the western mountains, it had withstood centuries of wind and rain. Black stones, stained with gray lichen, rose to a summit ten stories high. In the days of the Nagaree, thousands of captives had climbed the steps, to have their hearts cut out by obsidian knives and offered to the moons. Many of those captives had been resurrected as ghost dogs, and in the ruined temple complex surrounding the pyramid, scores of them still nested.

Exploring the area, the travelers discovered rooms and courtyards where the creatures sprawled on their backs or slumped against walls. Some of them scuttled away listlessly at sight of the intruders. Others only stared as though in trance.

At night it would be different.

For their campsite, the witch selected a pillared hall across the plaza from the pyramid. Part of the roof was intact, and storerooms adjacent to the hall had solid walls and no windows. Amlina would need a safe, enclosed place to weave her magic.

The Iruks spent the afternoon gathering broken rafters and scraps of dry wood. In one of the storerooms, they discovered sealed jars full of oil. From split beams and tattered rags, they fashioned torches. By nightfall, a bonfire blazed at the entrance to the hall, and torches burned along the edges of their camp. Amlina spied ghost dogs creeping across the plaza, their red eyes glaring in the firelight.

"I think as long as we keep the fires burning, we should be safe," she said. "But three of you should always stand guard."

Lonn nodded grimly. "Don't worry about that. We'll be ready if they come."

They cooked the last of the fresh venison and ate it with hard bread from their stores. Wilhaven strummed his harp, his tune a soothing counterpoint to the sporadic howling of ghost dogs across the city. After eating a healthy portion, Draven rested on one elbow by the fire. Amlina was heartened to observe his strength returning so quickly.

Before retiring, Amlina removed the queen's head from the basket and raised the eidolon body. Coming awake, Meghild stared around with lips parted, then drifted to the entrance of the hall. Amlina and Wilhaven followed her.

"Are you well, my queen?" the bard inquired.

The eidolon's eyes gazed at the pyramid. "We are here at last."

"Yes," Amlina said.

"I am weary," Meghild muttered, her voice barely audible. "So many visions, bright and harsh, but all have disappeared. And soon this one too will fade. How much time is left, Amlina?"

"Five nights till the moons align."

Meghild sighed. "One more task, and then I shall rest."

* O *

Glyssa was roused by a hand shaking her shoulder. She'd had only a few hours sleep after standing watch, but she came awake at once, pierced by a feeling of panic.

"I'm sorry to waken you." Amlina whispered. "I need your help."

Glyssa sat up, breathing hard. It was morning, a dreary gray light hanging over the ruined plaza. The remains of the bonfire smoked at the entrance to the hall. Eben, Lonn, and Karrol stood guard.

Amlina's face betrayed care and fatigue. "I did not mean to frighten you."

"I am all right."

Glyssa pulled on her boots. She followed the witch into a storeroom off the main hall. The small chamber contained dusty bales of fabric and a shelf with ancient pots and jars. Amlina had spread her bedding against the wall. Tiny lamps burned on the floor, arranged in a star pattern. The head of the queen floated in a ceramic bowl filled with water. Meghild's eyes were closed, and Glyssa had the feeling, for the first time, that she was looking at the head of a corpse.

Amlina sat down on the floor and directed Glyssa to do likewise.

"In four nights, I will forge the Mirror Against All Mishap," Amlina said. "But mentally and physically, I am so tired. I fear I will lack the necessary concentration. I've decided, since there is time, that I will enter the dark immersion. In this way, I hope to replenish my energy. Starting this morning, I must not be disturbed for any reason. Do you understand?"

Glyssa nodded, lips parted.

"The problem is," the witch continued, "I might not awake from the trance in time. That is why I need your help. To be summoned from dark immersion is dangerous, if not done properly."

"What must I do?"

"Four mornings from now, if I am not awake, you must summon me back. Come in here alone. Call my name softly, and reach for me in your thoughts. Just as you did on the bridge, when you were blindfolded, but gently."

"All right," Glyssa said. "Is that all?"

Amlina smiled and touched her hand. "You are strong and faithful, Glyssa. I know I can rely on you."

They stared at each other in the dim room, and Glyssa sensed the witch's mind touching hers.

"I am a poor teacher indeed," Amlina said. "I have not done nearly enough to help you. Or even paid attention to your condition. I know you are frightened."

"Surely there is good reason for that," Glyssa said. But even as she tried to make light of it, the dread welled up inside her, a dark, crushing force. Her voice faltered. "It is getting worse. I think it is the fishhook again. It started when we were on the river, but it grows worse all the time. And now, this place ..."

Amlina held both her hands and gazed into her eyes. "You feel something unknown, but powerful and terrifying, reaching into you, seeking to gain control—"

"Yes. It feels like before, when the sorcerer made me a slave. But it can't be he, can it? Because he is dead."

"No. It is not Kosimo. I am sure Beryl killed him. I suspect what you feel is something I also am feeling—the blood magic, rising in both of us. It calls to the spirit of this place. That spirit is known as the Devourer, and it is his power I must use to create the Mirror. I did not realize you would feel its presence too. It is a mark of your growing talent."

"What can I do?"

Amlina paused before answering. "Keep up your exercises, circulating the power inside you, to give you control and balance ... And call on your klarn-spirit. That is an energy unknown to the lore of Larthang, but I have come to know it is a wonderful protection."

* O *

Rain whispered and hissed in the night. Gray clouds had blown in from the west on the second day of the witch's deep trance. The rain had started in the afternoon, dripping through holes in the roof, forming puddles on the floor. Some of the stored fuel had gotten wet, forcing the Iruks to build a smaller fire tonight, in the roofed section of the hall.

Standing over the fire, Glyssa peered into the gloom of the plaza, wary for any sign of movement. Two of the ghost dogs had rushed the camp last night. And though they'd been easily beaten back, a dozen others had lurked just outside the circle of firelight, growling and yapping till dawn.

Tonight, with the diminished firelight, Glyssa thought they might attack in force. She heaved a deep breath, pushing down her fatigue and gnawing terror. The tension of waiting felt unbearable.

Draven stepped up and laid a hand on her shoulder. "Why don't you get some rest, mate? You look worn out."

Glyssa winced, remembering how his neck had looked when Wilhaven changed the dressing that morning—raw and shrunken, a chunk of flesh missing. "You're the one who should be resting," she said.

Draven harrumphed. "After five days flat on my back, this feels like a night in the tavern."

Glyssa responded with a cheerless laugh. She glanced around the camp. Lonn, Karrol, and Wilhaven also stood watch, with only Brinda and Eben sleeping. The weariness welled up and her shoulders sagged.

"Perhaps you are right," she said. "I will try to sleep a little."

She slumped over to the bed furs, took off her sword belt, lay down with her weapons close at hand.

* O *

Glyssa moved through a narrow passage. Beneath her feet, the floor lifted and sank. She was back on the ship, the Larthangan vessel they had traveled on from Kadavel—after her mates saved her from enslavement. She remembered the passages below decks, but this corridor was longer, endless. She was lost. She had to find Amlina's cabin ...

She drifted past doors hung with a silver sheen, like the looking glasses she had seen at inns in Fleevanport, and later in Gwales. You could see yourself, everything around you, reflected perfectly. They were called mirrors.

"What do the mirrors mean?" A voice sounded behind her. Glyssa spun around, but saw no one.

"Belach?"

"Yes, it is Belach. What do the mirrors mean? You must remember."

She was surprised to find Belach here, but the force of his question compelled her to search her mind for the answer. "Amlina is making a mirror, the Mirror Against All Mishap."

"Is she indeed?" Belach sounded surprised. "Where is she making this mirror?"

"Here, in Valgool. On the pyramid."

"So? And when? When will she be finished?"

Glyssa wondered why Belach was asking these things, and why she could not see him. But she trusted the shaman, and so felt she must answer. "A few more days."

After a pause, Belach said suddenly: "Amlina is in danger. You must go to her."

Glyssa sat up. She was unsure how she had come to be lying down, but this question vanished as she reached for her sword. Amlina was in peril. The serd had come for her, was going to enslave her as Glyssa had once been enslaved.

Glyssa rose to her feet, distantly aware that she was in the ruined city, rain dripping from the roof. Her mates stood guard with their backs to the fire. Silently, she crept to the rear of the hall, like a hunter stalking prey. She slipped into the storeroom.

In the flickering lamplight, Amlina lay in deep trance. A thin, black-robed creature hovered over her, leaning close as though to feed on the witch's soul. The sorcerer, the one who had once been Glyssa's master, the one she hated above all others in the world.

"Hurry," Belach whispered in her ear. "You must strike now."

Glyssa cringed, but the sword felt true and solid in her grip. She stalked past the lamps, lifted the blade to plunge into the serd's back.

But she hesitated.

The sorcerer was dead. Amlina had told her so.

The black-clad figure turned, changing. It was not the serd, but Belach!

"Stop, Glyssa, daughter of Sorcha!" he said. "You are about to kill your friend."

"Agh!" A gasp of rage sounded from behind.

Glyssa whirled and spied—not Belach, but another—a tall powerful woman she had seen before, in the cavern under Kadavel. Amlina's enemy, the one called Beryl.

The truth sprang to her mind. Beryl had bewitched her, possessed her, tried to trick her into killing Amlina. In pure fury Glyssa lunged, stabbing the Archimage in the belly.

Beryl shrieked and vanished in a flash of searing black. Pain tore up Glyssa's sword arm, and she was flung backward, cracking her head against the wall.

* O *

Controlling her rage with a grim effort of will, Beryl limped through the upper chamber of the Bone Tower. The Iruk's sword had struck her etheric body, of course. But Beryl had chosen to manifest the wound in physical form, to heal it more quickly. A puncture, an inch deep, just below the stomach—she had sealed it at once to stop the bleeding. The soreness, she knew, would last some days.

Now, pausing to lean on a heavy chair, the Archimage pondered her next move. She had been so close to killing Amlina and ending the threat. At the last moment, the Iruk shaman had broken free and wriggled out of her grasp. Then Glyssa had moved with stunning speed, stabbing Beryl's projected form before she could defend herself or break the link.

Once again, she had been caught off-guard by the toughness and tenacity of her opponents. Perhaps the long decades of dealing only with slaves and weak-willed minions had left her soft, over-confident.

Regardless, she could not afford any more mistakes. She needed to assess the danger now, coldly and clearly. She had learned Amlina's location, Valgool, and the name of the ensorcellment she meant to cast. The Mirror Against All Mishap—no doubt, an ancient Nagaree design, its purpose obvious enough from the name, a protection against all attack.

The Mirror would be forged in a few more days. Did Beryl have time to prevent its completion? Difficult, at this distance and with Amlina's barriers so effective—even if Beryl had her full strength. But with this wound ...

Too early to decide. First, she must replenish herself. Her gaze tracked to the far wall, the alcove hung with a black curtain. As she headed in that direction, the treeman emerged from under a table and followed her, his long tail twitching with anticipation.

Beryl pulled back the curtain and scanned the line of bronze cages. Four captives stood within, two male and two female, eyes closed, brains asleep. Beryl placed a finger to her lips and scrutinized their naked bodies, deciding which one she would feast on.

No. In this extremity, better to take two.

* O *

Glyssa walked through an empty landscape under a gray-white sky. Snow crunched beneath her feet, and white flakes drifted in the air. After walking some distance, she spotted a figure clothed in black feathers. Glyssa marched up to him.

"Belach? Is it you?"

"Yes, daughter of my tribe." He lifted the beaked mask, revealing his face.

"I thought it was you before, but it was another."

"Yes, I know. She is a mighty witch, that one. She bound me and stole my shadow. Only at the last moment, when she thought she had won, was I able to break free and warn you."

"She is the witch we mean to kill. She almost tricked me into killing my friend. I am glad you warned me."

"I am glad also." Belach's black eyes appraised her. "You have done well on your quest, overcoming your fears. But now you have met the second great enemy."

"What do you mean?"

"I mean *deceit!*" Belach clucked his tongue three times. "When you travel in the spirit worlds, many may try to deceive you. This time we were lucky. I was able to intervene. But you must learn to conquer this enemy yourself, just as you have the first."

"How can I do that?" Glyssa asked. "How can I know what is true?"

"By *clarity!* By looking carefully and fearlessly, not only with your eyes and brain, but with your heart. The eyes, the nose, the mind—all can be fooled. But never the heart."

"I'm not sure I understand."

Belach smiled kindly. "Clarity is not easy. As with facing the first enemy, it must be won again and again. But you are clever and *brave."* He laid a gloved hand on her shoulder. *"Be well, daughter. And be wary!"*

He spread his arms, the cloak moving like wings, closed them again and disappeared.

TWENTY-THREE

"Glyssa. Glyssa, my friend. Return to us now. All is well."

Glyssa's eyes blinked open. Amlina leaned above her—and behind the witch's shoulder, Lonn and Brinda and Karrol peered with grave concern.

After probing Glyssa's scalp with her fingers, the witch sighed with relief. "She will be all right now."

"How do you feel?" Lonn asked gently.

Her mouth was parched. "Thirsty."

Chuckling, the mates sat her up. Karrol fetched a cup of water.

"You had us worried," Lonn said. "We found you lying here and couldn't rouse you. We didn't know what to do. Finally, Amlina came out of her trance this morning."

Glyssa frowned, confused. "I was supposed to wake you."

"No matter," Amlina smiled. "I was able to wake you instead. What do you remember?"

"I'm not sure. I was on guard with Draven and then ... I must have fallen asleep."

"What else?" Amlina insisted.

Glyssa squeezed her eyes shut, straining to clear her thoughts. The memories rose with a surge of fear. "The master ... the serd, he was attacking you—No, it was not him. It was your enemy, the Archimage. She must have bewitched me."

"Yes." Amlina blanched. "I thought I felt her presence in the Deepmind. So now she knows about the Mirror ..."

Glyssa knew that was true. "She read it from my mind ... And then she tried to trick me into killing you."

The witch regarded her with surprise. "What prevented you?"

"Belach appeared, our shaman. At first Beryl pretended to be Belach, but then he appeared in truth, and warned me. And then I saw that it was Beryl, and I stabbed her with my sword."

"Indeed?" Amlina's surprise deepened. "Seems I owe Belach a debt—and you as well."

Wits returning, Glyssa looked around at her mates. "Are the rest of you all right?"

"Well enough," Lonn said. "We are holding the camp."

"Barely," Karrol interjected. "The ghost dogs attacked in force last night. We killed six before they retreated. And we are running short of fuel."

"That won't matter." Amlina stood. "Before nightfall we will climb the pyramid. I am almost certain they won't follow us there."

"So it's tonight," Glyssa said. "I was gone for two days?"

"Yes," the witch replied. "Tonight we cast the Mirror."

* O *

After the Iruks left the storeroom, Amlina knelt on the dusty floor. While she lay in trance, the tiny lamps had burned for four days and nights, fueled by energy channeled from the Deepmind. Now, with a word, she extinguished the flames one by one.

As Amlina had hoped, the dark immersion had revived her, balancing the vast powers of the blood magic in her body and spirit—leaving her with a cool, steady determination.

But while Amlina floated in trance, Beryl had learned about the Mirror. The Archimage had managed to pry into Glyssa's mind and seize control of her body. Yet, at the crucial moment, Glyssa had fought back and driven Beryl away. The untutored prowess of the Iruk woman continued to surprise Amlina. And now, looking at the problem with deepsight, Amlina perceived that Beryl had withdrawn, perhaps been damaged by the encounter. Had Glyssa's sword actually wounded her? Impossible to tell. And once Beryl comprehended the power of the Mirror, she might strike again to prevent its creation. Beryl was fully capable of piercing the veils of distance, to materialize lethal forces here in Valgool. Amlina would have to be on guard against that possibility.

In the hours between now and sundown, she had much work to do: weaving extra protections, fashioning trinkets, raising the eidolon of the queen.

But first, she must see Draven.

After putting away the lamps, Amlina walked out to the hall. The morning air was crisp, the sky a pale lavender here on the high plateau. The Iruks sat around a smoldering fire, sharing a meager breakfast. Wilhaven leaned on a column, somberly plucking his harp.

Amlina took some porridge and tea. She chatted with Lonn and the others, advising them of her plan to march to the pyramid at dusk, and warning them to be alert in the meantime. After finishing her meal, she took Draven aside, leading him by the hand to a portico at the rear of the hall.

She placed her palm gently on his bandaged neck. "You are still recovering, my dear friend?"

Draven grinned, took her hand away and hugged her in a crushing embrace. "Oh, yes. Better all the time."

Feeling his warmth and solidity, Amlina sighed. "I am so glad."

Draven held her at arm's length. "But you also feel stronger today."

"Yes. The dark immersion did its work. I am imbued with power." She gripped his shoulders. "You have so often lent your strength to me. I want to share some of this power with you now."

"Oh, there is no need."

"Yes," she insisted. "It will help you heal. Now I want you to relax and look into my eyes."

Draven shrugged, but obeyed. Amlina held both hands near his neck and envisioned cool, healing light penetrating the bandage, weaving new layers of muscle and skin. When she took her hands away, his body glowed faintly with witchlight. He stared into her eyes with a knowing grin.

"What?" she asked.

"I was just remembering the Star Road."

She lowered her eyes, warmth rising in her cheeks. "What do you remember?"

"I was traveling to join the Great Mother, but you found me and called me back. Because you love me."

Amlina hugged him, resting her head on his chest. "It is true. And I've never loved anyone else."

Draven kissed the top of her head. "Will we have time then, to be lovers?"

"I hope so. I hope when all this is over, we will find a place where we are safe."

Draven sighed with contentment. "That is good enough for me."

* O *

Amlina spent the daylight hours in her chamber, seated cross-legged on the floor. Using the top of her trunk as a work bench, she labored with her trinketing tools. Trinketing, the art of fashioning objects permeated with magic, had always been her favorite art. These few worn tools she had carried with her always, from the Academy in Larthang, to the Tathian lands and Far Nyssan, and on her long, dangerous wanderings since fleeing Beryl's court. With a bone-handled jeweler's saw, she removed a hand mirror from its frame and meticulously cut it into eight small squares—one for herself and each of her companions. With pliers and shears, she bent bezels of silver around each piece, and connected them to silver chains. Then she murmured incantations over each necklace so that, when the Mirror Against All Mishap was forged, its power would flow into each and protect the wearer.

As she finished this task, an inspiration came. Searching through the trunk, she found a tiny glass vial with a stopper—a vessel used to store oils or potions. She emptied the contents and scraped the dust and jagged fragments of the cut mirror into the vial. Deliberately, she pricked her fingertip and added seven drops of her blood. The Mirror would last only so long as the eidolon had existed in the world—60 days. Before sealing the vial, she spoke her intention: that after the Mirror had vanished from the world, its protection could be resummoned by breaking this vial—summoned for the length of seven heartbeats by her seven drops of blood.

None of the Nyssanian sources mentioned the possibility of extending the Mirror's power by such a device. But, according to Larthangan lore, any magic could be sealed in a trinket and summoned at a later time. Amlina saw no harm in trying.

Next she opened the talking book and rehearsed all the phases of the grand ensorcellment, whispering the verses and incantations in Old Nyssanian, imagining the flow of powers. As she worked, words and images appeared and vanished on the pages of the book— Nagaree characters and runes, pictures of the three moons, the fearsome dragon face of the Devourer.

Shadows were lengthening in the plaza when Amlina emerged from the storeroom. She nodded to the Iruks who eyed her solemnly, then asked Wilhaven to come into her chamber. The bard looked surprised, but followed without a word.

Amlina had rolled up her bedding and packed away all of her magical objects except for the book. Faint light slanted through the doorway. "I am going to raise the queen's body now for the last time," she told Wilhaven. "I thought you should be present."

The bard nodded, brow furrowed, the corners of his mouth pulled back. Amlina sensed his dismay now that the hour had come— perhaps an instinctive aversion to the blood magic, perhaps simple grief at parting with the queen he adored.

Amlina set the bowl of water on the floor and spoke the words to raise the eidolon. Light shivered into being, expanding into a foggy column that slowly lifted the head. Meghild's eyes came open. She glanced at Amlina, then Wilhaven, and recognition dawned on her features.

"So. It is time."

"Yes, my queen," Amlina answered.

Emotions rippled over Meghild's face—pain, fear, anger. She looked down at the open book, which showed a jagged image of the Devourer.

"I had thought ... I thought I would be ready. But now I do not feel ready." Her eyes showed grief and sadness. "It is strange. All the times I went into battle, I went gladly. I knew I might die, but I went with fury, without fear ... But that was different. This time, the end is certain." Hands appeared at the end of her eidolon arms. Meghild stared down at the fingers. "Now I want to cling to life, even this false reflection of life."

The bard turned to Amlina, whispered in remorse. "Is there no other way?"

Amlina swallowed. She had always known the queen might balk at the decisive moment. If Meghild did not go to her death willingly, all would be for naught. The Mirror could not be forged.

"No one can force you, my queen," Amlina said quietly. "It must be your decision."

Meghild's stare was suspicious, calculating. "If I do not go with you, Amlina, how long will I live?"

"I truly do not know. You might survive in that form for a thousand years, or it might dissolve tonight when the moons align. I also don't know what would happen to me, to all of us, if the powers I have set in motion do not flow to their intended end."

Meghild peered into the witch's eyes, her expression changing again—wariness, regret. Finally, the queen lowered her gaze, leaned over and closed the book.

"Make my song, Wilhaven, and sing it in all the halls of Gwales, so I will be remembered. And do not omit this scene. Let it be known that in her final hour, Meghild bespoke her fear, and yet walked bravely to her end."

* O *

In the crimson light of sunset, Amlina moved across the plaza, the ghostly figure of Meghild floating at her side. Behind them marched Wilhaven and the Iruks, carrying swords and unlit torches, wearing their Mirror talismans.

Glyssa walked in the center of the line, warily scanning the collapsed buildings at the edges of the square, searching for any sign of movement.

She was not afraid. Perhaps, as the witch suggested, the time in trance had balanced and restored her, just as it had Amlina. But Glyssa thought it was more than that. She knew now it was Beryl the Archimage who had opened the wound in her heart, insinuated herself into Glyssa's soul, nearly enslaved her. Aided by Belach, Glyssa had seen through the deception, turned and struck at her enemy. Now the wound seemed to be healing again, the fear fled away. Glyssa marched once more as an Iruk warrior, with the calm of a stalking hunter, the bravery of the klarn pulsing in her blood.

As they reached the pyramid, howls of rage echoed in the gloom. Across the square, Glyssa spied ghost dogs scuttling from the shadows. But they did not approach. As Amlina had predicted, they seemed to regard the pyramid with awe and terror.

Glyssa climbed the steep steps, her short legs straining with the effort. The pyramid was enormous, the summit far away. As they ascended in the fading light, the warrens and squares of the ruined city came into sight, then the roads and distant hills beyond. The view was as staggering as the mountains Glyssa had seen when flying with the torms, but beautiful only in its desolation. By the time they reached the top, a few stars glinted in the darkening sky. Rog, the red moon, rode at the zenith, a faint half-circle. Grizna, which would be full tonight, had not yet risen.

* O *

The summit was a platform, six paces square. Amlina had arranged her companions one level down, equidistant from each other, to form a seven-pointed figure. Light from their torches wavered and danced in the gloom. Far below in the square, the kul shira could faintly be heard moaning and barking.

As night fell, the spectacular view of the ruined city faded away. Grizna appeared, a pale disk peering over the flat rim of the plateau. At the culmination of the rite, it would hang directly overhead, with Rog and the lost moon Tysanni each sixty degrees away, forming the alignment known as the *Baleful Trine*.

Amlina waited until the large moon had cleared the horizon, then looked up at the eidolon. "Are you ready, my queen?"

Meghild's fierce visage shifted in shadow. "Aye. I am ready."

Amlina drew the dagger from her belt and held aloft the Mirror talisman. Heaving a deep breath, she began to chant. She carried no book, but repeated over and over, in loud and commanding tones, the Nyssanian verses she had memorized.

The moons align in triple light
Above Valgool the sacred place
I call your spirit in the night
Nargassa Hulgar, Eater of Souls.

From the caves beyond this world
From the spheres beyond the moons
I raise your power on this night
Nargassa Hulgar, Devourer.

Even from the first, power tingled up and down her arms. Amlina trembled and continued the chant. Her awareness focused on the power, circling in her body, swirling into the sky, making the stars and moons vibrate like bells.

* O *

Glyssa heard the unending chant, but from her angle could not see the witch. In her hand the Mirror talisman seemed to hum and throb. From time to time she glanced at her mates, Lonn at one corner, Draven at the other. What she could see of their faces looked solemn and wary in the shuddering torch light. In the plaza below, the ghost dogs howled ceaselessly.

Hours passed. Amlina continued the same incantation, over and over and over. Glyssa wondered that the witch's voice could stay so strong and steady.

Grizna climbed higher. It was nearing the top of the sky when a wind arose, blowing hard around the pyramid. Looking up, Glyssa saw pin pricks of light, flashing and blinking. Draven and Lonn watched also, their mouths gaping.

The lights grew more numerous, flickering sparks of orange and red. They seemed to form an enormous mouth with many rows of gleaming teeth. Above the mouth, eyes appeared, glaring fragments torn from the round moon.

"When I said it might be an interesting voyage," Lonn grumbled. "I was not expecting this."

Above them, the chanting stopped.

* O *

Amlina held the talisman and dagger before the burning eyes of the Devourer.

"Nargassa Hulgar, Beast of Valgool. I am the one who summoned you. By the magic of the three moons in baleful alignment, by the magic of blood and death, I command that your power bend to my will."

The eyes widened, the starry jaws fell open, and the Devourer roared with primal rage. The sound vibrated Amlina's bones. A voice of menace boomed inside her skull.

"What are you? What are you to summon me?"

She shouted the answer. "I am one who knows your name. I am one who knows the laws. I am one who offers blood and death. By these offerings, I compel you."

"You are no priestess. You are a stranger here."

"I am a witch of Larthang, but I know your name and the laws. I have summoned you, I offer blood, and so I command you!"

The terrible roar sounded again. Amlina stood firm, her garments fluttering in the wind. Now was the moment of testing. Had all her workings correctly aligned the forces? Would her will be strong enough? The roar continued, shaking the stone below her feet, rattling her knees. Pain erupted at the center of her skull. Against her will, she closed her eyes. She seemed to be falling.

But then the shaking stopped, the monstrous rage subsided. Amlina opened her eyes to find herself still standing. The voice in her head was subdued.

"What is your will of me, foreign witch?"

Gasping, she answered. "As in the ancient days of Valgool, by the rites of blood magic, I invoke the Mirror that is proof against all harm."

"The Mirror Against All Mishap? That construct has a confined span, and requires a sacrifice commensurate to the intent. What is your intent, witch?"

"The same that I offer." Amlina pointed the knife at the eidolon. "The death of a queen in exchange for the death of a queen."

"But does the sacrifice offer herself willingly?"

Amlina glanced at Meghild's face. "Now is the moment, my queen."

Staring at the Devourer, Meghild hissed with defiance. "I be Meghild, Queen of Tribe Demardunn. To aid this witch in her purpose, I offer my death willingly to your jaws. The death of a queen in exchange for the death of a queen."

The Devourer's defiant roar sounded again, reverberating in the night. But then the voice grumbled in defeat. *"So. The moons are aligned and the blood is offered. Call then my power, witch. I cannot refuse."*

Amlina thrust up her arms, grasping the talisman and knife. "By blood and death and sacrifice, in the triple light of the moons, I summon your power into this world, all protection for myself and my comrades, to achieve our intent, the death of a queen for the death of a queen. So must it be!"

As she screamed the last words, the eidolon's light flickered out. Meghild's head flew into the air and vanished into the glittering mouth. The Devourer exploded in a blinding flash that rolled down over the pyramid.

Below, the earth rumbled and the city shook.

* O *

Glyssa saw the Devourer expand into a burst of light. Next moment the whole world was convulsing. She stumbled, dropping her torch, bracing herself against the shuddering stone.

The quake lasted a dozen or more gasping breaths. When it ended, the pyramid was still again. The sky was empty except for stars and the two visible moons. The night hung deathly quiet.

Glyssa stooped to pick up her torch. She touched the Mirror talisman suspended over her heart. It no longer throbbed with power. At the corners of the pyramid, Draven and Lonn stared at her, uncertain.

Amlina descended the steps. She walked unsteadily, looking frail and weary.

"Are you all right?" Glyssa asked.

The witch nodded. "It is done. Let us leave this place."

Lonn and Draven motioned to the others, who came around the corners and drew near.

"It's over?" Glyssa asked the witch. "I don't feel any different."

"I know," Amlina said quietly. "I hope Meghild's sacrifice was not in vain."

Cautiously, they made their way down the steep stairs. Below them, the plaza lay dark and quiet. But as they neared the bottom, Glyssa saw the ghost dogs, throngs of them skulking near the base of the pyramid, red eyes glaring, mouths slavering.

Glyssa and Amlina stopped on the bottom step, the others clustered behind them with blades and torches held high.

"We'll have to fight our way through," Lonn muttered.

"No," the witch held up her hand. "Wait here."

Before anyone could react, Amlina darted onto the pavement, into the crowd of ghost dogs.

"No!" Draven shouted.

The creatures flung themselves at the witch, howling and snapping. But in the instant before the first of them touched her, a tingling noise erupted in the air and space itself tore open. Glyssa stared at a writhing tumult of bodies, flailing limbs, spraying blood.

The ghost dogs were attacking each other. It lasted only seconds. Then the creatures were howling in fear, snarling, skulking away into the dark. Six of them lay on the pavement, either writhing with death wounds or already dead.

Amlina stood in the center of the carnage, perfectly still and unharmed.

PART THREE
TO TALLYBA THE TERRIBLE

TWENTY-FOUR

The catacombs of Tallyba stretched underground beneath the various warrens of the city. The oldest and deepest were under the citadel, where hundreds of generations of priests and nobles lay entombed. Below the temple precincts, a maze of crumbling stairs and curving tunnels gave access to the most ancient crypts. Beryl threaded her way through the maze alone, walking erect and fearless. She had no need of lamp or torch, as a gem set on her turban cast an eerie red light that pulsed with her heartbeat. Rats and roaches skittered away on her approach. The stale, dusty air smelled of myrrh and corruption.

Seven days had passed since her wounding by the barbarian's sword. The blade must have been imbued with magic. It had taken Beryl this long to regain her full vitality—even after consuming the blood of four sacrifices. In her weakened state, Beryl had lacked the energy to weave designs that might have prevented the forging of the Mirror. Instead, she had devoted her efforts to learning what she could about the protective ensorcellment. She had found nothing about it in her library, and only scant mention in the temple archives. Now the quest had led her to the catacombs.

She entered a circular chamber lined by vaults. Stone faces of ancient priests stared down from carved ossuaries. Beryl strode to the exact center of the floor. From her robe she removed a silver vial and an ebony wand topped by a fist-sized ruby. After tracing arcane symbols in the air, she pointed the ruby at the wall, emptied the oil on the stones, and cried out an invocation.

"Hep-satt Lozari, Priestess of Rog, I raise your shadow from the shadows. Let this oil loosen your tongue. Let this light compel your speech. I, Beryl Quan de Lang, Supreme Ruler of Nyssan, command you."

From red light and crimson shadows, a figure like smoke slowly condensed. It drew near, a tall woman in clerical robes, with a wizened and glowering visage. She spoke in an archaic dialect from before the Age of the World's Madness.

"You are not of Nyssan. Who are you to disturb my long rest?"

"One with the power to compel you." Beryl gave the wand a slight twist.

The ancient ghost stiffened. "Agh! You have called me before. I remember—Usurper!"

Beryl twisted the wand harder, making the ghost hiss in pain.

"What do you want of me?"

"Knowledge of the Nagaree."

In the ghost's time, two nations had vied for supremacy in Nysan—Tallyba on the southern coast, and the Nagaree Empire in the highlands. The Nagaree were known as mighty wizards, and mages such as Lozari had been constantly occupied learning and countering their ensorcellments.

"What of them?"

"I must know about one of their designs—the Mirror Against All Mishap."

The face lowered in puzzlement. But then the eyes grew wide "Yes, I remember. You seek to create the Mirror? It will not be easy."

"No. I must learn how to counter its magic."

Now the eyes narrowed in malice. "So, you have an enemy who wields the Mirror? Then you are surely doomed."

Beryl gave the wand a violent turn, making the ghost cry out. "Tell me what magic can destroy the Mirror."

Lozari's shade writhed and yowled. "There is none! By its nature it reflects all power cast against it."

"Don't take me for a fool! Your mages must have discovered something, or Tallyba itself would have fallen." Deliberately, she screwed the air with the wand.

"Stop, stop!" the ghost screamed. "I will tell you."

"Well, then ...."

"I spoke truth. The Mirror casts back all power. What was found in the end to defeat it was the *absence* of power."

"Elaborate."

"Very well ... How do you render a mirror useless? By removing all light, so there is nothing to reflect. Our mages discovered they could cast a void into the minds of those who carried the Mirror talismans. The void drained all magical energies from their vicinity. They perceived unnatural darkness and wandered in confusion until the Mirror expired."

"Remarkable. I knew the Mirror must have a limited span. How is that determined?"

"Ah ... They learned that it lasts exactly as many days as the initial ensorcellments preliminary to its casting."

Beryl smiled. "That is good. Very good." She gave the wand a final twist, and the ghost gasped in agony. "Should I have occasion to summon you again, dead priestess, you will remember this pain and know to treat me with better courtesy."

Winding her way back through the levels of the necropolis, the Archimage contemplated what she had learned. The Mirror had a limited lifespan. Beryl believed she could estimate the time period based on when she had first sensed the magical disturbance in the far north—and suspected it was Amlina's doing. More importantly, the Mirror's protection was vulnerable to the *absence* of power, a withdrawal of energies. Beryl could use that knowledge to set a trap for Amlina and her followers.

No—*several* traps. Beryl would not underestimate Amlina again.

* O *

The torms arrived on the eighth day as promised and carried Amlina and her companions away from Valgool. They spent one night feasting at the torms' high place of ritual, where the witch expressed her gratitude with more gifts of coins and silver chain. But despite prolonged and vociferous invitations from the winged people, she insisted her party could not stay longer. Next morning, torm hunters flew them once more into the sky.

Three days later, they were set down in the hills behind Blaal's Landing. Izgoy and his people were amazed to find the travelers strolling back into the village. The headman had never expected them to return. Fortunately, erring on the side of caution, he had kept his promise to leave the *Phoenix Queen* unmolested and to care for the windbringers. After a joyful reunion with Kizier, the travelers purchased new provisions, loaded the boat, and set off that same afternoon. In just five more days they arrived in Borgova.

It was the first day of the second month of Second Summer. Of the expected lifespan of the Mirror, 47 days remained.

Despite Amlina's best efforts to enchant or bribe the master boatwrights of the town, none would agree to refurbish the *Phoenix Queen* and make it sea-worthy in less than three days. In the end, scowling, Amlina agreed to a contract with the same Master Bruel who had converted the boat for the river.

As they unloaded their gear, the witch reflected on how drained and weary her friends looked. After the long and arduous journey, three days for rest and comfort was perhaps a worthwhile delay. So Amlina opened the bag of gold coins Queen Meghild had left her. After reserving rooms in the best inn in town, she visited a clothier shop and had the entire party measured for new garments. While a cohort of tailors cut and stitched, the travelers passed the afternoon in the bath house, soaking in warm and scented water.

That evening, they feasted in a private alcove off the main dining room of the inn. The Iruks were dressed in new tunics and trousers of light linen, Amlina in a gown of yellow silk. The party dined on baked lamb and fish, roasted vegetables, apples, fresh bread, and plenty of dark ale.

Gazing around the table in the lamplight, the witch gauged the mood of her companions. The Iruks were joyful and contented, relishing the comforts and luxuries of the town with simple, unabashed delight. More, she sensed how they reveled in their mutual connection, the mysterious klarn-soul. For all the time Amlina had spent in their company, she still could not fully fathom the klarn, how it allowed them to share the deepest elements of themselves.

Seated next to her, Draven reached under the table and took her hand. She smiled at him. Of course, the love she felt for Draven was also a spiritual connection, a joining similar perhaps to the klarn. Amlina treasured the thought that someday, she and Draven would have the chance to explore that love.

Wilhaven sat at the far end of the table. Of all the group, he alone was subdued. Since Meghild's death he had been in mourning, solemn and morose, though he had fulfilled the duties of sailor and physician with his usual aplomb. Today he had purchased new harp strings, and now he threaded them, tightened pegs, and frowned as he tested the notes.

"Will you sing for us?" Glyssa asked him.

Glyssa. Amlina pondered again the remarkable heart of the Iruk woman, her gentle caring for everyone, her gift for smoothing relationships and binding the group together.

"Not tonight," Wilhaven answered. "My mood is not musical."

"Oh, but you should!" Eben declared. "Last time you had the whole room clapping and stamping."

The bard glumly shook his head. "Not tonight. Your pardon."

Eben shrugged and reached for his tankard.

Amlina glanced over to find Glyssa's eyes fixed on her. "And how is *your* mood tonight, Amlina?"

The witch responded with a brittle laugh. Glyssa too was observing the ebb and flow of feelings in the group, and had turned the tables on her.

"Grateful," the witch said, squeezing Draven's hand. "To be blessed with such company."

Glyssa tilted her head, eyes searching. "And yet, still troubled?"

The witch considered. "Perhaps ... I know this delay is good, that all of us need the rest. Yet I worry about the time remaining—how many days the voyage will take, how long our protection will last."

"Well, we Iruks have a saying," Lonn grunted. "You can't spear tomorrow's yulugg today."

Amlina joined their laughter. "Sound advice, to be sure."

"Is there something else?" Glyssa pressed her.

Amlina hesitated. Her witch's training taught her not to dwell on worries counter to her intentions, and never to speak of them without good reason. Thoughts and speech had power and could actualize undesired outcomes. Yet, she had come to feel such a bond of trust with these friends, and to know the relief of sharing her fears. Besides, they had a right to know.

"I am wondering about Beryl. I am sure she knows we have forged the Mirror. By now she likely knows what it means and is seeking to devise countermeasures. I have no idea what they might be, but not knowing, waiting for her to strike—this makes me uneasy."

"Nah! That's just another yulugg to kill tomorrow," Karrol said, reaching for the pitcher.

* O *

Swallowing her fear, Zenodia marched across the throne dais. One step ahead moved her superior Toulluthan, heavy shoulders slumped in his orange gown as he reluctantly followed the Archimage. At the conclusion of the Council meeting, Beryl had casually ordered the temple treasurer and his assistant to accompany her to the Bone

Tower. This of itself was ominous. Beryl rarely brought courtiers to her sanctuary, and then only for secret purposes. Many times, the invitees did not return.

In the month since Zenodia had attended the Archimage's salon, Beryl had shown no sign of special interest in her. Zenodia had kept her head down, focused on her duties and on watching the current of events in the temple and the court—alert for any sign, any hint of an opportunity that might help her achieve her sworn purpose, the overthrow of the tyrant. Now she wondered if Beryl knew of her secret enmity, if a lifetime of practice at hiding her true self had been insufficient after all, if today Beryl meant to put her to death.

They passed under a tall, pointed archway and into a corridor that receded into the distance. Without breaking stride, Beryl waved a finger over her shoulder. The gesture caused iron doors to roll from within the portal and clang shut. Toulluthan's bald head swung around at the noise, and Zenodia glimpsed rigid apprehension on his face.

"Do not be alarmed," Beryl called as she moved down the hallway. "I have just a few matters to address with you both."

The obese temple treasurer had to hasten to keep up with her. Zenodia walked deliberately behind, arms folded in her sleeves. The walls were formed of panels that gleamed like pearls. Rumor said that each panel was a door only Beryl could open, and that beyond lay vaults containing piles of gold, silver, and jewels—all the vast treasures the usurper had stolen.

Crossing beneath another arch, they walked into a courtyard paved with granite. The massive Bone Tower loomed ahead; Zenodia had never seen it so close. With a twinge of dread, she allowed her glance to slide up the rugged surface. The mortar joining the stones was said to contain the crushed bones of rivals Beryl had slain in her ascent to power. Twelve sentries were stationed at the tower gate, thralls with the bodies of muscular soldiers and the heads of lions.

Armed with halberds and scimitars, they stood frozen and stared with blank eyes.

Reaching the gate, Beryl turned. "Zenodia, come with me. Toulluthan, you wait here."

The treasurer stiffened, his shocked eyes raking over the lion-headed men. "Wait here, majesty?"

"Yes."

Zenodia sensed the delight Beryl experienced at the man's terror. With a mute glance at Toulluthan, she followed the Archimage into the tower. They crossed a cavernous chamber. A stairway on the wall spiraled upward. But Beryl led her to the center of the floor, beneath a round aperture in the distant ceiling. The queen turned to Zenodia, holding a black glass bead between forefinger and thumb.

"This little trinket is the easiest way to ascend. You will need to hold my hand. Do you understand?"

"Yes, majesty."

Staring into her eyes, Beryl spoke a few words in a foreign tongue and dashed the bead on the floor. Silver light exploded. Trembling, Zenodia grasped the queen's offered hand. With a jerk she was pulled off her feet. Together, she and Beryl rose into the air, twisting on a spiral of light.

Zenodia was awed by the sensation of flying, but even more by the touch of Beryl's icy hand and the terrible gleam in her eyes. They rose through the floor above, drifted sideways, and settled on their feet. Gulping, Zenodia looked around at the upper chamber, the Archimage's lair.

The monkey-like treeman scampered across the floor, jabbering with excitement, and jumped into Beryl's arms. "Hello, Grellabo." Beryl cooed and stroked the familiar's bald head. The treeman looked at Zenodia and hissed through yellow teeth.

Cradling the treeman, Beryl tilted her head for the priestess to follow. The chamber was crowded with shelves and tables strewn with books and magical apparatus. Openings in the curved wall led to other rooms and shadowy alcoves. Lamps burned in colored globes, and thrall servants stood stiff and unmoving.

Beryl led the way onto a parapet. From here, Zenodia could see the whole of Tallyba, all the way down to the harbor.

"An impressive view, don't you think?"

"Yes, majesty."

Beryl smiled. "But of course you are wondering why I brought you here. In fact, I have a little experiment. Wait here."

Beryl pivoted and went back inside. Zenodia gripped the balustrade, a painful dread writhing in her belly. The pavement of the courtyard stretched some 200 feet below. Would Beryl cast her down—or, more likely, force her to jump?

When the Archimage returned, she was clad in a wide-sleeved cloak of silver and black. "You might recognize this garment," she said. "It is the Cloak of the Two Winds, one of the most powerful artifacts in the world—if not *the* most powerful. In addition to the purposes it was made for, it can be used as a source of raw energy. Now, my experiment today does not require nearly so much energy. But this is a test for proving the design. Later castings will need to be potent indeed."

Zenodia stared, holding her head low.

Beryl nodded, thin-lipped. "You wonder why I should tell you all this. The fact is, I have decided to replace Toulluthan. Oh, he is able enough, but his constant wheedling and carping in the council wearies me. You, on the other hand, seem capable of performing your duties with a diffidence I find refreshing. As of today, Zenodia, I am appointing you treasurer of the temple."

Zenodia replied with a constricted throat. "Thank you, majesty."

"Well deserved. I have had my eye on you for some time. So that brings us back to Toulluthan. Since he has outlived his usefulness, I will allow him to assist in my experiment. And I want you to witness. I am sure you will find it a valuable lesson."

Beryl stepped to the edge of the parapet and raised her arms, the wide sleeves of the magic cloak hanging down. She uttered a string of phrases, again in the foreign tongue—which Zenodia took to be Larthangan. Beryl pointed a finger toward the base of the tower and whispered the name, "Toulluthan." Then she extended her arms, palms pointed at the ground. Light rippled along the threaded designs of the cloak. Beryl whispered again: "Kill him."

From far below, Zenodia heard Toulluthan scream. Next moment, he stumbled into her line of sight, fleeing away from the tower. Two of the lion thralls marched after him, curved swords held high. The terrified priest lumbered and howled. But rather than run for the open portal in the far wall, he blundered around the courtyard in a confused course, changing and reversing direction, as though unable to find an escape route. The lion-headed guards followed in relentless, unhurried pursuit.

Beryl leaned over the parapet, her face a mask of vicious excitement. "His brain is befuddled, you see? He cannot find his way."

Zenodia could hardly bear to watch, yet could not tear her eyes away. At last the exhausted priest fell sprawling on the pavement. He was just able to rise to his knees before the thralls closed on him. He lifted his hands in supplication to the tower, screaming for mercy.

Zenodia turned her face away. The screams rose to a frenzy, then died off amid the wet noises of blades chopping flesh and bone. When she forced herself to look again, the thralls were marching away, the butchered remains of Toulluthan lying in a widening pool of blood. Breathing hard, Beryl faced her, flushed and triumphant. Zenodia dropped to her knees and pressed her head to the floor.

"Congratulations on your promotion," Beryl said. "I know you will serve me well. And I am sure you will remember today's lesson and take it to heart."

Zenodia dared not lift her head. "Yes, majesty. I will remember."

TWENTY-FIVE

"Mind is all. When sensation is eliminated and thoughts are stilled, the personal mind merges with the Deepmind, the Formless One, in which all forms and forces originate, and to which they return ... "

Amlina read aloud from the *Canon*, translating so Glyssa could understand. They sat in the witch's cabin on the *Phoenix Queen*, eight days out from Borgova. Glass lamps burned on the floor between them, arranged in a star pattern with a spinner at the center. The salt air held a tinge of incense smoke.

"Yes, that much I understand," Glyssa said. "But how does that help me move the spinner?'

The spinner was a thing of brass, with fan-like blades set on a spindle. Normally, a small candle or lamp was set below the blades, the heated air rising to turn the device. As an elementary step in her training, Glyssa was attempting to turn the spinner with her mind.

"All forces emerge from the Deepmind," Amlina explained. "To the degree that you can merge your mind with the Deepmind, you can influence or control the energies that it continually pours forth."

"I suppose that is reasonable," Glyssa said. "But it does not *feel* like it can be true. We Iruks are taught to move things with our muscles, not our minds."

Amlina let out a sigh. "It is a difficult lesson for a novice."

But it was more than that. The entire Larthangan mentality was alien to Glyssa. Even translating the *Canon* to Low Tathian was a challenge, bound to alter some of its meaning. And to Glyssa, Tathian was itself a foreign language, a foreign way of thinking. As Buroof had once pointed out, training the Iruk required translating

Larthangan knowledge and modes of thought for a totally different culture.

"But you are talented, Glyssa. You have shown me that again and again. Do you remember when you helped me call the North Wind?"

"Well, yes," Glyssa replied. "But that was different. I was mostly following your lead. And we chanted, and I envisioned the cold fire ... "

"Indeed, that was an example of a *formulation*—what the Tathians might call a *spell*. That art requires creating a mental construct; imbuing it with power through singing, gesture, and visualizing; and then releasing it all at once. This exercise with the spinner is a lesson in the more basic art, called *quon-xing* or pure shaping. It requires the immediate, direct focusing of thought to create effects in the world."

Glyssa's look was earnest, but unsure.

Amlina offered an encouraging smile. "Try again."

The Iruk shrugged and stared at the spinner. Amlina shut her eyes and withdrew her thoughts, so as not to influence the effort. After twenty breaths, she looked again. Glyssa glared unhappily at the spinner, which remained stubbornly motionless.

"I think that's enough for today," Amlina said. "But do not be discouraged. Learning these arts is difficult, and power emerges only when it is ready. Many accomplished witches have been known to take a year or more of fixed effort to master the spinner."

Glyssa shifted her legs. "Who knows where we will be a year from now?"

"That is true." Amlina let her shoulders sag. "I suppose, if we survive Tallyba and all goes as we hope, you and your mates will want to return home."

Now Glyssa's eye lit with a touch of mischief. "I'm not so sure of that. Draven, I think, will want to be with you."

Amlina lowered her glance. "That would be my wish as well."

"As for the rest of us, we haven't talked about it much. Karrol and Brinda want to return to the Iruk seas, I'm sure. But who knows about Eben? And, Lonn,"—here she smiled—"he will want to be with me, I think."

"And where will that be, Glyssa?"

"I am not sure. I started training with you to heal my heart, and you have helped me greatly. It's not completely healed; maybe it never will be. But I feel there is a bond between us, Amlina—something like the klarn-soul, and yet very different. And I think there is still much you can teach me." Her mouth twisted. "If I can ever get this cursed spinner to move."

Amlina reached over and grasped her hand. "You will, my dear friend, if you persist."

After Glyssa left the cabin, Amlina straightened her spine and sought meditation. She was heartened at the thought that Draven and Glyssa might stay with her, that they might have a time of peace and joy when this voyage was over. But then thoughts of what they faced besieged her, disrupting the pleasant serenity.

Since sailing from Borgova, Amlina had sensed Beryl working in the Deepmind, fashioning some grand ensorcellment, some design meant to impede their voyage, to keep them from reaching Tallyba. Each day the energies of that unknown design seemed to coalesce, somewhere ahead, but drawing ever closer.

And yet, Amlina sensed with certainty that she *would* reach Tallyba. Over and over a vision recurred in her deepsight—the same vision she had glimpsed when she first decided to seek the Mirror. In that vision, Amlina faced the Archimage one final time, in the upper chamber of the Bone Tower.

Lately Amlina had also seen Glyssa there—and come to suspect that the Iruk had some crucial role to play. Amlina could not say why, but it seemed imperative to concentrate on Glyssa's training, to fortify her for that final confrontation.

* O *

On the tenth day of sailing, the *Phoenix Queen* left the Bay of Mistral and headed south along the coast of Near Nyssan. In these latitudes, the weather of Second Summer was warm and windy, perfect for sailing. Over the days that followed, Glyssa and her mates spotted numerous freighters and galleons plying along the coast. Tathians and Nyssanians had mingled here for centuries, creating a mixed and prosperous land of city states. The Iruks would have liked to put in at one of the thriving ports, but Amlina was anxious to avoid delays. Instead they stopped for just a few hours at a fishing village, to replenish water and supplies.

Glyssa divided her time between her duties crewing and bailing the boat, and studying with Amlina. She continued the daily practices of meditation and moving the cold fire through the nerve centers of her body. She spent hours in the witch's cabin, practicing the formation of mental constructs, singing in the strange, high-pitched Larthangan language, and attempting—still with no success—to move the spinner with her mind. She listened attentively as the witch read from her small red book about the basics of the *Five Revered Arts of Magic*. In addition to formulation and pure shaping, there was deepseeing, trinketing, and one called *weng-lei* or magical combat. Glyssa found that one most alluring, as she could relate the principles to the disciplines of Iruk sword-craft.

That vague connection comforted her. Increasingly, she felt divided within herself, between her normal life with the klarn and the strange, luminous world of witchery. The more Glyssa practiced with Amlina, the more a restless hunger stirred in her, to somehow bring those two lives together, to make herself feel whole.

* O *

A gray curtain hung over the sea. Glyssa spotted it from her perch on the masthead, when taking a turn as lookout. Dark and opaque, it wavered in the distance and then vanished, like some ominous mirage. They were sailing off a barren coast of black cliffs called the Cape of Moloc, 21 days since leaving Borgova. Of the lifespan of the Mirror, just 22 days remained.

Next day the curtain appeared again. Now, it lingered on the horizon, dark and forbidding. As the *Phoenix Queen* approached, it seemed to recede, as though beckoning them on. Standing with Lonn at the helm, Glyssa sensed an evil power.

"I don't think it's a fog," Eben called from the lookout. "No witchlight that I can see."

"Nothing natural about it." Lonn turned to Glyssa. "You'd best tell the witch."

Glyssa ran forward and knocked on the hatchway. Presently, Amlina crawled from the cabin, blinking and dazed as though roused from a trance. After a quick look at the horizon, she shook herself and hurried aft. Glyssa followed, past where Karrol was stationed at the lines and Wilhaven manned a bailing pail.

"Do you know what it is?" Glyssa asked.

"Not exactly," Amlina said as she climbed to the rear deck. "But I think I know who sent it."

"Aye. I've never known the like of it," Wilhaven called after them. "A thing of sorcery, there can be no doubt."

"Well then, the Mirror should protect us," Glyssa said. "Shouldn't it?"

Standing at the rail, Amlina stared intently at the horizon. "I don't know."

After a quick glance at Lonn and Glyssa, the witch knelt before the windbringers. She touched Kizier's stalk, and his eyelid rose.

"Kizier, my friend," Amlina said. "What can you perceive of the darkness on the horizon?"

The single eye peered into the distance, and Glyssa thought it widened with worry. "Nothing. Some kind of barrier ...?"

"Can you tell if it stifles the wind?"

"I cannot sense anything," the bostull answered after a moment. "It seems to swallow mental energy, and emit nothing."

Amlina nodded grimly. "My perception as well."

"Should we tack west?" Lonn asked her. "Try to sail around it?"

Amlina's mouth twisted. "I hate to risk the delay. But yes, I suppose you had better try that."

Lonn called out the order to trim sail and leaned on the tiller. The boat veered to starboard, heading away from the land. Their speed increased on the new course, hull and outriggers bounding over choppy waves.

But soon Glyssa saw that the mysterious curtain also moved, streaming along the horizon until it hovered once more dead ahead.

"Resume our former course," the witch said. "We cannot avoid it."

Lonn gave the order to come about, and once more they sailed with the land to port. The gray curtain still loomed before them, and now it no longer receded. Instead, it rose higher, and stretched to east and west to swallow the horizon. As the boat approached the weird barrier, twilight spread over the sky. The sealight faded, the water turning dull and metallic. Worse, the wind dropped off.

Amlina knelt in front of the three bostulls. "Kizier, can you and your comrades summon any wind?"

It took a few moments for his eye to open. His voice sounded dull and lethargic. "Amlina, I am sorry. It is hard to even speak. Our mental focus is draining away."

Presently, strands of darkness drifted over the cranock. The air grew cold and clammy, with a faint smell like rotting fish. Numb with fear, Glyssa watched Amlina, who stared into the gloom as though trying to pierce its mystery.

The gray vapor enveloped the boat. Glyssa could no longer see the prow. The sail hung limp, the hull creaking forlornly as it rocked in the water

"Now what do we do?" Karrol called fretfully.

"Lower the sail," Lonn ordered. "We'll hoist it again when the wind comes." He turned to Amlina, uncertain. "If it comes?"

The witch stared dolefully as the yardarm came down. "This is Beryl's sending. I am sure of it."

"Her magic is stronger than the Mirror?" Glyssa asked.

"She has found some way to counter it. I don't know how. I will have to study the problem." She took a breath and seemed to gather herself, then gripped Lonn and Glyssa's wrists firmly. "We will get out of this. I know we will. I have an appointment with Beryl in Tallyba."

But as Amlina stepped back toward her cabin through the clammy mist, her figure looked small and frail, and Glyssa wondered if she was truly as confident as she pretended.

* O *

Some hours later—Glyssa could not tell how many—the witch came back on deck. It might have been sunset, or even night; there was no way to tell in the perpetual gloom. Water lapped gently around the hull, the sea lacking both wind and wave. The entire crew was awake, Eben bailing amidships, the others on the rear deck, muttering dispiritedly to one another. The air was dank and cold, with the fetid rotting smell.

As she climbed the steps, Amlina's face emerged from the murk, looking pale and haggard. Draven stood and hugged her.

"Anything?" Glyssa asked.

"Not yet," the witch answered, taking a seat by the rail. "Can you bring me something to eat? I need to fortify myself."

"Of course." Draven moved down the steps to the food locker.

"What have we gotten ourselves into?" Karrol demanded. "And how do we get out?"

Amlina looked at her and said nothing.

"Did you try the talking book?" Wilhaven asked.

The witch answered wearily. "Buroof is silent. All magic has been drawn away from us—including the magic of the book."

Draven brought her a platter of dried fish and hard bread, and a tin cup of water. The witch ate in silence, her gaze wide and blank.

"It's not only magic," Glyssa said suddenly. "Remember what Kizier said about his mental focus being drained? I think it's happening to all of us. It's hard to think, like we are adrift in some dream."

"I've noticed that too," Eben called from his bailing post. "It's hard to string my thoughts together. I thought it was only me."

Amlina nodded. "Magic is a mental activity. I do believe this ensorcellment works by dulling our minds."

Karrol started to speak, then bit back the words. She jumped to her feet and stamped off in frustration. The other Iruks looked at each other helplessly.

"Do not despair," Amlina said. "I am going to perform the *Bowing* ritual and enter deep trance. Some way out will present itself. All of you must hold to that thought. Remember, all else being equal, the Deepmind tends to manifest that which we consistently believe in and expect."

TWENTY-SIX

Glyssa sat in the crawlspace below the rear deck, eyes shut in trance, moving tendrils of cold fire up her spine. The more difficult it was to concentrate, the more grim resolve she applied. She repeated the practice each time she finished a watch.

Seven watches since Amlina entered deep trance—that meant it was three or three-and-a-half days since the darkness had settled over the boat. With no sighting of sun or stars, this was now her only way to reckon the passage of time.

Beside her, Lonn shifted and moaned in his sleep. The unending darkness, the relentless feeling of helplessness, were taking their toll on her mates. Glyssa could feel the courage of the klarn-soul fraying.

She clenched her jaw, returned to the meditation.

When the envisioned light rose to the top of her spine, she slipped into a dreamlike state. She recalled the shaman, Belach, and the last time she had met him in a vision. He told her of the second great enemy that she must face, *deceit*. The knowledge came to her that this unnatural darkness was a kind of deceit, a magic sent to deceive their minds ...

But what use was this knowledge?

To overcome deceit, Belach said, she must find *clarity*, must look not only with her eyes and mind, but with her heart. Glyssa pulled a long breath and settled her attention on her heart.

She saw herself on the *Phoenix Queen*, a season ago, when they first sailed across the ocean. She leaned on the rail of the foredeck, Wilhaven beside her, playing his harp and singing. All around them, the bright sea was alive with the bobbing heads and rolling bodies of the dolphin people.

An insight arose in her brain. *Magic had been driven away, mind suppressed. But there was still music and song. That was the way out.*

Glyssa opened her eyes, reviewing the thought. It made no sense, and yet she knew it must be true—knew it as one knows there is food in her stomach or blood in her veins. Amlina had taught her that deepsight sometimes came in flashes of inspiration. Perhaps this was one of those.

And she knew what she must do.

She reached for her boots in the dark and pulled them on. She crawled over Lonn and Draven and opened the hatch. Stepping onto the deck, she moved in the direction of Wilhaven's sleeping tent. Karrol and Eben leaned on the rails by the mast, and Brinda was barely visible at the helm.

"What is it, Glyssa?" Karrol asked.

"I'm looking for Wilhaven."

Karrol tilted her head. "He's moping up at the prow."

Glyssa made her way to the foredeck. She found the bard sitting under the carved figurehead, knees up, feet spread wide. He held the harp, his fingers moving over the strings silently in a way he had—playing but not playing. So far as Glyssa knew, he had made no music at all since Meghild's death.

He watched drearily as she approached. "Lady Glyssa. Would you take a drink?"

He offered his silver flask, filled she knew with brandy.

She knelt before him. "Thanks, but no. Wilhaven, I need you to play and sing."

He frowned with bewilderment. "And why would you be wanting that?"

"I don't know exactly, but you must."

He took a swig from the flask. "Have a drink instead."

"Please. This is important."

A MIRROR AGAINST ALL MISHAP

"Nay, I cannot. My heart is broken, Lady Glyssa. To see Meghild give her life—my noble queen! And to have it all come to naught. I fear I will never play again."

Glyssa snatched the flask from his hand and flung it away. "We are not defeated. Not yet! If you will sing, it may save us. It may get us out of this."

"Aye, and how could that be?"

"I don't know. But Amlina has been training me, and I think it is deepsight that tells me this. The enchantment that surrounds us, it snuffs out magic and confuses thought, but perhaps not music. Perhaps music can pierce it."

He stared at her, considering but not convinced.

Glyssa shrugged. "What have you to lose? And if your singing and playing can break the enchantment, would that not make a glorious chapter of your saga?"

A gleam sparked in his eye. "Aye, that it would."

Glyssa took his elbow and helped him to his feet. The bard straightened, placed the harp against his chest, ran his fingertips over the strings.

"But ... what shall I play?"

Glyssa touched a finger to her lips, reflecting. "Do you recall the songs you sang for the myro folk, when we crossed the northern ocean?"

Wilhaven's lips parted, eyebrows flicking up. "Aye ..."

With a nod, he began plucking strings and tightening pegs. While he tuned the instrument, Glyssa waited in anticipation, thrilled and fearful all at once.

Presently, Wilhaven cleared his throat and started to sing. His voice, ragged at first, grew steady and clear, the song a mournful ballad. Glyssa gazed out over the murky water, listening keenly, hoping.

When the song ended Wilhaven looked at her inquiringly.

"Keep singing," Glyssa said fervently. "Please."

The bard shrugged and began again.

In the midst of his third song, Glyssa heard it—an unmistakable twittering out on the sea. Wilhaven paused, stiffening in surprise.

"Go on," Glyssa cried. "Don't stop!"

He resumed with new energy, singing louder. Other voices answered from the darkness, calling, whistling, drawing near. Soon Glyssa could hear swishing and splashing as the creatures swam close to the boat. She quieted her thoughts and called to them with her mind.

Lovely myro, dolphin people, can you hear my voice?

Answers came like whispers from several quarters.

We hear you, priestess of the air.

But faintly. The waves of your voice are muffled.

Why do you float in this darkness?

Glyssa put all her strength into sending her thoughts. *We are trapped in the darkness. We need your help.*

We would not have entered the dark zone, but that we heard the air singer.

He is known to our people.

Some have heard him before.

Can you please help us? Glyssa asked. *Can you move our boat?*

While Wilhaven continued singing, a babble of debate erupted among the myro—clacking, whistling, wheezing. Glyssa caught snatches of the communication in her thoughts.

We have never done such a thing.

Of course we can.

It will hurt our noses.

We can push with our heads.

It will make a fine story!

Suddenly a jolt shook the hull, then another. The deck lurched underfoot.

"What is that?" Wilhaven asked.

Tell the air singer to continue.

A lively song to help our pushing.

"Keep on," Glyssa cried. "Play a spirited tune."

Understanding dawned, and the bard burst out laughing. He strummed hard and launched into an energetic song. The deck rocked again, and the boat edged forward, more and more of the myro pushing on the hull.

"What is happening?" Karrol called from amidships. "We are moving."

"The myro!" Glyssa exclaimed. "They have come to help us."

Head toward the land. She heard the instruction in her mind. *The dark is weakest there.*

Which way is that? she replied. *We cannot tell.*

This way! This way! They called from off the prow.

"Brinda," Glyssa shouted. "Steer to port."

We could do better, the myro said, *but it hurts our brows.*

Glyssa had a thought and leaped down to the main deck. "Ropes," she called. "Throw out lines so they can pull us."

Lonn and Draven had just come out on deck. After a quick explanation, they joined Eben and Karrol in securing lines and flinging them overboard. The lines grew taut as the myro seized them in their teeth, and then the boat surged forward as if running before a stiff wind.

The Iruks hooted and laughed with glee, Eben jumping up and down, Lonn lifting Glyssa off her feet.

Wilhaven continued to play and sing. Scores of myro flapped and splashed around the *Phoenix Queen* as it streamed over the water. After less than an hour, the darkness began to disperse. Ribbons of light appeared in the sky. The air freshened, taking on a clean, salty smell. The sea began to gleam, and daylight shone on the horizon ahead.

When the wind rose up and the last of the darkness had faded, Wilhaven at last put down his harp. The Iruks retrieved their lines, and Lonn, standing at the helm, shouted orders to raise the sail. Leaning over the prow, Glyssa silently gave thanks to the myro.

They rolled their bodies in the bright sea and chortled in answer.
We are happy to help you, air priestess.
We honor you and the air singer.
Farewell. Farewell.

As the dolphin people swam away, Glyssa turned to find Amlina, her face serene and bright with wonder. The witch placed both hands over her heart and bent forward at the waist.

"I bow to you with respect, Glyssa, mage of the Iruk people. This day, your magic has saved us."

* O *

Beryl stretched and yawned, her fingertips touching the smooth pearly shell of the headboard. The enormous bed, fashioned of white marble and pink scallop shell, nearly filled the crescent-shaped room, one of several that adjoined the central chamber of her tower.

Long ago, lovers had shared the bed with her, sometimes two or three at once. But when she grew tired or displeased with these consorts, she had them killed, and soon all potential lovers grew too terrified to be pleasing. Later, the Archimage had fashioned drogs, made-creatures, to act as her sexual partners. Drogs had the advantage of tirelessness, and could be shaped into any form she desired. But over the years, these too grew boring. As Beryl extended her lifespan indefinitely, she had gradually lost the appetite for carnal pleasures.

Witchery provided all the stimulation she wanted.

Seeing her awake, the treeman crawled up and nestled against her shoulder. Beryl smiled and caressed the smooth head. Without Grellabo, she sometimes thought, she might actually feel lonely.

"Good morning, my darling," she cooed. "How are you today?"

The creature hissed fretfully, issuing sounds that she could interpret as words. "I am worried, mistress. I fear what is to come."

"Ah, naughty Grellabo. Have you been peeking into my mind again?"

"Yes, mistress. I have seen that the despicable Amlina has escaped your dark sending."

Beryl's mouth turned down. "She has indeed. She and her friends are proving most difficult adversaries. But do not fear. That trap was only the first. It was meant to delay her, and in that it was successful." She petted the furry back. "Now she is running very short of time, and still has many days to sail."

"Will you use the Cloak to send winds against her craft?"

"No, my dear. Because of her Mirror, winds called by magic would rebound against my intention, would likely speed her progress. But no matter, even if the natural winds are favorable, even if Amlina and her henchmen reach Tallyba before their protection expires, I will trap them. Then they will be ours to play with."

"But mistress, I am still worried. What if Amlina reaches you *before* her ensorcellment fades?"

"I think that extremely improbable. And yet, I have learned from my previous overconfidence. I will be prepared. Should she reach the tower before her Mirror vanishes, a Gate of Spaceless Passage will be ready, to take us both to safety. Does that ease your concerns, my sweet?"

"Yes, mistress. I was foolish to think you might not be prepared."

"Think of it no more, my precious. Think instead how much fun we will have tormenting Amlina and her followers." Beryl sighed, letting her head sink into the pillow. "Such pleasure. Such delicious, prolonged enjoyment ..."

TWENTY-SEVEN

"Have you talked with Amlina about this?" Brinda asked. "Or Wilhaven?"

"Not yet," Glyssa said. "If the klarn does not agree, there would be no point."

The Iruks sat knee-to-knee in a circle, in the dry space between the mast and the rear deck. The boat was sailing close-hauled, westerly wind driving a long tack south, away from the coast. The mast leaned hard to starboard, and the sail bowed against the pale blue sky. When they needed to change course, the mates would jump up and haul on the lines. They dared not heave to and delay sailing, even for the little while it would take to hold a klarn meeting. By Amlina's reckoning, the Mirror Against All Mishap would last only another seven days.

Wilhaven had the tiller, standing within earshot. But they spoke in Iruk, so he would not understand. Glyssa had called the meeting to make an unusual proposal. She wanted to add Amlina and Wilhaven to the klarn.

"Well, I have no objection," Karrol said, surprising Glyssa with her ready agreement. "We have sailed with them both for months, and we're going into battle together. It seems only reasonable."

"It is not so simple," Eben said. "They are not Iruk. Will they even understand what it means to be klarn?"

"Certainly Amlina will," Draven answered. "Remember when we sat with her in the circle, when we were searching for Glyssa in Kadavel? We shared our minds with her then. And Wilhaven has observed us together. He will understand."

"I am unsurprised that you like the idea, Draven," Eben said. "You have wanted Amlina in the klarn for a long time. But here is another question: Will Amlina acknowledge Lonn as leader? Or will we have to elect Amlina to lead us?"

The mates pondered this, and then Brinda spoke. "I think Eben raises valid questions. Will Amlina defer to Lonn in a battle? If not, is she fit to lead us? We have to know who will be in charge when the fighting starts."

"I don't see that as a problem," Lonn said. "If the klarn voted to keep me as leader, I would follow Amlina's word, as we always have. Remember, we once vowed to obey her commands, unless they were plainly harmful to the klarn. That rule has worked till now, and I'd see no reason to change it. But I want to hear more from Glyssa. Why do you bring this up now? You seem to feel it's important."

Glyssa gnawed her lip, all eyes fixed on her. "Yes, that is fair. I've been thinking about it for a while. Perhaps it is partly my training with Amlina. I have come to love her, like a sister. But more than that, I feel a division in myself—in all of us—between our old lives as hunters, and what we have become since leaving the Polar Sea, all the changes that have come to us. My heart tells me we must not be divided within ourselves, when we face what lies ahead. I hope that bringing Amlina and Wilhaven into the klarn will ease that strain, help us all be stronger."

Glancing around, she sensed the klarn-soul stirring in her mates.

"I think you speak with wisdom," Brinda uttered softly.

Eben lifted a shoulder. "I still have reservations. But I will go along."

"That's good enough for me." Lonn reached out his hand, palm down. The others placed their hands over his in a pile. "We will offer Amlina and Wilhaven membership in the klarn," Lonn said.

"Agreed," each of them replied.

Lonn gave the order to bring the yard about, then went and relieved Wilhaven at the helm. When the boat was streaming on its new course, he and Eben and Glyssa spoke to the bard.

"Are you ready to reveal your secrets?" Wilhaven asked. "I could tell by your faces it is something momentous."

"And not to be taken lightly," Eben said.

"We have voted to invite you and Amlina to join our klarn," Lonn announced. "If you accept, we will have a ceremony, disband the klarn, and re-form it with you and Amlina as our mates."

The humor fled from the bard's expression, leaving it startled—and reverent. "Sure, and that would be one of the great honors of my life."

"You need to be clear on what it means," Eben said. "We each give a part of ourselves to the klarn, and it becomes part of us. That, and we swear an oath: for as long as the hunt lasts, to live for each other and die for each other if need be—valuing our mates' lives more highly than our own."

"Aye, you only convince me further of how noble is the honor." Wilhaven spoke in sober tones. "I have learned a deep respect for you all, as shipmates and comrades-in-arms. But more than that, I owe a debt to Lady Glyssa. When I wallowed in self-pity, it was she who reminded me of my duty as a bard, and so gave me back to myself."

He ended by bowing to Glyssa, touching one knee to the deck. She laughed and embraced him.

"Dear Wilhaven, we shall be most honored to have you as a mate."

"That leaves Amlina," Lonn remarked.

"Yes," Glyssa said. "Let me go and speak with her."

In a jubilant mood, she ran forward and rapped on the hatch to the witch's cabin. "It's Glyssa. I have something to ask you."

* O *

The brass spinner twirled in one direction, then the other. The erratic movement reflected Amlina's mind, swerving back and forth as she considered the Iruks' offer.

At first glance, the idea was outlandish. All of her training decreed that a witch did not mingle her psyche with others—except in formal rituals or carefully controlled circumstances. Certainly, a witch of Larthang did not risk her powers by joining her soul with barbarians.

But if Amlina had always strictly adhered to her training, she would never have left Larthang in the first place, would never have dared to invoke blood magic, to raise the Mirror Against All Mishap. She would never have allowed herself to fall in love with Draven, and would certainly not have followed him onto the Star Road. But that risk, taken for love, had made her stronger—she was sure of it. And when she looked at the prospect of joining the klarn, her deepsight *seemed* to indicate that this too would give her strength, would add a new well of energy to her resources.

Still ... the cautious, rational side of her mind insisted that it was madness, a dangerous, unnecessary step at this most critical time, when she must focus all her attention on preparing to face Beryl in Tallyba.

Frustrated, Amlina uncurled her legs. She crept to the shelf behind her bunk and pulled down the talking book. Setting it on the floor, she opened the cover.

"Buroof: I Amlina call you."

In the shadowy compartment, the pages glimmered. "I hear you."

"What knowledge do you have of the Iruk culture—specifically their hunting bands, known as *klarns*?"

"Only what I've gathered from interacting with your primitive friends. Almost nothing is recorded of them. One obscure source asserts that their race migrated to the South Pole in prehistoric times from the Western continent, that racially they derive from the same root stock as the peoples of Zindu and southern Larthang. That unsupported notion constitutes the sum of my knowledge."

Amlina frowned. "What about ... any records of Larthangan-trained mages participating in foreign spiritual communities, specifically ones that involved derivation of a group soul?"

"Well, there are many such examples, but—Oh! I think I see where this is leading. But surely, you cannot be *that* foolish."

Amlina laughed grimly. "By now you ought to have learned not to underestimate how foolish I can be."

"Yes. Point taken. So you plan to join their savage hunting band? Will you dress in fur trousers and carry a spear?"

"Never mind the ridicule. About the historic examples—"

"None are relevant. All extant records relate to cults and temples in *civilized* lands. In all of history, if any mages of Larthang have sought to blend their souls with savages, they have not troubled to document the folly. Once again, Amlina, you are contemplating unexplored realms of lunacy."

"Very well then," she said and closed the book.

She ought to have known that speaking with Buroof would not be helpful. Wincing with indecision, she glanced at the spinner.

The brass arms moved, first one way, then the other.

* O *

Zenodia placed the wicker cage on the smooth dark wood of the altar. Inside, the gray finch fluttered in agitation, as if sensing what was to come.

"Daughter," Mawu the high priestess said, "I ask you again to reconsider. Let me summon the oracle instead."

Zenodia tightened her jaw. "The oracle is too vague. I need plain answers now, to clarify my visions."

Just over a month had passed since she witnessed the murder of Toulluthan and was appointed to take his place. That day had changed everything for Zenodia. Driven by horror and cold hatred of the queen, she had quickly consolidated her power in the temple hierarchy, dismissing assistants who might question her authority, appointing submissive acolytes in their places. Already possessing a masterful knowledge of temple accounts, she had begun siphoning off money. Some of it she dispatched secretly to a mountain village, where her family lived in impoverished exile. The rest she accumulated, building a private treasury to fund her activities. Her new position on the council gave her access to all parts of the temple compound. Zenodia had researched ancient archives, reading dusty scrolls, educating herself in forgotten arts of divination. In the tombs below the temple, she had practiced necromancy, summoning the ghosts of priests and sorcerers from long ago. In disguise, she had visited a squalid, crime-ridden neighborhood, purchased forbidden drugs to expand her visions.

All of these efforts were focused on her goal, to understand the tyrant's powers, to find some way to defeat her.

In these endeavors, Zenodia had been reckless. It was only a matter of time, she knew, till her improprieties drew notice, till some informer brought them to the attention of the temple council or the queen. Zenodia didn't care. Visions told her that a single, real opportunity was coming—perhaps the only chance in her lifetime to overthrow the tyrant. She was more than willing to risk everything on one daring gamble.

She drew a knife and turned a drugged, feverish gaze on Mawu. "The ritual is not improper. My studies inform me that sacrifices exactly like this were done in the Temple of Tysanni in ancient times."

"True," the white-haired priestess answered, thin-lipped. "But we have not offered blood to the Moon for centuries, and never in this shrine."

The knife wavered in her hand. "If you are squeamish, I can do the ritual in my own apartments. I just thought it might go better here."

"No, child," Mawu bowed her head. "If you are determined, it is better done here. If things go badly, I might be able to protect you."

"Thank you, High Priestess."

Zenodia set the knife down beside the cage. She prepared a brazier, laying out charcoal and dried herbs from jars stored in a cabinet behind the altar. She sprinkled in tinctures from two vials she carried in her robe. After lighting candles, she touched fire to the brazier.

With the high priestess watching somberly, Zenodia raised her arms high.

"By the power of Tysanni, the silver moon, I summon Ol-Thum-Nyarr, the Spirit of Foxes. By smoke and blood, I call you here that you may aid me."

Zenodia had never before attempted to raise a Nature Spirit of such magnitude. But she desperately needed elucidation of her disparate, confusing visions. She poured another vial onto the brazier. Flame sizzled and flared, gushing gray smoke. Zenodia reached into the cage and groped until capturing the frantic bird. She pulled it from the cage and picked up the knife.

"Ol-Thum-Nyarr, Spirit of Foxes. By smoke and blood, I command your presence."

As the high priestess watched grimacing, Zenodia set the struggling finch down on the altar. She sliced off its head with a quick motion, then tossed both body and head into the fire. The tiny carcass sizzled, and the smoke grew thicker.

As Zenodia called the invocation a third time, a vaporous face appeared in the smoke—canine snout, pointed ears, feral, gleaming eyes.

"What do you wish of me?"

"Ol-Thum-Nyarr, I seek verification and explanation of visions I have seen."

"And what have you seen, priestess?"

"That the tyrant queen can be defeated, that one is coming to Tallyba who might kill her."

The eyes stared for ten beats of Zenodia's racing heart. "Yes, I see this also. But the matter is far from decided. Vast powers have been brought to bear—much greater than you might hope to wield. The scales totter and may dip either way."

"How can I influence the outcome?"

"Difficult ... But there might be a way. I see darkness descending on the tyrant's enemies. It is just possible your sight may pierce it ... But even that looks to be too little, or to come too late."

Zenodia grunted as though seized by pain. *She needed clearer information.* From her pocket she drew a tiny sphere, like a smoky pearl.

"What about this? It is a bead of levitation such as the Archimage uses. I have had it fashioned at great expense. One of my visions told me it would be needed, but I do not know why. I do not even know if it will work. Perhaps I can use it to sneak into her tower, to learn some secret or steal some weapon ...?"

After a pause, the fox spirit said: "No. Such an attempt will bring your death. If the bead has a use, I cannot see it. Too many threads are still unwoven."

"Is there nothing more you can tell me?"

"Nothing more. And now the blood is consumed, and so I am free." The floating face disappeared.

Zenodia screamed and pounded on the altar in fury. "Why can my guidance never be clear?"

Mawu stared in stricken silence, her wrinkled face wet with tears.

* O *

In the quiet night, the *Phoenix Queen* floated on a calm sea, a shifting plain of witchlight. The sky was black and rich with stars.

Rog, the small moon, rose full-faced in the east, while a waxing Grizna dwindled in the west.

Just five days remained till the Mirror would expire.

Yet Amlina had agreed to lowering sail and letting the craft drift for the time it would take for the Iruks to prepare and hold their ritual. She stood now on the foredeck with Wilhaven, waiting. Each of them held one of the Iruks' short spears. Behind the mast, the Iruks were gathered in a circle. One by one they had set down their spears, and now were pouring libations—releasing the klarn-spirit so it could be reborn.

Why had she finally decided to accept their offer? Amlina still wasn't sure. Perhaps it was speaking with Glyssa, realizing how important it was to her that all of them be joined together, how necessary for the mending of Glyssa's soul. Amlina had promised to do all she could to help Glyssa heal, and Glyssa had saved them all more than once on this voyage.

No, it wasn't only for Glyssa's sake. In her heart, Amlina wanted this too. She loved Draven, of course. But in the end, she had realized that she felt a bond of love for all of them—all the brave companions who had followed her on this mad and dangerous venture. Now at last the journey was nearing its end. Win or lose, triumph or death, she wanted them to face it as one.

Down on the main deck, the Iruks picked up their spears. Lonn beckoned. "Amlina, Wilhaven, come forward."

As they approached, the circle opened. Draven grinned and squeezed her hand. Lonn lifted the bowl of water. He spoke in Tathian.

"Now is the time for hunting. We come together to re-form our klarn. The oaths of six of us still abide. But you, Amlina of Larthang, and you, Wilhaven of Gwales, will you now take up your spears and join us with all your heart and courage?"

"Aye, so I will" Wilhaven answered gravely.

"Yes," Amlina affirmed.

"And do you now swear on your soul, and on the souls of your ancestors, to sail with us, to be as one hunter, one warrior, to cherish our lives above even your own, to stand with your mates, protecting them with all your strength and skill, binding their wounds before your own, sharing with them your last food and sip of water?"

"I do swear," they both said.

"And do you take this oath freely and with a true and open heart?"

"Yes," they said.

Smiling, Lonn offered the bowl to Amlina. "Then drink and give an equal drink to the klarn, and so become our mate."

She took a sip and poured a bit out on the deck. With her witch's sight, she saw the klarn-soul rise up from the spilled water, a tenuous, misty thing, seeping into her body.

Hands trembling, she passed the bowl to Wilhaven. He drank and poured and passed it on. As the bowl went from hand to hand, Amlina felt the klarn-soul growing in power, a clear and living presence. It frightened her at first, so alien and wild. But as she accepted it into herself, it become a source of comfort—a being composed of the friends she loved, their passions and strength, their spirits and courage.

Now it was part of her too.

When the bowl was empty, the Iruks picked up their spears. They tapped them in unison on the deck and chanted. Amlina and Wilhaven joined them, intoning in the Iruk tongue, the words they had been taught:

Through wind and sharp wave
Through ice and blood
We hold to the klarn
We are fearless
Many hands, one heart
Many eyes, one soul
Many spears, one hunter
We hold to the klarn
We are fearless

Lonn closed the ritual by knocking his spear haft hard on the deck three times. The Iruks whooped and hooted and embraced their new mates.

"The klarn is remade," Lonn announced. "Now let us go and kill our enemy."

TWENTY-EIGHT

Black clouds floated over Tallyba, interspersed with shafts of sunlight. The city was vast, sprawling along a marshy shore, rising gradually in piles of stone and brick, mounting at last to the distant citadel and its highest point, the Bone Tower. A hot breeze blew off the land, carrying a dank and swampy smell.

Amlina stood at the prow, one hand resting on the carved wing of the phoenix figurehead, the other gripping an Iruk spear. She was dressed in her witch's robes, dagger and trinkets hidden inside, the Mirror talisman on a chain around her neck.

The lifespan of the Mirror ended tonight.

For the past five days the winds had slowed the cranock, blowing steady and strong from the west. Kizier and the other bostulls had worked hard to shift the wind off the prow. Still, they had been forced to mostly sail close-hauled, the hours dragging on Amlina's nerves. She had done her best to make use of the time: weaving protections, renewing the magic imbued in her companions' weapons, forging new designs and trinkets that might or might not be of use.

Would all her preparations be enough? Would there be enough time?

A hand settled on her shoulder, making her jump.

"Steady," Draven laughed gently.

He and Glyssa had approached without Amlina hearing. They were dressed for battle: leathers, wool cloaks, swords and daggers at their belts. Each wore a Mirror talisman and carried a quiver of spears.

They both grinned at her. Remarkable how the Iruks seemed actually to relish danger. And yet, when she touched on the klarn-soul with her mind, she too felt a strange thrill of excitement.

How she had changed since fleeing from Tallyba. And now at last she had returned. *Would it be her end, or a new beginning?*

"Odd to see so large a harbor empty of ships," Draven muttered, scanning the distant wharfs.

Only barges and small craft were tied there, or rode at anchor in the shallows. Foreign traders had learned long ago to avoid Tallyba the Terrible, docking instead at port cities to the north or south. Amlina thought of the unfortunate Captain Troneck and his crew. Forced to land here by a gale, they had been captured and condemned to be sacrificed in the Temple of the Sun—until Amlina rescued them in her desperate flight from the city.

"Seems odder that no one's trying to stop us," Glyssa said. "Letting us sail straight into the harbor—it feels eerie."

The witch nodded slightly. "Beryl is toying with us, I think."

But halfway across the harbor, Eben sang out from the lookout. "Ships astern! Galleys!"

Amlina spotted them: a squadron of six, rounding the stone jetty that formed the southern arm of the port. Small warships of the type Beryl used to patrol her coasts, they came on hard under oars.

"Cutting off our escape?" Draven asked.

Amlina nodded again. "Toying with us, as I said." She cupped her hands and called to the helm. "Bring us about, Lonn. Head for the closest point on the shore."

Under Lonn's orders the *Phoenix Queen* changed course, pointing toward the northernmost quays, away from the course of the galleys. The patrol ships pursued at speed.

When the leading galleys drew within range, they launched missiles from arbalests mounted in their bows. Bolts with flaming tips arced across the gray sky. The first two fell harmless in the

Phoenix Queen's wake. The third and fourth headed straight for the cranock.

Before they could strike, a weird singing noise rippled over the water. The air wavered and warped, and next instant the bolts were flying back the way they had come. They struck the decks of two galleys and set them burning.

The Mirror Against All Mishap was still in force.

But the galley captains had their orders from the Archimage, and they dared not relent. Crossbowmen stationed on the decks fired clouds of arrows. Many splashed about the cranock's hull. Others turned in the singing air and flew back at the warships.

Along the rails, the Iruks hooted and cheered. Beryl's ships charged on without pausing.

When the cranock had sailed within a few dozen yards of shore, the foremost galley closed, aiming to ram them. Once more the air rippled with silvery waves. This time the twanging song of the Mirror merged with the screech and groan of cracking timbers. As the air churned the galley buckled, breaking apart. The *Phoenix Queen* coasted on toward the quay.

The Iruks lowered sail, and Lonn brought the helm about. The hull glided into the shallows. Karrol and Wilhaven handled long poles, maneuvering the boat till the port outrigger scraped the submerged steps of the quay. Then Amlina and her party went over the side, splashing through knee-high water, rushing up the stone steps. Pausing just long enough to secure bow and stern lines, they headed down the wharf.

The waterfront was deserted, with none of the normal traffic of workers and boatmen. A fortified wall separated the quays from the city. The witch and her party ran for the nearest gate.

The gate stood open, but just as they approached it, creatures rushed out—squat warriors with scaly green skin and bronze armor. They carried long, three-pronged spears.

"Are they men or—?" Lonn called.

"Drogs," Amlina answered. "The Mirror should protect us. But be ready."

The eight companions huddled close, leveling their spears. Growling and slavering, the wave of drogs charged—only to be flung back in a whirling tumult of shrieking noise, twisting bodies, and splattering green blood. Amlina and her friends waded forward, shielded by an impermeable bubble, while around them the chaos raged.

They reached the gate unscathed. Behind them, a score of drogs writhed on the ground in death throes. Their artificial flesh bubbled and hissed, melting into gray slime.

* O *

Across the city, beyond the citadel wall, Zenodia lay on her back, clutching damp sheets. She stared at the ceiling, her head splitting. For two days and nights she had lain here, sick with agitation, obsessed with drug-engendered visions. The promised events were imminent—she knew it. Yet she still had no direction, no idea what they were or what she could do …

Consistently, her thoughts led her back to the prophecy of the oracle. "The queen would thrive for a thousand years, unless three prevailed." One of those three was the "student who returned." Amlina, the Archimage's renegade apprentice: it had to be her.

Amlina was in the city. Was that a fragment of dream? A dubious wish? Or a truth perceived by occult channels? So hard to tell with all the sorcery she'd dabbled in, all the opium and *saenna* weed …

She had to find out.

Zenodia sat up. Her brain swam with dizziness, and she clutched her throbbing skull. With a grim, spiteful effort, she crawled from the bed and groped for her clothing.

* O *

"How can the streets be so empty?" Karrol demanded. "Is the city dead?"

"Not dead, enslaved," the witch answered. "If Beryl decreed that all people stay off the streets, no one would dare disobey."

"Sure, and why would she order such a thing?" Wilhaven asked.

Amlina strode on deliberately. "To make it easier to focus on us."

They were crossing a district near the waterfront, of narrow streets and twisting lanes. Amlina sought the most direct route to the citadel, navigating by sighting the Bone Tower whenever they reached an intersection or open square.

But after some time, a faint dread simmered at the edge of her mind. *The tower was not getting closer.*

"Well and it might be my aging eyes," Wilhaven said. "But it seems the day grows dimmer."

"No, you are right." Glyssa answered with a shiver. "It feels like that darkness we were lost in before, at the Cape of Moloc."

Amlina halted, casting her gaze over the sky. "It is the same. The galleys and the drogs were just feints, designed to lure us in. This is the real trap."

Even as she spoke, smoky tendrils appeared over the rooftops. The companions stood still in the middle of the road.

"This trap worked before," Lonn observed.

"And this time there are no dolphin people to rescue us." Glyssa turned a worried face to the witch.

"That is exactly why I expected this," Amlina said, "and prepared counter-measures. Let us hope and believe they will prove effective."

From a pocket in her robe she produced a small white candle. After much meditation, study, and discussions with Buroof, Amlina had arrived at a strategy. No effect in the Deepmind was absolute. Beryl's summoning of darkness had undermined the Mirror by draining power from its vicinity. But the ensorcellment itself would likely be vulnerable to overloading—by forces sent back along the mental conduit to strike at its source, the mind of the Archimage. The theory seemed sound. Whether Amlina's candles would work in practice was another matter.

"I need a flame to light this," she said.

The bard and the Iruks looked at each other, shrugging. No one had thought to bring flints and fibers.

They knocked on doors and shuttered windows. No one answered. In the end, Lonn and Karrol kicked down the door of a chandler shop and acquired a burning lamp with a glass globe. The witch apologized to the terrified shopkeeper and left a gold coin on the counter.

Back in the street, the air had chilled. Banks of grimy mist drifted over the pavement. Amlina lit the candle and raised it in the direction of the citadel.

"We must all focus our thoughts," she said. "Visualize our arriving safely at the Bone Tower."

She marched up the street with determined steps, her companions trailing behind. Amlina could feel the power of her design in the fluttering of the candle flame, streaming out in all directions, holding the malevolent darkness at bay. But she could also feel Beryl's mind on the far side of the barrier, pushing back with tremendous power.

The darkness thickened. Still, it hovered gray and tenuous, not black and impenetrable. Overhead, Amlina could still see daylight, still track the movement of the sun.

They had landed in the morning; it was now past noon.

The ground rose. The streets grew wider, bordered by larger, more prosperous buildings. The Bone Tower, looming in the gray haze, seemed to inch closer. The magic candle burned low, and Amlina lit another—hoping the six she had fashioned would be enough.

* O *

A MIRROR AGAINST ALL MISHAP

Night descended on Tallyba. Grizna hovered in the east and Rog, nearly full, climbed over the horizon. At midnight, with both moons past zenith, the Mirror Against All Mishap would die.

All day they had trekked through the empty streets, the chilling gloom. Always they seemed to be making progress, yet whenever the Bone Tower appeared, it hovered still far in the distance, tauntingly out of reach.

They stopped to rest at the edge of a plaza. Wearily, Amlina sat down on a low wall, the others squatting on the ground or leaning on spears. The stub burned low in the witch's hand. She took out the last of her candles.

"We're not going to make it in time, are we?" Glyssa asked.

The witch turned to her, startled.

"I'm sorry. I know you told us to focus on the belief that we would. But now I think we must face the truth."

Carefully, Amlina touched flame to the unlit candle. "You are right." She looked at the faces of her friends, her *klarn*—shadowy and grave in the shuddering light. "At the least, we must decide what we shall do if we *don't* arrive before the Mirror expires."

The seven warriors looked around at one another.

"What choice do we have?" Lonn asked with a shrug.

Amlina let the question hang unanswered.

"We still have our weapons," Draven said. "And you still have magic of your own, don't you, Amlina?"

She nodded, lips clenched. She *had* made other preparations. She had her dagger, imbued with a poisonous force designed to paralyze Beryl's nerves; a glass bead that, broken, would emit a blinding light; and the vial containing seven drops of Amlina's blood—which might or might not summon back the power of the Mirror for the span of seven heartbeats.

But she would not lie to herself, nor to her companions. "Yes, we can fight her. But make no mistake, without the Mirror, to defeat the

Archimage in her own stronghold ... The odds will be long. Very long."

"We faced Beryl before," Eben said. "It would be unseemly to hide from her now."

"We are Iruks," Karrol said stubbornly. "We don't run from our enemies."

"Sure, and if we did run," Wilhaven said, "'what a sorry climax that would make to Meghild's song. No, I say we must go on."

All of them were nodding. Their courage almost brought the witch to tears. She gathered herself and rose to her feet.

"Then let us go and make the best song of it that we can."

They marched quietly across the plaza, through darkness disturbed only by the witch's candle and the faint pink light of Grizna. They entered a warren of brick-walled enclosures: trading establishments and warehouses. The streets here were wide and straight, and it should have been simple to stay on course. But, after traversing several blocks, Amlina caught sight of the tower again—and realized they had unaccountably been moving in a sideways direction. She halted, hissing in frustration.

Off to the left, she spotted a light. After a moment, she realized it was a single figure carrying a lantern, moving toward them.

"What do you think?" Lonn asked her.

Amlina glanced at her candle, a third of it already consumed. She turned up her other hand with a fatalistic gesture. "Let's find out who it is."

They set off toward the approaching figure. Soon Amlina could see it was a woman in the robes of a temple official. A few yards from them the priestess stopped, lifting her lamp, squinting in the gloom.

"It is you!" she cried in the local tongue. "It is you, Amlina—is it not?"

"Who are you?" the witch demanded.

"Zenodia. I was assistant to Toulluthan when you were here. Now I am high treasurer."

"Yes, I remember you," Amlina said. "But why are you here, wandering the empty streets?"

"I have been searching for you ... for many hours."

"Why?"

"I do not know. Except—if you have come to Tallyba to kill the tyrant, I would help you. In any way I can. Even at the cost of my life."

"Who is she? What is she saying?" Lonn demanded.

"She appears to know Lady Amlina." Wilhaven had understood parts of the exchange.

Amlina stared into Zenodia's eyes. She read the effects of narcotics, of reckless sorcery. But also a sincerity born of desperation and agony.

"Can you lead us to the Bone Tower?"

"Yes, of course," the priestess answered, confused. "But you must know the way."

"We are ensorcelled," Amlina replied. "But you perhaps are not. If you can lead us there, do so now—quickly!"

Zenodia's eyes widened. "Yes. Yes. Follow me." She whirled and hurried off.

With an abrupt wave to her companions, the witch followed.

"We are trusting her?" Glyssa asked, rushing a step behind.

"We are," Amlina replied. "We have very little to lose."

TWENTY-NINE

They raced up tree-lined avenues, past shops and wealthy manors. The Bone Tower and then the citadel walls came into view, consistently drawing nearer. As Amlina had suspected, Beryl's ensorcellment was aimed at the Mirror and those who shared its power. Zenodia was immune.

In less than an hour they approached a grand square. Lamps winked atop the citadel wall, with sentries visible on the battlement. The bronze Gates of the Sun stood thirty-feet tall and closed.

"We'd better go in by one of the lesser gates," Amlina said. "That will be easier for me to unlock." She spoke now in Tathian, of which, it turned out, Zenodia had a limited command.

"The door to the temple garden" Zenodia said. "I have a key."

They followed her to the left, along the base of the citadel hill, through narrow, high-walled alleys. Another quarter hour brought them near the temple complex. An enormous dome curled beyond the fortified wall, its gold surface borrowing a sheen from the brightening moon.

Finally, Zenodia stopped before a door set three steps down from the pavement, dark wood reinforced by black iron. She set down her lantern, found a key in her robe, turned it in the lock. She pushed, and the door creaked inward.

Amlina led the way inside, her companions close on her heels. They stood in a formal garden, pools and topiary shrubs arranged along pebble walkways. The rear of the huge temple lay to their right, the palace and the Bone Tower straight ahead up the hill.

The moment Zenodia shut the door, brightness like a meteor tumbled out of the sky. A flash erupted, and Beryl appeared, tall and menacing in blazing gold robes.

One of the Iruks flung a spear. It flew into the figure and vanished.

"Don't bother," Amlina said. "It is only a *sending*, an image."

Beryl laughed mockingly. "Such delightful ignorance. But welcome, welcome Amlina, and to your crew. I have waited a long time for your arrival." Her eyes sought out Zenodia, hunched behind the others. "And, Zenodia ... It seems I underestimated both your hatred and your nerve. I will enjoy punishing you for this betrayal."

"Come on," Amlina shouted to her friends. "She can't stop us in that form. We must hurry."

"Yes. Come. Come!" the phantom voice called. "You are running out of time, aren't you? Soon your defense will vanish."

Amlina in the lead, they charged directly at the figure. It faded as they passed, leaving Beryl's scornful laughter tolling in the air.

* O *

Rog and Grizna floated near the top of the sky. Glyssa knew the Mirror's time was almost gone.

They had traversed the gardens, circled past annex buildings, crossed a huge paved area where, Amlina said, other temples had once stood. At one point a patrol of sentries had tried to stop them— only to be flung back by the Mirror. Now they dashed up the steps of a building Amlina identified as the palace.

Beyond a shadowed portico stood tall golden doors embossed with lions and emblems of the sun. Amlina walked up and touched one door with her palm.

"They are barred to us, but not by magic," she said.

"How do we enter?" Glyssa asked.

"Quiet. I must visualize and move the locks."

Shutting her eyes, the witch raised both arms, her long fingers extended. Her hands circled slowly in the air. Glyssa and her mates glanced around, wary and impatient. Zenodia shrank back near a pillar.

Behind the doors, a noise sounded, a dull groan of metal. *Pure shaping*, Glyssa thought, remembering her lessons with the spinner. Amlina dragged her hand three times through the air, and Glyssa heard three bolts moving. The witch swept her hands back toward herself, and the heavy doors slipped open.

"Hurry!" Amlina cried.

They squeezed through the gap. Inside they found a vast circular chamber, silent and empty. Amlina led them across to a distant throne on a high platform. They mounted the steps and rushed to a pointed arch sealed by iron doors. This time when they approached, the air shimmered and the doors shrieked and rolled open.

They ran down a long, high corridor with black floor and light gray walls. Passing through another arch, they emerged in a courtyard under the night sky. A glance told Glyssa that the moons had wheeled past zenith. The Bone Tower they had struggled all day to reach lay across the courtyard. At its base stood soldiers armed with long pikes or halberds. Without pausing, Amlina ran toward them and the gate they guarded. Glyssa and her mates charged after.

Before they had crossed halfway, the world shuddered and the air sizzled. Glyssa stumbled, touched a hand to the ground to regain her balance. Something burned the skin on her chest. Instinctively, she grabbed the Mirror talisman and pulled it from her tunic.

The surface was leaden, no longer a mirror, all of its power gone.

O

The klarnmates climbed to their feet, tense and wary. Amlina stood at the front, shoulders slumped and head bowed. At the base of the tower, the dozen guards widened their stances and leveled their weapons. Glyssa could see now they were not human, but creatures with men's bodies and lions' heads.

From above came the sound of Beryl's mocking laughter. Her face appeared on the stones of the tower, like an enormous reflection in a pool.

The lion-headed guards stalked forward.

"Let's make a fight of it." Lonn growled, hand flying to his hilt.

"Yes. At last!" Karrol gave a fierce cry.

The Iruks drew their blades and lifted spears to cast.

"No!" Beryl's voice rolled like thunder. "You cannot move. Your limbs are stone. Your blood is ice."

The power of the voice shuddered inside Glyssa's body. She strained, growling with the effort, but could no longer move. Fear welled in her, the remembered sensation of the fishhook, the terror of being enthralled. Sword and spear slipped from her fingers.

"On your knees, my slaves."

Trembling, Glyssa obeyed, chin sinking to her chest.

* O *

Amlina saw her companions drop to their knees, heard their weapons clatter on the ground. In helpless rage, she lifted her eyes to the top of the tower.

"Come in, Amlina. Up the stairs." Beryl's voice purred in her mind. "I have something special to show you."

Amlina weighed the Iruk spear in her hand, then tossed it away. She walked forward calmly, past the thrall sentries—who stood frozen now that the intruders were subdued. She entered the tower, made her way along the curved wall to the base of the stairs. As she climbed, Beryl's voice taunted her.

"My dear Amlina, you are finally here. I saw all along it must end this way, you and I meeting one last time, in my tower, where we spent so many interesting hours together ..."

Amlina tucked her arms in her sleeves. She still had her dagger, the blinding bead, the vial containing her blood and the Mirror fragments. *If she could distract Beryl for a just moment, she might yet have a chance.* She tightened her lips, pushed the hopeful thought from her mind. She must hide the existence of her weapons from Beryl's probing ...

She reached the top at last and entered the Archimage's lair. Beryl awaited her, tall and erect, dressed in gold robes and jeweled turban. Candles in glass globes cast trembling islands of light and shadow across the chamber. Behind Beryl, on an ivory perch, the treeman bounced and jabbered, tail curling. Nearby, draped casually over the back of a chair, lay the black and silver cloak.

"Oh, yes." Beryl read the direction of Amlina's gaze. "The Cloak of the Two Winds. I used it, you know, to cast the darkness that befuddled you."

"I thought you might have."

"Kneel," Beryl commanded. "I want to relish this moment."

Offering no resistance, Amlina sank to her knees.

"You have caused me a surprising amount of trouble," the Archimage said. "The fight in Kadavel, your impressive journey to Valgool, even today with your little candles—clever, if not very effective. And the Mirror Against All Mishap. I don't know where you acquired the knowledge. And I never would have guessed you had the nerve."

"Seems you underestimated me," Amlina murmured.

"Yes, but never again!" From the table behind her, Beryl picked up a glass sphere, roughly the size of a human head. Inside Amlina glimpsed scissors, a razor, needles—all floating in a viscous solution with drops of blood.

"Something I made just for you, Amlina. Something that will let me enjoy my revenge indefinitely."

Thoughts of what that design might do loomed in Amlina's mind. In desperation, she fought to move her arms, to defend herself. But Beryl's will had locked onto her body, holding her paralyzed.

* O *

On hands and knees, Glyssa had watched Amlina walk through the ranks of the lion men and into the tower. Glyssa's breathing came in ragged gasps as she struggled with fear and impotent rage.

At first the fear was stronger. For the first time in many days, Glyssa experienced the wrenching pain of that thing she called the fishhook, felt the wound in her heart torn open again, remembered the icy dread and despair of being a thrall, a slave to another mind. Now that fate was upon her again—and not only on her, but her mates.

That thought fueled the rage. She had weapons to fight back now, the cold fire, all the control of mind and soul she had learned from Amlina. Slowing her breath, Glyssa brought those weapons to bear. She envisioned the cold fire pulsing along her nerves, lightening her leaden muscles, freeing her.

The Archimage's sorcery fought back, dragging Glyssa down into hopelessness and fear. But the enthrallment seemed weaker. Beryl believed the Iruks were conquered; her attention now must be fixed on Amlina ...

Slowly, with calm determination, Glyssa focused her mind, seeing herself rising, straining to hold on to that vision. After long moments, her limbs began to shake. Heat like a fever burned behind her eyes.

Suddenly, she tore free, arms flying up.

Glyssa scrambled to her feet. Behind her, her mates stirred and started to rise. She had broken the Archimage's hold over all of them.

But as they gathered themselves, the lion men growled. Awakened by the prisoners' movements, the creatures stepped forward.

Glyssa crouched to pick up her weapons. Spears flew over her head, striking two of the guards, sending them stumbling backward. Roaring, the Iruks rushed to the attack. Glyssa parried the blade of a halberd, stabbed at a thrall's neck. Her mates leaped around her, wheeling and thrusting.

Then a thought screamed in her mind: *Amlina needed her.*

Throwing herself under a swiping blade, Glyssa rolled on the ground, then jumped to her feet behind her attacker.

"Can you take them, mates?" she shouted. "I must help Amlina."

"Of course," Karrol laughed, smashing aside a halberd shaft. "I've been itching for this!"

"Go!" Lonn told her.

From the corner of her eye, Glyssa spied Zenodia. The priestess must have hidden back in the corridor when the rest of them were immobilized. Now she moved furtively, darting around the edge of the fighting.

Glyssa spun and dashed for the tower. Passing the gate, she entered a cavernous chamber. Light shone from a hole in the distant ceiling. Along the wall, stone steps curved up.

Glyssa was racing for the steps when Zenodia cried out to her in Tathian. "No, this way. Faster!"

She was making for the center of the floor, pointing at the ceiling. Amlina had trusted her, Glyssa recalled. She rushed over to join the priestess. The woman's hood was back, revealing a shaven head, red-dyed skin. Her eyes shone round and pleading.

"You kill the queen, yes?"

Glyssa lifted her spear. "I will certainly try."

Zenodia held a black bead in her fingers. "Take hold of my hand."

Glyssa shoved her sword into its scabbard and grasped the woman's hand. Zenodia uttered some words and smashed the bead to the floor. A gush of silver light appeared, spiraling, lifting them off their feet. Glyssa's stomach lurched as they rose, twisting into the air. The floor rushed away below their feet; the light in the ceiling drew closer.

They ascended through the hole and into the chamber above. Some distance away stood the Archimage, her back to them. In front of her, Amlina knelt on the floor.

With a clear line of sight, Glyssa did not hesitate. Still floating in the air, she cast her spear. Even as it flew across the chamber, Beryl whirled.

"No!" she screamed and swept out a hand. The spear swerved in mid-air, dropped, and skidded uselessly across the floor.

Glyssa still held Zenodia's hand. The action of throwing the spear had flung them both backward, out of the shaft of silver light. They fell sprawling on their backs, beyond the rim of the hole. Glyssa rolled over and scrambled partway to her feet. But then Beryl's gaze bored into her mind.

"Kneel!' she commanded. "You cannot move."

Glyssa sank down, powerless once more. Beside her, Zenodia whimpered.

* O *

The moment Beryl turned, distracted by the darting spear, Amlina moved. Still on her knees, she reached into her robe. Her left hand found the vial containing the Mirror fragments and drops of blood. Her right hand clutched the hilt of her dagger. Her hands slid back to her sides as Beryl faced her.

"Oh no, Amlina." Beryl flung out a hand, the sharp gesture causing the dagger to fly from Amlina's grasp.

Amlina locked eyes with the Archimage, keeping her left hand motionless, the vial hidden.

"Now, no more interruptions." Beryl raised the globe containing the blood and sharp instruments and smashed it on the floor.

At the same instant, Amlina squeezed the glass with her fingers and thumb, breaking the vial open.

A cloud of crimson erupted and roiled toward Amlina. Before it touched her, the power of the Mirror burst into life. Space tore open with a thrum like harp strings. The red cloud reversed and rushed at Beryl.

Her face contorted with shock just before the cloud reached her. Swirling and churning, it swallowed her body.

From within the red shroud came Beryl's screams, mixed with the sounds of ripping flesh. The chaos lasted for nine or ten beats of Amlina's pounding heart. Then the shroud folded in on itself and vanished.

On the floor lay a pink, naked thing, like a withered human torso. It had no arms or legs, just useless, wiggling flippers. But the face on the shrunken head was unmistakably Beryl's. The lips flapped soundlessly. The eyes gaped with horror and impotent fury.

Amlina had gotten to her feet and inched closer. Now she sank to her knees again, averting her face, unable to look at the loathsome thing.

Presently, Glyssa and Zenodia walked up beside her. They gazed down at the monstrosity, neither speaking. Glyssa gripped Amlina's elbow and helped her to rise.

"It must be destroyed," Amlina whispered at last. "Beryl's mind is still in there. We cannot risk that she ever find a way out."

Zenodia shuddered. "All my life ... all my life I have longed to kill her. But now ... this ... I have not the stomach for it."

Glyssa looked at them both, surprised. "Well, I have."

She drew her sword. With the toe of her boot, she kicked the torso over onto its belly. Gripping the hilt with both hands, she took careful aim, lifted the blade back behind her head, and swung it down with all her strength.

The blade severed the neck cleanly and rang on the stone floor. A thunderous force exploded. Glyssa was tossed back off her feet and landed on her side, bruising a shoulder. Amlina and Zenodia cringed, shielding their eyes. The Bone Tower rumbled, and the floor beneath them shifted with a groan.

Regaining her feet, Glyssa looked wonderingly at the witch.

Amlina's voice was soft and solemn. "All her designs are overthrown."

THIRTY

Moments later, Lonn and the rest of klarn came charging up the stairs. They looked around wildly, holding weapons splashed with blood.

"It is over," Glyssa told them. "Our enemy is slain."

The Iruks roared with jubilation and shook spears and swords in the air. The energy of the klarn-soul surged into Amlina, lifting her weary spirit.

Laughing, Glyssa ran over to embrace her mates. "Are all of you all right?" she cried. "Any wounded?"

"Oh, a few bumps and scratches," Lonn said.

"The lion men were strong, but slow," Karrol boasted. "Hardly fit to challenge Iruk warriors."

"I guessed Beryl might have been slain," Eben observed, "when the tower started shaking."

"Aye, I do believe the foundation split," Wilhaven said. "I fear the whole structure will need to be rebuilt."

"More likely, torn down," Amlina said, with a meaningful glance at Zenodia.

The priestess was staring at them all, dumbfounded. Suddenly, she dropped to her knees and seized Amlina's hand. "You have fulfilled our greatest hopes," she cried in the Nyssanian tongue. "I pledge to support your rule in every way I can."

Aghast, Amlina snatched her hand away. "No. No! I have no intention of taking Beryl's place."

"What did she say?" Karrol demanded.

"I think she just offered Amlina the throne," Wilhaven said.

Amlina nodded curtly, then spoke to the priestess in Nyssanian. "I intend to leave Tallyba at once. I will take only the Cloak of the Two Winds and ..." Distracted, she looked around the chamber. Thralls kept by Beryl as attendants had come awake. Two had dropped to the floor, moaning. Two others wandered around in confusion. The treeman, Grellabo, was nowhere to be seen.

"... There are also some scrolls that the Archimage stole from Larthang," Amlina said. "Oh, and we'll take a modest measure of gold, to recompense my brave companions."

Eben grinned wolfishly. "Did she just mention loot?"

Zenodia was still on her knees. "But, if you don't take her place, there will be chaos, factions fighting for control ..."

"No doubt." Amlina gathered the Cloak in her arms. "You seem like a capable woman. I expect you could be influential." She waved a hand, indicating the magical lair. "Especially with all of Beryl's books and tools to help you."

Zenodia eyes followed the witch's gesture. Realization seemed to dawn in her. "Yes. You are right." She struggled to her feet. "I am a priestess of Tysanni—and for now, at least, I have access to the temple treasury. I will devote myself to reestablishing the old gods, to bringing our nobility back from exile."

"You are speaking like a leader already," Amlina said, as she hunted for the scrolls. "I'd be careful with the narcotics, though. In the end they will muffle, not sharpen your powers."

Zenodia hastened over to the witch's side. "Yes. I will. I promise you."

Amlina rummaged through one of Beryl's chests. The Archimage possessed so many interesting trinkets and documents. How tempting to examine them all at her leisure, to take more than a few things with her ... But no, her intuition was awake and definite: She must get herself and her friends away from Tallyba as soon as possible, taking only the Cloak and the *Nine Scrolls of Eglemarde*—

the national treasures Beryl had stolen long ago from the House of the Deepmind.

"Can I help you?" Zenodia asked. "What can I do to repay you?"

Amlina considered. With Beryl's demise, she could feel the city beginning to stir. "Can you arrange an escort to take us back to the harbor?"

Zenodia touched her chin, brow lowered. "I suppose so ... Yes. The temple guards will obey me. I will say that I act on the queen's authority."

She turned to leave, but hesitated. "One thing I must ask you, Amlina. The oracle of Tysanni made a prophecy. She said the tyrant would rule for a thousand years, unless three prevailed: 'The student who returns, the queen who was already dead, and the spear that was melted and forged again.' I thought you must be the student, which is why I expected your return. But does any of the rest ring true?"

"Aye," said Wilhaven, who stood nearby. "That queen would be the lady I served, Meghild of Demardunn. She sacrificed her life so Amlina could cast the mighty Mirror."

"Indeed," Amlina replied. "And it was the last energy of the Mirror, encased in a trinket, that turned Beryl's vile magic back on herself and caused her defeat."

"Was it so?" the bard cried. "Then I have a fitting end to my noble queen's song."

"That matches the prophecy truly," Zenodia said. "But the final part, the spear that was melted and remade?"

"That's easy." The witch pointed her chin across the chamber to where Glyssa stood rejoicing with her mates. "That would be Glyssa, a mage true and skillful, and the bravest soul I have ever met."

* O *

One hour later, Zenodia climbed the steps of the Bone Tower, leading three of her assistants. Clerics from the office of the treasury, they wore orange gowns and sandals, their faces and scalps dyed red. Arms folded in sleeves, they followed, mute and obedient, though Zenodia knew they must be terrified. For lower-ranking clerics to be summoned to the palace at all was a rarity, but to the tower of the tyrant queen—never. Zenodia could not even imagine what they must think.

She had woken them by pounding on their doors, ordered them to follow her as soon as they could dress. Emerging on the temple's main portico, they had been joined by a company of guardsmen.

Acquiring the guards had been more difficult. The captain on duty had looked askance when Zenodia ordered him to turn out a company in the middle of the night. This coming on the heels of the queen's bizarre command, requiring the whole city spend the day behind locked doors and shuttered windows. But Zenodia had refused to explain, only repeated her order coldly, and stated that she spoke with the authority of not only the temple council but the queen herself. The captain had not dared to refuse.

Arriving at the palace with three clerics and thirty guardsmen, Zenodia had found Amlina and her followers emerging from the corridor behind the throne. The barbarians carried sacks Zenodia knew must contain treasure. Small enough recompense, she thought, for slaying the tyrant. She kept her promise, dispatching ten men to escort the witch's party to the harbor. The rest she left to guard the audience hall, telling the captain that the queen was involved in deep magical work and must not be disturbed on any account.

Now Zenodia turned at the top of the stairs, the entrance to Beryl's lair. The assistants stared up at her, their faces confused and distraught. Two were in their early twenties, a young man and woman, neophytes whom she had elevated and who owed her loyalty for that alone. The third was Ilse, a middle-aged woman Zenodia had known for years, a fellow worshipper of Tysanni.

"As you may have guessed," she said, "I was not entirely truthful with the captain. There is momentous good news for our land, which will be known to all soon enough. But for these next hours—however long we are undisturbed—I need your help. We will make an inventory of the books and artifacts in these chambers, and begin to ascertain how these things may be used as we seek to re-establish a just order in Tallyba."

The clerics stared as if she had gone insane.

"But ... where is the queen?" Ilse managed.

Zenodia smiled. "Come, I will show you."

Hesitantly, they followed her to the place where the body lay—a pink, shriveled thing in a puddle of blood. Nearby, the severed head showed Beryl's ghastly countenance. The clerics stared in shock and revulsion.

But the sight no longer troubled Zenodia at all. *Amlina has made a strong impression on me*, she thought, *her composure, her fearless determination.* From now on, Zenodia would emulate those qualities.

"It is true," she said. "The tyrant is dead, slain by that young witch and her followers, who even now are leaving the city. And so, we have a chance to rebuild our land." She nudged the bloody, flippered thing with her foot. "This atrocity, we shall burn."

A rustle of movement drew her attention. The treeman crept from under a bookcase, hissing softly, staring at them with frightened eyes.

"Her familiar," Ilse said.

"Yes." After a moment, Zenodia knelt and held out her hand. "Come here, Grellabo. Come here. It's all right."

The creature hesitated, glancing nervously at the clerics, at his dead mistress' remains. Anxious, flinching, he edged toward Zenodia's hand.

The moment he came within reach, she grabbed the fur on his back. Grellabo hissed and spat, tried to scratch her with his claws. But Zenodia stood calmly, holding him away from her body.

Deliberately, she walked to the hole at the center of the floor, her assistants shuffling behind. The treeman screeched and tried to writhe out of her grasp. Zenodia extended her arm, holding the creature over empty space.

She opened her hand. The treeman plummeted, twisting and tumbling through the air, his howl of terror fading.

Zenodia watched as the body was smashed on the stones far below. The three assistants looked at her, open-mouthed. She loosed a sigh of relief.

"So let all the tyrant's evil be destroyed."

* O *

Dawn slipped over the sky in shades of maroon and gold. Glyssa marched with her klarn, exhausted but happy, along the quay toward their boat. The Iruks carried spears and sacks full of loot. Amlina walked in their midst, holding a satchel of Larthangan scrolls and the Cloak of the Two Winds folded in her arms. Ten temple guards accompanied them as escort.

In the long corridor across from the tower, they had discovered all of the wall panels rolled away. Beyond them lay vaults stuffed with treasure. Only Amlina's insistence that it was dangerous to remain long in the city kept them from picking through it all. In the end, except for a few rings and a jeweled cup, they agreed to limit their loot to gold coins. They filled seven sacks—more than enough, Eben judged, to keep them all in meat and drink the rest of their lives.

Reaching the *Phoenix Queen*, they made haste to load the treasure on board. While the mates handed the sacks of coins over the rails, the temple guards stood watch, shielding their activities from a growing crowd of curious spectators. The city was waking up, people returning to the streets and quays. Did they sense something in the air, Glyssa wondered, or was word already spreading of the queen's death?

Karrol went to open the rear hatch. Suddenly, she jumped back, drawing her sword. "Whoever you are, come out of there!"

The Iruks stopped their work and reached for their weapons. They glared as a figure crept from under the rear deck—a small, bearded man with boney shoulders, wrapped in one of their bed furs.

"My apologies, but I found myself naked and had to put on something. Perhaps one of you can lend me a garment?"

"Who in the Mother's name are you, and what are you doing on our boat?" Lonn demanded.

But Amlina, standing by the mast, smiled affectionately.

"Hello, Kizier."

EPILOGUE
EAST OF ALONE

"I am thinking again that this course was not the best decision." Karrol grunted, marching with two water casks balanced on her shoulders.

"You were anxious to get home," Glyssa replied, trudging behind her on the beach. "A straight course is the fastest way."

"That's obvious," Karrol answered. "But it hasn't been so fast, has it?"

Six of the mates walked single file along the shore, carrying water and sacks containing a few shellfish and eggs they had managed to scavenge. The *Phoenix Queen* rode at anchor in a cove a short distance away. The island, named Alone, was as barren and desolate as the tales told—a pile of rock in the midst of the ocean, home only to seabirds, crabs, and ferocious fire turtles. At least the dry grasses and stands of stunted conifers would provide fuel. They'd be able to cook tonight.

"Just be happy we found the island," Draven told Karrol. "We won't starve or die of thirst."

"I *am* grateful for that," Karrol allowed. "But it's hard to be merry anticipating many more days on skimpy rations."

"Aye, and with our ship riding heavy with sacks of gold," Wilhaven mused. "It's tragic, mates, as if the Fates were mocking us."

"We'll be in Fleevanport soon enough," Lonn said. "Then you'll have all the meat and mead your bellies can hold."

That thought lifted their spirits. Laughing, trading rough jests, they carried the supplies across the shallow water and hoisted them onto the boat.

Leaving the harbor at Tallyba, the klarn had decided to head straight out to sea. Word of the queen's overthrow would spread quickly along the coasts, Amlina had warned, with turmoil and lawlessness sure to follow. A cranock, laden with treasure and carrying a small crew, would make a tempting target for pirates or naval squadrons suddenly unleashed from disciplined command. Besides, sailing southwest was the most direct route to the Iruks' home seas. They had decided on Fleevan as their destination, a Tathian colony where they could hold up and rest.

The plan had been for Amlina to use the magic cloak to summon the freezewind and drive them expeditiously over frozen seas. But the second day of the voyage, Amlina fell sick. Exhausted by her confrontation with Beryl and the long ordeal of carrying blood magic, the witch had fainted on deck while wielding the Cloak. For two days she lay unconscious, and the mates had feared for her life. Draven or Glyssa sat with her constantly, sponging her brow, stroking her hair, calling on the klarn-soul to strengthen and heal her.

Finally, she had awakened. Yet now, after a full 17 days at sea, she was still too weak to leave her bed. So the mates had sailed on soft water, the prevailing northerly winds on the starboard stern. Navigating by the stars, they had arrived at this near-mythical island just in time to replenish their fresh water.

Climbing aboard the cranock, the mates set about sorting the supplies, lighting the cook stove, and boiling water to make soup and tea. As twilight gathered, they sat in a circle on deck, sharing the light meal and musing on what they would do after arriving in Fleevanport.

Eben bragged that he meant to drink mead all day and night for a year—perhaps buy his own tavern. Wilhaven said he would likely rest in the colony for some time, before arranging passage back to Gwales. He still had much work to complete Meghild's saga—and also, he hinted, other songs that were tugging at his mind.

Kizier for his part planned to stay with Amlina and, when the time came, accompany her back to Larthang. He aspired to write a detailed account of their voyages together and the far-flung places they had seen. Kizier spoke softly, looking uncomfortable in his ill-fitting Iruk garb. He was finding it difficult, Glyssa knew, to readjust to human form. He still spent long periods seated on the rear deck with the two remaining windbringers, seeking to attune his mind with theirs.

Lonn and Draven were noncommittal as to their plans, saying only they would wait and see. Draven, Glyssa thought, had become more subdued and reflective since being wounded and nearly dying at Valgool. But he felt bound to Amlina—as did Glyssa herself—and would no doubt stay with her, at least until she recovered.

Only Karrol and Brinda were intent on returning to Ilga, the klarn's home island. With all the loot they had won, there would be plenty to pay off any reparations the tribal elders deemed they owed to their neighbors. It was almost a year ago that the klarn had left the hunt and plundered Amlina's ship—then later been forced to refuse to share their catch with the other boats of the hunting fleet. Of course Glyssa herself had not witnessed that confrontation, having been enthralled by the sorcerer and carried away to Kadavel ...

Sitting close to her mates, she put those evil memories aside. The nights of Third Summer were warm and pleasant, especially in these mid-latitudes. With myriads of stars overhead and the bright sea lapping gently at the hull, Glyssa felt calm and content, whatever the future might bring.

* O *

Amlina moaned and opened her eyes. A dream had disturbed her—or rather, an intuition of danger. From the stillness of the boat, she could tell they were still anchored off the island.

She felt terribly weak, even after so many days of rest. The ebbing of the Mirror's power had drained her vitality, far more than she would have expected. In retrospect, the attempt to heal herself by entering deep trance had been a mistake. Once scattered by the dark immersion, her soul had resisted coming back to itself. The *Bliss of Unknowing* had proved all too tempting. She might have dissolved entirely, a gentle path to death sometimes taken by witches, except...

She gazed fondly at Draven, asleep on a cushion, his head and arm resting on the edge of her bunk. Her will to live was still strong, because of the time she wished to spend with Draven, and with her other friends. Also, she still had ambitions, to return the Cloak and the Scrolls of Eglemarde to Larthang, to claim just honors ... though all of that seemed less important now. Amlina let her fingers toy with Draven's black hair.

He raised his head and gave her a sleepy smile. "Are you all right?"

She reached for his hand to kiss.

Loud pounding shook the hatch.

"Amlina, Draven!" Glyssa called. "You're needed on deck. There's trouble."

The witch bolted upright. Shaking off a wave of dizziness, she reached for a robe. Draven helped her pull it on over her nightdress. They crept across the low cabin and onto the deck.

It was morning, the sky deep blue with towering white clouds. The island rose to the west in tumbled boulders and crags. To the north, a line of ships was coming around the headland. Legs weak, Amlina gripped the rail and stared. Ten—no, twelve—of the vessels appeared to be *drommons*, Tathian galleys. Farther away, a pair of galleons were visible on the horizon: supply ships.

"Sure, and it's a Tathian war fleet." Wilhaven stood at the witch's elbow. "But by the Three Sisters, what are they doing here at the end of the world?"

"Hunting for us," Amlina replied with a dread certainty.

The Iruks were on deck, strapping on harnesses and weapons. They had already raised the anchor stone.

"Should we hoist sail?" Lonn asked the witch. "Try to outrun them?"

"No chance of that on soft water," Wilhaven answered solemnly. "Not with forty oarsmen per vessel."

"Well, we plainly can't outfight them," Lonn said.

The whole party stood at the rails, watching the oncoming fleet. Each drommon carried a troop of marines armed with bows, lances, and swords. The galleys featured high fighting decks fore and aft, and iron-shod prows for ramming.

"Perhaps an offer to parley?" Kizier suggested. "Let them know about the power that we hold."

Amlina fought to keep her head clear. "Yes. I will attempt to bluff them. If that fails, I will have to use the Cloak." She turned to Lonn. "I suggest you hoist sail and come about. Approach to within hailing distance."

Lonn ran to the helm, shouting orders. The Iruks untied the sail and bent their backs to the halyard. With the yard in place, they adjusted the sheets, and Lonn set a course to bring them abreast of the drommons. By then, Amlina could see the red and gold flags flying from the masts.

"The Dragon-Amid-the-Waves," Wilhaven remarked, "the flag of Kadavel."

"So it is." Amlina gave a faint, bitter laugh. "Hagen, their Prince-Ruler, developed a certain interest in the Cloak of the Two Winds when it was held in his city. His desire to possess it must have grown strong indeed."

"But how could they have tracked us here?" Eben asked from beside the bard.

"Hagen's state sorcerers," Amlina replied. "They bent much labor and attention on the Cloak and must have developed an affinity for it. If they perceived the possibility of it being torn from Beryl's grasp, they could also have seen it would pass this way."

The drommons had moved into position to block the *Phoenix Queen* from escaping the cove. From the high rear deck of the flagship, a herald in red livery blew a trumpet flourish, then called out through a megaphone.

"Greetings to the ship of Gwales. You are blockaded by a war fleet of the Princely City of Kadavel."

Amlina cupped her hands and called back with the strongest voice she could muster. "We are a free vessel. Why do you molest us unlawfully on the open sea?"

A man dressed in maroon with gold-colored armor conferred with the herald. Amlina recognized Hagen himself, the Prince-Ruler.

"We believe you are in possession of an item stolen from our city," the herald called, "a certain black and silver cloak of magical properties. Our Prince-Ruler wishes this item returned. We propose to send a boarding party under a flag of truce to search your vessel. If you surrender the Cloak, or if it is not found, you will not be inconvenienced further."

"Oh, I remember that Prince-Ruler well," Karrol called from amidships, two spears in her grasp. "Threatened to execute us when our hands were tied. Maybe he'd like to come over and fight us for the Cloak."

Amlina considered, then shouted back to the Tathians: "You may send your boarding party, but only to discuss the matter. And be aware, we are able to defend ourselves, with spears and magic both."

"Why let them board us?" Glyssa asked.

"Yes," Eben said. "If the Cloak will get us free, why not use it now?"

Amlina answered wearily. "I might be able to beguile or bluff them. Using the Cloak must be a last resort." *And I'm not sure I have the strength for it.* But she kept that thought to herself.

The klarnmates watched as a pilot boat was lowered from the flagship. Amlina went below to don the Cloak. When she came back on deck, the pilot boat was crossing the water. It held a crew of five—four rowers and a helmsman—plus three passengers. Two were sorcerers, bearded men in long robes and tall pointed hats. The other was an officer in armor and plumed helmet. The Prince-Ruler himself still watched from the high deck.

As the boat neared the bow of the *Phoenix Queen*, Amlina arranged for the Iruks to stand in front of her, spears in hand. Light-headed, her palms perspiring, she worried that she might faint before this parley ended.

Three of the boat's crewmen clambered over the side, glanced grimly at the Iruks, then turned to help haul the sorcerers aboard. Last came the officer. When he removed his helmet, Amlina recognized the bearded face.

"Who is in command?" he said. "Where is the lady?"

"Stand aside, my friends," Amlina said.

The Iruks parted ranks. The eyes of the sorcerers gaped wide and one of them pointed.

"My lord, it is as we foretold! She has the magic cloak and wears it brazenly."

Amlina ignored him and addressed the commander. "I believe we have met before, sir. Admiral Dantonius, is it not?" Dantonius had commanded the fleet blocking the channel to Kadavel when Amlina's ship first sailed there.

The admiral stared hard. "Yes, I remember. But last time we met you claimed to be merely a ship owner's daughter, not a powerful witch."

"I claimed what suited my purpose," Amlina said. "And now I tell you this: the Cloak of the Two Winds belongs to Larthang, and I am returning it there. Kadavel has no valid claim."

Dantonius surveyed the stern faces of the Iruks, and their hands tight on their weapons. His eyebrows flicked up when he noticed Wilhaven and Kizier.

"It is a rag-tag crew you have here, Lady. Barbarians from the South Pole—I remember them from before—and these two, a pirate of Gwales, if I am not mistaken, and a skinny beggar, who cannot be much good in a fight." He spread his hands. "I am not here to debate the validity of claims. My prince has you trapped by blockade and outnumbered more than a hundred to one. He will take the Cloak if you do not surrender it."

Glaring, Amlina gestured at the sorcerers. "I imagine these two learned men have some knowledge of the Cloak. But I'm not sure they have informed your prince of its full powers. By summoning both winds at once, I can easily create a storm to wreck your fleet and drive the remnants hundreds of leagues away."

The Admiral hesitated, turning to the sorcerers. "Well?"

The men looked at one another, perplexed. "Uh ... There are *certain* accounts in the annals," one stammered.

"But those are usually discounted as *highly* improbable," the other said.

Dantonius sighed unhappily. After a moment, he unbuckled his sword belt and handed it to a crewman. "Lady, if I may approach for a private word?"

Amlina smiled and beckoned him over. Eyeing the Iruks warily, he stepped close to the witch and spoke in muted tones.

"I am only a seaman and know nothing of scholarship or sorcery. I certainly cannot judge whether your threat is plausible. But in the interests of protecting the lives of my men, I tell you this: Prince Hagen has become obsessed with recovering this Cloak. Remember, its appearance in our city caused turmoil, unnatural weather, unrest. The Empress of Far Nyssan, the Archimage, brought her war fleet near our shores. Then, as riots were breaking out in the city, the High Priest of the Temple of the Air was assassinated, and that same night you, the Archimage, and the Cloak all disappeared. The Prince-Ruler was left looking weak and ineffectual. He faced challenges to his government, bordering on open revolt. But rather than meet those problems head on, he made tracking down this Cloak his mission. He has committed many months, many ships, and much treasure to the effort. As I said, it has become his obsession. Now it is nearly in his grasp. He will not be deterred."

Amlina's head was swimming. She remembered that Beryl had planted the idea of winning the Cloak as a seed in Hagen's mind. Small wonder if that seed had grown into a mania.

She lowered her eyes. "I am sorry for your men, Admiral. But I also cannot be deterred. The Cloak must go back to Larthang. Your fleet must make way for us to pass."

Dantonius bowed his head in resignation. "I regret your decision, but I will convey it to my prince."

As the pilot boat was rowed back to the flagship, Amlina and her mates watched from the rail of the *Phoenix Queen*.

"So you will have to use the Cloak after all," Eben said. "I assume you were not bluffing about its power?"

"Oh, no," Amlina answered. "It will raise a tempest—if I have the strength."

"Are you not well enough?" Glyssa asked with concern.

"Yes," the witch answered. "I have to be. But let us wait until the admiral makes his report. Perhaps it will not be necessary."

They watched in silence as the party of the pilot boat climbed back onboard the flagship. Dantonius marched quickly aft and climb the steps to the rear deck. Amlina discerned by his gestures and stance that he was trying to convince Hagen to relent. But Hagen stood with arms folded. He questioned the state sorcerers as soon as they arrived on the rear deck. Then he turned to the herald, barking orders.

The herald raised the megaphone and hailed the cranock. "By order of Hagen, Prince-Ruler of Kadavel: Surrender the Cloak of the Two Winds or you will be boarded and then sunk."

Amlina waited no longer. She raised both her arms, hands pointed at the Tathian fleet. The Cloak's left sleeve called the freezewind, the right sleeve the meltwind. Both raised together could summon limitless powers of sea and air. Closing her eyes, Amlina lifted her mind from her body, cast it into the sky. The Cloak came to life and her hands trembled.

Pain flared inside her skull. Her legs wobbled, and she gripped the rail to keep from falling.

"Are you all right?" Draven cried.

Amlina scanned the anxious faces of her mates. "I do not have the strength."

* O *

At the edge of the cove, the drommons were lowering their oars, maneuvering to begin the attack. Glyssa laid a hand on the witch's arm.

"What shall we do?"

Amlina's face was ashen. "You will have to do it."

Glyssa leaned back. "But—I don't know how."

Amlina was already shrugging off the Cloak. "You remember when we called the North Wind? This is very similar. I will guide you."

"But—" Glyssa cast her glance at the drommons. "Very well. I will try."

She received the Cloak and pulled it over her shoulders. Immediately, she felt its magic, hot and freezing cold, as if all the weather in the world was woven into its fabric. She tugged the sleeves over her arms.

"Raise your hands," Amlina instructed. "Stretch your fingers. Point them at the ships."

The drommons were turning, oars striking the water, bows pointing at the cranock. With a flicker of panic, Glyssa recalled all of her attempts at pure shaping, all of the failures.

"Cast your thoughts into the sky," Amlina said, "the source of all winds. Then remember that the sky is but a manifestation of the Deepmind, the true source of all. Its power is linked to the Cloak you wear."

"Yes," Glyssa answered. "I feel it."

"Good," Amlina whispered. "Now call the power, Glyssa. Summon it through both your arms, call it into the world as a mighty wind to scatter our enemies."

Glyssa's mind flew away into the sky. Deep in trance, she recalled every wind and storm she had ever witnessed. She gathered them all together into one, the Father of All Winds, and called it down through the Cloak and into the world.

About the *Phoenix Queen*, the water lapped mildly.

But away to the west the sea lifted, tossing and churning. Wind came whistling out of the blue sky. Even as the sun shone on the cranock, thunderheads appeared, rushing together over the Tathian fleet.

Lightning flashed and thunder cracked. Breakers rolled toward the drommons' bows. Sailors' shouts of fear and confusion sounded in the turbulent air.

Still more power poured through Glyssa's arms. The waves mounted higher, pushing the hulls of the drommons, crashing them into each other. The storm clouds blackened. Winds howled louder and louder, moving the fleet away from the island, sweeping it off to the west.

Amid the roaring and thunder, Glyssa heard Amlina shouting. "Send them far away! Will the storm to last all day and night."

Glyssa poured that intention into the Cloak and into the sky. The fleet and the black clouds flowed away toward the horizon. The deafening tumult slowly diminished, and finally died.

At last, Glyssa lowered her arms. Standing on the gently rocking deck, she stared down at her hands, stunned.

Her mates had gathered around her, mouths hanging open, expressions of awe on their faces. Amlina stood with her back against Draven, cradled by his arms.

"Now Glyssa can call the freezewind," she murmured, "and take us far away."

* O *

Glyssa slept fitfully that night. She lay under a fur, sharing the crawlspace below the rear deck with Lonn, Eben, Karrol, and Kizier. There was no roll to the boat. The cranock, she remembered, rested on ice. Even in the warm season, the ice would last a day or two, according to the witch.

Of course, when it melted, Glyssa could put on the Cloak and call another freeze.

She could summon the winds. That staggering thought came back again and again. She could not cease reliving the events of the morning, the vast energies that had flowed through her body, the power of magic to shape the world.

She might have fallen asleep and dreamed, or it might have been a vision ...

She found herself crawling into a lodge house somewhere in the Iruk Isles. Blue flames rolled over oil, burning in a circular stone hearth. A lone figure was bent over the fire. Iridescent raven feathers gleamed on his shoulders. The beaked mask lay by his knee.

"Welcome, Glyssa, daughter of my tribe."

She sat down at the fire. "Honored Belach. I am happy to see you."

"Are you? I am happy to hear it." He examined her with his eyes like black beads. "I see you have done very well, on your quest to become a woman of power. You have overcome fear, and you have also conquered deceit, using clarity of vision. But now, I see, you have met the third great enemy, the most dangerous of all."

"Have I? What is it?"

"It is power itself! Power can make you think much of yourself. It can tempt you to cruelty, to idleness, to indulging foolish whims, to neglecting what is truly important."

Glyssa realized, with embarrassment, that she had been thinking much of herself. "I see the wisdom in your words, honored Belach. But tell me: What is truly important that I must not neglect?"

"Ha ha!" the shaman laughed. "That, young woman of power, is something you must answer for yourself."

She opened her eyes and sat up. Touching the space beside her, she realized Lonn was gone. Musing on what Belach had said, she pulled on her boots and went out on deck.

The wind was calm. Both moons could be seen, floating among the stars. Sea-ice stretched in all directions, glowing with witchlight. Brinda stood the watch. She raised a hand and smiled at Glyssa. Up on the prow, Wilhaven sat silently working his harp, composing music purely in his mind.

Glyssa climbed to the rear deck and found Lonn seated under the tiller, a fur wrapped around his shoulders. He showed a half-smile as she sat down beside him.

"Why are you not sleeping?" she whispered.

"Restless." He spread the fur to cover her. "Thinking."

"About ...?"

He sighed. "Wondering what will happen after we reach Fleevanport. What will become of us?"

"I have been wondering the same."

Lonn fretted. "We may have enough gold to last the rest of our days, but what then? Eben thinks to live in idleness. But that is not a good life for Iruks. Karol and Brinda say they will go back to hunting and sailing. But after all we have seen, I am not sure any of us can do that. We have crossed so many lands and seas, met so many kinds of people. It seems to me we have won everything, but also lost everything."

Glyssa nodded, smiling wistfully.

"And you, Glyssa, you most of all. Today you raised a storm, called the freezewind into being. You have become a mighty witch, like Amlina. Could you ever go back to the simple Iruk ways?"

She searched her heart for the answer. "You are right. I don't know what will happen after this voyage. I don't know what I will become. But I *do* know what is important to me."

"Oh, and what is that?"

"My mates. To support them and love them for whatever time we have together. That goes for Amlina and Wilhaven too, even Kizier."

Lonn grunted. "That is well, I suppose."

She leaned over and kissed him on the cheek. "But it goes for you most of all, Lonn."

He smiled at that and wrapped his arm around her. "Well. That's all right then."

GLIMNODD CALENDAR, MAP, AND GLOSSARY

Glimnodd has two moons. Grizna, the larger, has a period of 32 days. The small moon, Rog, has a cycle of 11 days. A *month* always refers to the 32-day Grizna cycle. The cycle of Rog is called a *small-month* or simply a *rog*.

A year has six seasons, each two months or 64 days long:

 First Winter
 Second or Mid-Winter
 Third or Late Winter
 First Summer
 Second or High Summer
 Third or Late Summer

A map of Glimnodd is available online at http://triskelionbooks.com/Glimnodd/Map of Glimnodd.pdf

Glossary

aklor - a tall, six-legged animal used as a mount or pack animal in the Three Nations

Archimage - official title for the chief witch or mage of a nation

bostull - a windbringer

cantrip - a minor spell or 'mind trick'

cranock - Gwales ship constructed of wooden planks and with a single mast

Deepmind - the formative realm of which reality is a reflection

deepseer - one skilled in the Larthangan art of deepseeing; that is, seeing outside the boundaries of time and space

deepshaper - one skilled in the arts of shaping reality through magic design - any magical working

desmet - a hanging trinket used to enhance mental power

dojuk - Iruk hunting boat, agile on sea or ice

drells - a delicate winged people whose land lies to the south of Larthang

drog - literally 'shell', a creature formed of magic, animated by the will of a deepshaper, guided by a single purpose

drommon - a Tathian warship, propelled by sail and oars

ensorcellment - a great act of magic

falchion - curved hunting sword used by the Iruks

fire turtles - sea turtles that breathe fire. Normally considered non-sentient.

Fleevan - Tathian colony in the South Polar region. The capital is Fleevanport.

flizzard - a small winged reptile

formulation - the Larthangan magical art of creating and casting power through mental constructs

gallwolves - large wolves native to northern Nyssan

ghost dogs - corpses of human sacrifices, reanimated to serve as guards in ancient Valgool

Gwales - mountainous land north of the Tathian Isles

Gwelthek - native language of Gwales

Iruks - hunting people of the South Polar region

Khylum Destrae - also called the Missing Mountains, an impenetrable region in central Nyssan, formed in the Age of the World's Madness

kiia - edible fern of the tundra; leaves are used to wrap dried fish

klarn - Iruk sacred hunting group, consisting of five to eight warriors. Members of a klarn share a group-soul that gives them strength and courage.

kul shirra - ghost dogs

lamnocc - large deer of the Polar region

Larthang - Westernmost of the Three Nations. Home to a race of powerful witches.

mage - any skilled practitioner of magic

myro - sentient sea-creatures spawned from dolphins

Nagaree - ancient empire of northern Nyssan

Nyssan - Easternmost of the Three Nations. Home to several races. Normally divided into Near Nyssan and Far Nyssan.

Ogo - Larthangan name for the Deepmind. Literally, 'drift.'

pure shaping - the Larthangan magical art of creating immediate effects through the power of thought

quon-xing - pure shaping

serds - a sentient race evolved from deep-sea fishes; powerful sorcerers who ruled Glimnodd during the Age of the World's Madness

skimmer - small boat for ferrying cargo

Tath - Middle realm of the Three Nations. A group of islands, home to a race of seafarers and traders.

thrall - a sentient being whose mind and will have been subjugated by sorcery

torms - winged people of northern Nyssan, spawned from birds

trinket - any object fashioned to contain or enhance magic power

trinketing - the Larthangan art of constructing trinkets

Tuan - the ruler of Larthang, a sacred king or queen

Tysanni - Glimnodd's legendary third moon, which disappeared in the Age of the World's Madness

volrooms - tusked, white-furred bears

wei-shen - the Larthangan art of deepseeing

wei-xing - general term for the Larthangan arts of deepshaping

weng-lei - the Larthangan art of magical combat

windbringer - a sentient fern-like plant; skilled at attracting winds and therefore prized by mariners of all nations witch - broadly any female mage; strictly, a woman trained in the Larthangan arts of the Deepmind

yulugg - giant sea mammals, similar to whales

AUTHOR'S NOTE

Once again, sincere thanks to my Beta Readers, Marilyn Massa and John W. Kelly, and to my editor, Jaime Henriquez.

The Glimnodd Cycle includes these books:

Cloak of the Two Winds

A Mirror Against All Mishap

Tournament of Witches

If you enjoyed this story, please consider leaving a rating and review on Amazon, as well as other sites. The algorithms of the publishing business make this extremely important to a book's success.

To learn about other books and get free offers and chances to win free prizes, sign up for the Triskelion Books newsletter at: https://triskelionbooks.com/list/

You can also connect with me at:

Web: triskelionbooks.com or jackmassa.com
Facebook: www.facebook.com/AuthorJackMassa/
Twitter: @JackMassa2

Made in the USA
Coppell, TX
13 December 2022